James Calbraith is a Poland-born writer, foodie and traveller, currently residing in South London. His debut historical fantasy novel, "The Shadow of Black Wings", has reached ABNA semi-finals. It was published in July 2012 and hit the Historical Fantasy and Alternate History bestsellers list on Amazon US and UK.

Praise for *The Shadow of Black Wings*

"Fast paced and full of energy."
— Adrian Tchaikovsky,
author of the *Shadows of the Apt*

"This manuscript is full of highly crafted detail that will make readers shiver at times with fear and delight...a familiar yet highly original fantasy that is a worthwhile read."
— Publishers Weekly

"The real-world cultures are incredibly well-researched and truthful, and yet well-balanced with the fantasy elements. An intriguing and impressive series."
— Ben Galley,
author of the *Emaneska Series*

By James Calbraith

THE YEAR OF THE DRAGON

Book One: The Shadow of Black Wings

Book Two: The Warrior's Soul

Book Three: The Islands in the Mist

Book Four: The Rising Tide

The Year of the Dragon Books 1-4 Delux Edition

Transmission

Dragonbone Chest

Visit James Calbraith's official website at
jamescalbraith.com
for the latest news, book details, and other information
Or sign up for the newsletter at:
tinyletter.com/jcalbraith

The Rising Tide

Book Four of
The Year of the Dragon

James Calbraith

FLYING
SQUID

Published April 2013 by Flying Squid
ISBN-13: 978-83-935529-7-9

Cover Illustration: Daniel Kordek
Map Illustrations: Jared Blando and Flying Squid
Cover Design: Flying Squid

TABLE OF CONTENTS

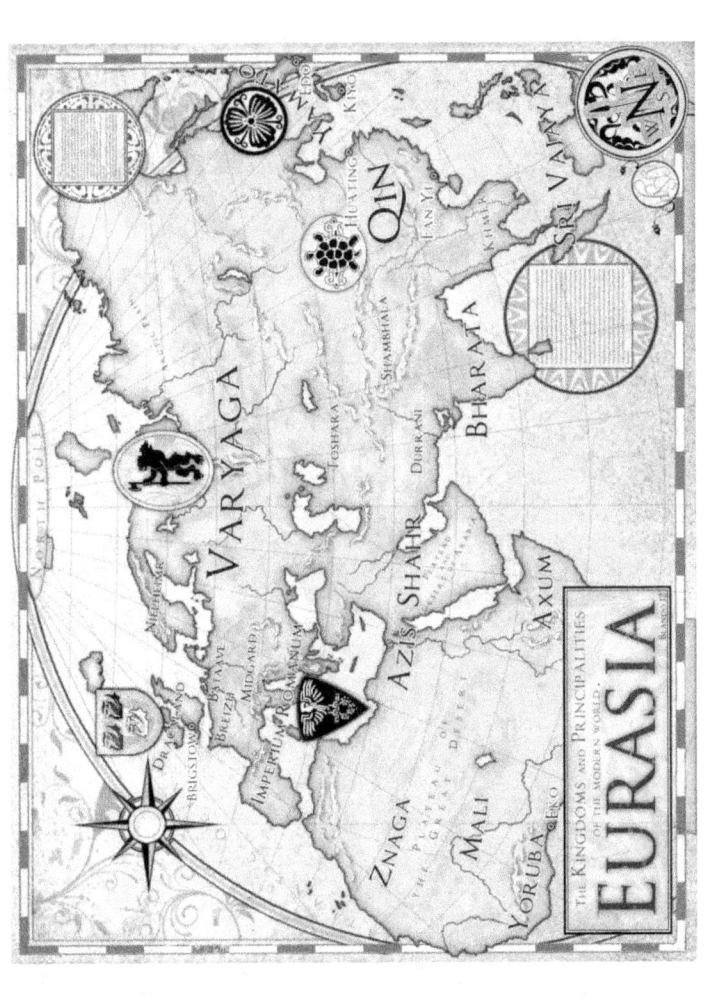

EURASIA

THE KINGDOMS AND PRINCIPALITIES
OF THE MODERN WORLD

CHINZEI
IN THE BEGINNING OF THE
ANSEI ERA

BIANDO 12

TANEGASHIMA

YAKUSHIMA

KAGOSHIMA

KYOMACHI
KIRISHIMA
HAYATO
SENDAI
KOTODA RIVER
AKAE

GOTO
ISLANDS
DETAIL

GOTO

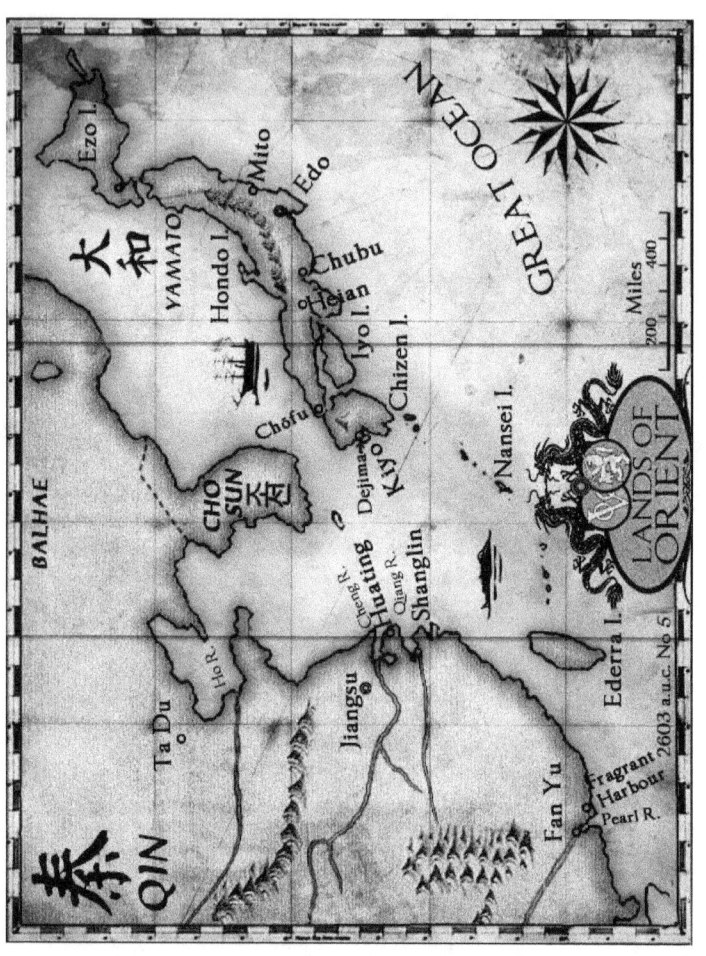

QIN

秦

Ta Du

Ho R.

BALHAE

大
和

YAMATO

Ezo I.

Mito
Edo

Hondo I.

Chubu

Heian

Iyo I.

Chizen I.

CHO
SUN
朝
鮮

Chofu

Dejima

Kiyo

Nansei I.

Cheng R.

Huating

Qiang R.

Shanglin

Jiangsu

Fan Yu

Fragrant
Harbour

Pearl R.

Ederra I.

GREAT OCEAN

Miles
200 400

LANDS OF
ORIENT

2603 a.u.c. No 5

If I see a bridge of flying magpies
Across the frost-white sky
I know the night is almost over.

Chunagon Yakamochi

PROLOGUE

The grounds of the Imperial Palace of the Divine *Mikado* were as tranquil as the blue, cloudless sky above. Noble men shuffled along gravel paths in silence. Thrushes sang softly in the gingko trees. Water trickled in the canals along the avenues into the ponds where frogs croaked the coming of the evening.

Crown Prince Mutsuhito sat down on the springy grass beside one such pond, looking at the great white wall stretching all around the palace gardens. Beyond lay the bustle of Heian, the Imperial Capital. The streets of the city he had seen only once, when, as a child, he had to run from a fire to the Shimogamo Shrine across the river.

"Trapped in a palace like *Butsu-sama* himself," he said quietly. Nobody heard him beyond the silk curtain. Since he was three years old and could express himself formally, the Crown Prince had insisted that his path, wherever he went, was concealed from the outside world. Nobody protested, of course; nobody questioned. The word of the imperial heir was a command of the God.

"How is my Divine Father doing today?" he asked louder.

"His Imperial Majesty is busy writing another letter," an unnamed servant answered from beyond the curtain. All his servants were nobles themselves, of course, from the finest aristocratic families.

"He is angry, then," the prince guessed. He imagined his father's jowls shaking with fury. *Mikado* Kōmei was often angry, and when he was angry, he wrote letters.

"There is... disturbing news from the Taikun's court."

"Oh?"

"I am not sure, *denka*. We did not have an official report yet, so we must rely on rumours."

"What is it, then?"

"There is a rumour of – unspeakable as it sounds – the barbarians landing in Edo."

"Invasion?"

The prince stood up abruptly. A frightened frog leapt from under his feet.

"A scouting party, perhaps... I believe if it was indeed an invasion, we would have more news about it by now."

But how? The Divine Winds were supposed to be impenetrable... have the Bataavians betrayed us?

"Prepare the curtain," Mutsuhito ordered, "I think I shall visit my Father."

An acrid, unpleasant smell filled the imperial chambers; the stench of alcohol and women. Mutsuhito covered his nose with a handkerchief and entered his father's study.

The *Mikado* ordered the woman away. The Prince recognised her – one of the ladies-in-waiting. The woman picked up her kimono, giggled and disappeared through the back door.

"I thought you were writing letters, Father-*sama*."

The *Mikado* tried to rise with dignity, but swayed back onto the silk cushions. His face was purple.

"I was! I am! Look, here it is. It's almost ready."

Mutsuhito reached for the scroll and browsed through. Despite his state, his father's writing remained calm and dignified. It was a missive reminding the *Taikun* of his duty to protect the Divine Land and the need of expulsion of any barbarians who dared to stand on it.

"What happened in Edo?" the Prince asked.

"The barbarians have set up a camp south of the city and demand to speak to the *Taikun*. Why they have not yet been annihilated or how they even got so far inland, I don't know. They are not telling me everything – but I *will* find out. I have my own ways."

The barbarians, Mutsuhito thought, *what were they like?* They were not all bad – he touched the burned-out circle of skin on his arm where he had been secretly vaccinated against the pox by a red-haired physician. Not even his father knew about it – all Western medicine was forbidden in the palace.

"I like the toys the Westerners make," he said, "the dolls that move of their own accord, the birds that sing when you turn the key..."

"Mere tricks to gain our confidence!" the *Mikado* cried. "I will order these toys burned!"

The prince said nothing, not risking his father's wrath turning against him. There would always be more toys sent from the south.

"I can see you are busy, Father-*sama*," he said, glancing towards the back door. "I will leave you to your... duties."

The *Mikado*'s lips wobbled. He raised his hand feebly, holding the wooden sceptre, the symbol of his power.

"It's all my fault," he said.

"What is?"

"If the land suffers it means the sovereign is to blame. It's the punishment of the Heavens. The fires, the earthquakes, and now this... I have been frail and I have neglected my duty as the Divine Father."

"There has never been a more dutiful *Mikado* than you."

His father hid his face in his hands and started sobbing. Mutsuhito felt it best to leave him alone.

The Prince studied his reflection in the round bronze mirror. He untied the ribbons holding his long black tresses in place and the hair fell down onto his shoulders.

His fingers smelled of fish, despite frequent washing. It was customary to present the Crown Prince with fresh sea fish on any special occasion, these having been of old an item of luxury in the landlocked capital city. Neither jewels nor gold adorned his room. The Imperial Family lived in traditional austerity and was dependant on gifts from the courtiers and a meagre yearly stipend.

There were some more gifts coming his way, and slightly more opulent. His Coming of Age day was swiftly approaching. Soon his long boyish hair would be cut off and his plain robes replaced with the clothes of an adult.

It seemed to him ominous to have such an important ceremony at such a critical time. There was more news of the barbarians coming from Edo and none of it served to calm Mutsuhito's father down. The *Mikado* had ordered prayers for Yamato's prosperity in the seven shrines and seven temples of the capital and then sat down to write another angry missive to the *Taikun*.

Mutsuhito wondered if anyone ever read the letters. *Probably not.* Why would the all-powerful overlord and Commodore of all the Yamato armies care what the Imperial Puppet had to say on matters of state? The *Mikado* represented a symbolic and spiritual power without any real influence. It was said that all the healing power of the shrine priests depended on the *Mikado*'s well-being, but Mutsuhito suspected this was just a story made up by the chroniclers in the ancient times to justify the need for the existence of the Imperial Family. His father had only very limited command over the spirits. His biological mother, he remembered, a daughter of a noble family from Chinzei, had become a skilled healer, but only once she had retired to a temple in the mountains.

A tiny bell tinkled, signifying the water had reached the desired temperature. He stepped towards the bath, untied the silk sash and dropped his red robe. Nobody attended his baths, not even the chamber maids. This was a breach of the custom but, again, nobody dared to question his command. They just assumed it was one of his divine whims.

But there was another, much more important reason for his seclusion. One that only his mother and his physician knew about. At first – they told him – it was just a small spot of infarction on his upper thigh, a bit of hard, dead skin. But as the prince had grown, so had the blemish and by now it covered most of his thigh, descending below the knee in places.

It didn't hurt or itch. In fact, somehow it felt even more natural than his human skin. He sat on the bath's edge and scratched the thigh absent-mindedly; the soft light green scales shimmered in the candle light.

CHAPTER I

There was fresh blood on Dylan's boots.

It came from a puddle he had stepped into, a street earlier. Or maybe from another, a block away. There was no way to know for certain; all the streets of Shanglin were bathed in blood.

He walked over a dead body and stumbled over another lying just beside it. He didn't look down; not anymore. They were all the same, anyway: stripped naked, mangled, slashed with swords and burned with gunshots. Only the size and gender differed. The conquerors of Shanglin did not discriminate. Old men, children, women... all were piled along the walls and blood-filled gutters. The dead, black window holes of the burnt-out houses stared down at the carnage in silent accusation.

Dylan didn't bother to count the slain. How many people had lived in Shanglin before the war? Ten thousand? Twenty thousand? How many more gathered here fleeing from the besieging Imperial Army? Only a few hundred women survived, spared for the soldiers' entertainment. Another hundred may have fled into the marshes. That was all.

There's always war in Qin, he thought. *But not like this...*

He heard cries. He rushed into the narrow cul-de-sac between a burnt out brick warehouse and a ruined inn. Three Imperial soldiers, flushed with drink, were standing over an old woman, beating and abusing her. The woman was still alive, though barely, and her cries for help weakened with every blow.

Red mist swam before Dylan's eyes. He raised both hands. *"Rhew!"* he cried, letting the dragon's fire flow freely from his fingers, at full force. The nearest of the soldiers stood up in flames and screamed in agony before succumbing to the fire and folding down like burning paper. The other two swayed drunkenly at Dylan. He dodged a clumsy blow, grabbed the attacker's arm with one hand and pressed the other to his chest.

"Gwrthyrru!"

The repelled soldier flew back, his shoulder torn right out of the socket. He put a hand to his chest and pink foam spewed from his mouth. He made a few steps and fell on the ground, trashing in dead throes. One man remained, sobered by the deaths of his comrades; he raised the broad Qin sword. Dylan did not waste magic, and simply punched him in the throat with the edge of his palm, smashing his windpipe. The man dropped his weapon and fell to his knees, gasping and choking.

Weakened by the magic outburst and anger, Dylan knelt by the old woman; she was breathing rapidly, her eyes wide open. She noticed him and shuddered. She reached shaking fingers out to him, crooked into the sign against evil.

"Curse you, Westerner! Curse your guns and your dragons!"

She took one last, hoarse gasp, and died.

He climbed the arch of a wide bridge spanning one of the city's many canals, and passed Qin soldiers guarding the passage. They let him through without a word, or even a bow. Dylan was too numb to take offence, although he did make a mental note of the guards' behaviour.

Beyond the canal lay the Tianyi Gardens, where the conquering army had made their headquarters. Traces of destruction and fire and blood had been scoured from the gravel and all the dead had been removed from the paths. Rose and camellia bushes had been cut down to make place for tents. Soldiers sat on moss-covered boulders and stone benches around ponds, playing *ma jiang* for bits of Cursed Weed. Gold and silver coins, looted from the city's treasure houses, were strewn all over the grass.

No discipline at all, thought Dylan bitterly, *this rabble would never have taken the city without our help.*

The words of the dying woman echoed in his head.

She blamed me for her fate, not the Qin soldiers torturing her.

The Bohan set his staff up in the main lecture hall of the great Library Pavilion; a long, two-storey building with eaves like sickle blades pointing to the skies. Dylan found him there, studying a large map; several other maps lay scattered around the floor and tables. The upper half of a discarded automaton lay in the corner, its glass eyes and metal hand raised accusingly into the air.

"Ah, Commodore *Dí Lán*!" the Bohan welcomed him with a grin and open arms. "Come, join us. We are planning our next stratagem. What do you think of moving on Chansu?"

"Another siege?" Dylan asked. He dismissed a servant who offered him a cup of tea.

"I know you Dracalish like moving swiftly, but this is how this war will have to be fought for now, until we push those vermin beyond the walls of our cities."

Vermin.

"Perhaps it would be easier to capture the cities if the defenders were given a chance to survive."

The *Bohan* looked him in the eyes and smiled.

"You don't approve of our methods, Commodore."

"No, I can't say I do. I will write a report to Fan Yu of all that's happened here."

Bohan's smile vanished. He stood straight, letting go of the map; it rolled up with a rustle.

"These... rats dared to stand against the Mandate of Heaven. They got what they deserved. Besides, they had plenty of time to surrender without bloodshed."

"Plenty of time? The siege lasted less than a week – thanks to *our* guns and *our* dragons."

"That was a week too long."

"Her Majesty will not take kindly to having her troops associated with this massacre."

The *Bohan* smirked and stroke his beard.

"Do not presume to deceive me, Commodore. I know your orders as well as you do. You are to provide us with any assistance we require in defence of your country's trade interests – and provide us you shall. Speaking of which, I will need half a dozen of your dragons to-"

"Enough!" Dylan slapped his hands on the table. The outburst surprised him. The *Bohan* raised a sharp eyebrow.

"My men are not butchers! You can capture your cities yourself. Huating is safe, and that's all that matters for our trade interests."

The *Bohan* blinked, and then laughed.

"You want to teach *me* about butchery? You, a Westerner? I know *you*. You've destroyed entire nations and you'd destroy Qin if you thought this was in your… *interests*. Oh, but you're too shrewd for that - you prefer to kill slowly."

"I don't know what you're talking about," said Dylan.

"You don't know? How many of my people died because of your accursed trade? How many died of famine in Bangla because you took their fields to plant more Weed? Don't *you* lecture *me* about butchery, Commodore *Dí Lán;* unless you want me to get better at it. Play war like the nice soldier you are, and we'll all be free to go home in no time. Isn't that what you want?"

Dylan gritted his teeth. He knew he couldn't give the Qin official the satisfaction of another outburst. He inhaled and exhaled slowly.

"Tell your soldiers to stay out of my way," he said, forcing himself to sound calm. "I'm going back to the main camp."

"I will send my requests to your tent, Commodore," the *Bohan* replied.

"You will have a prompt reply."

Dylan nodded sharply, turned on his heels and stomped outside.

Makino Tadamasa returned to his apartment at the guesthouse, put his two swords on the rack and the padded raincoat on the chest, and paid homage to the household spirits at the tiny shrine above the entrance. He then slid away the paper panels forming the western wall of the room and sat down on a narrow veranda overlooking a small garden.

As one of the inner circle of hereditary *fudai* daimyo, Tadamasa could easily afford a private residence of his own, but he preferred to live in one of the lavish, extravagant guesthouses in the middle of Edo, near the walled pleasure district. He had his wife and son neatly cooped up in a mansion just outside the city; near enough for them to fall under the rules of alternate attendance which required the daimyo's family to live under Edo's surveillance as glorified hostages – and yet too far to interfere in Tadamasa's everyday duties and entertainments. These days the visitors would arrive mostly from the nearby pleasure district, but sometimes they were his feudal clients or representatives of other, lesser daimyo, basking in the light of his influential position.

He had just spent half a day negotiating an important contract for the delivery of cannon barrels and compressed air to the *Taikun*'s new harbour fortress at Daiba and all he wanted to do was to soak in a relaxing bath and watch the moon reflecting in the pond in the small garden. He was understandably annoyed when a servant knocked on the door of his apartment and announced a guest.

"I told you I'm not seeing anyone today!"

"I beg your apologies, *kakka*, but it is the esteemed Councillor Hotta-*dono* who wants to see you."

"Keep it brief, Naosuke, I have a bath waiting," barked Tadamasa, sitting at the low table.

"I will, Councillor-*dono*. I come to you with a proposition. As you well know, I need one more vote behind my motion for the next month's meeting. The Matsudairas are beyond my reach for now; young Kuze is – well, I have not found any leverage on him yet. So, only you remain, Tadamasa-*dono*. Now, before I tell you what my offer is, I wonder if there is anything that could sway you to my side?"

"Nothing," the old man said and grunted. "I don't know what makes you think I would do such a thing. I have made up my mind."

"Money? Prestige? Women? Men? How about a little blackmail, no?" Naosuke pressed.

"Listen, Naosuke. I am an old, rich, powerful man. You may think to threaten me or bully me or bribe me or whatever it is you have done to your opponents to get as high as you have, but none of this will help you with me."

Naosuke nodded sadly.

"I was afraid you'd say that."

He clapped his hands and, out of the shadows, came a burly *rōnin* pushing before him a young boy who was bound and gagged. Tears streamed from under the blindfold. Tadamasa recognized his nine-year old grandson.

"Tadakuni! How *dare* you..." He raised an accusing hand at Naosuke. "My family is under the *Taikun's* personal care!"

"That may well be," Naosuke said with a self-confident shrug. "But it makes you wonder, *eh* – if I can get my hands on the *Taikun's* hostages, what more *am* I capable of?"

Tadamasa's shoulders slumped in defeat. If he was younger, he would find more strength to fight; but he was old. Next year he was planning to retire from the Council altogether...

"What do you want from me?"

"I only need one vote. That is all. And your immediate retirement after that, of course. I already have a more... pliable... replacement prepared to take over your position."

"You have it. Now give me back my grandson."

"After the vote, dear Makino-*dono*. After the vote," said Naosuke, smiling.

Hanpeita crouched at the roof of the guesthouse, observing the entrance. He first saw the burly *rōnin*, carrying a large rolled *futon* on his shoulders. Councillor Hotta followed, deliberately turning in the direction opposite from the *rōnin.*

Hanpeita waved a lantern. From a roof across the street another lantern waved; one of his men – he didn't know which one, it was safer this way – confirmed he was going to follow the *rōnin,* letting Hanpeita and his group follow the Councillor.

They moved softly from roof to roof, using the skills Hanpeita had learned in Tosa, his home province, before coming to Edo.

When is Gensai-sama *going to arrive?* He wondered briefly, leaping noiselessly across a narrow cul-de-sac. No action could start without the master swordsman joining the group. But it was a long way from Kumamoto and the spring storms kept delaying the journey.

Hotta stopped in the middle of a brightly-lit alley running towards the southern gate of the city. Hanpeita and his men lay flat on the roof; the Councillor looked around slowly, his hand reaching for the short *kodachi* sword. His eyes glinted gold in the light of the lanterns.

It is *him,* Hanpeita thought, clutching the hilt of his katana in a sweaty hand. He felt as if the Councillor was looking straight through him, even though he couldn't possibly see any of them hidden in the shadows.

The contact was right. He is no longer human.

Hotta smiled and his grip on the hilt relaxed; he continued on his way. Hanpeita bade his men stop.

"It's too dangerous tonight," he whispered. "He'll spot us. We'll have to try again some other time."

A clay beaker rested on Nagomi's chest, with the spirit light burning bright orange. She couldn't remember where she got it from – it wasn't the Suwa light, that one she had lost on the road from Hitoyoshi…Something inside her body hurt. She heard the whining sound of a bamboo flute that soon grew louder and louder and then the whinging of a *hichiriki* oboe joined in. A waft of a breeze brought with it the scent of cherry blossom.

It's too late for cherry blossom, she thought.

She sat up carefully and the pain inside made her wince. She touched her chest and looked around. In the flickering orange light, she saw Bran and Satō sleeping on the cave floor, entwined in an embrace. She turned her eyes away, towards the shimmering waterfall and a babbling stream flowing from it into the forest.

A cloud of gold and green fireflies, the tiny flickers darting to and fro, hovered over the brook. The heady scent of cherry blossom made Nagomi dizzy. She took a deep breath and felt warmth spread all over her body. The pain subsided.

A cloud of white mist appeared on the other side the stream, and from it emerged a wispy shape of a woman in a long flowing robe the pink colour of cherry blossom. Her face was lime-white, her thick eyebrows were painted with charcoal in the ancient fashion. The fireflies surrounded her, drawn to the soft light emanating from her body. A white fox purred and rubbed against her like a cat. The woman beckoned the priestess with a slender hand.

Nagomi stood up and staggered towards the figure across the stone cave floor and grass moist and cold with dew of the coming morning. The white fox perked up, its ears twitching. The figure reached out her arms across the stream. Her face beamed white light, too strong for Nagomi to bear; she lowered her gaze and raised the beaker up.

The woman's hands touched hers; they felt like warm, soft leaves. The beaker's flame burst bright; Nagomi closed her eyes and shivered, as strong, cold wind blew against her naked skin. The sound of the flute and oboe grew faint, until it was barely audible.

When she opened her eyes again, she was standing on the peak of an imposing steep mountain, shooting high above the layer of dense white fog. The wind whirled and parted the mists and she could see all of the Chinzei Island and further, all the way towards Heian, the Imperial Capital. Somewhere beyond the curving horizon lay Edo and the Northern provinces.

The dawn rose threatening and ominous, blood red over the eastern seas. Black clouds were gathering over the northern horizon where the *Taikun*'s castle lay, in Edo, and more dark billows were coming on the Westerly winds over the sea from the direction of Qin. Nagomi saw that the clouds were giant flocks of carrion crows and ravens, circling the skies in hungry anticipation.

The beaker in her hands burned brighter again, the cold wind blew once more, and she found herself back in the forest. The woman in the cherry blossom robe was smiling sadly. Nagomi felt an overwhelming desire to join her on the other side of the stream, feel the warm, motherly embrace of her willowy arms, to never again feel the pain and sadness... She stepped forward into the water. But the woman shook her head and floated back towards the white mist behind her.

The fireflies buzzed over the stream towards the priestess, and gathered around her. One by one, they landed on Nagomi's body, extinguishing their flame and dying. As they touched her, she sensed their tiny, burning spirits; they seemed familiar, as if she had met them before somewhere.

It's the old Mushi from Shofukuji Temple, she realized. *And the homeless woman from Shinbashi. And the porter from Omura. All my strays...*

She felt the pain inside slowly disappear, the fatigue give way to vigour. The spirit light in her beaker was vibrant and dancing.

The music intensified again, the unseen zither and drums joining the flute in quick, mad rhythm. The woman waved her hand, showing Nagomi the cave behind her. The white mist enveloped her and she disappeared. Gone were the fireflies, but the white fox remained, staring at Nagomi with cunning, glowing eyes. The priestess turned and walked towards the cave. On its threshold she looked back; the fox was still there, twitching its whiskers anxiously.

The music grew to a frenzy and then stopped. Nagomi lay down on the cave floor, wrapped herself back in the tattered clothes and cloaks and put the spirit light on her chest. The white fox barked once and vanished into the forest, its bright white tail visible among the trees for a second more.

She smiled and closed her eyes.

CHAPTER II

Bran's first thought was that he did not wish to wake up. The world outside was cold, and he was warm and snug here, nestled as if in his mother's embrace.

Five minutes more...

Someone sighed. He opened his eyes.

He shuddered as the freezing wind blew against his back. Satō must have felt it too, for she huddled up closer. Her black hair tickled his nose. He caressed her head. She stirred and frowned, but she did not waken.

Through the haze of exhaustion, he was remembering the battle in the Shrine, the dragon, his transformation, the Crimson Robe, and the flight into the tunnels. His side was sore from lying on the rocky floor of the cave. The makeshift campfire burned out. Dawn peered through the trees, faintly illuminating the cave with greyish gold.

He unwrapped himself carefully from Satō's embrace, threw a few more pieces of wood and summoned a little spark; barely enough to light the fire back again.

This was the last of my dragon magic left.

He squatted by Nagomi's side and brushed hair from her forehead; she was running a slight fever, but her breath was calm and stable. He adjusted the cloaks around her – she must have been stirring in her sleep – and then went to the stream to wash in the icy cold water. This helped him clear his mind a little. He scratched his cheek where the *shinobi's* sickle blade had drawn deep blood. The scar was still fresh and painful.

What now?

Getting help for Nagomi was the priority, as was finding some food. He could only hope they were safe enough from any pursuit in the cave. He patted the sword at his side reassuringly.

At least I still have the blade.

He felt a stir at the back of his mind, a nudging presence. At first he thought it was the Farlink returning and a jolt of joy came through him, but his delight was short-lived.

"What do you want?" he asked, annoyed.

"*I will overlook your impertinence considering the circumstances, boy,*" said Shigemasa graciously. "*I have something very important to tell you.*"

"Do you know a way out of here, *Taishō?*"

"*That I do not…*"

"Then whatever it is will have to wait until we're safe."

By the time Bran returned to the cave, Satō was awake and leaning over the unconscious friend.

32

"She is still feverish," he said.

"And the wound is swollen again," Satō said and sat down; her face crumpled.

"This is hopeless."

"She will all be alright," he said. He sounded unconvincing even to himself.

"I'll go look for help. There must be some village nearby where those people came from," he added, pointing at the remnants of the hunting gear strewn on the cave floor.

He stepped outside and heard loud voices and the sound of several people trudging noisily through the forest somewhere downhill.

"Somebody's coming," he said and frowned.

"The hunters! They will help us!" Satō stood up, excited.

"*Shh*! We don't know if they're friendly. Let's hide and see what they're up to, first."

He extinguished the campfire and helped Satō move Nagomi into the bushes, from where they observed the men arriving at the cave.

There were three of them, all in crude hunting gear – deerskin trousers and fur hats, bows and long knives in tree bark scabbards. A large yellow hound accompanied them, its nose to the ground. They were loud, not caring for stealth. Two of the hunters carried their game hung over a bamboo pole.

"Look!" Satō whispered with horror, pointing at the pole. Tied to it by the wrists and ankles was a tall man, naked and hairy. The third hunter prodded him with a stick and baited him with the tip of his knife. The man's body was cut and slashed in many places and full of bruises.

"What are they? Slave traders? Cannibals?"

The hunters came into the cave's entrance and threw their prey roughly at the cold rock.

"That's 'nuff. Throw t'trinket back on it," said the third hunter, and one of the other two took a string of jade jewels. Bran could not see what he did with it from his hiding place.

"Make sure it's tied up well," the chief hunter warned.

"Wait! Somebody's been 'ere," said the man holding the necklace. Immediately the hunters fell silent, pulling out their long hunting knives and eyeing the forest around them suspiciously. Bran and Satō dropped to the ground.

The birds chirped and the wind rustled the bamboo leaves.

"Do you have any power left?" whispered Satō.

"No dragon magic. I can do simple illusions, but-"

Before he could finish, the hound stood rigid, sniffing towards them.

"Look at the dog!" the chief hunter cried. "Over there, in the bushes!"

The other two aimed their bows at the hideout.

"Come out of there!" the chief hunter ordered.

Bran waved his fingers. A growl and a roar rang out at the back of the cave.

"What the…"

The hunters turned back in fright. The dog started to bark madly.

"Was that you?" asked Satō. He shook his head and focused on the illusion.

"*Ystlumod*," he spoke.

At that moment, a dark, large flock of bats flew out of the cave over the heads of the bowmen, who released their arrows, aimless, into the air, shouting in surprise.

"Now!" cried Bran, drawing his sword. Satō leapt out with a katana in her hands, releasing a rain of icy sparks on the leader and his dog. Hoar covered the animal's hair and it yelped in pain. The hunter shielded his eyes with his arm.

Bran cast bright sparks into the eyes of the other two and attacked them with the flat of his blade. He did not wish any more men to die; he still remembered the nauseating stench of blood and death from the battle at the Shrine. With a couple of hefty blows, he forced the two men to drop their bows and run off down the hill.

But Satō's opponent refused to give up easily. Her sword clashed against the hunter's long knife. The man was stronger than the wizardess, and well-rested. His dog caught on the girl's hakama and tugged at it with a mad growl, making it harder for her to move. In short quarters, Satō's long blade was a hindrance; the hunter pushed her against the tree, grabbed her wrist and forced her to release the weapon. He let out a leering chuckle, noticing the curves under the girl's torn kimono. He dropped the knife and reached for her.

"Stay away!"

Bran lashed out at the man blindly, only for his face to meet the hunter's fist. Lightning flashed before the boy's eyes; he reeled back, stunned and disoriented. Blood sprouted from his broken nose again. An irritated voice spoke in his head.

"*Good. I'll take it from here.*"

In an instant, Bran's sword arm drew a perfect curve which bypassed the hunter's parry. The blade lodged itself in the hunter's neck. Blood spurted from the wound and the man fell gurgling to his knees.

Bran could do nothing to prevent the hunter's death. Shigemasa's spirit was as strong as ever, unlike the weak and spent boy.

"Let me back in," he protested feebly.

"*I don't think so,*" replied Shigemasa.

"You fiend! Of all the moments…"

"*It is a pity,*" admitted the General, "*but you were too keen to die lately, and that doesn't suit me at all, boy.*"

Satō noticed the change in Bran's posture before he turned around and looked at her with eyes as black as the night. She picked up her sword and pressed its sharp, icy edge to his neck.

"Drop your sword and let him go," she said calmly.

The General licked his – Bran's – lips, eyeing the blade.

"Thou wouldst not hurt him. "

"It would hurt *you*, first."

"I will be of much more use to thee than the lad," the General said, smiling. "I know my way around this island. I am a better fighter. I could protect thee... young woman."

In response she pressed the sword closer. A droplet of blood appeared on his skin.

I can't keep it up for long.

"We are of the same stock, thou and I," he continued with a smile. "Samurai both. Thou canst trust me." He began to slowly raise his hand towards the blade, but before he could move it away from his neck, she pressed even harder.

"I trust *Bran!*"

His sword-hand moved faster than she could blink, but somehow she managed to pull back and parry the powerful blow aimed at her neck. Sparks flew from the clashing blades.

Bran stood right in front of the door to the red-light tower, trying to calm himself down.

Don't panic. Focus. You can do it.

It was his body; he managed to get it back once already.

But I had Emrys then. And my ring.

He looked at his ring-finger; it was empty.

So it's gone here as well.

But Shigemasa was in a hurry, and had made a sloppy job of banishing Bran from his mind. The boy pressed at the door and it budged a little with a creak. He sensed the General was trying to push him back, but at the same time was distracted by Satō. At last, the strain of dealing with two diversions at once irritated Shigemasa to the point of bursting. Bran read his quick thought: he was going to *kill the insolent bitch!*

No!

Bran rammed at the door with all his strength at the same time that Shigemasa's sword flashed towards Satō's neck. He leapt inside the tower and, with great effort, he tore the General away and cast him far out onto the red dust plain, into the deepest recesses of his soul.

Exhausted, he fell down onto the forest floor.

Satō splashed water on Bran's face. He opened his eyes and she breathed with relief – they were jade green.

She helped him up. The dead hunter's dog was sniffing its slain master, whimpering. She stomped her feet and the animal ran away into the forest with a yowl.

"What about the other two?" asked Bran.

"I don't think they'll come back," she replied. She was still shaking after the encounter. "Can you get Nagomi into the cave? I'll check on that poor man they were carrying."

She passed the threshold and reeled back in terror.

In the back of the cavern, instead of the naked man, lay a large black bear. Its fore and rear legs were tied with strong rope. Its fur was shaggy and dirty and its sides collapsed with hunger. She fought the primal fear taking her over, making her want to flee. She stepped back and bumped into Bran, who had just brought Nagomi over the cave's threshold.

"What's going – ? Oh…"

The dragon rider laid the priestess down and moved carefully forward.

"Look out!" Satō warned him earnestly, "it can slice your head off with one blow!"

"It doesn't look like it has any strength left.." Bran said. "And what happened to the human?"

She studied the bear more closely. The animal looked at them with strangely intelligent eyes, exposing its teeth in an effort to look threatening. Around its neck was hung a necklace of jade stones.

"You don't think…"

"I don't know, you tell me! Have you ever heard of something like this?"

She scoured her memory for the old tales.

Nagomi would know better, she always loved those stories…

"Well, there are… there were foxes and raccoon dogs which could shapeshift… but I never heard of bears. Can you use True Sight?"

He shook his head.

"I'm too exhausted for that. But that necklace..." Bran walked past her. The bear grunted and waved its head. The boy jumped back, startled, but then slowly came even nearer the animal.

"*Eeh!* What are you doing?" Satō cried, as the boy reached for the jewels.

"I want to see what that necklace is for."

"Maybe it keeps the bear sedated! Maybe it's sapping its strength and if you take it off, the bear will jump and eat you! Why can't you just leave it alone?"

"I... I'm just curious, that's all. I think...Look, it's letting me touch it."

The bear lay its head sideways on the cave floor and did not move, only breathed heavily as Bran examined the jade gems wrapped around the animal's huge neck on a piece of leather cord.

"Yes, of course it would let you touch it, if it meant it could get its strength back and kill us all."

But Bran did not listen. He reached out his hand.

"Give me your dagger," he said.

"You're insane," said Satō, but she gave him the weapon. After all a man was thrown into the cave where the animal now rested...

The boy cut through the cord. The jade gems scattered on the floor of the cage with a tinkle. Nothing happened.

"Well at least it didn't bite your a– look out, it's moving!"

40

The bear started writhing on the cave floor. Bran quickly jumped back and Satō pulled out her blade by a few inches. But the bear did not attack. The animal's body twisted and tossed around as it groaned in agony.

"Is it...dying?" she asked.

"No. And I know what's happening..." whispered Bran. "It's *transforming...*"

The bear muscles and bones started to relocate and half a minute later a tall, muscular, hairy naked man lay unconscious on the cage floor.

"The day just keeps getting better," said Satō, sighing. "Now we have *two* casualties to take care of."

With some effort, Bran and Satō carried the man towards the campfire.

"I've never heard of bears changing into humans, or the other way around," repeated Satō, "I wonder which way it is. The hunters treated it like an animal."

"I've heard stories... Of werebears and other such creatures living in the frozen forests of the deep north, beyond the Varyaga Khaganate."

"But what's it doing here? It looks almost like a Yamato, only taller."

Bran shook his head.

"I don't know. But we really need to find some help now. For both of them," said Bran. He stood up from the campfire.

41

"Don't leave me." Satō tugged on his sleeve. "What if that bear-man wakes up and attacks me? What if the hunters return?"

He looked at her surprised. She suddenly seemed frail and vulnerable as never before.

Is this the real Satō … or just another mask?

As if in answer to the girl's fears, the hairy stranger stirred and moaned. Satō jumped away, reaching for her sword, but Bran remained motionless. The man raised himself on his arms, his movements still resembling an animal. He shook his head and looked up. He saw them and stepped back on all fours. His body was covered in old and new scars. Powerful muscles bulged on his shoulders and thighs, but he was visibly famished, with a stomach caved in under the protruding ribs. Long hair and a short, shaggy beard surrounded a sunken face, with eyes rounder and the nose longer than those of the Yamato. The hairs on his chest were discoloured in the shape of a white crescent that the black bears bore below their necks.

The stranger opened his mouth to speak, but produced only a low growl. He coughed a few times, clearing his throat before trying again.

"You… you're not the hunters."

"The hunters are gone," said Bran. "You're safe now."

"Safe," he repeated hoarsely, sitting down in a bear-like manner, with his legs straight and supporting himself on his knuckles. For a while he bobbed sideways, before speaking again.

"They… took my clothes."

Bran untied his sash and gave it to the man, who wrapped it around his waist like a loincloth. He grunted in thanks.

"Who – or what – are you?" asked Satō, tapping her fingers on the hilt of the sword.

The man bowed, or rather, rocked deeply forward.

"I am Chief of the Kumaso, the Bear People. Torishi."

"*Bear People*? There are more of you?"

"No more," the man shook his head.

"Not much of a Chief, then," Satō remarked.

"But I thought… *werebears* only lived in the far north," said Bran.

The bear-man looked up and squinted.

"Before the Yamato came… my people lived on these islands. Then we were pushed to the edges."

"And now you're the only one left?"

"That I know," the bear-man said, lowering his head, "and what of you?" He glanced at their tattered, bloodied clothes and noticed the unconscious priestess.

"We lost a battle yesterday and had to run," explained Satō in as vague terms as she could. "Our friend was wounded. We need to go down to the valley and find help."

"Help?" Torishi shook his head and stood up. He towered above them, taller even than Dōraku, and more broad-shouldered. He did not seem as weak now. He ran his hand sideways across his beard.

"The Chief of the Bear People will help you."

Satō eyed him suspiciously.

"You look as if you need help yourself. I'm afraid we don't have any food to share."

"Come with me," said Torishi, "I have plenty."

"*Bear* food?"

The man guffawed. "Come!"

He stooped over Nagomi and hesitated. Finally he reached out and gently caressed her red hair. Then he frowned.

"Your friend… is a priestess?"

"Yes," said Bran. "What of it?"

Torishi laughed wistfully.

"To think I would help one of their kind…"

He leaned to pick the girl up.

Satō bit her lips. The man lifted the priestess's limp body without effort.

"My house is not far," he said and without waiting for them, walked off into the forest. Satō looked at Bran. They both shrugged and followed outside.

CHAPTER III

Satō trudged alongside Bran and the bear-man for about a quarter of a *ri* through the thick undergrowth, slipping and cursing, out of breath and out of strength. At last, they reached what looked like an impassable tangle of poison ivy stretching from tree to tree, and stopped. The man nodded at them.

"Move those two branches away. Do not touch the leaves."

The ivy parted with ease, revealing a comfortable entrance to a large, round, open glade. Stepping through it, she saw a large hut with walls of bamboo and straw, and a roof of tightly-woven grass. It stood beside a small stream flowing across the glade. There were remnants of several other huts, all dismantled or burnt down a long time ago.

"But – this is like a normal house!" she cried out.

"This used to be a village," noticed Bran, stepping over a few broken bamboo poles.

"Eight families lived upon this stream," the bear-man said, "the last of the Kumaso."

He entered the house, and she followed hesitantly. It was dark and tight, with just a little light falling through a tiny window, but it was also warm and dry. An unpleasant, sweet smell was coming from the opposite wall, but she couldn't see through the gloom. Torishi laid Nagomi on a long, low bench beside the fireplace in the middle of the hut and covered her with skins.

"There is food in those crates and jugs by the door."

"What about Nagomi?"

"The young priestess? I need to prepare while you eat."

Satō opened one of the crates and reeled back.

"What is this?"

Bran picked up what looked like a dark-red log and sniffed it.

"It's smoked meat." He licked it. "Venison," he said. "Wild boar?"

She gave the boy a stare, but he was busy biting his teeth into the tough meat and didn't seem to notice.

Torishi laughed again.

"Tasty, eh? There is more here, fresher. Deer."

He reached into the gloom and took a long haunch, blackened with age and glistening with fat. He then put on a long tunic of light brown cloth that reached to his knees. He offered Bran his sash back, but the boy raised his hand in protest.

"Er... you can keep it."

46

"Meat, meat and more meat," Satō opened one crate after another, holding her nose with her fingers, "you wouldn't have anything without legs?"

"Fish in that round box," the bear-man said. He threw some wood on the fireplace and started lighting it up with a flint.

"Thank *Butsu-sama* for that!"

There was about a dozen small, silvery fish inside the bamboo box, cured in some sour-smelling paste. The girl devoured them quickly.

"I suppose rice is out of the question," she said. Torishi shook his head; every time he did so, his thick, long mane of black hair shook wildly from side to side.

"We grew millet, when there were hands enough to work… And we used to buy rice from the valleys. But it's been a long time since I ate either."

The fire started and was now crackling merrily. Smoke rose up through a hole in the grass roof. Torishi reached for some clay pots on the wooden shelf by the only window and put them around the bench where Nagomi lay.

"Now. What happened to her?"

"She's been stabbed through her lungs," Satō said grimly. "She's lost a lot of blood, and I don't know what's going on inside her."

The bear-man sucked air through his teeth and stroked the back of his head. He reached under the bed – a sleeping platform raised about a foot over the floor on wooden logs -

and pulled out a small deerskin drum, and a sealed lacquer box.

"What are you doing?" she asked.

"I must commune with the Spirits."

"*Eeh!* You're a *healer* then?"

"I am Chief of the Kumaso," he said, as if that explained everything. "I did not save my people from the Blistering Sickness, but I can deal with injuries."

"Blistering Sickness?" Bran whispered.

"He means smallpox," replied Satō. "Is that what happened to your village?"

Torishi opened the lacquer box carefully.

"The hunters brought the Blistering Sickness into the forest," he explained. "And we, shamans, could not deal with it. But I survived. The Spirits chose me to witness my kindred suffer and die."

His face took on a grim, determined expression as he tied a tightly woven scarf around his head. He picked up a spruce twig, a blade of grass and some dried leaves from the box and tossed them on the fire. A dark, thick smoke spewed from the fireplace.

"The young one will live. The Spirits owe me that much."

He then poured water into a small bowl, mixed in something that looked like dried seaweed, and drank it, wincing. He stuck two small carved bamboo slats into the ground by Nagomi's head.

"Into these sticks I move the pain and the sickness," he said, "when the sticks turn black you must throw them out."

Bran nodded and moved closer to the window. The bear-man started banging out a simple, steady rhythm on the deerskin drum and chucked a few more twigs and leaves onto the fireplace. Thick white smoke filled the inside of the house. The drumming grew faster and louder. Torishi threw back his head and started chanting in a strange, ancient-sounding language.

Ku koh tobochi tan anchi kanne

tani asi ku kon tuntumi ku-tata

Tamb e'tahne ku shirao venara

Ku koh tobochi utarakhe echi mauhe pirikano

Inkoshishchuka yanua, Isomaraykire!

Tan ven ainu kuru-kasihi

Esiohteya mau tambe, ponno ponno

Tan ukuran echi-kochari chiki, pirika!

His body started writhing in a trance, the drum beating grew frenzied. His chanting became garbled, eventually turning into a simple, wordless "*Ya, ya, ya, ya!*" interspersed with whistles and groans. Sweat trickled down his brow.

"Nothing's happening," Bran said when a good half an hour had passed.

THE RISING TIDE

The white smoke hovered over Nagomi's body like a dark spirit.

"Look, the sticks!" Satō whispered, pointing. The pieces of carved bamboo turned solid black, obsidian. Bran grabbed them and scowled.

"Hot!"

"Get them out!"

The boy threw the sticks out the window. They fell into the stream with a hiss of steam. The black smoke disappeared; the air in the room was clear again.

Torishi was still in a trance, but his movements were slower now, more relaxed, and the beating was steady again. She could once again make out words in his chanting.

Ashim puhara,

kamui akah kata

E-kom pashuhi

Tu kamui sonko,

Re kamui sonko,

Anokote!

He stopped and dropped his head until his chin touched his chest. He rocked back and forth for a moment yet, eyes closed, murmuring some quiet prayer.

The priestess moaned and stirred. Blood started returning to her cheeks. She opened her eyes and gasped for air.

"Nagomi!" Satō leapt to her feet. The priestess winced, but smiled weakly.

Bran came up to the bench where the priestess lay. He took her hand and held it tightly, not saying a word.

"I'm... sorry..." Nagomi said with effort, "for worrying... you."

"Don't be stupid," said Satō with visible effort. She turned to the bear-man.

"Is she really alright?"

He nodded heavily.

"See for yourself."

Satō uncovered the place where the sickle blade pierced Nagomi's chest. There was barely a trace of a wound, little more than a white scar she traced down with her finger.

"Are you... are we safe?" the priestess asked.

"We're safe," said Bran. "Here, have some water."

The priestess lapped up a few mouthfuls from a clay pot and lay back on the bench, closing her eyes.

"You must rest now. We'll tell you about everything later," he added.

"It looks like we are even, Torishi-*sama*," Satō said, bowing before their host.

"The Spirits repaid their debt," the bear-man said, shaking his head. He leaned towards her. He smelled of raw meat and soil. He touched her arm with a long, dirty finger. She fought the urge to step back.

"You too are wounded."

He took a small container from the box and handed it to her. It reeked of animal fat.

"Put it on the wound. *Kudzu* root. Keeps it clean."

She looked at Bran, slightly panicked. The boy glanced at Nagomi.

"He helped her – maybe he can help you, too."

The blood-soaked and tattered sleeve of her kimono fell apart in her hands when she tried to roll it up. She tentatively scooped some of the white goo and put it onto the red, swollen wound. It stung, but she endured in silence.

The noon turned to afternoon, and the inside of the hut grew even darker and gloomier with all the smoke and soot. Nagomi was still asleep, but her skin had a healthy glow again, and her breathing was regular. Satō had her arm bandaged and was eating the last of Torishi's fish, while Bran devoured another portion of cured venison. He caught her repulsed gaze.

"Stop looking at me like that," he said. "I'm not a Sun Priest. I haven't had meat for a month. Why don't *you* eat meat, anyway?"

"I… I just don't," she replied, realizing she had only a faint idea of the reason. "It's gross."

Torishi handed them each a wooden cup filled with some misty liquid. She smelled it suspiciously.

"Another medicine?"

The bear-man chuckled.

"Yes, medicine… for the head."

She sipped. It had a bitter and fermented taste, like bad saké. She gulped the cup in one go and felt the warmth spreading throughout her body. She reached out for seconds, but Torishi took the cup from her.

"One is enough."

"So…" Bran started. "What happened to your people? Did they all die from this sickness?"

Torishi shook his head again.

"That was just the end. First the Valley People kept on coming… always up, always deeper into the forest," he said in a monotone, resigned voice, staring at the flames. "Cutting down trees… building homes of wood and paper… planting fields… hunting our game… taking our women."

He raised a hand to the light. His arm was covered in ancient scars and burns.

"They had metal and fire, and the Bear People only had wood and stone and claw. After they took our land they started hunting *us*."

"Like the hunters we fought today," said Bran. "But *why* hunt you?"

"Our insides hold powerful magic. Or so the Valley People believe. But only if cut from a bear. That's what the

53

jade necklace was for – to seal me in bear; strong but dumb. Easy to trap."

"And they would've left you to starve?" asked Satō.

"Bad luck to slay one of us. Much better to let one die of hunger."

"Somehow I... I knew I had to remove the necklace," said Bran. "Was that you?"

Torishi nodded.

"It's a call from one Kumaso hunter to another. But there are no more Kumaso hunters in the mountain." He looked into the darkness. "And the Valley People were deaf to our calls."

Nagomi stirred and moaned. Torishi touched her head with a fatherly gesture and the girl calmed down.

"You asked whether Nagomi was a priestess," remembered Satō.

"Your priests were the chief of our enemies. They rallied the Valleys against us. But... it doesn't matter now. The crimes of others are not her fault."

He paused. "My daughter had fox hair, too."

Satō blinked, surprised.

"A Dejima child? In this forest?" Satō could think of no other reason.

"Many fox-haired cubs laughed and played in this village before the Blistering Sickness silenced them forever."

He lowered his head and let out a long, sad grunt, then looked back up at them with a smile.

"No, let's not dwell on the past. You must be tired."

It was still early, but Satō felt weak and weary. She nodded. Torishi stood up and moved Nagomi gingerly onto the raised bed.

He unrolled a couple of old boar skins on the floor.

"I need to check the traps," he said, heading for the door. "Maybe catch a fish."

He left the house. Satō ran her fingers through the bristles and a few bugs skittered onto the floor. She recoiled in disgust.

"Blistering Disease," she murmured.

"What?" asked Bran.

"What if it's still here? Aren't you worried?"

"Don't be silly, nobody dies of smallpox anymore."

"Not here. At least Nagomi's vaccinated, but I…"

"You'll be fine. The disease must be long gone."

It wasn't very reassuring, but there was little else she could do. *He's our host,* she thought with her eyes closed. *And saved Nagomi's life. I have to take what he has to offer.*

She saw Bran shake the skin with a swift motion and tried to do the same, but a needle of pain pierced her arm.

"Are you alright?" the boy asked.

"I'm fine."

She lay down on the boar skin, carefully, trying to touch as little of it as possible, and closed her eyes.

"Looks like we were lucky again," she heard Bran's voice nearby.

"Yes... the *kami* take good care of Nagomi – and us."

"Did you mean it?" he asked.

"Mean what?"

"When you said you trusted me."

There was a long pause as she mulled over the answer.

"We have to trust each other. There's nobody else left."

"Thank you."

He sighed. She heard the fur rustle underneath him.

"I killed a man today."

"It was the old Spirit, not you," she said, not sure where he was going with it.

"I think I slew some more yesterday."

She tried to recall the details of the battle, but it was all a blur; only the death of the man in the black *yamabushi* robes she remembered clearly, the sound of cracking skull, her blooded sword.

"I thought you were a soldier."

He sighed again.

"I was taught how to fight, yes, but not how to take a life. It's... not at all how I imagined."

56

"I wouldn't know," she said, "I am a samurai. Killing is in my blood."

But when she closed her eyes she could still see the anguish on the slain man's face; after all it was her first kill, too.

Does death hurt that much?

"An old doctor once told me," said Bran, "not to dwell too long on killing. If I do, I might start... enjoying it."

"That's what my Father taught me, too. Not to give in to bloodlust. The doom of the samurai, he called it. But I yearned to kill this demon so much!"

Father...

Shūhan's gentle face appeared before her eyes. What would he have said about the way she conducted herself in the battle?

"It was close. We could have all died there."

"Nagomi almost did."

"Eh... Our host is right. No point dwelling on the past. We're alive, that's all that matters. As soon as Nagomi is healed and rested, we will..."

He hung his voice.

"We will go down from these mountains," she finished for him. "And the first thing I'll do when we get to a town is take a bath and buy some new clothes. Good thing I still have my gold."

This was as far ahead as she could think right now.

Bran turned on his side; from the soft rhythm of Satō's breath he could tell she was already asleep. The priestess lay on the platform on her back with her hands clasped over her stomach, hair spread like red fire on the dark skins. The door to the hut squeaked open and in came Torishi, quietly, with three large fish tied to a pole. The bear-man sat down in the corner and began to work on his catch in utter silence.

They had avoided the subject all day, but now that Bran was alone with his thoughts it had returned at last.

What are we going to do now? What am I going to do?

There was a void in his mind; the dragon was gone. Broken away, it was roaming somewhere over Yamato.

I could still hunt it down, he thought, *follow the news and rumours. A rampaging dragon is an easy thing to track after all.*

But he dreaded what he had to do to Emrys, as he also knew, after the Farlink was gone, it was too late for anything else.

Father was right, he thought bitterly. He imagined Dylan, shaking his finger.

"*I told you. You can't trust a dragon.*"

I still need to get back home after that. The Bataavian ship will be here in a month, if I manage to get back to Kiyō. He sighed. Suddenly everything seemed that much more complicated and depressing. Get to Emrys, and fly away; that was all he had ever thought about - until now.

And what about the girls? It had been an insane idea to take Nagomi on this dangerous journey in the first place.

Whatever had Lady Kazuko been thinking? And Satō? Without a dragon, was Bran still a target for the Crimson Robe?

Unlikely. She would be better off chasing him on her own. Or better yet, find somebody more suitable for the job... like that Gensai man from Kirishima.

He didn't sleep much that night; by morning he had made up his mind.

"I'm going after the dragon. Alone. We will get you two down to the Valleys and find a way to transport Nagomi back to Kiyō."

They looked at him puzzled.

"It's my dragon and it's my quest," he proceeded to explain. "You both are no longer a part of it. Satō, you had better look for your father without me. And I don't care about the Prophecies or whatever the High Priestess told you, Nagomi – it's got too dangerous."

"Do you think... I followed you because... Kazuko-*hime* told me to?" asked the priestess quietly. Talking still was an effort for her.

"No, that's not what I –"

"It was not your decision to have us join you, and it will not be your decision to make us leave," said Satō.

"Look, you got it all wrong!" Bran struggled, "I only do this because I don't want you to get hurt! Because I *care* about you."

"And you think that we don't care... about you?" Nagomi said and turned her face to the wall. She would not say anything more.

"Idiot," said Satō, standing up. "Don't make her angry, she's still not well. Come, let's talk outside."

Bran followed her and they sat on the bank of the cold stream.

"I want to track the dragon down. But I can do it all by myself," he said, scratching the scab on his cheek. "You don't need to follow me anymore. You can go searching for your father, and Nagomi can rest in some shrine in Kagoshima. I would only be getting in your way."

Satō sighed and wrapped her arms around her knees.

"I'll tell you a secret, Bran. I don't think my old man is still alive."

He looked at her, surprised.

"I never said anything because I didn't want to worry Nagomi, but... it's been so long. The Crimson Robe must have decided it's not worth keeping him around anymore."

"Then why...?"

"I want revenge. And don't you want one too? It's partly because of that demon that your dragon has gone – how do you say it?"

"Feral."

She pondered it for a while.

"I understand what you're trying to do, and I think it's very honourable," she said at last, "but it's too late."

60

She put her hand on his arm in a gesture she must have picked up from him.

"We're friends now, Bran. We fought together; we've been through hardships together. We've saved each other's lives. And if there's anything you need help with, you can count on us."

He nodded slowly and smiled, somehow relieved.

"And you can count on me."

"Great." She stood up. "So what's the *real* plan?"

By the next morning, Nagomi stood up from the bed on her own. She swayed at first, but refused the support of Satō's arm.

"I'm fine, really. I need to stretch my legs, they're too weak."

She paced slowly around the hut; there wasn't a lot of space in the low, dark building, so she stepped outside, where Torishi was preparing a morning soup of bracken and roots. The bear-man saw her and smiled, welcoming her to sit beside him.

"You're well, little cub."

"Yes. All thanks to you, I hear, Torishi-*sama*."

She bowed.

"Thanks to the Spirits. You know it as well as I do."

"You're a priest, too?"

A shadow marred his face for a moment.

"I speak to the Spirits, but in a different way."

In the silence that followed, she sensed the presence of many *kami* all around her. They studied her in curious silence; the place felt almost like… like…

"This entire glade is a shrine!" she said, astonished.

Torishi nodded. "We do not build shrines. Our Spirits dwell with us."

"Did you stay here to keep the Spirits company after everyone died?"

"You might say that," he said and threw another split root into the pot. There was little emotion in his voice, but Nagomi suddenly felt an overwhelming sadness and loneliness.

"I heard that you… your people lived here before the Yamato came."

He nodded.

"Are you one of the Ancients, then?"

"Oh, no," he said, shaking his hairy head. "But I know *of* them. They lived alongside us, a long time ago. The Little Folk, we called them. We learned the bear lore from them, and the secrets of the Forest."

"What happened to them?"

"They were already a dying race when we came. That's what the legends say. Sick and poor. They hid in the tunnels they dug deep into the mountains, in the earth barrows… praying to their dragon gods to come and save them. None ever did."

62

The dragon gods?

"This is ready," he added, picking up the pot. "Time to put it on the fire."

"There's no point wasting your time because of me", said Nagomi, "the sooner we leave, the sooner we will find Bran's dragon and your honoured Father."

Satō cast Bran a meaningful look and said, "It shouldn't take us more than two, three days to reach Kagoshima, and it's a city as big as Kiyō."

"Did your father know anyone in Kagoshima?" asked Bran.

"There are a few wizards who moved there from Kiyō. I'm sure I can ask around. We'll be safe from the *Taikun* there, too."

She noticed the bear-man listening to their conversation with great interest and, as soon as they finished planning, he stood up and started packing his belongings into a large canvas bag: his shaman's box, little drum, ointments and herbs.

"What are you doing?" she asked.

"There is nothing to keep me here."

He reached for the weapons hanging on the wall – a long, curved hunting knife in antler sheath and a bow with two dozen flint head arrows.

"But what about the Spirits?" asked Nagomi.

"They agree. Your coming was a sign. Time to forget about the past."

"You don't even know our purpose."

"I don't need to."

Satō leaned over to Bran and whispered in his ear.

"What do you think?"

"We could use his protection," replied Bran, eyeing Torishi's muscular arms and chest, "if we can trust another stranger. He seems kind though..."

"He is a *werebear*. What if it's dangerous, like your Dragonform?"

Satō felt Nagomi's hand on hers.

"I believe in this man's good intentions," the red-haired girl said. "Please, Sacchan, let him join us."

"All right, then," said Satō with a sigh. "We're moving out in an hour. I just hope the people in the valleys don't shoot you on sight."

The noon sun stood high in the sky. Satō picked up her bundle – thanking quietly the servant girl from Kirishima for salvaging so much of their belongings – and headed towards the fence of poison ivy.

"Wait, please," said Torishi. He entered the bamboo hut and emerged with a burning log from the fireplace.

What is he doing?

The bear-man chanted in his strange language and started walking around the building, singing and setting fire to the dry straw walls. The hut quickly burst into flames, like a giant funeral pyre.

He cast the burning log into the stream and stood for a while in front of the blazing house with his head hung low; a giant black silhouette against the yellow flames. In his light brown tunic, woven of bark cloth and richly decorated with black patterns, and embroidered red and blue headscarf, he looked truly regal, as the great chieftain of a proud race should. Finally, he turned around. His face was grave, but calm.

"Thus perished the last village of the Kumaso," he said. "Let us leave this forsaken place."

THE RISING TIDE

CHAPTER IV

"We will now vote for the second time on Hotta-*dono*'s proposal from the previous meeting. And if this time we have a stalemate, then, according to the law, we will refer to His Excellency's decision. Are we all in agreement?"

Chief Councillor Abe waited until all the other councillors grunted their confirmation.

"In that case, please raise your hands if you believe we should initiate our secret negotiations with the Barbarians."

He raised his hand, as did Naosuke; this was expected. The two Matsudairas voted in the same split way as before. Young Kuze looked at them with contempt. It seemed there would be a stalemate again, after all. This suited him; the *Taikun* was bound to disagree with the motion.

But then the old Councillor Tadamasa also raised his hand, slowly, with a visible effort.

"Makino-*dono*," the elder of the Matsudairas asked with a frown, "are you sure you understood the question?"

"I may be old, but I'm not senile," replied Tadamasa angrily.

"May I ask what changed your mind?" asked Kuze, struggling to keep calm. His right hand twitched close and open.

"No, you may not," the old Councillor said and lowered his eyes, seemingly fascinated with the dark lining separating the *tatami* mats on the floor.

There was a long silence. At last, Chief Councillor Abe coughed and spoke.

"Then I declare the vote to have passed. We will send the message to… no… I will go meet the foreigners myself. Hotta-*dono* will accompany me."

Kuze Hirochika rose in indignation.

"Then there is nothing for me to do here. While you talk like weaklings, I shall prepare the defences of the capital. Let's see whose way will prevail, a clerk's - or a warrior's."

He turned to Naosuke and seethed through his teeth.

"It's your fault, Hotta-*dono*. I don't know how, but I know *you* did this. It's another one of your tricks. But you'll regret this, mark my words. Your days as the Councillor are numbered."

"Titles are meaningless. I exist only to serve the *Taikun*," said Naosuke and bowed.

The interior of the Inner Palace was austere, contemplative, compared to the lavishness of the Outer and Middle courts. Those ones were designed to awe and overwhelm the *Taikun*'s guests with gold flakes, priceless paintings, ancient scrolls and vases, and rich gardens. The Inner Palace was

68

where the *Taikun* and his family relaxed. The walls were plain black and white lattice of bamboo and paper, with all the effort put into harmony and balance rather than decoration. Beyond the *Taikun*'s private rooms lay the great Ōku hall, the many-corridored harem where his wives and concubines spent days painting, playing instruments and engaging in ceaseless intrigues and power struggles. And surrounding all this was the *Taikun*'s private garden, with moon viewing verandas, tea houses and delicate pavilions overlooking decorative ponds teeming with koi carps and small brown turtles.

It was on one of the garden verandas that the great *Taikun*, Tokugawa Ieyoshi, lay on his side, admiring the plum trees growing around a small, circular pond. They bloomed for the second time this year and were an unusual colour of pure scarlet, their petals floating like drops of blood on the surface of the pool. Ieyoshi was not superstitious, but even he wondered if it wasn't some kind of an omen.

The *Taikun* was an old man; tired of life. His efforts at reforms had failed, his treasury empty, his borders undefended; he was all too aware of the shortcomings and dangers facing his nation. He glanced with worry at his only son, Iesada, who sat beside him, observing the flowers with a blank look. A weak-minded and weak-bodied boy, he was not an heir fit for the challenges of ruling a country in these difficult times. Ieyoshi could have only hoped he would live long enough to guide the Yamato nave across the seas of trouble before an untimely death.

The squeaking of the nightingale floor in the Corridor of Bells announced the arrival of the boy messenger at the veranda. The *Taikun* slowly turned his aching body towards him.

"What news of the Council, boy?"

"The Council has voted to open secret negotiations with the Western Barbarians, *kakka*."

The *Taikun* suddenly jumped to his feet with agility defying his age and health.

"What!?" he roared. A flock of startled sparrows flew from the peony bush. "How did that happen? Abe was supposed to make sure there would be no talks!"

"Word in the palace is, Makino-*dono* was convinced by Councillor Hotta to support the motion. Abe-*dono* was simply outvoted."

"And who proposed the motion in the first place?"

"Councillor Hotta, *kakka*."

The *Taikun* closed his hands in fists and gnashed his teeth.

"He will pay for the insolence. His usefulness has at last expired. I will force the little pale devil to resign. Come, Iesada, you should learn from this."

Reluctantly, the *Taikun*'s heir picked himself up from the veranda floor and followed his father down the Corridor of Bells to the Room of Scrolls, where the old *Taikun* liked to prepare his edicts and despatches before officially dictating them to his secretary.

"Make me some ink, son, my arm is weary. Now, let's see... we shall do it the old fashioned way. *To Hotta Naosuke, the esteemed Councillor, etc., from Tokugawa Ieyoshi, Great Commodore of Yamato, etc.* The secretary will fill up all the required titles. *Please accept this gift as an expression of our gratitude for your services. We trust this ancient cha ceremony set, said to belong to Sen Sōsa himself, the first headmaster of the Omotesenke School, will be to your liking. We know how fond you are of the Ceremony, and we hope in the near future you will find sufficient time to fully appreciate its beauty."*

"That's it? We're sending him a tea pot?" Iesada blinked, his face showing utter lack of understanding.

"Have none of my teachings reached through that thick skull of yours?" Ieyoshi said and sighed. "Read between the lines, boy! You need time to practice Way of *Cha*, time you can't spare if you are busy running the government. That's the way we deal with things at the court. *Subtle and refined.* Do you understand?"

"Yes, Father..."

"Do you? Sometimes I wonder. Come with me to the Middle Palace, we shall make this letter known. And you," he said to the boy messenger who waited patiently in the door. "Get me Abe. I need to remind him the Council is just an *advisory* body."

Dōraku examined the surroundings of the shrine, discovering the tracks by the burned-out remains of a gate leading into the forest. It was the middle of the night, the forest was pitch black, but his eyes could easily spot the signs of a battle which had taken place around the *torii* gate: the earth torn and the trees shattered by magic, the discarded weapons; the charred remains of an oxcart and a few links of a shattered iron chain. But the bodies had been taken away for funeral, and the rain washed off the footsteps; even he could not tell them apart.

Everyone in town spoke of nothing else but the fire and devastation of a large part of the shrine and the death of many priests and samurai in the conflagration. Those who spoke the loudest were blaming it on some careless kitchen maid or a rogue lightning strike. After greasing a few palms here and making a scary face there, Dōraku soon learned a different story: that of a flying monster, coming down the mountain and destroying everything in its path.

Two days had passed since he had come to his senses on the rocky slope of the Takachiho Mountain. The day before, he had to kill a deer; but an animal's blood was not enough to sustain him after the exhausting regeneration.

Cursed thirst. If only I had more time to rest…

There was an odd set of tracks leading east, up the slope; it seemed as if some bulky giant had run through the forest, followed by more hurried steps in the same direction. He traced all these tracks down to a line of tall, grey rocks. Here the first set seemed to disappear into thin air, while the other group scoured the ground searching for clues, much like Dōraku himself was now doing. They then departed north along the rock face.

"They aren't here anymore." A young voice surprised him. He turned around to see a girl dressed in the simple clothes of a shrine servant.

72

"And how do you know who I'm looking for?" he asked and frowned. He didn't like being surprised.

How can she see me?

"I helped them escape. They went up there," she said, pointing to the east, over the rocks, "but I can't tell you how they got away. It's a secret."

She covered her lips with her hand and giggled.

"Who are you? How did you find me?"

"I'm just a servant girl, samurai-*dono*. But I can see… things."

"Have you seen the battle?"

"No, samurai-*dono*. I can't stand the sight of *blood*."

He stepped closer and saw the girl was blind.

She senses my thirst.

"Are you going to help them?" she asked.

"I'll try," he replied and turned north.

"What are you doing, samurai-*dono*? That's not where they went!"

"Now that I know they survived, I can see where those people have gone too," he said.

"But they may be in danger."

"And *are they* in danger now, girl?"

"N…no," she admitted. "For the moment they are in safe hands."

Dōraku looked at the servant girl carefully.

"That's a remarkable gift you have, child."

"The priests think it comes from a demon."

"The priests are all dead," he said, "and believe me, I would know if it was a demon. Here," he added, throwing her a large silver coin, "this should pay off whatever debt is keeping you here. Move to some other shrine, where they will recognize your talent."

"Thank you, samurai-*dono*."

The old, bald Nanseian, Shō, threw a thick piece of firewood into the air and chopped at it with the edge of his hand. Two cleanly sliced parts fell to the ground. He grunted, satisfied.

"Show off," mumbled Azumi.

She was crouching against a cedar tree, clutching a large straw basket in her arms.

"Why can't you just use an axe, like everyone else?"

"I need to stay fit. You could do with some exercise too."

She shrugged.

"I don't care."

"You may want to watch your tongue, woman."

She stared at him in cold fury.

"And who's going to tell him? You can't even find three lost kids!"

"You were there too," he barked.

74

"I'm not a tracker. And *I* was wounded."

"They used magic. I can't deal with magic."

"Neither can I. Makes you wonder why he chose *us* to pursue them."

"The Master is after the *dorako*. His magic is needed there. We'll be fine, they can't have just disappeared. It's only a matter of time."

She kept staring at him. He ran his hand over his bald head. He was always uneasy near her.

Is it because I'm an shinobi… or because I'm a woman?

"What did he promise you, Nanseian?" she asked. "What would you do with the Reward?"

"My father is the king of Nansei," he replied proudly. "A *rightful* king. Yet he has to pay tribute to Satsuma. I would change that."

He punched a nearby tree, to show what he would do with the masters of Satsuma. The blow left a satisfying, fist-size crater in the trunk.

As if in answer, the bushes parted and a tired, grey-clad swordsman appeared on the glade before Shō.

"What is it?" the Nanseian asked.

"We found this in the forest, Shō-*sama*." The *rōnin* handed him a tattered, bloodied piece of white cloth. Shō studied it for a moment.

"The priestess," he said, picking up a red hair. "You haven't found the body, then?"

75

"No, just this. The rest of the group followed the tracks into the woods; they sent me here to report."

"Very well." Shō nodded. "Get up, Azumi. We have a hunt on our hands."

The assassin rose and started tying the straw basket to a sash on her back.

What was that?

She turned around swiftly, but there was only the forest.

"What is it?" he asked.

"I thought I saw something, over there in the trees."

"Must have been a deer."

"A climbing deer?"

"A monkey, then. Hurry up, woman."

There are no monkeys in these forests, Nanseian.

It was already dark by the time Azumi and Shō reached the camp the grey-clads had set up around the waterfall cave.

"We found them running through the woods," one of the swordsmen said, casting two frightened men onto their knees before Shō. The Nanseian squinted to see their faces better in the light of the torch.

Poachers.

"They have an interesting story to tell."

One of the men told the tale of their meeting with two armed, spell-casting youths.

"Only two?" the Nanseian asked.

"Yes, Shō-*sama*."

Shō nodded at the *rōnin*. One of the poachers understood the gesture and raised his hands in despair. His pleas for mercy were cut abruptly by a quick sword cut. His companion jumped up and tried to run away. As he was passing Azumi, she raised her hand in silence. The sickle blade pierced the poacher's neck; the man fell to the ground, clutching the wound and gurgling.

"Have you found anything else in the cave?" Shō asked, turning away from the dying poacher crawling in the grass.

"Only traces of campfire and this," one of the men presented a handful of jade comma-shaped jewels and a piece of string. The Nanseian furrowed his brow in thought.

"Magic", he said and spat. "Who's the best tracker here?" he asked.

"That is me," said the swordsman who spoke first.

"Take a torch and try to figure out what went on here. As soon as the day breaks we follow the trail further. They can't have gone far; they're tired and injured. Somebody finish that man off!" he added, annoyed.

The tracker returned shortly before dawn.

"There were two of them coming in – and one carried – but three left. They either got help or somebody captured them. Big feet, lots of hair," he added, presenting a bundle of long, black hair he had gathered from the branches around the cave.

"Black hair? You recognize any of this?" the Nanseian asked Azumi.

How can you not *recognize it?*

"It's a bear," she said.

"Right. A big man in bear skin should be easy to find. Wake up you lazy oafs!" he shouted and started kicking those who would not get up quickly enough, "the trail is fresh."

In half an hour the camp was packed and the group made ready to follow the tracker up the mountainside, deeper into the forest. They walked for a quarter of a *ri* when the tracker stood up and sniffed.

"Smoke."

He wrinkled his nose.

"Strange smoke. That's no campfire. Stay here; I'll see what's going on."

Minutes passed, and the tracker failed to reappear. Shō scratched the top of his bald head.

"You," he said to another of the grey-clad swordsmen. They all looked the same to him.

"Check what's up with him. But be careful."

As soon as the swordsman disappeared in the bushes, Shō selected three others.

"Shadow him. Run back if there's any danger. Don't get heroic."

He didn't have to wait long before an abruptly cut shout echoed through the forest.

"Shō-*sama!* It's a tra-"

The Nanseian clapped his hands and motioned others to follow him. There were six warriors still left, and a few hired hunters, armed with bows; Azumi followed behind. They all hurried in the direction of the shout and ran through an opening in the wall of poison ivy out onto a wide, sunny glade. Remains of a small house built of straw and twigs were still smouldering near a calm stream. A tall man, clad in a purple hooded cloak, stood in the middle of the glade, with his back, towards Shō. He held twin swords in his hands; the blades dripped with blood. Her heart skipped a beat.

"No… no, no, no," said Azumi, stepping back.

"What's wrong?" asked Shō, but he couldn't wait for an answer. The man in the hooded cloak turned around to face them. His eyes were golden, and his face pale like old paper: just like Azumi remembered. The six grey-clad swordsmen surrounded him in a narrow circle.

The Nanseian took a long, cautious look at the two bloodied swords and ordered his men to step further back. The hunters drew their bows and targeted the man, but Shō told them to put down the weapons.

"Arrows can't hurt him."

He stepped closer, though sweat covered his bald head.

"What is your quarrel with us, Fanged?"

Fanged?

79

"I will have no quarrel if you turn around now and go back to your master, Nanseian," the Swordsman spoke.

"That I cannot do. Step aside and let us continue the hunt."

"I said, leave this place now - while you're still alive."

"I serve one of the Eight Heads. You *will* stand aside."

"Your master told you of the Serpent? How reckless of him." The Swordsman smiled wryly. "I do not care for them, and do not fear them."

What are they talking about?

"Cut him to pieces," Shō ordered, and the six warriors leapt into battle.

As soon as the grey-clads launched their attack, Azumi decided discretion was a far better part of valour and vanished from the glade. From a nearby tree, she observed the fight. It was brief.

The Swordsman's eyes turned from gold to black; his face seemed even paler in contrast. His body became one with his swords, a whirlwind of blades, a flurry of cuts. He undercut the first warrior's grip with such force that the man's katana flew high into the air. The swords moved faster than the eye could see, with inhuman speed and unnatural strength, whistling through the air, breaking through mail and bone with ease.

His opponents were highly trained swordsmen and killers in their own right. But before the flying katana dropped to the ground, the fight was over. The demon stood

80

alone in a pool of red; the six swordsmen around him dead or dying, some sprawled on the grass, some still kneeling, clutching their gushing wounds in agony for a few more seconds. The hunters fled into the forest. The Swordsman shook the blood off his swords, in the same move wiped and sheathed them. His kimono was splattered with crimson, but there was not even a scratch on his body. Shō reeled back; he looked to his sides, searching for Azumi, only to discover that he was alone.

You may think me a coward, she thought, *but at least I will live to warn the Master.*

"Did you not know who I am, Nanseian?" the Swordsman spoke, his voice icy cold. "Did my name not reach the southern islands yet?"

The old man shook his head, speechless.

"I am Niten Dōraku; I am Shinmen Takezō; I am the Immortal Swordsman. I have never been defeated in a fair fight. I gave you the chance to live, but you threw it away. And now, because of you, I hunger even more…"

Shō raised his hands in combat stance; the Swordsman leapt towards him. The sinewy man struck a powerful blow on the demon's chest, but it made no impression on the samurai, who grabbed Shō's outstretched arm and snapped it at the elbow like a twig. Glistening fangs plunged into his neck and the demon started lapping up bright blood spewing from the vein. Shō gurgled and flailed his arms desperately.

The Swordsman threw the bloodless body to the ground and wiped his lips. The colour of his eyes returned to gold. He looked at the Nanseian's corpse.

"Poor fool… were Ganryū's promises really worth so much?"

He closed his eyes, bowed his head and started praying.

Azumi did not wait to see him finish.

CHAPTER V

Bran felt as if he had seen all this before. They were climbing down a narrow, forested gully, following their new guide, just as they had been following Dōraku not that long ago.

How come we keep doing this?

The gully had been carved in the slope of the Takachiho Mountain by the same stream that ran through Torishi's village. By now it had grown into a raging mountain river, foaming and skipping over the boulders on its journey down to the sea. It was nearing the end of the day and the rain started pouring down again.

"There is a village right below that ridge," the bear-man said. "Good people, if easily frightened."

"What do we tell them?" asked Nagomi. "We don't look like normal travellers."

Their clothes were still tattered, singed and bloodied in places. Satō and Torishi had tried hard to repair them over the previous couple of days, but they could only do so much with bone needle and vine thread and cold stream water. The wizardess had her arm wrapped in bandages, Bran's broken nose was still bruised and swollen.

"We don't need to tell them anything," replied Bran. "They're just peasants."

Satō raised an eyebrow but said nothing.

Nobody welcomed them at the entrance to the village; the only road was empty and quickly turning into a quagmire in the rain.

Another desolate hamlet, thought Bran, and his heart sank.

The sharply angled thatched roof of the headman's house loomed over the centre of the village. As they drew closer, heads started appearing in the doors and windows of the huts, curious faces of children and their mothers.

We must be the most visitors this place has seen in years.

That the two of them wore noblemen's clothes – albeit torn and tattered – made it even more of an event. By the time they reached the village centre – a wider and less muddy bit of the road in front of the headman's house – they were followed by a small, silent, curious gathering.

A far larger crowd had gathered on the square, made up of men and women in field clothes. They were not there to welcome the visitors; in fact, Bran saw only their backs. The crowd listened to the headman, who was standing on a tree stump, shouting and waving his arms, trying to calm the agitated villagers down.

"Yes, there will be new taxes," Bran heard him say, "and we will have to work harder through the harvest season to rebuild our shrine."

So they know already.

Angry murmurs rippled through the crowd.

"But who knows – there may be work at the rebuilding! Carpenters, porters, all sorts of construction workers… I'll send a man to Kirishima tomorrow to see if there's any word of what they may need."

"There's never any work in town!" somebody cried. "They have their own craftsmen."

"All they want is more rice, more barley, more buckwheat, never more workers," complained another. "At this rate we'll have no grain left for the sowing season!"

Others hollered in agreement. Bran turned to one of the old women in the group that had followed them through the village.

"What's going on?" he asked.

"Oh, terrible news, *tono*," she replied, bowing. "The Great Shrine has burned down! Many dead, many wounded. Priests and even… some samurai."

"How awful!" he said avoiding her gaze.

The men in the square finally took notice of the strangers, as did the headman. He raised his hands again.

"Be quiet, all of you!" he cried, "let me welcome our noble guests."

This had the effect opposite to what he intended. The villagers became even more aggravated, their anger now turned toward the mysterious visitors.

"Noble guests?" said one, a burly, strong-looking fellow with a few teeth missing and a bruise under his eye. "They don't look noble to me! Look at the girl's hair - only demons have hair like that! And that bearded giant, isn't he one of the mountain goblins?" He spat.

Bran's hand wandered to the sword at his side.

How dare you...

"What noblemen have no horse, no bags, no servants?" added another peasant, a woman in dirty-brown *monpe* and red headscarf.

"First a burned shrine, and now *they* are coming down from the mountains?" shouted someone else. "Funny that!"

"Silence, serf!"

Bran stepped forward, with the sword drawn by a few inches. The crowd pulled back and quietened, but then the woman in the red headscarf cried again.

"Look at his eyes! Bright green! It's a goblin! A goblin!"

She grabbed his kimono and shook him, as if to see if he was real. A handful of gravel flew towards his face. Sudden outrage turned his vision red. In one swift move, Bran drew the sword and slashed her across the chest.

"Aiyeeee!" She fell down with a brief, shrieking yell. Red splattered over the mud.

Everything fell silent for a brief moment; and then the crowd charged. They fell on Bran with fists, clubs and stones. He slipped in the mud, letting go of his sword. Instinctively, he summoned a weak *tarian,* but the sight of magic only roused the peasants into further frenzy.

The barrage stopped as abruptly as it had started. A villager was thrown aside with great force, then another, and the crowd scattered in fright. Torishi's bulking frame loomed over Bran and a muscular, hairy arm reached out to help him up. Satō was standing in the middle of the road, waving her blade threateningly at any peasant who dared to get near. A man was lying at her feet, screaming and clutching a stump of an arm.

The bear-man handed Bran his bloodied and muddy weapon. He stared at it, as if seeing it for the first time, then at the peasant woman at his feet, and the wide gash across her chest still spurting blood in a weakening rhythm, its edges bright red and glistening in the rain. He felt nauseous. He looked around. Only the headman remained on the road, prostrated, not daring to look up.

He felt somebody grabbing him by the arm.

"We'd better go," Nagomi said quietly. "Looks like we won't be staying here for the night, after all."

It was too late to look for another village, so they decided to break camp off the road, an hour's walk down the mountain. The forest here was not as wild as higher up, with young trees planted in place of the old ones by the woodsmen, and all the fern and bracken cleared regularly.

"We'll find a bed and bath tomorrow," said Satō, smiling. She bumped Bran in a friendly way, trying to cheer him up. The boy had been gloomy and silent since leaving the village. He nodded, absentmindedly.

"What's wrong with him?" Torishi asked.

"It's complicated," she replied, herself unsure.

Bran looked up, overhearing their exchange.

"It was me this time," he said in a blank voice. "Not Emrys, not Shigemasa. I slew her because I was angry. Because she touched me."

"You did nothing wrong," said Satō. "They were about to attack you, right? She showed no respect for a samurai. She got what she deserved. You should rest now."

"I'm fine," Bran replied and stood up. "I need to be alone for a while."

He followed a path deeper into the woods and a clearing freshly cut by the lumberjacks. He sat down on a stump of cedar tree and closed his eyes.

He was trying to recede from consciousness the way he had all those days ago in Mogi. At last it worked; when he opened his eyes, he found himself looking down from the top of the red-eye tower, out onto the measureless red dust plain.

"*Taishō!*" he cried at the top of his lungs. The shout echoed throughout the flatland, the only sound in this vast emptiness.

He waited. Eventually, a lonely dot appeared on the horizon, moving slowly. When Shigemasa neared the tower, Bran shouted again.

"That's enough! Don't come closer."

The old General looked up to him with a wry, mocking smile.

"What are you doing to me?" the boy asked.

"I haven't done anything," Shigemasa replied. "That's just the way things are, boy. You didn't think there wouldn't be a price? You're becoming one of *us*."

"No!" Bran cried and the power of his protest raised a gust of wind so strong it slid Shigemasa away by a few feet.

"It's your whispers, your... mind tricks!"

Shigemasa chuckled.

"I told you, didn't I? The old hag from Suwa had no idea what she was unleashing. To bind the spirit of a Barbarian with that of a samurai... Nobody ever tried anything like it."

"I don't care. I want you to *stop*."

"I can't - ! As long as I'm here, you will keep changing. You should be happy, Barbarian."

Bran gnashed his teeth.

"Why are you so upset anyway?" the General asked. "It was just some peasant scum. They should *all* have been put to death."

"No. You wouldn't understand. It's not how things are done in *my* country. We are *not* killing innocent people."

A smile vanished from General's face.

"Oh but I *do* understand. I understand you Barbarians very well. I fought alongside the Red Heads at Shimabara, remember? You like to think yourselves all high and moral. You don't kill like us, facing your enemies. You'd rather stab us in the back…"

"Shut up," said Bran.

"*Insolent brat!* You think I came here just to listen to your childish whinging?"

There was a short pause. Brain sighed.

"Oh, yes," he said, "You had something to tell me. That *very important* thing a few days ago. *Before* you tried to steal my body."

Shigemasa shrugged.

"You were about to be killed. I had no choice. I saved you."

"Your help is much appreciated," said Bran with an angry sneer.

Shigemasa looked at him with amusement, and Bran expected another outburst. But the General started laughing, patting himself on the belly with glee.

"You even *talk* like an old samurai now!"

He's right. I sound just like him.

He shook his head and stood straight.

"All right. I'm listening now."

The General stopped laughing and scratched his beard in a slow, deliberate manner before speaking.

"It's about the man who was your guide. The one who called himself Dōraku. What you must know is that he's –"

"The Immortal Swordsman?" interrupted Bran. Shigemasa opened his eyes and mouth wide, in genuine surprise.

"*You knew?*"

"It was obvious. There were too many clues. All I needed was some time to gather my thoughts and remember all the facts. But why bring it now? He's long dead."

"It's not that easy to kill one like him, boy. 'Immortal' is not just a *name*."

This did intrigue Bran.

"How do you know him?"

"He was at Shimabara, too, as one of the *Taikun's* assassins. Back when all the Abominations like him were yet under our control... or that of the Rebels."

Our control...

"The Rebels used the Fanged?"

The General nodded gravely. "They were the first to do so. No trick was beneath them."

"So you *did* recognise Dōraku at once. Why didn't you tell me sooner?"

"I had my reasons then. I have my reasons now."

You were scared of him.

"You think he's still alive, then? That he will come after us?"

"That the wolves did not kill him, I'm certain. I've seen him come out of worse in the war. But who knows what his plans are now..."

Bran closed his eyes.

We have enough trouble as it is.

"I...thank you for letting me know," he said with a sincerity which surprised even him. The General opened his mouth to speak, but Bran warped himself back to the real world before Shigemasa could add anything else.

He opened his eyes to see Nagomi appearing from among the trees. Her face beamed with relief.

"There you are! You've been gone for hours."

"I was... meditating."

The priestess sat down beside him on the tree stump.

"Sacchan said you shouldn't be so upset about what happened."

"That's just the thing. I'm *not* upset. No shame, no remorse. And I should be."

It was clear from her expression that she did not understand.

"Weren't you just defending yourself?"

"What I did stands against everything I was ever taught. It's one thing to kill in a battle, but to slay an innocent..."

"Sacchan said —"

"Yes, but what do *you* think?" he interrupted her. "You are a healer, from a family of physicians. Isn't it your duty to save lives?"

"I…" she pulled back at first, but then composed herself.

"Look – we are all tired and strained. With everything that's been happening to us lately… all the fighting and running away, and – you just made a mistake, that's all."

"A *mistake.*"

He laughed, bitterly.

"When this is all over, if you're still worried about that woman, we can come back here and pray for her."

"And that will… help?"

"Of course! This will placate her soul and restore the peace in yours. Everything will be fine."

He stifled a bitter laugh, not wanting to hurt her feelings.

Is killing really that simple here?

Despite their doctrinal differences, most wizards shared with the Sun Priests the ideal of the sanctity of life. As the ancient Roman philosophers had taught, it was a spark of the Divine Essence, identical in its nature to the Creator, and intended to return to its holy origin in its own time. Any other fate destined it to roam the vastness of the Otherworld, diminishing the Creation forever.

In a more down-to-earth version, slaying was believed to decrease the magic potential in the vicinity of the killer, as well as his own. The theory, though never fully scientifically proven, was popular among the Dracalish and Prydain scholars. That the magic academies like Llambed ostensibly trained future soldiers did not contradict the belief and wars were acceptable as long as they were fought far from Dracaland's vulnerable shores.

Bran wasn't sure if the weakness he had been feeling after the incident was just the power of suggestion, or a true loss of energy.

Placate her soul and restore the peace in yours.

The Yamato, living in a world crowded by the Gods and Spirits, had developed more practical ways of dealing with death. He wondered if these were just meaningless gestures, or was there something in the priestly rituals which helped restore the balance of nature.

A nighthawk began its long, loud call, and they both sat for a while listening to the haunting shrill.

"There's something else bothering you, isn't there," said Nagomi, observing his face.

He shrugged with resignation.

"It's all just too much. My *dorako* … the battle… and you almost died…"

He looked up at her and smiled.

"Back then in the shrine you said we wouldn't fail – so there is still some hope I guess."

"I lied," she said.

"What?"

"I have dreamed of the battle at the shrine, the night before it happened. I saw your *dorako* burning the place down. I saw myself die."

"Then *why* didn't you tell us?"

She looked down and played with the loose straps of her travel cloak.

"I believe... sometimes you can change what the vision shows. I hoped I could... I had to try."

"You knew and yet you threw yourself on the blade."

She nodded.

He reached out and pulled her to himself, hugging her tightly.

"You're the bravest of us all," he told her. She protested feebly.

"My dragon is gone," he said after a short pause, "I may have to kill it."

He caught a glimpse of Satō's vermillion kimono among the cedar trees.

"Dōraku is still alive," he whispered quickly in Nagomi's ear. "He's the Immortal Swordsman."

He let her go and stood up. It was beginning to rain.

It rained for four days straight.

Where is the damn sea?

THE RISING TIDE

Satō cursed the moment they decided to cut short across the valleys in their race towards the sea. Their new guide seemed at ease just wandering around the woods, the concept of being in a hurry meaningless for him, leading them only roughly south as much as his knowledge of the forest allowed. Finally, they got lost among the gullies and hills. What was supposed to be a two-day trek now reached into its fifth, with no end in sight. The food was running scarce; they were left with thin barley gruel and some forest vegetables and roots found by the bear-man, tasteless and smelly, and some bitter herbal concoction Torishi brew in place of *cha*. It gave her energy enough to walk on, and staved off illness, but did nothing to improve her mood. Bran and the Kumaso ate an occasional hare or wood pigeon caught in Torishi's traps, but neither Satō nor Nagomi could force themselves to swallow flesh.

I'm not starving yet.

The forest seemed to spread endlessly in all directions, a grey-green wall of cedars, cypresses and camphor trees overgrown with weeds reaching into the air to swallow the moisture, and lichen hanging in great curtains from the branches. Any other time, she would find this a wondrous sight: there were great camphor trees on the slopes of Suwa, but not that tall and in such great numbers. But the rain and the cold made her look only down, to the sodden ground, where Torishi's big footprints marked the path through the thick cushion moss and dense bracken. She noticed a reddish-brown *habu* adder slithering away slowly among the roots.

We need to get out of here.

She worried about her friends more than herself. The priestess claimed to have fully recovered from her wounds, but she was pale, silent and gloomy, struggling to put on a brave face whenever she noticed somebody was looking at her. Bran was absent, spending most of his evenings and mornings trying to make contact with his *dorako*, apparently to no avail.

On the third evening she had noticed Torishi leaning down to Nagomi and saying something quietly. The priestess smiled, nodded and stood up from the campfire, wiping tired eyes.

"Where are you two going?" Satō asked, putting down the book she'd been reading – the collection of samurai stories she had received as a gift from Master Kawakami in Kirishima. She had just finished the chapter about a nameless swordsman of the Bunroku era, during the Civil Wars, who had slaughtered one hundred students of the Ichijōji fencing school in a single battle. She was disappointed with how far into the realm of fantasy the tale had gone.

A hundred men defeated by one swordsman? What a ridiculous idea.

"She asked me to teach her the bow," replied the bear-man. "All the Kumaso girls knew how to shoot."

"A bow? What do you need that for?" she asked Nagomi.

"I can't rely forever on Luck and the Gods to help me," the priestess said, "and it sounds like fun, too."

97

Nagomi followed Torishi towards a nearby open glade. Satō reached for the book, but did not open it again. Her eyes fell on Bran, leaning against a camphor tree. He was staring into the fire.

That's not such a bad idea, she thought. *Training helps take one's mind off life's hardships.*

"I can teach you how to use a Yamato sword, if you want," she offered. Bran looked up.

"I'm sorry?"

"I was a teacher in my father's dōjō, after all."

"I know how to fence. I had a soldier's training."

She couldn't help bursting out with laughter.

"You call that waving about fencing? Come with me, I'll show you fencing."

He looked wounded for a moment, but then smiled and stood up.

A hot spring burst forth from among the stones, covered with white, sulphurous residue, and ran down the glade a pale blue, steaming stream. Satō put her foot into the rippling brook and sighed.

"Too bad it's so small. I could really use a hot bath."

Bran inadvertently imagined the girl naked in the water. The jarring sound of a sword being unsheathed brought him back to reality.

"Stand like this," she ordered. "Left foot forward, right foot to the back and at an angle. Both bent slightly. A bit more."

Bran obeyed, although the stance felt unnatural to him, strained.

"Bring the sword to your right shoulder, pointing straight up, a bit towards the rear. Elbow up. That's the Shadow Frost Stance, the basic form of the Takashima School."

"All right."

"My form is the standard Metal," she said, hiding the blade behind her so that he could only see the pommel. Bran didn't really try to remember the names.

"Try to strike me from above."

"The girl is good," Shigemasa's voice spoke in Bran's head. *"Her footwork is flawless."*

Bran raised the blade and brought it down at Satō, half-heartedly. The girl dodged aside without moving the sword.

"No, no. You have to really try to hit me. Don't worry, you won't manage," she said, grinning.

"She's right. There's no way you can touch her."

He repeated his strike harder, and this time her sword flashed and clanged against Bran's blade; its tip hovered by his neck.

"Good," she said.

"That was good?"

"Yes," she laughed. "For a beginner."

They clashed a few more times, each time Satō's blade ended flawlessly near one of Bran's vital points, while his own sword flew in some random direction.

I don't see how this is teaching me anything, he thought, growing annoyed. *Hold on, I can show you a trick or two as well.*

He raised the sword deliberately too high. He noticed her loosen her stance, certain of herself. He stepped forward and, when she was raising her weapon to block him, pretended to slip on the wet moss. Satō's sword swished past his head as he lunged forward, grabbing her by the waist and pulling her to the ground with him. He pressed the edge of his blade against her neck.

They were both covered in mud and breathing heavily.

"Well… done," her lips moved in a whisper. He put the sword aside slowly and leaned down to kiss her, gently at first, but when she didn't resist, more passionately. She ran her fingers through his hair, pulling him closer.

"Bran? Sacchan? Where are you?"

Satō broke off the kiss and pushed him off. She stood up hastily, adjusting her kimono. She leaned over the hot stream and washed her face.

"You did well," she said, not looking back at him. "We… we should try it again some day. Fencing. We should try fencing again."

"What is this silver ribbon? Mist?" Torishi asked, pointing to the southern horizon when Satō and the others joined him on the bald top of the pass. The bear-man was always in front of the group, his long legs carrying him eagerly onwards despite the heavy bag of supplies he carried. His strength was inexhaustible.

"It's the sea," Satō corrected him and sighed with relief. "This is the Kinko Bay. And look, that must be Sakurajima – just like in the pictures. At last!"

The mountain rose in a perfect cone from the middle of the bay. Looking down from the ridge, Satō saw an affluent-looking market town, surrounded by citrus orchards and tobacco fields.

"The Sea!" Torishi said with wonder. His hand encompassed the coastal flatland.

"Then this must be the ancient kingdom of my people."

As if in answer, Sakurajima billowed a puff of thick smoke and ash. The cloud rose tall and wide, shaped like a giant sprawling pine tree, until it dwarfed the mountain itself. The perfect cone of the mountain rising from the middle of the round bay was the most beautiful sight she had ever seen. She expected at any moment to hear ringing of alarm gongs and panicked cries in the town below, but nobody seemed to pay any attention to the eruption. Before long, the winds scattered the cloud over the bay, and all the ash fell down from the sky like grey rain. They watched the spectacle for several long minutes in complete silence.

"The Fire Mountain…" said Torishi in an awestruck whisper. "The first thing the Kumaso kings saw when arriving from the Sun Lands. They settled in a flat valley beside the Great Lake in the shade of the Fire Mountain."

101

"Try not to exert your birth right too keenly," Satō said finally. "The people down there may be more terrified of you than peasants. Come, let's try to get to the town before nightfall."

By the time they reached the lowlands, Satō understood why none of the locals paid any attention to Sakurajima's eruption. The mountain spewed ash and smoke twice more that day, each time the cloud dispersing harmlessly before reaching the land.

Everything seemed calmer, brighter and nicer on the plain. The sea breeze pushed the rain clouds northwards up the mountains – which explained the wretched weather the travellers had had to suffer for the last couple of days. The sky over the lowlands was the colour of pure, bright azure, the air crisp and fresh, smelled faintly of damp and sea salt. For the first time in a very long while, Satō had to shield her eyes from the bright sun.

As they passed through the fields and orchards, the farmers stopped their work and watched them with curiosity; their eyes were focused mostly on Torishi's great, hairy form, much to the bear man's unease.

But the farmers, or rather their equipment, were an equally curious sight to Satō. Even Bran halted in surprise when they had first encountered the strange machine.

In the middle of a tobacco field stood a black cylinder, taller than a man, with a narrow funnel spewing white steam. Attached to it was a set of gears, pulleys and flywheels increasing in size; the last one, as big as an oxcart wheel, pulled a thick hemp rope. At the other end of the rope was a plough, pulled against the dirt by the power unleashed by the cylinder. There were three such machines in the fields around them, each serviced by a team of samurai and scholars bearing Satsuma crests on their clothes.

"That's a traction engine," said Bran, astonished. "Only the richest farmers in Gwynedd have them."

"Welcome to Satsuma," said Satō with a grin.

THE RISING TIDE

CHAPTER VI

At the edge of the town stood a wooden watchtower; it was empty. A single samurai rested in a ditch on the side of the road, chewing on a straw, his face covered with a bamboo hat. He heard them approach and raised the brim lazily. Seeing Torishi, he jumped up immediately, spitting out the straw and straightening his clothes.

"Halt!"

He put on the air of a proud, militant bureaucrat. He bowed before Bran and the girls, before turning to the bear-man.

"You can't carry those here," he said, pointing at the bow and the long knife. "You're far away from your forest, hunter."

Torishi looked helplessly to his companions.

"He's right," said Satō. "We will carry your weapons for the time being."

She took the bow and quiver and Bran took the knife. With their clothes and hair in disarray, they could both easily pass for the mountain hunters, if it wasn't for the clan crests still visible on their kimonos through the dirt and stains.

The samurai let them pass, eyeing them curiously. Before long, Satō heard his feet thumping on the dirt road.

"If I may be so bold," he said, after catching his breath, "you seem to be in some distress. May I offer you lodgings in my house? It's not far, by the harbour."

"My son has gone to the wizardry school in Kagoshima," explained the samurai, showing them an entire empty wing of his residence. "You can use any room."

"You're very kind," said Satō weakly. The warm, cozy inside of the house made her drowsy; she was wearier than she had realised.

"The servant will prepare a bath. If you excuse me, I need to send for somebody to take my place at the tower."

The samurai's plump, rosy-cheeked wife appeared to take over the duties of a host. Seeing the state they were in, she raised her hands to her head in a comic display of grief.

"*Eeh!* What terrible thing happened to you? Did you get lost? Were you attacked?"

"Both," said Satō, quickly coming up with a story of a group of bandits they had to fight off in the deep forest, with the help of Torishi, who had agreed to escort them for the rest of their journey.

"So close to Hayato! I always knew you shouldn't trust those highlanders," the woman said, glancing nervously at Torishi, before leading Satō and Nagomi to the bath room. "It's all those vapours and fog up the mountains, makes them go crazy. Do you have any other clothes?"

The wizardess shook her head. Nagomi's travel clothes almost fell apart as she took them off; Satō's vermillion kimono was in no better shape.

"I'll take you to the market tomorrow," declared the samurai's wife, "for now, please use our *yukatas*."

"We are in a hurry to reach Kagoshima-" started Satō, but the woman interrupted her, waving her hands.

"Nonsense! My husband will get you a fast boat, you'll reach the city in no time. You take your time, girls."

"Well, this is nice," said Satō after the woman had left them alone. The cypress-lined bath was almost as large and luxurious as the one at the Takashima Mansion and, for the first time in many weeks, the wizardess allowed herself to completely relax.

"I can't believe we survived so much," she added, shaking her head, "it feels almost like a bad dream right now."

"I'm just glad we're all still together," Nagomi said, splashing her face with hot water.

"Don't ever do that again," said Satō, turning serious.

"Do what?"

"Sacrifice yourself for me! Bran told me about your vision."

"I had to do *something*…"

"I understand, and I'm grateful. But we can't lose you. *I* can't lose you."

107

Satō reached out and touched the thin scar running between Nagomi's breasts.

"If I'm wounded, you could just heal me, right? But if *you* are injured, I am helpless. I never want to feel that helpless again."

Nagomi submerged herself till the tip of her chin touched the hot water.

"It's not like the old days, when I could mend your broken bones without breaking a sweat," she said and smiled.

"I'm not *that* old," said Satō in a pretend indignation; she smiled too.

Nagomi regarded Satō's naked body.

"You're a woman now," she said, "everyone can see that. When you are not wearing your male clothes, all men turn their heads. No wonder Bran – "

She stopped and covered her mouth with her hand. Satō blushed; they both fell silent. A magpie screeched outside.

Bran lay in the darkness of the vast, eight-mat room he had been given all to his own and felt terribly lonely. It had been long since he had to spend the night alone in a single room, without so much as hearing any of the girls' breath as they slept. They always chatted in whisper for a while before going to sleep.

He wanted to go home. He wanted to see his mother again, reading a book by the fireplace. He wanted to find out what had happened to his father, to Edern, to Gwennlian, to all those people he had so much more in common with. The girls now called him a "friend" – and he appreciated this rare privilege – but how many times had Satō pointed out he was a stranger here?

The wizardess never mentioned the episode by the brook again; she avoided his gaze, his touch. It was driving him mad. *What is wrong with me? Am I not good enough for her? Too alien?*

Out of nowhere, Atsuko's face appeared in his thoughts. The alabaster skin, the almond eyes, the smell of rosewood... the faint touch of her lips on his, like a butterfly landing. He was not too alien for *her*. She might have been attracted to him because he was a spark of unfamiliarity to her dull life, but what was wrong in that? Who could tell what reasons compelled people to be with each other, to spending time in each other's presence?

The silence inside his mind only exacerbated the loneliness. With the Farlink gone even Shigemasa's brooding murmur could not replace the resounding hollowness left by Emrys.

"I may have found something that will help you with that," said the General.

"I really dislike it when you read my thoughts."

"I can't help it, boy. You think I enjoy your wallowing? I preferred it when you were in a rage."

Arguing with the old Spirit was the last thing on Bran's mind.

"What have you found?"

"It will be best if you follow me."

Bran closed his eyes and transported himself onto the red dust plain. It was getting easier every time. The General was already waiting for him. He seemed haggard, wind-worn. His lacquer armour had lost its sheen and several of the metal scales.

"When you last cast me away I found myself in a strange part of this place, one that I have not seen before," Shigemasa explained, leading the way towards the horizon, "it takes a while to get there, but with little else to do around here, exploring it was a welcome distraction."

The plain, flat and featureless so far, began to rise and fall in a chain of hills and canyons. The earth turned from red to grey and then black. Bran cast a worried glance behind: the red-eye tower was barely visible.

Will I be able to get back on my own?

They climbed to the top of a tall black mound and the General pointed into the narrow canyon below. Something moved at the bottom, glinting green. Bran started down the slope to look closer. Half-way down he finally realised what he was seeing.

"Emrys!" he cried and ran the rest of the way.

"Be careful, boy," the General shouted a warning, his voice surprisingly anxious, almost afraid. "It's completely wild."

He was right. The dragon paid no attention to Bran. It hopped madly from rock to rock, from crag to crag, flapping its wings in vain and roaring helplessly. Something was keeping it from leaving the canyon. As the boy approached, the beast calmed down a little, but there was no recognition in its snake-like eyes. The dragon crouched with its claws forward, baring its teeth and hissing.

Bran sensed fear suffused with anger. It took him a while to realise what it meant: whatever this creature inside his mind was he could reach it with his thoughts. Did it mean anything in the real world? That remained to be seen, but he *had* to try.

He came forward with a hand reached out, sending soothing, calming thoughts. He had no idea how to tame a wild dragon, and didn't even know something like this was even possible.

This is not a real dragon, he reminded himself. *This is all in your head.*

"Easy, easy," he said, "good boy, good Emrys…"

The beast's flared nostrils narrowed, its jaw clenched. His snake eyes glinted. With a great effort Bran took another step, and then another. He was trembling, affected by the dragon's aura of fear. He summoned a *tarian* almost inadvertently. With one more step he was close enough to touch the beast. He moved his hand slowly.

The dragon spat fire; it was just a warning shot, but without the *tarian* it would burn him badly. The boy ignored the flames and pressed on. The dragon twitched its wings. Finally Bran laid his trembling hand on the warm, jade green scales and a jolt came through his body, like an electric spark. The dragon snorted and puffed sparks and smoke, but did not move away. Bran felt its emotions flow clearly without disruptions; he sent back an order. The dragon lowered its head in submission. The Farlink between phantom dragon and its rider had been established.

Bran leapt onto the mount's neck. Even though the dragon wasn't real, it felt great to be able to fly again. He flew back to the top of the black hill and landed – with some effort – near Shigemasa.

"Come, *Taishō!*" he said, laughing. "This will be faster than walking!"

"You seem perky today," said Satō. She was grinning herself, wearing an over-sized blue kimono she had borrowed from their host – her vermillion *Rangaku* outfit sadly damaged beyond repair. She still avoided looking him too long in the eyes, though.

"Things don't look as bleak when you're rested," the boy replied with a smile. He had no heart to worry today.

"Are we going already?" he asked, seeing her and Nagomi step down from the porch and into the sandals. "I thought – "

"We're going to the town. And so are you. Hurry up."

"No, I'll stay here with Torishi. I don't need anything."

Satō covered her month and sniggered. "Have you seen yourself lately? You need new clothes. And a *barber.*"

A barber?

He picked up a small glass mirror lying on the shoe cupboard and studied his still unfamiliar Yamato face. His hair had grown long and unruly, sticking out in tufts and clumps. The scar left by the sickle had healed up by now, but there seemed to be a layer of dirt on his cheeks... He touched his face.

I need a shave.

He hadn't shaved before; the Prydain grew beards late and slow. He wasn't even sure he knew how to do it. Dylan used magically imbued razors, which made the task much easier, and Bran doubted they had such devices here.

"All right," he said, putting the mirror down. Only now did he notice the Bataavian runes 'V.O.C.' on the back.

Western glass.

"But let's try to be back before lunch."

It was well past noon when, rested and refreshed, they followed the samurai and his wife to the Hayato Harbour. They were all wearing their new clothes: Satō wore a plain grey kimono and black hakama; Nagomi's travel clothes were pale yellow, and Bran managed to find a robe of the same dark indigo colour as his previous one. The Aoki crest of a mountain reflecting in the water had been hastily transferred onto the shoulders of the new outfit by the old tailor.

Their new travel bundles had been filled with necessary supplies: a waterskin and a small flask of saké, seaweed-rolled rice buns and dried rice crackers, straw sandals, bandages, a folded razor marked with Bataavian runes and a

113

sharpening stone for the swords. To Bran's delight, the Hayato cobblers had a small supply of sandals large enough for his Western feet. For the first time in a long while he could walk the cobbled streets comfortably.

Hayato was just a small fishing port, but their host managed to find a merchant boat heading for Kagoshima that was big enough to fit all of four of them.

"I hope you will have a swift and pleasant journey," the samurai said.

"I'm sorry for your trouble," said Satō.

"It's no trouble at all!" the samurai's wife replied, waving her hands, "it's the least we could do after what happened to you in the mountains. We wouldn't want you to think badly of Satsuma."

"I forgot to ask," Bran turned to the samurai just before boarding the boat, "were the machines in the fields yours?"

"Oh, no, no. They belong to His Excellency, Shimazu-dono. He's just testing them out on my fields. You should check out the wizardry school near His Excellency's castle, if that's the sort of thing you're after."

"And if you happen to meet a young man named Sugimoto, tell him his mother is very proud," added the woman, wiping a tear from her eye.

The couple stood on the pier, waving to the departing boat until they were just two specks on the horizon.

"It must be a long time since they've seen their son," said Nagomi, waving back. "I wonder what my parents are doing right now…"

A sudden gust of wind filled the ship's sail and she had to sit down and hold on to the bench.

"A school of wizards…" said Satō after a while, "I wonder if they were the ones we met in Kirishima."

"I'm surprised they haven't heard anything from the shrine yet," said Bran, scratching his cheek; his skin felt itchy after the barber's blade, especially around the scar. "It's been what, a week?"

"They are a bit out of the way here," replied Satō, "I suspect the news has to reach Kagoshima first."

"What's it like, this Kagoshima? Have you ever been there?"

The wizardess nodded.

"A few times with my father. It's a big city, almost as big as Kiyō. Maybe even larger, now – it keeps on growing."

The boat rocked again on a rogue wave. The enclosed bay was calmer than the open sea; still the girls sat tightly on their bench, not daring to look over the edge of the boat. Bran looked up to Torishi who stood on the prow proudly, like some old sea dog, unflinching as the salty waves splashed against his face. It was the first time Bran saw him happy.

"I've never seen anything so flat before," the bear-man yelled over the wind. "All the way to the horizon in every direction. It's like standing on top of the tallest mountain in the world! And look, the Fire Mountain is ablaze again!"

The boat slowed down, entering the narrow strait. They were approaching Kagoshima Harbour, and the waters of the Kinko Bay grew crowded with fishing boats and cargo ships. The wharf was flanked by a massive, slanting, stone wall, topped with what looked to Bran like modern cannons. On the opposite side of the strait the majestic Sakurajima loomed over the bay like a fist aimed towards the Heavens in defiance.

The ground shook as if in earthquake as three hundred *kin* of flesh slammed against the sand of the arena.

The crowd went wild, shouting the name of their champion: *Kyūkichi! Kyūkichi!* The wrestler stood calm, with his head modestly bowed, grinning discreetly.

The referee waited until Kyūkichi's opponent gathered his huge bulk off the ground, and then pointed the wooden paddle at the winner.

"Undefeated for a record twenty five games. The strongest man in Chinzei – Unryū Kyūkichi!"

The spectators cheered for more than a minute before the referee raised his paddle once again, prompting them to silence.

"This concludes today's tournament – unless there is another contender amongst you?"

Shakushain pushed his way through and stepped into the light.

"I will fight."

The crowd jeered and booed him. Not only was he too lean and slim to be a wrestler, his thick beard and long hair betrayed a foreigner. There was no place for the likes of him at the sacred arena.

The assistants rushed to remove him from the sand, but the reigning champion raised his hand to stop them.

"No, wait. Let him in."

Shakushain took off his cloak and handed it to the little dark-skinned man standing beside him. The crowd fell silent; they had never seen anyone whose muscles were so taut and perfectly toned; the geometric tattoos which covered his entire body were also a sight to behold. He basked in the spectators' amazement for a while before crouching down to the starting line.

"I know you," said Kyūkichi. "You're the Northerner who defeated Taniemon last year."

"He said I cheated. I was banned from the East Division."

"He was lying. I saw the fight. You beat him fair and square. I haven't seen a *Mitokorozeme* like that in a long time."

Shakushain smiled and bowed. The champion performed a brief ritual dance and stomped his legs, then entered the ring, threw salt on the sand to banish evil spirits, and crouched in front of his opponent.

Will he be the one who gives me a good fight? The Northerner thought, hopeful, assessing Kyūkichi's frame and stance.

His quest so far had been a series of disappointments. The *Shamo* – or Yamato, as the Southerners called themselves – liked to brag about being the greatest warriors on Earth. But most of them learned to fight with spears,

117

swords and bows; and he had defeated all the sumo wrestlers with little difficulty and no satisfaction. The bears and sea lions in his frozen northern homeland had put up more of a fight than these walking mountains of fat.

The referee marked the start of the fight. A lesser wrestler would have charged instantly at Shakushain, hoping to throw him off balance with the pure mass of his body. Kyūkichi just stared at the Northerner, studying his posture, the way his muscles rippled underneath the tattoos. Shakushain did the same, looking for weak points; there was no flaw in Kyūkichi's stance.

"Go on! Go on!" the referee urged them.

At last, the *Shamo* wrestler charged. Shakushain's muscles tensed and he let out a cry when the full weight of his opponent slammed into his chest. His feet slid dangerously on the sand, but he managed to hold just before the edge of the arena. The two men grappled with each other, trying to force one another to make an error of judgment. Sweat made their bodies slippery, making it difficult for Shakushain to get a grip.

This is no time for cheap tricks.

The *Shamo*'s skill left no place for special throws or undercuts; however Shakushain tried to pull or push, Kyūkichi responded in kind, his body nimble and pliable.

Only pure strength can settle this one.

At last, Shakushain managed to grab his opponent's thick loincloth in both hands. The crowd gasped as Kyūkichi's feet left the ground. The *Shamo* twisted and turned in Shakushain's grasp, but in vain. Straining his

118

muscles almost to the limit, the Northerner took a step back, then another. His calves trembled under the wrestler's weight. Feeling the rope surrounding the ring touch his heels, he turned around and let go; Kyūkichi flew outside the arena and landed, with a great thud, on the wooden floor.

In the silence that followed, Kyūkichi's laughter and clapping resonated loudly.

"Come with me!" the wrestler said, not bothering to get up from the floor. "Join my stable! I will make you rich."

Shakushain forced a smile, bowed, took his symbolic trophy from the stunned referee's hands and picked up his cloak from the little dark-skinned man. He had no mood for celebrating the victory. He spotted a glimpse of crimson in the audience and that spoiled his humour for the rest of the day.

The Crimson Robe found him outside the hall. He slid his hand across his chest in the Northern greeting.

"*Irankarapte,*" he said.

"*He.*"

"And who might that be?" the Crimson Robe looked at the little man at Shakushain's side.

"A friend from the North."

"That's a curious necklace."

The little man was wearing a jagged shard of blue glass tied on a leather cord. He covered it with his hand.

"What do you want?" barked Shakushain. "I don't need you anymore."

The Fanged smiled. "It is I that needs you. For a hunt."

"I don't hunt people."

"I know. This time I'm after a beast."

A beast?

"I'm listening."

CHAPTER VII

The fine black dust screeched under Bran's feet. The street sweepers may have all gone to sleep, but the Sakurajima Mountain was still awake, blowing up ash almost incessantly through the night, among the silent lightning strikes. The city of Kagoshima was the first he had seen in Yamato where the streets had not been immaculately clean. Not even an army of dedicated cleaners could defeat the inexhaustible power of the volcano.

Bran walked the swiftly darkening streets of the trade district, past the shops and inns closing, and saké stores and pleasure joints opening for the evening. He had an unusual guide into the night life of the bustling city: the General Itakura Shigemasa.

It started with a conversation they had had a few hours earlier. Bran and the others had eaten a rich supper at an inn Satō remembered from her travels with her father. Almost all the dishes served were fish – deep-fried in bronze paste, tiny marinated herrings, big chunks of rockfish, which tasted remarkably like the chicken, slices of succulent raw tuna – all this served with lashings of buckwheat noodles, polished rice and crisp pickles, and doused with *cha* and best local shōchū mixed with hot water. Later they had been asking around for some news and rumours that could lead Bran towards the dragon, but with no results, and Satō had decided they would have to visit the wizardry school the next morning.

"*They* will know," she said, before going to the room she shared with Nagomi.

Bran had retreated into his mind again and found the jade dragon still there, strolling about the red dust plain not far from the tower. Shigemasa was sitting at a safe distance from the beast, observing it curiously.

Bran approached the dragon, and this time it let him touch its scales without objection. The buzz of the Farlink once again filled the boy's head. It was very faint, barely a murmur, but Bran was almost certain this time that he had reached through to the *real* Emrys. There was no trace of sentience in the stream of emotions he received, just the beastly rage, the confusion and the hunger… He let go, and the dragon trotted off by a few paces before lying down to sleep. Bran turned to the General.

"Why have you shown me this, *Taishō*?"

Shigemasa chortled and stroked his beard.

"For too long I had to watch you and your little troupe wander aimlessly the length and breadth of Chinzei. A dragon hunt sounds much more exciting. But tell me boy, did it work?"

Bran looked back at the phantom dragon.

"It… seems to be working. But I never heard about anything like this being attempted before. When a dragon goes wild it cannot be re-tamed and there is no other way but to kill it."

"But isn't that what you were planning to do?" Shigemasa raised his eyebrows. "I thought I was just giving you a way to track the beast down and slay it."

"I don't want to slay Emrys," Bran said, "I want to *save* him."

The General scratched his chin in thought.

"I can't say I know a lot about these things, boy, but I trust your judgement. I'm glad we can start doing something useful for a change."

Bran felt a change in the way the Spirit was treating him.

"We," he said.

"I'm grateful for your help," said Bran. "If there's anything I can do…"

The samurai's eyes glinted and his face brightened in a grin.

"Tell me, did the wizard girl give you some more of her gold coins?"

"We split the treasure among the three of us, but what —"

"Put on your kimono, boy," said Shigemasa, standing up, "I'll show you the side of Yamato you haven't yet seen."

Kagoshima was a narrow city, hemmed in between the sea and the hills, and there was only one direction to cross it — north to south along the main street, across the river, past the merchant storehouses and into a district that was built-up more densely. Two- and three-story buildings lined the narrow, criss-crossing alleyways.

"I've only been in this city once," said Shigemasa, *"but it shouldn't be hard to find the right place. Just follow the noise!"*

There was nothing of Kiyō's nightly quiet here. The part of the city Bran ventured into seemed more alive after dusk than by day. The streets, illuminated by red paper lanterns, teemed with people, a forest of colourful paper umbrellas protecting their heads and clothes from the omnipresent dust. It didn't take Bran long to realise that the crowds were made predominantly of adult men, and that all the women either hung off the shoulders of their male companions, or stood in small groups in the doorways, laughing and shouting at the passers-by, revealing their painted necks and white ankles seductively.

"Wait a minute," said Bran, stopping in the middle of the street, "I may not be experienced in these matters, but even I know what this place is."

"Ignore them, boy. Tonight we seek a more refined pleasure. Turn here, after that palanquin."

Bran followed the ornate vehicle carried by four tall porters into another street. This one was wider and not as crowded, paved with small square stones. There were only a few buildings here, sprawling mansions hiding behind tall earthwork walls daubed with red plaster. Armed guards stood before each gate.

Shigemasa made Bran stroll the street up and down, while he assessed which residence they had the best chance to get into.

124

"The best one will be fully booked," the General said, *"so will the cheapest one. Try the one with the plum blossom on the* noren.*"*

The guard eyed Bran carefully, studying his face, clothes and the crest of the Aoki clan on his shoulders, and then bowed slightly – *too slightly,* for Bran's liking – and stood aside.

The inside of the strange residence was lush, by Yamato standards. The walls and floors were laid of delicate, sweet-smelling timber; the corridors were decorated with vases, paintings and flowers. A group of young women in the vestibule studied Bran unabashedly as he approached the counter. He heard them whisper and giggle among each other.

"Look at his eyes! He must be from Kiyō. One of them half-bloods."

"Impossible! He's far too high born for that."

"He seems so shy – do you think he's unbroken yet?"

The last sentence amused them greatly and they broke into another fit of giggles.

Bran felt his face burn bright red. Following Shigemasa's advice, he asked for a single table in the common room and "one shamisen girl".

"We don't want to spend too much on your first time."

He was then led into a large hall where several other men were already sitting at the low benches, drinking and conversing in hushed tones, accompanied by women in opulent, many-layered kimonos and elaborate make-up. They reminded Bran of the high-born ladies he had seen in his dreams.

A flask of saké and two cups waited for Bran on his table and, before long, a young girl came into the room. She headed towards him, holding a long-necked string instrument. She smiled gently and nodded her head. Her every move and gesture was deliberate, yet perfectly smooth. Underneath the thick make-up, she was almost as beautiful and gracious as Atsuko.

"Does my noble guest have any wishes for the music?" she asked in a soft, sensuous voice.

"A... anything you like."

She plucked the strings with the grace of a prowling cat and started humming a sad, slow song.

Hana wa Kirishima, tabako wa Kokubu

Moete agaru wa Sakurajima

Kawaigararete neta yoru mo gozaru

Naite akashita yoru mo gozaru

Flowers of Kirishima, tobacco of Kokubu

Fires of Sakurajima

Caressed in the evening

I cried until morning

126

Bran stared at her, transfixed. Her fingers were long and slender; her voice was like that of a nightingale, and her lips…

"Don't fall for her, boy," Shigemasa chuckled, breaking the solemn mood, *"she's just one of many. Offer her some saké."*

The girl batted her eyelashes and sipped like a sparrow from the white cup. She re-tuned her instrument and started on another melancholy song.

The *shamisen*'s sound brought him a memory of a bard's harp back in Gwynedd. His mind was transported by the melody to the sprawling green hills and the slow-rolling rivers of his homeland, the calm, golden-leaved forests where the only danger awaiting a traveller was getting lost in the subtle beauty of the hazel groves, the sea-side dunes of Cantre'r Gwaelod, the narrow, cobbled streets of Caer Wyddno… He saw the stone towers of the Academy; the dried-up marshes of the Teifi; and, as the song grew to a chorus, the red-washed walls of his home.

Wasuregataki furusato

Iika ni imasu chichi haha

Tsutuga nashi ya tomogaki

I miss my home town,

How are my mother and father?

Are my friends alright?

He saw Rhian holding a basket of freshly cut herbs and talking to Dylan who was cleaning the scales of the Azure dragon. They were laughing and both looked happy then.

How old is this memory? Bran wondered. He hadn't seen his parents together like that in years. The dragon was not Afreolus, but one of Dylan's previous mounts.

Home. It was strange; he had spent months out on sea without ever missing Gwynedd, but now, this beautiful girl's sad song made him almost weep from home sickness. His eyes welled up. He shook his head.

"Stop," he croaked, then coughed, pretending there was something in his throat. The girl blinked in confusion. "Sing something else."

The girl nodded and retuned her instrument to a more cheerful key. He gulped his saké and poured himself another cup right away and then another.

The evening passed briskly; the girl sang and played some more and once, at Shigemasa's request, performed a slow, graceful dance with two paper fans. By the end of the night – and of the third or fourth bottle of saké – Bran's thoughts and emotions were elevated to the point where he wanted to write a poem or paint a picture that would capture an impression of the scene.

The girl sat back down after another dance; the sleeve of her kimono dropped, revealing a naked shoulder. She did not adjust it; Bran leaned forward, his face burning. The girl was more subtle than the eager, flirty women from Shigemasa's memories, but she made him burn with the same desire; he recalled the vivid dreams he shared with the

General, including one he hadn't remembered before – of a pale-faced woman in a red kimono, in what looked strangely similar to his inn room back at the Hitoyoshi …

"You won't get that sort of thing here," the voice in his head said with a lewd chuckle.

"That's not… I've never even…"

"Oh, but you have. *I should have told you earlier."*

This sobered Bran somewhat.

Hitoyoshi wasn't a dream…?

"You…you took the liberty of my own body to…!"

"I'm not a monk, boy! But I can make it up to you. There was a place not far, I bet it's still in business. If you want I will take you there."

Bran hesitated for longer than he thought he would.

"N-no."

"Why not? It's only natural. The little wizardess does not seem willing to give you what your body needs, so I thought…"

"I'll be just fine," he replied, his mood soured.

The girl looked at him patiently, waiting for another order. He smiled and raised a silent toast to her. She put her instrument down and relaxed a little.

He could now hear the conversations by the neighbouring tables. Saké seemed to have enhanced his hearing at the expense of other senses. It was clear that the other men came here not just to admire the girls' performances, but to discuss important matters in a tranquil atmosphere. The two samurai to his left deliberated on the prices of rice and sweet potatoes, but the group to the right – three men whose clothes of soft silk were all marked with the cross-circle emblem of Satsuma – dropped a name in their conversation which made Bran prick his ears.

"I heard the daimyo's plan fell out."

"Some terrible disaster. All news is suppressed."

"Might be wise to invite daimyo's honourable brother to our next get-together."

The elder samurai nodded. "I will let Hisamitsu-*sama* know. But, have you heard? The *Daisen* Heishichi has returned from Kirishima. I passed him at the castle gates. He'll be with the daimyo now."

Bran had heard enough. He faked a yawn and dismissed the girl.

"You have been exquisite, but I am tired now."

"Of course, noble guest."

She remained with her head bowed until he left the hall. Once out of the residence and onto the sudden cool quiet of the street outside, he stopped and leaned against the red-plaster wall for a moment. His head was spinning a bit.

"That was…" He searched for the right word, "magnificent."

The General said nothing, but Bran could sense his satisfaction.

"Are you sure you don't want me to take you to that other place now?"

"Maybe later," he said with a smile. "I have to go somewhere else first."

He looked around; the street was darker and emptier than when he had entered the establishment. He breathed in the scent, not unlike that of Kiyō on that first fateful night. The noises on the main street were muffled, and in the silence, Bran heard a nightingale singing in the garden of one of the mansions.

I will miss this place, he realized, *just as much as I miss Gwynedd now.*

Once past the trade district, Bran drew the hood of his travel cloak over his head and returned his face to its Gwynedd look. He crossed a narrow canal and approached the deceptively small castle of the daimyo of Satsuma. The guards stopped him before the narrow bridge over the castle's moat.

"Halt! The gates are closed for the night. Whatever your business with the daimyo, come tomorrow."

Bran threw down the hood and looked up, noting the effect his foreign face had on the captain of the guards.

"I only seek tranquillity," he said, using the archaic code word *'shōhei'*. The captain drew breath loudly, then said "keep him here until I come back," to the other guard and left in a hurry.

He returned five minutes later.

"Come with me," he said and led the boy, not to the main gate, but to the southern side of the castle wall. He

131

pulled a hidden lever; steam spewed from a concealed valve. Bran heard brass pulleys turn inside the wall, and a small postern opened with a clunk. They walked down the narrow, winding corridors, up the stair to the second floor of the keep.

"Wait here, you will be announced," the captain said and left the dragon rider in the company of a servant.

Upon entering the daimyo's room, Bran became acutely aware of the magic energies permeating inside. A round paper lantern hovered over the floor on its own, illuminating the room with a faint light. A grid of magic trip-wire ley alarms was scattered around the painted walls and paper-covered windows. Even the inkstone glowed slightly with some minor enchantment. This was the room of a man who was not afraid of magic and did not care much for the *Taikun*'s restrictions in its use.

Shimazu Nariakira was a broad-shouldered man, with a long, oval face, a large, straight nose protruding between close set, clever eyes. Bran tried to find similarities between Atsuko and her father, before recalling she was an adopted child. The aristocrat was sitting at a table made of a single slab of walnut wood, supporting his head on his hand, studying a board game in complete silence. A thin wisp of white smoke rose from the incense bowl on the table, filling the room with the familiar scent of sandalwood.

Bran said his greetings and stood, waiting, for a minute, then another; his patience began to grow thin. The daimyo remained unflinching. Bran cleared his throat.

Lord Nariakira raised his head slowly. There was something odd in the nobleman's eyes and face, but Bran

132

couldn't quite put his finger on it. The atmosphere in the room, and the alcohol in Bran's head unnerved him. The daimyo still did not speak.

"I... I was hoping I could request your assistance, *kakka*," said Bran at last.

A deep chuckle came from beyond a thin wall. It slid open, revealing another room, almost a mirror image of the one Bran was in, except brightly lit. A man who could have been Lord Nariakira's twin looked at Bran with great amusement.

"*Gaikokujin!*" he said. "Insolent as ever. Do you not know you should always wait until your superior speaks, no matter how long it takes?"

The boy glanced from one man to another in confusion. At last, he used True Sight on both of them.

"An automaton!"

"Yes," said the real daimyo. "A new creation of my mechanicians. You have the privilege to be one of the first guests I have tested it on."

"It's... remarkably life-like."

In the West, automatons were mere toys, their practical pursuit abandoned long before Bran's birth. Now he understood what Atsuko had meant when she spoke of her chaperon.

"Come here, boy, let me look at you in better light."

The daimyo studied Bran for a while.

"You are shorter than I expected," he said at last.

"Kakka?"

Bran was ready to provide the *daimyo* with a long explanation regarding his presence in the castle and his knowledge of the secret password, but Lord Nariakira's blatant statement threw him off guard.

"Sit down," the daimyo gestured at another walnut table identical to the first one in every detail. Even the pawns on the game board were all in the same position.

"Two days ago I received a letter from my dear daughter Atsu," he continued, "in which she describes a meeting with a young Westerner whose name she fails to mention."

Bran gulped. *How much did she tell him?*

"In describing the man, my daughter paid particular attention to his, as she puts it, 'emerald green eyes.' By the end of the letter, she entreats me to hear his fascinating story and provide him with anything he may require, if we were to ever meet."

He paused. Bran kept silent, waiting for him to continue. The daimyo grunted with satisfaction.

"You are either brave or unwise to come here," he said. "I could easily have your head off. Maybe I should, *eh?* I can only imagine the circumstances in which you two have met. My daughter was to be kept under strict surveillance, so you had to be pretty sneaky - or reckless. Those responsible for allowing your meeting will, of course, be punished."

Bran opened his mouth to protest, but thought better of it.

They can't be helped and I'm in enough trouble as it is.

"However," the daimyo continued, "my daughter is not easily impressed, and I put great trust in her judgement of people. If she puts a good word in for you – and grants you access to our family code word – my interest is piqued. Let me hear you out first – and bear in mind, your life is in my hands. Let us start with introductions – who are you, boy?"

"I am Bran ap Dylan gan Cantre'r Gwaelod - the *dorako* rider," Bran replied.

Lord Nariakira digested the information before clapping his knee in joy.

"*Unnh!* It makes sense now. I take it you know it was I who kept your *dorako* imprisoned – and yet you come to me of your own will? "

"I... I hoped you might help me... find it, *kakka.*"

"You seem to have done it with no problems before."

"I lost that ability after what happened at Kirishima."

"And *what* happened at Kirishima? Tell me about it, or better yet, tell me all about your adventures. I need to know what kind of a man comes alone at night requesting the help of a daimyo."

Of all the people Bran had recounted his adventures to since coming to Yamato, Lord Nariakira was by far the best, most informed, and avid listener. His knowledge of the outside world, familiarity with matters of global politics, and Western magic was uncanny. The story took Bran much shorter to tell than he had expected. When questioned about it, the daimyo chuckled.

"Yes, I suppose I do know a bit more about the world than your average country samurai. But, you shouldn't be so surprised. You have seen some of my machines and workshops on your way here."

"Yes, *kakka*."

"So, Kirishima... you did not see the battle to the end, then?"

"We ran away to save the priestess."

"And have you?"

"Yes, *kakka*. She is alive and well. If I may inquire, have there been any survivors?"

"Yes, though not many. My soldiers reached the shrine just in time to drive the attackers off."

"Is... Captain Kiyomasa among those alive?"

"He suffered the worst injuries, but I am told he will survive."

"That makes me glad. He was... is a good soldier."

"That he is," the daimyo said with a nod. "*Yoshi!*" he added, standing up, "I will not have your head just *yet*. Whether or not I will assist you, is another matter. Tell me, young *dorako* rider, what were you planning to do once you got to Kagoshima?"

Bran had realised by now that honesty was the only way to gain this odd man's trust.

"I thought I might sail north following any hints and rumours I could find."

Lord Nariakira turned his back to Bran, looking out the open window. This seemed a reckless gesture – they were alone in the room, and the dragon rider had not been searched for concealed weapons. Bran cast True Sight again and saw the shimmering magical shield protecting daimyo's body – as well as silhouettes of two men sitting behind yet another fake wall. One of them was a wizard, protecting the Lord with his magic. The other's power signature was strangely familiar…

"It's a shame you haven't seen for certain who stole that ring of yours," said Lord Nariakira.

I'm sure you already know whom to suspect, Bran thought, but refrained from commenting.

"There is one more thing left out of your story, boy," the daimyo said, running his finger along a wooden slate in the window frame, "what do you know of this… Dōraku-*sama*?"

"I know that he's the Immortal Swordsman. An *Abomination.*"

"That's a very loaded word."

"That's what the stories call him."

The daimyo turned around and stepped towards Bran.

"I take it he did not manage to gain your trust during the journey."

The boy hesitated.

"Even though he saved your lives twice," Lord Nariakira pressed.

"He… I may have misjudged him in the end. Did you know of him, *kakka?*"

The daimyo smiled.

"I knew *of* him, yes."

"And… would you trust him?"

"I am a daimyo. It is my job to trust no one. But I would like to have him on my side; in battle and in a debate."

"But I thought… Immortal Swordsman… *a blood-sucking demon,*" Bran recalled the words of the Unganzenji abbot. The daimyo raised a finger to his lips in thought.

"Yes, he is all that. But he is also an outcast of his own kind. A renegade. One day the other Fanged will find a way to dispose of him for good, and it will be the biggest loss for Yamato since Taiko-*dono* mentioned to Rikyū-*sama* he no longer enjoyed his *cha.*"

"You embarrass me, Shimazu-*sama.*" A familiar voice spoke from behind the fake wall. It slid open and a looming figure in a purple cloak emerged from the hidden alcove.

"Let us hope we'll never find out whether you were right."

"You!" Bran jumped up, reaching automatically for his sword, before remembering he had to leave it with the servant outside.

"The same," the Swordsman said with a slight bow. "And let me congratulate you on impeccable timing, Karasu-*sama* – or should I call you Bran? I have only arrived in Kagoshima last night. Are the others alright?"

"*Eh*... yes. They are resting at the guesthouse."

"That's splendid news. I'm glad you came out of this alive."

Lord Nariakira waved his hand dismissively.

"It's time for you to leave," the Swordsman added, noticing the gesture. "Shimazu-*dono* and I still have a lot to discuss."

A servant slid open the door to the study and waited to accompany Bran outside.

"*Kakka.*" The boy bowed.

"Dōraku-*sama* will notify you of my decision," said the daimyo, and with a voice used to giving orders that could not be refused, added, "and you shall accept it, whatever it may be."

THE RISING TIDE

CHAPTER VIII

At Lord Nariakira's invitation, Dōraku sat down to the shōgi board.

"That was a performance worthy of Ginza, *kakka*," he said, taking out his pipe and stuffing it with tobacco.

"I needed to know if the boy was telling the truth. Or what he thought was the truth."

"And what do you make of it all?"

"Combined with what Heishichi and Atsuko have told me? All very disturbing news. That Crimson Robe is one of *yours* – do you know him?"

"Yes."

"Whom do you think he serves?"

"No one. I have never seen him do anyone's bidding – other than the Eight-headed Serpent, back in the days."

"Not even the Kumamoto?"

"He did mention not wanting to irritate Hosokawa. So there may be an alliance of convenience. But working for a mortal… no, if anything, it would be the other way around."

"I see. Either way, between this and the rumours of my brother Hisamitsu conspiring against me, it looks like Hosokawa Narimori-*dono* is no longer a useful ally. Now, where were we…"

The daimyo moved the Foot Soldier piece, reinforcing his defensive position. Dōraku chuckled.

"How very much like you, to worry more about your alliances than about a dragon let loose," he said, picking up a Lance and moving it two places forward in a casual scouting movement.

"The dragon, according to my spies, is rampaging in the north, far beyond the borders of Satsuma. Before the boy came, I thought it was no longer my concern."

"One *dorako* may be enough to tip the balance to one side in the conflict."

Nariakira moved another Foot Soldier one field forward.

"A valuable asset lost, certainly, but nothing worth losing my sleep over."

"And you are not at all worried about the *Taikun* learning you had a dragon – and then lost it?"

"The *Taikun* has plenty enough to worry about for the moment."

"Oh?" Dōraku reached for a captured Angle Mover, to put it back onto his side of the board.

"There was some disaster at Uraga Bay. Complete lack of communication from Edo since."

The Swordsman's hand hovered over the board.

"That is new."

"Of course, no word of it was supposed to get out to the outer provinces."

"I take it the town criers of Kagoshima will have an interesting tale to tell tomorrow."

The daimyo smiled. Dōraku finally put the Angle Mover down in an offensive position.

"Uraga Bay is the gate to Edo. A gate to all of Yamato."

"Indeed."

"You don't think it's an attack?"

"Anything is possible. But they wouldn't keep a tsunami or a typhoon in such secrecy, would they?"

"I heard the soothsayers are anxious. All they can see is Darkness."

"*Unnh*," Nariakira grunted in agreement. "All the more reason to secure one's position against whatever may happen." He slid his Flying Chariot to the left to fill up an empty slot in the wall of his castle.

"I am surrounded by enemies on all sides."

"You said you will consider the boy's situation, *kakka*, but something tells me you've already made a decision," said Dōraku. He moved a Lance forward, capturing Nariakira's flying chariot. The daimyo frowned.

"I will not let another *asset* out of my hands. The rider stays in Kagoshima until I decide what to do with him." The daimyo moved another piece back towards his Great General, strengthening his castle. This was his usual tactics, building up a strong position on one side of the board, from which he would send out massed attacks against the enemy's flank. Loss of one piece was insignificant in the long run.

"An *asset*," said Dōraku. "You mean like Anjin-*sama*, all those centuries ago."

Nariakira looked up. "That Seaxe in the first Taikun's employ? You remember him?"

"I met him once. Most curious fellow. Old Ieyasu was very fond of him. But in the end, he wasn't of much use to anyone."

The daimyo shrugged.

"We all know the story. When he arrived to Yamato, there wasn't anyone like him, and Ieyasu needed him to play the Vasconians. But we're in another age now. I have my wizards, I have my Bataavians... the boy is not as unique and precious as he likes to think."

"And what about the wizard girl? Wasn't Takashima-*sama* one of your allies in Kiyō?"

"Oh, Shūhan is safe," the daimyo said with a wave of his hand. "I have it on good authority. Keep this a secret, though, I may yet use this knowledge as leverage."

"Hmm." Dōraku puffed on his pipe.

"You disagree."

"You have plenty of wizards and scholars at your disposal. What good is another one?"

144

"I don't follow."

"A dragon rider without a *dorako* is just a minor magic user."

One of the Swordsman's lances charged the castle head-on.

"Better to have this than nothing at all. If I let him go, he'll only get himself killed or captured by my enemies – that Crimson Robe, whoever he is, or Hosokawa. And if he succeeds, it's even worse: he will fly away to Qin." The daimyo moved another Foot Soldier into sacrifice position to defend the Generals. "No *dorako*, no rider."

"He could be… *coerced* to help us." Dōraku duly gobbled up the sacrificed pawn.

"I hope so! That's why I need him here. As an advisor, not a fighter. I don't have many scholars of dragon lore in my court."

"And you would give up on the *dorako?*"

"There will be more where that one came from. If one got through, others will follow. For now I'm glad to leave the *dorako* where it is. Maybe it will fly to Kumamoto and deal with Hosokawa before I get my hands on him," the daimyo chuckled gleefully. He moved the first of his Lances, building up to a massed assault on Dōraku's right flank. In a few moves he was going to smash through Swordsman's defences and gain total dominance of the field.

"I'm afraid that, as usual, you underestimate the power of an individual's actions, *kakka.*"

Dōraku took the captured Flying Chariot from the wooden stand and placed it one field away from the promotion zone. The daimyo's eyes widened as he reasserted the situation on the board.

"Impossible."

"Do you see now? The Flying Chariot on its own is just a pawn, useful only for a sacrifice. But transform it into a Dragon King..."

A skilled player like Nariakira could clearly see there was only one possible outcome. The Dragon King was one of the most powerful figures in *shōgi*, and in the position where Dōraku had put his piece it posed a danger to the entire meticulously prepared castle. It was not enough on its own to threaten the King General, but it would require the daimyo to reconstruct his whole strategy.

"Hmpf," was all Nariakira had to say for a long time as he leaned over the board. "Hmpf," he repeated.

"*Yoshi*, you've made your point, Fanged," the daimyo spoke at last, straightening his back. "But what guarantee can you give me that your plan will work?"

"Only that of my honour, *kakka*."

The daimyo nodded and grunted approvingly.

"*Unnh*. Well said."

He stood up, indicating the audience was over.

Bran found Nagomi sitting at the doorstep of his room, in the darkness, wearing her sheer night *yukata*.

146

"What are you doing here?"

"I couldn't sleep."

He sat down beside her, drowsy and tired.

"Bad dreams?"

"Too many dreams. I saw you with Dōraku-*sama*. He looks fine."

Bran nodded.

"I just met him. He's coming here tomorrow to bring us news from the daimyo of Satsuma."

"You've had a busy night."

"And you don't seem at all surprised."

"We need to tell Sacchan," she said, ignoring his remark. "She will be mad we've kept it from her."

"I didn't think it mattered. I hoped we wouldn't see him anymore."

"Is he going to join us again?"

"I don't know. He seems to be mingling with more important men now."

He saw the silhouette of her head nod in silence.

"You saw something else," he guessed.

"Your *dorako*."

He lit a faint flamespark and looked at her. The light danced on her hair, making it seem like a roaring flame.

"Emrys? Was it alive?" he asked.

"Yes, just… asleep. I don't know… it was dark and cold. A metal box. Underground, I think…"

"Then it's captured already…"

She shook her head. "I don't think it's happened yet. But it will, soon."

"Have you…always been able to see the future?"

Nagomi nodded.

"When I was little, I had… intuitions. Vague premonitions. If I had visions, I did not understand them without hindsight. One summer, when I was ten, I sensed a great misfortune approaching, but I didn't know what it was and whom to warn."

"And what was it?"

"A typhoon. It would have been disastrous to the city, luckily the priests of Suwa foresaw it too and there was enough time to prepare."

"So you went to Suwa to train your talent?"

"Kazuko-*hime* requested it. And with her help my skills grew… I used to need to get into a trance, inhale the sacred fumes to see the visions, but since…"

She stopped and bit her lips.

Since the High Priestess died, Bran guessed. *She can't bring herself to say it.*

"You mean since you've become a priestess," he helped. She nodded again.

"It's as if a window had been opened into the future. I've been having more of these dreams, even on ordinary nights like tonight."

"You do seem more tired than the rest of us," he said. He hadn't noticed it before, but there were deep blue bags under her eyes. He felt sorry for her.

"If there's anything I can do to help…"

"*Un-n*, it's fine." She shook her head and yawned discreetly, standing up. "I'd better go. Maybe I can still catch some sleep tonight. Don't worry about Sacchan, I'll explain to her somehow."

"Thank you."

Bran stood up as well and for a moment they were standing against each other, face to face. Suddenly, Nagomi stood on her toes, threw her arms around him and pressed her lips firmly against his – then ran off down the corridor, without looking back.

"Is it true? Are you really the Immortal Swordsman?"

"Hush!" The samurai put a hand to his lips with an amused smile. "This is supposed to be a secret."

It's a joke, she thought. *They're all playing a joke on me.*

Satō was still reeling from the revelation Nagomi had shared with her the night before, when Master Dōraku entered the Sugi Inn and approached them with arms open, as if welcoming long lost friends. Even though a lot about the samurai suddenly made sense, she still didn't want to believe it.

We didn't see him die, after all.

Master Dōraku finished greeting everyone else – bowing deeply and rubbing his chest in front of Torishi – and cast a doubtful glance around the inn. "This is not a good place to discuss important matters. Why don't you come with me?"

"So... how *old* are you?" asked Satō, as soon as they sat down to breakfast. The place Master Dōraku had led them to was an opulent teahouse, adjacent to the castle walls. She noticed everyone else in the common room was either an aristocrat or a member of the daimyo's family. The guests were staring at Torishi far longer than was considered polite, but the staff had welcomed the Swordsman like a frequent guest and led the group to a cozy, secluded alcove, where the cast iron tea-kettle hovered, suspended on a rope over the fireplace.

"Let's see... I was born in the twelfth year of Tenshō era, in the Yoshino district of Mimasaka province," recited Master Dōraku. The wizardess paused, doing quick calculations in her head. The Yamato reckoning of years was needlessly complicated, she had always thought.

"That's two hundred and fifty years ago!" Her eyes widened.

If it's really all a joke, it's a very well thought-out one.

"You're thinking of the Bunroku era, Tenshō was the one before. So it's two hundred and seventy."

"*Eeh!* But that would mean... you'd have seen all those wars, all those battles...!"

Master Dōraku nodded, twirling his moustache.

"I was a young boy in the rear echelon at Sekigahara, yes. I climbed the walls of Naniwa Castle. I fought the rebels of Shimabara."

"This is where you have met the *Taishō*," added Bran. "And you've made a great impression on him."

"I'm honoured to hear that."

"Not a *good* impression," said the boy. "I can sense he loathes you."

The samurai chuckled.

"When you've lived – or sort of lived – as long as the two of us have, some differences of opinion are inevitable."

"Wait." Satō put her hand on the table with a loud smack. "Hold on. How do we know you're telling the truth? How do we know you and this old Spirit did not make it all up?"

Before any of them could react, a *tantō* flashed in his hand and a long, straight gash appeared down his forearm. The stench of blood filled the alcove momentarily, but the wound was dry and dull in colour. As Satō watched, it began to mend rapidly, as if under a priest's spell. Within seconds, it vanished without a trace, leaving just a patch of smooth skin.

She sniffed. The smell was unmistakable.

"Blood magic," she said.

The samurai nodded and wiped his dagger before sheathing it.

151

"Blood magic, yes. It's what keeps me alive. We were all born out of a Blood Magic."

"We?"

"Whatever you call our kind," he said and smiled. "All the Fanged. Abominations. Blood-sucking ghosts."

"*Demons*. But you look so… human. Not like him."

He looked straight at her. For a blink of an eye so brief she wasn't certain if she really saw it, his face turned paper-white, his eyes golden and his teeth long, sharp and black.

"We can disguise ourselves well. He just chooses not to."

Torishi, silent until now, smoothed his beard and spoke in a solemn voice.

"I've heard of you, Swordsman. Or at least someone *like* you. Stories about an immortal man visiting the Kumaso villages, in the days of my grandmother and her mother."

Dōraku smiled. "I'm surprised your people remembered me. I was just a passing traveller."

"You can certainly make an impression," remarked Satō.

She had not touched her food since the Swordsman's demonstration. All she could think of was the "curse".

Blood magic can make you immortal.

The energy drawn from the tiny needle in her glove was enough to make her spells fantastically powerful. What would it be like to use more blood? For example, all blood drawn from some animal? Or… *a human*?

152

JAMES CALBRAITH

"The addiction," she blurted. The others looked at her blankly, except Master Dōraku.

"You have truly a scholar's mind," he said. "Inquisitive from the start. Yes, the blood is addictive. But there are ways to deal with it. If you try hard enough – "

"Why are you here, Dōraku-*sama*?" interrupted Nagomi. She positioned herself opposite the samurai, as far away as was possible, in the small alcove, and kept her eyes fixed on him all the time. Bran was sitting close beside her, their knees almost touching. For some unfathomable reason this annoyed Satō.

The samurai turned serious. "I bring word from Shimazu Nariakira-*dono*."

"The daimyo?" Satō reeled back. "What does *he* want with us?"

Master Dōraku turned a meaningful glance at Bran.

"I… I asked him for help," the boy said.

"*Eeh?* What exactly is going on here?"

Questions rushed through Satō's head. *How did he get to meet a daimyo? Why nobody ever tells me anything? Why is he sitting so close to Nagomi?*

"I figured he would be the best-informed person on the matter."

"And you've made the right choice," said the Swordsman, filling his pipe. "The Lord of Kagoshima Castle has agreed to your request. You are all invited to his summer palace tomorrow morning," the samurai said with a mysterious smile.

"*Another* day's delay?" Bran slumped. "I was hoping we would move out as soon as possible."

"I'm sure you will not be disappointed with what His Excellency will show you tomorrow. Ah, the *cha* is ready," said Dōraku, reaching for the iron kettle.

"Let's eat. I'm eager to hear of your adventures since we parted company."

Bran closed his eyes and descended into the red dust plain. It was easier every time he tried it, and he was beginning to enjoy those moments. At the top of the tower there was complete silence and isolation, disturbed only by the wind blowing from nowhere to nowhere.

Earlier Satō had tried to convince him he should prepare himself for their meeting with Lord Nariakira.

"These are not the clothes you wear to meet the lord of the province," she insisted.

"B
ut I already *met* him."

"Yes, but that wasn't formal. There is a hierarchy to these things even *you* can't ignore."

"The Shimazu are one of the Great Clans," added Nagomi, "above them are only the *Taikun* and the Divine *Mikado*... A common physician's daughter like me would never dream of meeting such an esteemed person."

"Is that why you are putting on make-up?" Bran didn't think much of the priestess's efforts with the white paint and lip carmin. Satō, too, was at her most feminine, practicing a girly giggle and blushing on command.

"I just don't understand why suddenly – "

"It's *what's proper*," said the wizardess, futilely trying to put charcoal paste on her eyelashes. Her hand shook.

"Now go away, you're making me nervous with your staring."

The *Taishō* was nowhere to be seen. Had he wandered somewhere off, or was he not *always* present here in a physical form? Either way, his existence on this featureless plain must have been excruciatingly boring. Bran felt sorry for the old General. At least in the cave back in Suwa there were other Spirits to keep him company.

Bran came down to the green dragon and touched its neck. This time he penetrated farther, trying to learn more about Emrys' whereabouts. For a moment nothing seemed to happen; but when he pressed harder, his head began to spin and he found himself in the middle of a storm of unintelligible signals, a hurricane of raw emotions, impressions and visions. Wild yearning. Anger. Bloodlust. Fear. Freedom. The idea of a forest, a mountain-top, a rice field; the taste of fresh meat; the buffeting of wind.

Exhausted, Bran let go of the jade-green phantom and slid down to the ground. It seemed the dragon was both further away physically, and further into the process of going wild and Bran was unable to pick up any sense of direction.

The General appeared out of nowhere and came up to the boy.

"Trouble, eh?"

"I can't get through. I need to... I need to stop thinking, somehow. There's too much noise in my head."

"I can teach you how to do that."

"Really?"

Shigemasa scoffed.

"All well-educated samurai know how to meditate. Of course, it takes years of training, but I can teach you a trick or two today. Now sit straight, like a Man."

Bran knelt down with the body resting on his heels, with feet turned outwards. He usually could not withstand this position for longer than a few minutes.

"Good. Fold your hands like this and don't move. Now we need something for you to focus on. Look at the red light on top of the tower, and don't let your eyes wander off it."

The boy duly stared at the light. He waited for about a minute for further instruction, but nothing happened.

"What – "

The General hit him in the back with his sword's scabbard.

"Quiet! Think of nothing but your *breath*. In and out. In and out. Look at the light."

Bran soon lost track of time – there was, after all, nothing on the red plain to help him to orient his thoughts.

He tried to count seconds, but lost count after a hundred. He continued to force his eyes on the gently pulsating red light...

Another slap on the back woke him up.

"No sleeping!"

"Surely I'm ready now-"

"It's not even ten minutes since you started. Your mind is still full of random thoughts."

It feels like school now, Bran was annoyed, but stared into the light again. He focused on his breath. Finally the light at the top of the tower began to subdue, its pulsations grew slow and soft, as did Bran's heartbeat. The *Taishō* grunted with satisfaction.

"Enough. Try your magic now."

Bran felt light-headed and awake, but mostly, he felt his feet and legs burn with terrible pain. He stood up, made a few steps and staggered; falling, he reached out a hand and touched the warm, green scales again.

Images and sensations flooded him. An enormous, lush green valley, perfectly round. Tall, sheer cliffs on all sides. White-washed villages scattered about its bottom like snowflakes. In the middle, a high fire mountain, gushing steam from several outlets.

A ruby-hued light on the top, a beacon he couldn't resist, summoning him closer...

"Then it's captured already..."

No, don't go there!

Bran tried to call the dragon away; he sent out a powerful Word of command, but the strain of conflicting pulls proved too much. The thin link broke, and the beast cast him away.

He swayed back; the General supported him and helped him stand straight.

"Did it work?"

"I saw – a great round valley, with steep edges and a fire mountain inside."

"*Unnh.* Must be Aso-san. Anyone on Chinzei will know how to get there."

"Aso-san. I'll remember."

The General smiled lightly.

"Be careful in your dealings with the daimyo of Satsuma. I knew the first one, Tadatsuna-*dono*. He drew off hundred thousand Qin soldiers with just eight thousand men. His descendant looks equally cunning."

"I'll be careful," Bran replied.

When he departed, the image of the green valley and the ruby-hued light was still clear in his mind; but there was something else he recalled from the vision: a nagging, odd feeling of *another* Farlink. As if there was another dragon and rider pair somewhere near – somewhere in Yamato.

Is my father coming to my rescue at last?

CHAPTER IX

The naked torsos gleamed with the omnipresent black pumice powder, covering the body with a thin layer the moment the porters cleaned themselves. The men lifted the four boxes marked with the circle-cross crest of Satsuma and carried them swiftly down the streets of Kagoshima, along its main road. One of the vehicles remained empty: Torishi insisted on running along with the porters.

"I don't like being locked," he said. Bran quietly agreed with the bear-man.

Sakurajima loomed on the right; this meant they were moving north. Soon they entered the outskirts of the city, passing at least one "great workshop", belching white and yellow smoke from its red-brick chimney stacks, and started climbing up and down some low hills, before crossing the gate of thick wooden beams.

It was a long journey, and as Bran left the confines of his black box, he felt pins and needles running all over his limbs. He was still jumping up and down trying to relax his tense muscles, when Lord Shimazu Nariakira came down from a flower-topped hill to welcome them. The porters immediately fell to the ground while Bran and his party bowed deeply.

"How do you like my garden?"

Bran looked around and spotted the garden's most striking feature: from where he was standing, the trees and flowers seemed to form a window frame through which the mighty Sakurajima appeared like a part of the continuing garden arrangement, with the blue waters of the Kinkō Bay flowing before it like a decorative pond.

"It is magnificent, my Lord," replied Satō, her eyes hidden behind a paper fan. She was wearing a many-layered, long-sleeved kimono with summer motif she had rented a day earlier especially for the occasion. Tense and nervous, she had already tripped on its hem a couple of times; the blush of embarrassment visible even through the thick make-up which seemed to freeze a trained smile in place.

"You're Takashima Satō, aren't you?" Lord Nariakira said and smiled. Satō looked as if she was about to faint.

"I met your father once, you know. What a mind! Didn't he tell you to come to me if there was any trouble? Naturally, I would do anything to help Shūhan-*sama* and his family."

The wizardess could only nod.

"And you are Itō-*sama*'s daughter! How is he these days?"

"He... he is well, *kakka*. He's in Chubu, fighting smallpox."

"The man's a hero! Just think of the lives he's saving with his art... Men like him should be rich and powerful – not us, old wrinkly bats who've inherited their wealth because of what their great-great-great-grandfather did in one battle or another."

The daimyo chuckled and then turned to the towering Torishi – who hardly broke a sweat along the journey – and pretended to flinch.

"And who is that? A forest giant of the Kumaso! I never thought I'd meet one of your people."

"I am the last one," replied the bear-man. Meeting Lord Nariakira didn't seem to make any impression on him. The daimyo's face turned serious for a moment, "I'm sorry to hear that. My power does not reach far enough into the mountains."

Finally, the daimyo looked at Bran. He stared at the boy's transformed Yamato face for a moment, perplexed, before bursting with laughter – though his eyes remained ever serious.

"Yes! I see, I see. Come, come, my noble guests. I will show you something of interest!"

They followed him down a steep flight of stairs carved in stone, to a narrow inlet, cut off from the rest of the bay with a tall, thick lock gate. Moored to a wooden pier was a ship unlike any Bran had seen in Yamato. It was about sixty feet long, its hull was sleek, narrow, streamlined, covered with copper plate and painted black. Three masts rose from the deck, but there was also a thin funnel above a long, rectangular cabin. A brass lightning box hung from the foremast in place of a storm lantern and brass tubes and vents pierced the stern deck above the boiler room.

"But this is a... mistfire ship!" Satō forgot her decorum momentarily, picked up the hem of her kimono and ran down the pier to see the vessel up close. Lord Nariakira climbed on board and looked down an open hatch in the middle of the deck.

"Captain Kawamura! Are you there?"

A tall, robust, solemn-eyed man emerged from the hatch in a hurry. He was stripped to the waist, wearing only a pair of baggy *monpe* pantaloons. His upper body was smeared with oil and soot, and he held a big wrench in his hand, which he dropped, and pressed his forehead to the ground before the daimyo.

"*Kakka!* I did not expect you today!"

"Get up, Kawamura. How is she?"

"Ready to set sail at your command, *kakka!*"

"So, what do you think of my *Iroha Maru*?" Lord Nariakira said, turning to his guests, beaming with pride. "You won't find a faster ship in all of Yamato."

"This is incredible! I had no idea anyone was building something like this!"

Satō ran up and down the deck, before leaning down the hatch and examining the boiler room, "How big is this engine?"

"There's sixty-four elementals trapped in the Great Cauldron, noble lady," replied Kawamura, visibly abashed at being questioned in matters of engineering by a woman and guest of the daimyo.

"Sixty-four! To think Hisashige-*sama* was so proud of his eight!"

"Old Tanaka is pretty close to building such an engine himself, last I heard," said the daimyo. "And how do you like the ship, young *Gaikokujin-sama*?" he asked Bran, "How does it compare with what you're used to?"

"Very favourably, Nariakira-*dono*. I've seen yachts in the Brigstow harbour not unlike this boat."

The boy did not say out loud what his immediate thought was.

I could take it out to the open ocean and sail back to Qin.

At this moment he felt he was closer to home than ever since he woke up in Kiyō. Even if something happened to his dragon, even if the daimyo would not agree to lend him the ship, he could just steal it. With some effort and a bit of luck, using the knowledge he had gained on *Ladon*, Bran was sure he would be able to navigate his way towards the Qin coast.

All I have to do is to follow the setting sun...

He was nudged out from his musings by Nagomi. Her eyes pointed at Lord Nariakira.

"I'm sorry, *kakka*... I was admiring the lightning box."

"Ah yes. An intricate piece. I got it freshly made in Bataave. Anyway, Captain Kawamura will be in command of the ship on your journey. He will show you around. Kawamura, you will sail wherever these people tell you to."

"Of course, *kakka*."

"There is one more person I'd like you to meet. Heishichi!"

A lanky man came down the stairs onto the pier, wearing a long, hooded vermillion robe.

Heishichi!

"You're the Chief Wizard! You are the one that kept Emrys in its cage!"

The man dropped the hood, revealing his face. The entire left half of it was scorched into terrible, swollen scars and blisters. His left eye twitched constantly.

"Is that... did my dragon did this to you?"

Heishichi nodded.

"But the priests at Kirishima...!" said Nagomi.

"I wear these scars as a reminder of my disgrace."

"He wanted to kill himself," said the daimyo. "I didn't permit it, of course. My best wizard," he patted the *Daisen* on the back.

Heishichi bowed his head.

"I allowed my Lord's possession to be stolen. I have brought shame upon myself and all my family."

"Yes, well, you'll pay it back with your continuing service, of that you can be certain. You may start by joining these four noble travellers on their journey."

Heishichi bowed again in silence; the right half of his face twitched. The daimyo turned to Bran again.

"I will have your things brought from the inn before long."

"When do we leave, *kakka*?" asked Bran, darting away from Heishichi's pained stare.

I don't suppose we get to choose our travel companions.

"At dusk. I will be sailing before you, in my own official ship. This will draw the eyes of the spies."

"Will Dōraku-*sama* be joining us?" asked Satō.

"For now he's coming with me."

"I'm sorry, *kakka*" intruded Nagomi, "but where are we going?"

"That's a good question, young priestess-*sama*." The daimyo looked at Bran. "What do *you* think?"

"I think... I think we should go to a place called Aso-san," the boy replied.

"You managed to contact your *dorako* then?" Satō asked.

Bran nodded.

"Heishichi?" the daimyo turned to the wizard.

"It makes sense, *kakka*," the *Daisen* replied. "It is a nexus of power even greater than Mount Takachiho. A creature attuned to the magical energies would be drawn to it."

"But it will not be there by the time you reach Aso," added the daimyo. "Even on *Iroha Maru* it shall take several days to sail that far north. You will have to adjust your course along the way."

"I will try my best," Bran said, bowing.

"Of course you will", Lord Nariakira said, smiling; Bran felt uneasy under his stare. The daimyo seemed to be guessing at his deepest thoughts.

"And now I must leave you. I have to prepare for my own journey."

The daimyo bid them farewell and climbed back up the stone stairs. Captain Kawamura shifted his wrench nervously from one hand to another.

"Follow me, please, I will show you the cabin..."

Satō had spent half a day in the engine room, observing preparations for the launch and making note of the various valves, gauges and transformation chambers. The entire engine was of Bataavian make, and built so that even a person without magical talent could maintain it with ease.

The great cauldron had a small glass window in its cast iron wall, through which she could observe the elementals inside. The orange and blue wisps seemed to dance, or fight with each other within the confines of the chamber.

"I never really understood what the elementals are," she said, more to herself than to the Captain, who was busy adjusting a flange on a copper pipe. "They look so... alive."

"In a way, they are," a hoarse voice spoke behind her. She turned around to see the *Daisen* Torii Heishichi. His scarred face was hidden in the shadows.

166

"They grow, like crystals, but they can't multiply on their own, so they can't be said to be alive like us or animals."

"Some of them seem to have little faces," the wizardess observed. She had never seen elementals as big as these. The ones her father had worked on, obtained at a great cost from Dejima smugglers, or products of his own experiments, were just wisps of luminous air, barely longer than a man's thumb.

"Yes, that's something my students find most disturbing when they start working with the elementals. As they grow, they are beginning to look more and more human. Some Western scholars believe that that's how the magical creatures came about in the first place. And I've even seen an elemental larger than a new-born child."

"What did it look like?"

"Almost like a new-born child," the *Daisen* said, smirking. "It had a face and what could almost pass as limbs... But it was very unstable and soon perished. With a terrible cry."

With that, the lanky man stepped back into the shadows. Satō felt a shiver running through her spine. She wasn't certain if the wizard was telling the truth or was having a dark joke at her expense.

A cry? Does it mean the elementals feel pain?

She looked into the cauldron once more. The wisps whizzed back and forth all around the chamber and whenever one of fire met with one of water, a white flash of mistfire was produced which travelled up towards the funnel outlet.

Does it hurt when they do that?

Captain Kawamura finished working with the flange and clapped his hands.

"Right, time to increase the pressure."

He turned a great red valve, and even more elementals poured from their holding chambers, now a full thirty-two pairs of fire and water sprites. The inside of the cauldron filled with white smoke and its walls heated up.

Satō tried to listen to the tiny cries of the elementals, but all she heard was the rushing of mistfire up the pipes and the rhythmical beat of the firesteel and brass pistons.

In the quickly falling dusk, the *Iroha Maru* puffed inconspicuously away from the secret wharf. As the boat increased its speed, cutting through the waves of Kinkō Bay like a frolicking whale, excessive emanations of the elementals' magical energy transformations rose in a column of grey smoke from a narrow chimney. The paddle wheels rammed the water with a rhythmic roar, like a dozen waterfalls at once.

"We will sail her far into the open ocean," the Captain explained to Satō, "and circumnavigate Chinzei beyond the range of patrol boats."

"How far have you sailed this ship before?" she asked.

"She's been to Amami and back once. That's seventy *ri* each way. She's quite capable," Kawamura patted the steering wheel with a caring smile.

The fishing boats had all come back for the night already, and the waters of the strait between Sakurajima and the city were still and empty, cleared for the passage of the daimyo's ship. Satō could barely see anything before her, except the ominous shadow of the mountain concealing the stars lighting up in the darkening skies.

She was about to ask the Captain how he was planning to steer them in the night, when a bright yellow spark appeared in front of them.

"What's that?"

"That's the lighthouse on the Okagashima battery, Takashima-*sama*. There's five more between us and the Kaimondake cape where we turn westwards. I've sailed this route many times at night. Before dawn we'll be out in the open ocean – and then you'll see what she's really capable of!"

It was *Minazuki*, Month of Water, according to the Yamato calendar, Bran remembered; somewhere between May and June by Western reckoning, he guessed, but had no way to be certain. He had lost count of days a long time ago, when wandering the dark forests and high mountains of Chinzei.

The scorching sun stood high at noon, a slight cooling breeze having blown all the clouds away towards the land. The ocean was still and the weather was as perfect as they could ever wish for. Everything had a warm, fuzzy, dreamy quality to it.

Nagomi decided to stay on deck during the day, lying lethargic on a bench with her face turned to the sun and her eyes half-closed.

"This is like a holiday," she sighed, relaxed, "I never knew sea travel could be so pleasant."

Bran grunted back too lazy to answer. With Captain Kawamura at the wheel, there was nothing for any of them to do but watch the sea. He was leaning on the stern bulwark, munching on a juicy mikan. They had a whole crate of the fruits in the ship's hold, and in the heat of a summer's day this was about all the food they needed to sustain themselves.

Heishichi came out of the engine bay and sat on a bench, studying some square-shaped measuring instrument. Bran turned serious at once. He threw the fruit into the sea, wiped his hands on his clothes and came up to the wizard.

"I'm sorry," he said, "for what my *dorako* did."

Heishichi looked up, blinking with one eye. The burned half of his face remained still.

"At least I'm *alive*," he said, darkly. "Your *dorako* snapped one of my men in half."

A faint half-memory, half-dream returned to Bran; a sense of dread and fear.

"I… I didn't know."

The *Daisen* shrugged.

"We all understood the risk. It doesn't matter now. All my men are dead anyway."

Bran felt sorry for the wizard, and slightly guilty until he remembered this was the man who had held Emrys in its cage all this time, preventing their reunion until it was too late.

Heishichi returned to studying the device and adjusting the dials. He frowned and raised it to the sun.

"How good are you with Octagonometry?" he asked Bran.

"Terrible," the boy replied with a weak smile. He sat down on the bench beside the wizard and played with a piece of thin copper wire he had found lying on the deck.

It looks like Nagomi's hair, Bran thought.

"Riding a dragon is my only talent, really."

"When you got separated... how did you know how to find it again?"

Bran scratched his nose in thought.

"It's a power all dragon riders have... we call it *Farlink*. We can command dragons during flight and in combat. But I can also sense my mount wherever it is."

The wizard listened intently, from time to time turning to his device to adjust another gear.

"And what happens when your *dorako* dies or is lost for good?"

"The rider will be assigned a new mount, but it takes a while to readjust. A few weeks to make it listen to basic commands, months to reach the full union. Some riders are better at it than others."

"And are *you* better than others?"

Bran hesitated.

You are a good rider, he remembered Madam Magnusdottir. *One of our best.*

"So I've been told," he said at last.

Heishichi nodded.

"So you can't just take a *dorako* and make it yield to your will in an instant?"

"No. That would be a great feat."

"Then how did this… Crimson Robe manage to steal your beast at Kirishima?"

So that's what he's been getting at.

"He had some kind of an artefact. A ruby orb, about this size," Bran said, showing a clutched hand, "he could control my dragon and weaken *me*, when I transformed."

Heishichi looked at him sharply.

"A ruby orb? Are you sure?"

Bran nodded.

"I almost touched it. In True Sight it glowed like the Sun. Do you know about it?"

The *Daisen* didn't answer. He leaned over his instrument and carefully bent a thick copper wire. A bluish electric arc sparked across the device.

He stood up abruptly and pointed one edge of the device towards the horizon.

"Captain Kawamura, I have the radius!"

Bran stared in the direction Heishichi to which had pointed. All along the southern edge of the sky ran a thick, black, ominous wall of clouds, illuminated from inside by countless flashes of lightning; a massive storm, the likes of which he had never seen before.

The *Iroha Maru* continued to skirt the edge of the great storm all through the day. By evening a worried Bran joined Satō and Captain Kawamura in the helmsman's cockpit.

"Shouldn't we be turning back towards the land soon?" he asked, studying a navigation chart. It was oriented with the West to the top, so it had taken him a while to learn to read it.

"Soon, *tono*. We'll be taking a wide turn around these islands here, and I hope to get you near Aso-san in two days."

"And where is Aso-san?"

The Captain put his finger roughly in the middle of the map of Chinzei.

"So we're going back to Kumamoto," remarked Satō, pointing to the nearest harbour.

Kawamura shook his head.

"No, Takashima-*sama*. We can't be seen anywhere near the city. That's where His Excellency will be heading to draw attention from us. We will land somewhere in the marshes of Saga, to the north. Unless you tell me otherwise, *tono*."

"Me?" Bran looked up, startled.

"That's what I've been ordered. Listen to the boy with green eyes if he orders a change of course."

"Oh."

When Emrys moves somewhere else.

"Of course."

What if I order him to sail to Qin?

He looked through the left window, where the black wall of clouds still loomed, crested with white billows, neither grown nor lessened since he had first seen it.

"And if we had to go through this storm?"

The Captain blinked and laughed.

"That's no storm, *tono*. Those are the Divine Winds, *Kamikaze*. And we're not going *there* even on *Taikun's* orders."

Divine Winds?

There was something his father had told him… what seemed a very long time ago…

The Sea Maze! We're so close!

"How do the Bataavians get through that?" he asked.

"Believe me, if we knew the secret, His Excellency would have already sent ships to survey the Great Ocean."

Emrys got through on its own. And if it did, so could others.

He had sensed the other beast – or beasts – again last night, soaring through the dark sky. He was certain now the dragons were somewhere in Yamato.

The air cooled a little by the evening. Bran stepped out of the bridge, leaving Captain Kawamura leaning lazily over the steering wheel, chewing a chunk of tobacco.

The middle deck was illuminated by a single evertorch, powered by the lightning box on the mast. The faint beam obscured all but the brightest stars in the dark blue sky, and Bran moved to fore to see more of them. It was a curious thought: despite Bran being half-way across the globe, the stars looked the same as in his home country. There were one or two constellations he had only seen in the southern seas, but all the old summer familiars were there. He recalled Doctor Campion's lessons: Pisces, Aquarius, Capricorn... The Moon was just beginning to wane. Venus rose proudly from the East, and Vega, Bran's favourite, shone brightly to the Northwest. The Polaris hung to the right of the bowsprit, indicating they were headed north-west.

Nagomi stood on the prow with Torishi, eagerly discussing something. Her hair glowed warmly in the evertorch's light. Bran came up to them. The bear-man gave him a quick glance, smiled and left.

The priestess lowered her eyes and stepped aside to let Bran stand beside her by the gunwale.

"Do you know the names of the stars?" he asked.

"Some of them, yes."

"What do you call that big one?" he asked, pointing at Vega.

"That's Orihime, the Weaving Princess. And that's Hikoboshi the Shepherd," she replied, nodding at Altair hovering low above the horizon on the other side of the Milky Way.

"Her... lover," she added and flushed.

"What did you talk about with Torishi-*sama*?"

"His people have... had... a different way of communicating with Spirits than the priests. It's more... intimate. They did things I didn't think possible."

"Such as?"

"Travelling into the Otherworld or speaking with the *kami* directly."

Otherworld?

"Did he tell you what that place looked like?" he asked.

"A great, flat plain of red dust at first. A spirit guide can help you to reach other lands, where the *kami* dwell. For the Kumaso a spirit guide was the bear."

Is Emrys my spirit guide, then?

The waves lapped softly against the hull of the ship. The deck vibrated lightly under Bran's feet. Underneath, in the engine room, Satō and Heishichi were working on some experiment. With the bear-man gone to his cabin, Bran and Nagomi were all alone on the deck.

The priestess was clutching the rail tightly, facing the breeze.

176

"The years I spent in the shrine were an endless cycle of …seasons, festivals, rituals and chores," she started, "I was sure that was how I would spend the rest of my life. I got used to it. This… simplicity and repetitiveness. I felt at home with it. But when I was… dying," her voice broke a little, "all I could think of was 'too short'. 'My life was too short.' Those last few weeks with you and Sacchan… I was so scared that would be all I would ever know and – " She paused.

She's cute when she's sad, thought Bran. He shuddered, remembering her heartbeat slowing down, her body growing cold in his hands as he carried her up the forest path. Then he remembered her kiss – clumsy, naïve, and so unlike Satō's thirsty caress. It had taken him completely by surprise.

It must have been her first.

He reached his arm around her and pulled her close. She didn't resist, but didn't look up to him, either. She let out a quiet sigh and he felt her body relax; it seemed she was content just standing near him. She looked up to the sky and sung in a soft voice:

Ohoshi-sama kirakira

Sora-kara miteiru…

The stars twinkle in the sky

Looking at us from above…

"I've never heard you sing before."

"It's a song of the Tanabata festival… the story of Orihime and Hikoboshi. They can only meet once a year, on a bridge of magpies thrown over the River of Stars…"

She fell silent again. He didn't know how long they stood like that, looking at the moon and the sky splattered with bright pin pricks. His breath slowed down and his mind was clear; he realised he inadvertently slipped into the meditation Shigemasa was teaching him. Outside the red dust plain – the *Otherworld* - he couldn't quite sense his dragon yet, just a certain weak buzz, like a droning insect. He raised his hand and focused. A tiny flame, no greater than a burning match, appeared in the middle of his palm.

"Oh!" Nagomi clasped her hands. "You can do magic again!"

The flame disappeared.

"Yes, though only this much, and with great effort."

"Does that mean you'll be able to ride your *dorako* again?"

"I hope so," he replied.

A sudden movement in the water caught Bran's eye.

"What in *Annwn* – "

A long, black shape cut swiftly through the dark sea across their path. Captain Kawamura had no chance to avoid it – it was too low and too fast for him to see. At the last moment, the shape swerved aside – but it was too late. *Iroha Maru*'s prow jumped up and the entire ship rocked from side to side, throwing Bran and Nagomi onto the deck.

By the time Bran scrambled to his feet and helped Nagomi up, the ship was listing at a few degrees to starboard. He had spent enough time on sea to know what it meant; the hull was breached and they were taking in water.

Not again…

THE RISING TIDE

CHAPTER X

Wulfhere of Warwick woke up, raised a hand to wipe his tired eyes and hissed in pain.

"Careful. That arm is still healing."

I don't remember being wounded in the arm.

He opened his eyes. Hywel was sitting by his bed, half-smiling, his shoulder in a binding, his head swollen and wrapped in thick bandages.

"What happened?"

"They say it's because you struck that... *thing*. It will be sore for a few days."

"What was it?"

Hywel shrugged with one shoulder.

"Only the Qin know."

Wulfhere spotted two Qin faces in the tent's entrance. They disappeared the moment they saw him look at them.

"And who are they?" he asked Hywel.

"Your worshippers," the Prydain boy said with a chuckle.

A Qin man entered the tent; round-faced, sporting a crescent moustache over narrow

lips.

"You've made quite a name for yourself, Lieutenant," the Qinese said in good, slightly lisping Seaxe.

"I'm just an Ensign."

"Not anymore," said Hywel. "You were promoted."

"Why? And what do you mean, 'worshippers'?"

"You've struck down a Black Lotus," the Qin man said.

"Black Lotus… is that what you call it?"

"It, and others like it, yes. They are members of a secret society, attaching themselves to any disturbance in hope of profit."

"But I… I didn't kill it."

"Nobody can kill a Black Lotus – or so they say… but you've harmed it and made it leave the battlefield, Lieutenant. That is a feat worthy of a great warrior," the Qin main said. He wrapped his right fist with his left hand and bowed.

"I was lucky," replied Wulfhere in a subdued voice.

"What is wrong with you, Wulf?" Hywel said, laughing. "I thought you'd be bragging about this to everyone!"

The Seaxe closed his eyes and took a deep breath. The sight of Nechtan, twitching and dying in the creature's grasp, flashed under his eyelids.

"I'm still tired, that's all."

"Sure, sure. I'll let you rest."

Hywel stood up and left the tent. The Qin man remained.

"Who are you?" asked Wulfhere.

"My name is Li," the man replied, bowing again. "I am merely a servant of my Lord Bohan, the Commander of the Imperial Army."

"What do you want from me?"

"To see the hero and wish him good health."

"Thank you."

Uninvited, Li pulled himself up a stool.

"I hear you have royal blood in your veins."

How in Hel *does he know that?*

"My ancestor was a king of Dracaland, yes."

"Forgive me asking, but why then were you a mere ensign until now? And one without a dragon, too? In Qin, you would be a high-ranking officer already."

As I should be!

"My commanders aren't fond of me. They are mostly *waelesc.*"

"*Waelesc?*"

"Prydain. They are of a different, older race. A race we once conquered. They hold many grudges against us, Seaxe."

Li nodded. His face brightened.

"Ah, now I understand. My commander is of the Hunan people, from the South. We seem to have similar… misunderstandings. But, Commodore *Dí Lán* is a Prydain, no?"

"I don't know much about him. His son…"

"His son?"

"Why are you interested in the Commodore anyway, Li?"

"I am a curious man," Li replied with a smile. "And the Commodore is an interesting person. I didn't know he had a son?"

"I studied with him at the Academy. He would be here if it wasn't for the disaster at sea."

"He is dead, then. How unfortunate."

"No, no," Wulfhere said, waving his hands excitedly. "He's got a Llambed Seal. That would have saved his life."

"A Llambed Seal?"

"A spell all graduates of Llambed have. The rumour has it he's been transported out of Qin, nobody knows where. Somewhere safe."

"Out of Qin? And the Commodore is not trying to look for him?"

Wulfhere shrugged. "He's a soldier. He's got his orders."

"Fascinating. Well, it's been an interesting chat," the Qinese said, standing up. "I certainly enjoyed it. Do you mind if I come here again?"

"Not at all."

Li bowed and left the tent.

What a nice fellow, thought Wulfhere.

Gwenlian woke up; in the darkness of the tent, she saw the silhouette of a man sitting on the edge of her bed, with his head in his hands.

She was just a Flight Leader when they had first met, five years earlier. He was commanding her regiment at the time. Dashing, handsome, bright, with a scarred, mature face, he was popular among both the women and men of the Second Royal alike. They all loved and respected him and it was no surprise that she had fallen for him at once.

She preferred not to ask, but sometimes she wondered about his feelings. Who was she for him? Their relationship lasted too long to count as a passing distraction in time of war. She knew he had a wife in Gwynedd, Bran's mother, but he never talked about her and she was grateful for that.

She reached out to him and caressed his back.

"What's wrong, Dylan?"

He raised his head slowly.

"Do you think Edern would make a good commander?"

What brought that on?

"He's proving himself well in the field," she replied.

"Yes, he does, doesn't he? He's got an affinity with the Qin he trains. They like him."

"They like you, too. They like anyone who brings guns and victory. What's wrong?" she repeated, twirling the jade necklace he gave her at Shanglin.

Dylan sighed and lay back by her side.

"I can't do it anymore. I think I'm growing old."

"Is it about Shanglin? This has nothing to do with us."

"You know they couldn't have done it without our help."

"I warned you there would be trouble."

"What was I to do? I had my orders."

"Well, you're thinking of doing something *now*. I can tell."

"I can't betray my country. I've sworn to serve until… until…"

"What? You're not planning something *stupid*, Dylan? Think about your son."

"I am thinking about him. Gwen, I was wrong. I should be out there, looking for him. I should be in Yamato."

"*Yamato?* How do you know – "

"I *know*. I was guessing before, but now I'm certain."

"You've already decided," she said, after studying him for a while. She knew that look; there was nothing she could say or do to change his mind.

186

"Will you help me?" he asked, taking her by the wrist.

"We'll be court-martialled if they find out. You'll be stripped of rank, and your family will get no pension. We'll be lucky to get out of it alive."

"But you *will* help me."

"I know you, Dylan ab Ifor. You've already planned how to get out of all possible trouble."

He smiled and leaned to kiss her.

Dylan knocked on the flaps of Edern's tent.

"Banneret?"

"Coming!"

The Tylwyth's head appeared in the opening. His face was flushed, his hair unkempt. "Yes, Commodore?"

"I need you at the headquarters."

"What's going on? I didn't hear an alarm."

"We have to plan our next attack. I want to move before the Imperial Army does."

"Oh. Right, I'll be there in ten minutes."

"Who have you got there, Edern?" Dylan asked.

Edern glanced around with shifty eyes and then grinned, mischievously.

"Admiral's *aide*," he whispered.

Dylan chuckled.

"You sly fox. You have ten minutes. I'll be waiting."

"What's all this about, then?" asked Edern, running his slender fingers through his silver hair.

Dylan traced the staff map with his finger, leaving a golden trail where he touched the paper. A grid of such lines in different colours marked the imagined movements of the wings and squadrons, all concentrating on a small town, some forty miles north-west of Huating.

He stood up and looked around. There were just a few of them in the room – the Ardian of the Twelfth Light, the Commander of a small squadron of gunboats which had recently arrived to replace Admiral Reynolds's fleet, Gwen and Edern; it was still the same sparse brick warehouse in the Concession he had been using when the Second had first appeared in Huating. Dylan preferred this place to any other of the proposed locations for the staff headquarters: it was the only one where he was certain there were no Qin spies.

"Chansu," Edern deciphered. "That's in an opposite direction to where our main forces are."

Dylan nodded. "But this is where the *Bohan* will strike next. I want that city *ours*."

"Why the hurry? Were there some new orders from Lundenburgh?" asked Seton, the Ardian of the Twelfth. Dylan glanced at him and caught himself inadvertently biting his lips. The man had an indecipherable, blank face, hidden behind a great Seaxe moustache.

"Yes," replied Dylan, looking Seton straight in the eyes.

188

They had met once before, a year earlier: Seton was the commander of the Foot detachment saved from the Birkenhead disaster. His exemplary conduct on board the ship had earned him quick promotion.

Since arriving in Huating, he had made it clear on several occasions that he would not let the debt of gratitude get in the way of his sense of duty.

"May we see those orders, Commodore?" Seton asked.

"They are for my eyes only."

I won't have another massacre on my hands.

Seton's eyes narrowed, but he said nothing. Edern leaned over the map, rubbing his chin. "Will we make it, though? With just two regiments of dragons and without the *Bohan*'s infantry…"

"The city lies near the coast. The gunboats will be more than enough replacement for the Imperial Army."

The navy man nodded sharply. He didn't seem to be bothered with the sudden change of plans.

There would be no trouble with this one, at least.

"I want us to fly in three days. The Rebels will not expect us so soon; they think the *Bohan* is still in the South."

Seton's finger traced a red line between Chansu and the rebel headquarters at Suchou, and stopped at a complex of several large bodies of water.

"That's only twenty miles to send reinforcements, and we won't be able to stop them beyond those lakes."

"Me and my men will take care of the left flank," said Dylan.

"Oh?" Seton raised an eyebrow.

"I will leave the glory of entering the city to yourself, Ardian." Dylan smiled.

Maybe that will get you off my back.

Wulfhere's task required discretion and skill, but he struggled to even keep his dragon in a straight line. His arm was still sore, his command of reins not up to scratch and proper Farlink was out of the question; this was one of the fresh batch of mounts, barely broken. And it wasn't even a typical military breed, but a Highland Grey – a Shadowcloud, like the one ridden by Dean Magnusdottir.

The other soldier in his detail was a quiet, dark-haired Kernow girl, Keyna. She was riding a tiny Kernow Crimson, a most unusual mount for a Light Dragoon.

It's even smaller than that frog Bran was riding.

The Crimson was fast, but not very strong. Together, the two riders were an odd pair. Wulf had no say in who was assigned as his newly acquired command. Keyna accepted his orders with just a nod of the head and a mumbled *yessir* from under a long fringe. She had expressed no surprise when he told her where they were going.

"We are assigned to the Royal Marines, to Commodore's guards," Wulf had said, "at Ardian Seton's request. It's an honour, you see. Because of what I did."

Keyna nodded, not impressed in the slightest. He sighed; he was getting used to everyone knowing him as the Hero of Qiang River.

Commodore Dylan was leading a charge of Silvers and Azures on a rebel column trying to get across a narrow strip of land between two large lakes. The battle was brief; the rebels had only a few dragons of their own, and there were no heavy weapons or mysterious tricks like at the Shanglin. Below, the footmen of the Ever Victorious Army were moving in to mop-up the survivors and secure the perimeter among the burning remains of the oxcarts and walking machines.

But the Commodore did not seem satisfied with the outcome of the fight. To Wulfhere's surprise, he and several other dragons split from the main skein and flew north, across one of the lakes, towards a line of old rebel fortifications.

What's he doing?

Wulf spurred his mount to fly higher, into the low-hanging clouds, and follow the Commodore. He noticed Keyna dragging behind.

She can't keep up. He rolled his eyes. *That's the problem with those small dragons. No stamina at all.*

"Go back to Ardian Seton," he cried an order. "Tell him what happened."

The girl nodded and turned around. Wulf was now alone inside the grey-white fog. He could still see the Commodore's silver mount clearly, but his own dragon's scales turned a shimmering, semi-translucent grey that made it so perfect for the mission he had been tasked with.

He hadn't told Keyna the other reason for his assignment.

"Keep an eye on the Commodore," the Ardian had told Wulf after the main debriefing. "That's why I'm giving you a Shadowcloud. Let me know if you see anything suspicious."

Well this is certainly suspicious, he thought. The Commodore's detachment – five riders altogether, Wulf counted – dived towards the fortifications. The rebels manning them opened fire from all sorts of weapons – rockets, cannons, muskets and repeating rifles; the sky filled with smoke and explosions. The dragons spewed fire and lightning, but where one gun was silenced, two more barrels answered in a hellish cackle.

A squadron of Qin *long* appeared from over the hills to the West – a dozen beasts at least. Wulf was reminded of his own patrol mistake, when he had lost his own dragon.

There's too few of them. They will be massacred!

A tactical error of this scale was very unlike the Commodore. The Qin descended upon the five Western mounts from three sides. One of the Dracalish dragons broke off and, in a wounded zigzag, headed back across the lake, then another. The third spiralled down, its rider stunned by a near explosion; the mount recovered just above the ground and retreated as well.

When just the two riders remained, the Commodore turned sharply north and, breaking through the cloud of enemy with ease, sped along the lake shore, soon finding himself out of the range of the rebel guns. The *longs* soon abandoned their pursuit, unable to keep up. Only Wulfhere's Grey could match the full speed of a Mountain Silver.

This was a no-man's land between the frontlines of the two armies; camps of marauders strewn among abandoned villages and ruined fields, flooded by swollen rivers and canals unbound from the confines of shattered dams and broken levees.

What are they doing here?

Wulfhere kept up a safe distance, unnoticed by both the pair of riders and anyone on the ground. Trying to navigate in the thickening clouds, he almost missed the Commodore and the other dragon land beyond a ridge of low, steep dunes bordering the lake on the north-east, lined with birch and willow.

Wulf pulled on the reins and directed his mount to the bottom of the ridge; he flew below the tree canopies, thankful for the new dragon's natural stealth.

I would make a mess of this landing on any other mount, he thought.

The dragon touched down in the sand silently like a cat. Wulfhere jumped off and climbed carefully to the top of the dune, where he dropped to the ground and crawled the rest of the way through wild wheat and tall grass.

He found the Commodore and the other rider – Wulf recognized the Reeve of the Second Marines – in a narrow ridge on the dune slope. The Commodore was tracing a complex pattern on the sand with black powder.

"But you used up all three charges of your Seal years ago," said the Reeve.

The Commodore finished the rune and shook the powder off his hands.

"Only you and Edern know that."

"And have you told Edern of your plan?"

"He will guess what happened when he sees this. Now move back. I know it's just an illusion, but it's the most powerful one I've ever made."

The Commodore knelt down and touched the pattern. He spoke a sequence of spell words too quietly for Wulfhere to hear. The sand exploded with blinding white light.

When Wulf's sight returned, he saw a column of radiance rising high above the dunes, piercing and tearing through the clouds.

This must be visible for miles around... he thought, and then he realized what it was – or rather, supposed to be.

The Seal of Llambed! He's faked the Seal!

He looked back down. The Commodore and the Reeve were mounting a dragon – only one, the great Silver of the Commodore.

The other Silver was in its death throes, tearing the dune's slope with its claws.

She used the Kill Word, Wulf realized with a shudder. The Commodore raised a hand and shot a tongue of flame at the dying dragon. It added little to its suffering, but the scorched scales made the death seem even more violent.

194

"I'm sorry, Gwen," the Commodore said to the Reeve, "it was the only way."

"I understand," she replied, "but are you sure we'll make it to the Bataavian ship on just one dragon?"

"It shouldn't be more than a day's flight from here. They couldn't reach to Yamato yet. And Afroleus is strong."

"Edern will be angry you didn't take him with you."

"He will understand. The Ever Victorious Army needs a commander if they are to reach Chansu before the Imperial Army."

The great Silver beast spread its wings, oblivious to the fate of the other beast. Wulf shuffled to the side, to hide himself underneath the branches of a weeping willow as the Commodore flew above him. He waited a couple of minutes to make sure neither he nor his Shadowcloud were spotted, and then made his way back down the slope.

He had heard a lot – but it didn't mean anything to him. And something told him Ardian Seton would know just as little.

But there was somebody else who *might* know…

The ocean was big, empty and the colour of pure lapis lazuli under the cloudless sky.

"I'm having second thoughts, Dylan," said Gwen. They had been flying in a zigzag line for a whole day. Since leaving the shores of Qin and passing through the Barrier, they saw no ship or even a boat.

She removed her goggles and put the spyglass to her eye.

"How can we possibly find anything in this vastness?"

"I've studied these seas. There are only so many ways a sail ship can pass through. The winds, the currents... the Bataavians *must* be here somewhere."

"What if we missed them?"

"Let's hope not."

Afreolus roared and buckled. Dylan sensed the beast's irritation with the long journey, and growing restlessness.

"Afreolus is nasty today," remarked Gwen.

"Yes, it's been like that for a while."

"It can't be going feral yet? You only got it after the first Panjab."

"It's been ten years now."

"I remember your previous mount. An Azure, not Silver."

"I lost it to the jungle madness. Pity. I liked it."

"You always said you preferred the Azures."

He nodded. "They make fine companions."

He regarded his mount's long silver neck and horned head. Always an unruly beast, Afreolus was growing ever more stubborn as years went by.

Not long now, he thought. *A year at best, if all goes well.*

"Are you alright?" he asked Gwen. "After the Kill Word, I mean."

"I'm fine, really. A bit disoriented without my dragon's wind sense. Where are we?" asked Gwen, looking at the featureless sea below. Dylan traced the rough light map in the air.

"About two hundred and fifty miles south-east of Huating. Another hundred miles this way there's a chain of islands which lie beyond the Sea Maze."

"Can we land there?"

"If we fail to find the ship. But there's still a day or so of flying left in Afreolus. Let's make the best of it."

Gwen rummaged in the saddle bags.

"Do you want some bread?"

"No, I'm fine. I'll have *cwrw*, maybe, if there's still some left in the canteen."

She leaned back to open another bag.

"There! Look! Five o'clock!"

Dylan turned his head and followed her finger with his eyes. On the edge of the curving horizon a sharp, white, triangular dot stood out against the canvas of lapis lazuli. The unmistakable trace of a ship's wake.

"Could be them," said Dylan and spurred Afreolus around. The dragon growled, struggling in the reins.

"Come here, you dumb beast!"

The mount resisted again, ignoring the Farlink command and the tugging reins. Dylan cursed and summoned a Soul Lance with a buzz. He touched the dragon's scales with its tip; he knew to a dragon it felt like being prodded with a red hot poker. Afreolus yowled and shook its head but obeyed at last.

The brass letters on the stern spelled the name "Soembing".

"It looks so… ancient!" cried Dylan.

The Bataavian ship was a two-hundred feet long three-master, with a single thin funnel between fore- and mizzen-masts. The engine was silent; the wind was good, and all the sails were up. The single row of six antique cannons may have been impressive in native ports, but were useless against any modern vessel.

Dylan scratched his scar.

"I've seen Bataavian ships. They're just as good as ours. I don't even know if I can land on this shell."

"They don't seem to expect a fight," said Gwen.

They swooped towards the ship. Afreolus sensed an incoming fight and shook its head triumphantly, nearly tearing the reins out of Dylan's hands. The Bataavians noticed them when it was almost too late. Most sailors fled under deck, unable to withstand the dragon fear. A few remained, valiantly, and responded to the attack with small arms fire; rifle bullets and lightning bolts struck the *tarian* surrounding the dragon, bouncing harmlessly off. Dylan circled the ship a couple of times, looking for a good place to land.

I could sink it in moments, he thought. *It should be in a museum!*

A hatch on the bow opened and the multi-barrelled mouth of a rocket-launcher spat missiles after Afreolus. Dylan pulled on the upper reins, turning the dragon on its back in a half-roll. The beast spewed flame, scorching the first wave of the rockets. But one got through; it exploded underneath the dragon's right wing in a hail of sparks and shrapnel. The *tarian* held, but the noise and flash angered and frightened the beast. For a second, Dylan lost the link with his mount altogether.

It's over, he thought in sudden desperation. *I was wrong. Its mind is gone.*

"Dylan, we need to land!"

"I'm trying!"

It's on the brink of going feral! How in Annwn *did I miss that earlier?*

Struggling to retain control over the dragon, Dylan dived for the poop deck, the only surface wide enough for a landing. Just as the dragon's claws were about to touch the deck, another, stray rocket burst above his head. The dragon landed with a huge crash, rolled on its side and, losing its grip on the boards, slid down onto the quarterdeck with a terrible crackle; it broke through the rigging and smashed against the mizzen-mast, snapping it in two with the force of the massive impact. With a deafening creek, the mast slowly fell, covering Dylan, Gwen, the dragon and some of the Bataavian crew with the heavy shroud of white canvas sails.

Dylan felt the dreaded *snap* in his mind, and then the all-too-familiar emptiness. The beast growled and threw both riders off in a spasm of fury, tearing its way out through the sail, helping itself with bursts of dragonflame. Dylan dodged the splinters of timber flying all over the place; a stray tongue of flame reached the main mast, and the course sail caught fire. Some of the Bataavian sailors tried to stop the beast with their thunder guns, but that only made it more angry and frightened.

Dylan finally found his way out from under the fallen mast. He saw Gwen standing against the gunwale, defending herself with the Soul Lance and shield from several panicked Bataavians. She was staggering. A long gash ran down her left leg. The sailors' efforts to subdue her were half-hearted; they were more concerned with the dragon wrecking the ship behind their backs.

He focused and sent a command through the Farlink; then another, stronger. A wave of anger was the only response. The beast was too far gone. It attacked a man now, ripping him in two with its claws and biting the other through with the mighty jaw. Blood and guts spilled on the deck.

It's too late.

Dylan closed his eyes and focused again. His lips moved noiselessly as he pronounced the Kill Word.

Afreolus raised its head and screamed an ear-splitting, devastating yell; it buckled in spasms, tearing the planking apart with its claws. It coughed, spitting several great balls of flame, which ignited everything in its path. It beat its wings and jumped, trying to fly away. Its death throes rolled the ship from side to side, and the beast started sliding off the bloodied deck. In a last effort, it held on to the gunwale with teeth and claw. The ship listed dangerously, and for a moment it seemed the dragon would pull it down to the bottom of the sea with it. At last, the wooden planks snapped away and Afreolus fell, splashing, into the water.

Dylan fell to his knees; the backlash of the dragon's death made him briefly deaf and blind, leaving what he knew would be a great mental scar – another one to add to the many. He wiped a nose-bleed and as the sight slowly returned to him, looked up.

He was staring straight into four barrels of a repeating air gun.

"What are we going to do about them, *Kapitein?*" a sailor, holding Dylan at gunpoint, asked a tall, red-haired, long-faced man in a black-and-orange uniform.

"We can't risk any more delay," the Captain replied. "Throw them overboard."

Dylan smirked. He was standing against the shattered bulwark next to Gwenlian, with his hands on the back of his head. He glanced at the planks and noticed something curious: from under the wooden boarding torn off by Afreolus military-grade steel showed through.

This is an ironclad, after all!

"What are *you* laughing about," the sailor barked, pushing the barrel closer.

"I've survived worse," said Dylan.

"You speak Bataavian?"

"I've spent two years at Bretten, Captain... Fabius, isn't it? I remember you commanding a rather more... contemporary vessel."

The Captain frowned.

"Who *are* you?"

"I am Commodore Dylan ab Ifor of the Royal Marines. I need to get to Yamato."

"Commodore? Dracaland is at peace with Bataave! Why did you attack us?"

"I'm not here on behalf of my country. All the damage was unintended, and I will recompense you as soon as we reach a friendly shore."

"I have men dead."

"I'm sorry."

"Why *are* you here, Commodore?"

"I'm looking for my son."

Captain Fabius gave Dylan a long, curious look, then waved his hand at the sailor with the gun.

"Lock them down. I want to hear this story."

Before Dylan opened his mouth, a cry came from the quarterdeck, where the Soembing's crew was busy putting down fires started by the dying Afreolus.

"Kapitein! Andere draak!"

The Captain looked up; the Commodore and the Reeve did the same. High above the Soembing's two remaining masts, beyond the range of any of the ship's cannons, circled a great Qin dragon, gleaming golden in the sun.

"Friends of yours?" Fabius asked.

"No," said Dylan, "but I think I know who it is. I would advise you let *this* one land."

THE RISING TIDE

CHAPTER XI

Shakushain breathed in the crisp, sulphuric air and gazed down from the summit of the volcanic cone. The peak of the fire mountain rose tall from the bottom of a vast, bowl-shaped valley, the rim of which loomed in a vertical cliff on the horizon. Several craters spewed yellow smoke and grey ash all over the rough slope. The raw, savage landscape reminded Shakushain of his homeland, far in the freezing North.

"This is a good place, demon!" he cried. The Crimson Robe turned around with a grin.

"Glad you like it."

"Are you sure it will come *here?*"

"Sooner or later. This is where all of Chinzei's magic is centred. And a beast like that will follow the lines of magic, unbeknownst to itself. When will your trap be ready?"

"Soon, demon. Soon."

He picked up a couple of wooden stakes from a pile and proceeded to insert them into holes dug in the living, steaming rock. He had spent two days preparing the stakes – shaving the wood of the young alder tree; carving the magic patterns; summoning the *kamuy* spirits to inhabit each and

205

every one of the pieces of wood. This was going to be the greatest sacred enclosure the world had seen. Only fitting for the greatest prey ever caught.

He reached the seventh slot when a quarrel caught his ear. He saw three of the Crimson Robe's men – the grey-clad *rōnin* – standing over his dark-skinned companion, mocking him and laughing at the orders the small man tried to give them in his strained, guttural accent.

Shakushain threw the stakes to the ground and in few quick strides approached the laughing men. Without warning, he punched the nearer one in the face. The swordsman fell down senseless; blood trickled from his ears and nose.

"You will all do as Koro says," he said, pointing a finger at the remaining two. "He's a better man than all of you put together."

They bowed and departed quickly, mumbling curses. Koro followed after them, waving his small fist. There was still a lot of work to do before the circle was finished.

He bent the last of the willow boughs, slotted it through a loop made of stripped bark and stepped back to admire his work. The figure was as tall as a man, and twice as long, woven densely out of willow, bamboo and birch. The wings were the most difficult, a delicate structure tied together with vines. A covering of butterbur leaves imitated the green scales.

Shakushain hadn't seen the dragon he was trying to replicate in the sculpture, but it didn't matter. The figurines of bears and wolves he made as a young shaman's apprentice always came out resembling disfigured pigs, but they worked nonetheless. This one was the same – only bigger.

With Koro's help, Shakushain carefully transported the fragile structure into the middle of the sacred enclosure, then he tied its delicate limbs and wings with a chain woven of poison ivy. *Like for like,* such was the rule of the Northern magic. To trap the real dragon, he had to first shackle the imitation.

He lit up two bonfires, one on each side of the circle – beacons for the crazed beast. It was near; the demon's spies had brought the news of it ravaging the pastures on the southern rim of the Aso Valley. That meant they should see its flames tonight; he hoped the beast would fall into the trap by midnight.

Koro cried out excitedly and waved his hands. His blue necklace was glowing. Shakushain ran up to him and looked in the direction where the little man pointed. A dot of light flashed against the dark shadow of the southern cliff-side, followed by a blast, and a bright line of flame. A second later a whoosh of hurricane-like wind and a sound of explosion reached where they were standing.

It's coming.

Samuel fell off his bunk and slid across the floor, hitting the opposite wall with his shoulder. The entire ship shook from some heavy impact, rolling to one side and then back again.

All the alarm bells rang out at once, all the evertorches lit up. The bearded sailors ran past Samuel back and forth, shouting orders and repeating them further. The ship was listing and, as far as Samuel could tell by the changes in air pressure, rapidly descending.

The doctor's instincts kicked in.

There may be wounded. I should be in the infirmary.

But the layout of the vessel was yet unfamiliar to him and instead of the infirmary, he found himself in a corridor he hadn't seen before. It was eerily empty and quiet compared to the chaos everywhere else. A door at the end caught his eye. It was unlike any other on the ship. He approached it slowly. Made of a slab of patinaed bronze, it had no visible handle, just a red locking rune blinking slowly where a keyhole should be. Samuel touched the metal surface; it was freezing cold.

I shouldn't be here.

He realised his hands were shaking and his throat felt dry. He turned back and hurried down another corridor, down a flight of metal stairs. This led him straight to the ship's bridge. An officer shot out through the round door and Samuel had never been so happy to see another human being. The crewman looked at Samuel in bewilderment, waved him aside and ran on with some important orders. Inside, the Admiral was sitting at his desk of many knobs and buttons, holding the steering wheel with one hand and pushing levers with another. He, too, was shouting something at the navigator, who was clutching a broken, bleeding nose and trying helplessly to plot a course on the map which seemed to consist mostly of a blank space and a few scattered navigation points.

Samuel's grasp of the basics of the Varyagan language allowed him to understand some of the Admiral's yells and curses.

"*Vad fan!* That was a *mistfirer*! What's a *mistfirer* doing in these waters?"

"I don't know, *Amiral.* We are definitely in the right place."

Somebody pushed Samuel aside and barged into the cabin.

"Nobelius!" the Admiral hollered, "do you have the *skaderappor?*"

"The *komandotorn* is breached and the *roder* is stuck."

"Can we hold her up?"

"Only if we blow all the ballast."

The old engineer and the Admiral began to exchange technical naval jargon at great speed, and Samuel lost track of the conversation. He decided to depart from the bridge and look for the sick bay elsewhere.

"*Doktor!*" the Admiral shouted after him. "Shouldn't you be at the infirmary?"

Satō woke up in pitch-black darkness. Her head throbbed and her left shoulder was sore from where she had hit the floor. She stood up on wobbly legs; the cold seawater, rushing through the narrow, jagged breach in the ship's iron hull, reached her knees and was rising fast. The only light she could see was the small glass window in the cauldron, where the elementals frantically continued to exchange their magical energies.

The ladder should be somewhere to the left… or was it right?

She stumbled and grabbed some handle; a valve opened, letting out steam.

Oh no! I broke something!

She tried to set the handle back to its original position, but slipped and dropped to the floor again with a splash.

The trap door opened above her head and somebody leapt into the water. A strong arm grabbed her and led her towards the ladder.

"It's alright," she said weakly, "I can manage…"

Somebody pulled her up onto the deck, somebody's hands loosened her clothes and held her while she retched out the seawater.

"Get this hose down," somebody shouted.

Captain Kawamura.

She was beginning to recognize the voices and the faces around her. Red hair – Nagomi, standing closest, worried. The Captain, setting up some heavy iron device with a long leather hose attached. The bear-man's storm of hair.

"Where's Bran?" she asked.

"Downstairs," answered Nagomi.

The Westerner appeared up the ladder, soaked through, spurting water.

"I got him out of the water, but won't manage to bring him up here."

"Bring whom?" asked Satō. She had a nagging feeling she was forgetting somebody.

"The *Daisen*! He's unconscious."

"I can help," the priestess stood up, but the Captain stopped her.

"Nobody's coming down until we stabilize the ship," he said. "If that cauldron floods, you'll be boiled alive. Come, Kumaso, I will need all your strength."

Torishi rushed up to the device Captain Kawamura had set up.

"Keep pressing that end of the lever," the Captain ordered. "Try to synchronize with me. Can you do that?"

Torishi nodded.

"One of you needs to make sure the hose isn't crooked and the water flows freely," the Captain said to Bran and Nagomi. The priestess straightened the coils and dropped the end of the hose overboard.

"What about the breach?" asked Bran. "The water is still coming in."

"One thing at a time. We'd need a wizard to fix it and our only one just got himself knocked out."

"I'm a wizard," said Satō. The Captain looked at her and stopped pumping for a moment.

"You're hurt," he said.

"It's just a bruise. What needs to be done?"

"How good a swimmer are you?"

She slumped.

There was never time to learn...

"Not very good."

"I'll help you," said Bran. "The sea is calm enough; I can hold you while you cast spells."

He dropped his clothes quickly, leaving only the linen loincloth, and leapt into the sea. She heard him yell and, fearing something terrible had happened, ran up to the bulwark.

"Cold!" he shouted, spitting. "Come on, I'll catch you!"

She stood against the rail, paralyzed with fear at the thought of leaping into the dark abyss.

He's shaming me again. I can't swim, I can't ride a horse... what kind of samurai am I?

She took a deep breath and jumped over the edge. Freezing water enveloped her.

I'm drowning, she thought. *I'm going to die.*

She started thrashing about in panic, until a strong pair of hands embraced her tightly and pulled her up to the surface.

"Calm down," said Bran. "It's harder when you move about."

With one arm wrapped around her waist, he swam slowly towards the stern, helping himself along the way by

212

holding onto the spokes of the silenced paddle-wheel. The pistons were quiet, and the ship drifted sideways on the waves.

"The breach is under the water-line. Can you hold your breath for long?" he asked.

She nodded. She was certain she could do at least that much. He pulled her down and she inadvertently opened her mouth. Instantly, they emerged back to the surface.

"It's all right, we'll try again. Did you see the breach?"

"No," she said, coughing. "I had my eyes closed."

He chuckled. "I'll try to guide you. Can you cast with your eyes closed?"

"I have to say the word."

"As long as you remember to only exhale. Right, one more time – on the count of three. One, two, *three!*"

They submerged much more gently this time. She felt his hand on hers, holding it straight and steady. He tapped her gently on the waist with his other hand.

"*Bebblubblu!*" she cried. The sound of the spell word was distorted by the water, but it didn't matter, what was important was her mental focus on the incantation. She felt her hand turn cold as the bolt of ice shot from her fingers, freezing the water around it.

They were back on the surface.

"Almost there. One more try," said Bran. "Deep breath. One, two, three."

213

She repeated the spell, this time trying to keep her eyes open. The salt stung, but she endured, making sure she covered the bubbling breach with a thick layer of frost.

"I've never… done… magic under water," she said, coughing and spluttering and trying to wipe salt from her eyes.

"Don't touch your eyes," said Bran, "it will only make it worse. You need to wash it with fresh water."

They swam back towards the stern, where Nagomi threw down a rope ladder. Now that the immediate danger was gone, Satō relaxed, letting Bran drag her freely against the waves; she felt the warmth of his body pressing against hers through soaked clothes.

No, she scolded herself. *You promised yourself.*

She climbed down to the engine room to secure the breach from inside. The water was now just up to her ankles, too low for the pump to be of any use, so Bran, Torishi and the Captain were pouring it out with buckets.

"That was quite a whale," said Captain Kawamura, assessing the breach.

"A whale?"

"What else? There are no reefs here."

"That spell won't last long," said Satō.

"We'll bring her to port in the morning," the Captain replied, "I know a place where we'll be safe from prying eyes."

214

Satō came up to Nagomi, who was kneeling by the still unconscious Heishichi, trying her best to wake him up.

"How is he?" the wizardess asked.

"Not badly injured."

The priestess's fingers glowed light blue, and the girl murmured a brief prayer. The *Daisen* coughed, gasped and opened his eyes. He sat up and shook his head. Satō turned her eyes away; the wizard's scorched face still made her nauseous.

"My glasses…"

"Here," said Nagomi, handing him the wire-framed pair. "I'm afraid one of the lenses broke…"

"Thank you."

"You should thank Bran," said Satō, nodding towards the boy. "He got you out of the water."

Heishichi stood up, cast Bran an empty stare and went to examine the damage to the ship.

"Did you do this?" he asked Satō, pointing at the ice.

"Yes."

"We could use a talent like you in our school. Our last ice mage died in Kirishima."

She couldn't help smiling.

"Thank you, but I have my own *dōjō* to run in Kiyō."

He smirked. "That's not what I heard."

The smile perished from her face.

215

The *Iroha Maru* moored at a low stone pier with a bump. Bran jumped off under Kawamura's direction to assist with tying the ship's hawsers to the bollards.

The place they landed in was a small town, little more than a village, hidden at the northern end of a long, narrow gulf. It was surrounded on all sides by tall, steep hills covered with lush green forest, except for one narrow pass to the west, where some farmers toiled what looked like barley fields.

There was only the one pier in the harbour. The small fishing boats used by the villagers had been towed out onto the wide beach of fine grey volcanic sand. Sparkling in the noon sun, the shallow sea had the colour of bright jade.

"This is wonderful!" said Nagomi. "What is this place?"

"Sakitsu on Amakusa Island," the Captain said. "We're almost at the edge of Yamato."

"Wait," said Satō, stopping half-way down the gangway, "I know that name. Isn't this part of *Taikun*'s personal domain? Are we really safe here?"

"They can answer your question, Takashima-*sama*," the Captain replied, nodding towards the end of the pier. There was already a group of curious children waiting there, and one or two fishermen coming to see the strange boat. An official looking man came up to greet the newcomers. He was wearing a long black robe, tied with hemp rope, and a tall Phrygian cap. He greeted them with a singing accent. Bran hesitated.

"If I didn't know better, I'd say you were..." he struggled to find a Yamato word, but could only come up with a Latin equivalent, "a *pater*."

"I am, indeed, *pater*. My name is Kukai."

"You are a Sun Worshipper!"

The man nodded.

"Driven to these islands by persecution, we remain faithful to the religion of our fathers. What is this strange vessel?" he added, pointing at the ship.

The Captain leaned over the edge.

"This is the private yacht of His Excellency, Shimazu Nariakira of Satsuma," he said. "We need to stay the night to make some repairs, if it's alright with you."

"Any subject of Shimazu-*dono* is welcome on Amakusa. We have long enjoyed his friendship and assistance."

"You kids go see the town," the Captain said, spitting tobacco discreetly into a handkerchief, "me and *Daisen-sama* will get to work."

"Please, let me show you around," said the man in the Phrygian cap.

The settlement had just a few narrow streets, lined with modest, simple houses, huddled on the edge of a cliff. The farther from the pier Bran went, the stronger a certain emotion he failed to recognize grew within from the very depths of his soul. It was directed at the *pater* and his congregation and absorbed him so much he barely noticed what went on around him.

"So many children..." he heard Nagomi say. "The town must be rich."

"On the contrary," said *pater* Kukai, "the soil here is poor – what little of it there is – and the fish avoid these coasts. But the *Taikun* keeps sending new colonist families every year."

"So I was right. This place does belong to the *Taikun*," said Satō.

"In name only... There is a *bugyō* on the island, but he lives across the mountains, on the Kumamoto side. All he's interested in is sending the colonists as far away as possible. Most of them end up here."

"And you turn them all into Sun Worshippers?" asked Bran.

"If they so wish. Whatever scary stories you might have heard in the past, we're a peaceful people. And here is our place of worship," said *pater* Kukai, stopping in front of a dark, windowless, foreboding building, imitating a vaulted cavern.

The girls went in, followed by Bran, who instantly recognized the shape of a *mithraeum*. The inside was also familiar with long benches along the walls and a painted altar opposite the entrance.

"Today is a special day: Mercuralia," *pater* Kukai said, "you're welcome to witness our ceremony."

For the first time since his arrival in Yamato Bran could tell the proper date.

Mercuralia – the Feast of Water. That's mid-May...

218

"Who is this man fighting an ox? And the woman in the blue robe? Are they your ancestors?" Nagomi asked, approaching the altar with great curiosity.

"These are their main *kami*," replied Bran, before the *pater* could answer. "*Isis,* the Earth Mother and *Mithras,* the Sun Warrior. A mockery of our Gods."

Eh, our Gods? What am I saying?

"I see you know something of our faith, young man" the *pater* said, dryly, "but we do *not* mock your beliefs: ours are much older. You're welcome to see our rituals for yourself tonight."

"I... I don't..."

Bran shook his head, trying to clear his mind. He realized his hands were clenched tightly into fists, and his breath was quickened. He felt sick.

"Are you alright?" Nagomi touched him on the shoulder.

"I... I'm sorry. I don't feel that well. I'd better go back to the boat."

He left before they could stop him. He knew now the emotion surging within him, making his hands shake, his teeth chatter. It was hate – pure, seething hate.

He looked down on the red dirt plain from the top of the tower. A great storm blew across the plain, shrouding the horizon in red haze, raising billowing clouds of dust. In the middle of the hurricane stood Shigemasa; fierce and somehow taller than usual.

"What is the meaning of this?" Bran cried against the wind.

The General raised his head but did not answer. The storm changed again, forming the clouds of dust into images. Haunting visions, moving sand sculptures.

Bran saw the Sun-worshipping rebels attack temples, shrines and those of the villagers who refused to join them. He saw a boy, Bran's age, wearing a black cape and the Western-style ruff collar, leading thirty thousand blood-thirsty masterless samurai and peasants against the castles throughout Chinzei. All the horrors of a civil war were laid before him: bodies hacked to pieces and strewn over the battlefields; limbs torn away by bullets and cannon balls, cripples wading in the mud; babies taken from their mothers; priests tortured, monks hung and quartered; the beleaguered defenders starving to death behind the walls of Hara, forced to eat their horses, dogs and corpses. Death, destruction, suffering brought through actions of those worshipping the Warrior God on the pious Yamato and on themselves alike.

At last the vision changed. He saw another boy, green-eyed, on some black metal ship, sneaking up to a man crouched over a map, with a large wrench in his hand. With a deft stroke on the head, the boy knocked the Captain out. He then dropped the wrench and took a sword from under one of the bunk beds. At that moment Bran realised this was no longer a vision - this was reality.

He looked down. Shigemasa was gone; the tower was locked from inside.

In the middle of the vaulted hall a large feast was being prepared. Nagomi sat beside Satō, just before the altar, slightly uncomfortable on the reclining bench. Heishichi observed the proceedings from further at the back, making notes. With Bran and Captain Kawamura back at the ship, the other missing member of the party was Torishi. The bear-man had disappeared into the woods for the night.

One of the townspeople stood up, holding a heavy stringed instrument, beaten and ancient; to its plucking sounds, the rest of the gathering started a chant in a language unknown to Nagomi. It was more a recitation than singing, not unlike the official prayers of the High Priests in Yamato shrines, but faster and more rhythmical.

After the singing, *pater* Kukai stepped onto the altar, with a staff in one hand and a bronze sickle in another.

"Bring out the *haoma!*" he announced, stamping the staff on the floor.

Several girls in long, white, translucent flowing robes came out with clay pitchers. Nagomi presented a small cup she had been given at the beginning of the ceremony and one of the girls filled it with a milky liquid, smelling of pine needles.

"What do you think it is?" she asked Satō.

"Maybe some kind of saké? It's got a strong smell."

The wizardess quaffed the drink, but Nagomi hesitated. These, after all, were the *Sun Worshippers*. They may look benign now, but she was raised on the tales of their blood-thirst and cruelty. What if it was poison, or some strange drug? She looked around and poured the liquid on the floor.

Just when she was about to ask Satō about the taste, the door burst open. Bran ran into the building, holding his sword in outstretched hands. The children and women screamed. A man rose from the back bench to stop him but Bran slashed his sword and the villager fell among the plates and pots with a cry, bleeding from his forehead. The rest of the townspeople rushed in panic towards the altar, leaving only Heishichi sitting on his bench, observing the scene with bemusement.

"Bran! What are you doing?" Nagomi stepped forward, but Satō held her back.

"Wait, that's not him."

The wizardess put her hand on the hilt and approached Bran, who now stood in the middle of the aisle, ready to strike. His eyes were deep dark and burning with hate.

"Itakura-*dono*," she said.

The spirit in Bran's body looked her straight in the eyes.

"Step aside, girl. I have no quarrel with thee. Or have they converted thou as well?"

"These are peaceful people, *Taishō-dono*. Not rebels from Shimabara."

"They are all enemies of the Divine *Mikado*! Step aside, I said!" The General tried to push his way past Satō, but the girl drew her own sword. The blades clashed.

"I *knew* thou wouldst be on their side. Thou art half-barbarian thyself."

Shigemasa pressed forward, but Satō was strong too. They were in a clinch. The General looked around. He was surrounded by the congregation, closing in on him from all sides. A few of them held walking sticks or fishing knives threateningly.

"Nngh!" The General pushed once again; Satō slid dangerously on the stone floor, but still had her sword raised. A few of the townsfolk leapt between her and the samurai.

At the back, Heishichi stood up with a half-frown, stretching his knuckles. Shigemasa cast him a furious glance, then turned back to Satō and the men before him.

"I'll get thee yet, traitor. I'll get all of you!" he cried, then spun around and ran towards the temple door, slashing his sword at one more worshipper who failed to get out of his way fast enough. Heishichi made no effort to stop him.

"Help the wounded," Satō told Nagomi, sheathing her sword. The priestess nodded and crouched beside the man lying on the floor bleeding onto the stone slabs from a deep cut across the chest. When she looked back, the wizardess was already gone. She focused on the healing ritual. She cleared her mind, took a deep breath and put her hands on the man's wound. But before she could start, she felt a heavy hand on her shoulder. She looked up.

"We do not wish assistance from your demons, priestess," *pater* Kukai said.

Demons?

"He is dying. I can heal him."

"He will die a warrior's death, then. It is better to die and join the ranks of the Sun Warrior's army than to live through a pact with the demon."

Nagomi raised herself uncertainly. A few townspeople picked up the two wounded men and carried them away.

"We take care of our own," said the *pater*, "and we will seek revenge on the one who harmed them. The *Taikun* spy will not get away far."

"Bran is not a *Taikun* spy! He… he wasn't himself."

"Go on," the *pater* said with a frown.

"He shares his soul with a Spirit, who – "

"A Spirit? You mean a *deva,* a demon! I'm not surprised," the *pater* interrupted in a solemn voice, "in the presence of the Divine the *deva* often become agitated and angry."

He turned to his congregation, and raised his arms in a calming gesture.

"Behold! *Mitorasu-sama* brings us another sign of his power!" he cried. "To show us the dangers of the outside world, he brings a *deva* into our midst."

The townspeople cowered as the preacher continued. Heishichi appeared beside Nagomi.

"Stay close," he said. She nodded.

"Yes, this is how playing with the demonic rituals always has to end. Do not think I am blind or foolish. I know some of you still cling to the old ways. I have seen the shrines and statues in the forest. But I have ignored them for too long, and now we have been reminded all too well what the consequences of worshipping those demons are. The sword of the Sun will fall on them all."

He climbed the altar and picked up the bronze sickle.

"Bring out the bull," said *pater* Kukai.

"The bull! The bull!" the gathered cried. Nagomi's hair stood on end as she felt the crowd's growing frenzy. A short, stocky man in a black *gi* jacket opened the door to what looked like a pantry and carried out a small, terrified calf. One of the young girls in translucent robes approached the animal. Only her eyes, bright and blue, were visible above the veil and Nagomi could see fear and fascination in them as she reached out and put a circlet of silver thread and bells between the animal's horns. The crowd fell quiet in patient anticipation.

"Is that a… *symbolic* sacrifice?" she asked Heishichi. "Bran said they don't kill the innocent…"

"I don't think so," the *Daisen* replied, half of his mouth twisted in a sneer.

Pater Kukai spoke again to the agitated crowd.

"As the beloved Mithras had slain the Bull sent from the Otherworld," the priest intoned, "and brought life to the barren world, so do we bring the life of this bull to its end, to renew our bond with the Sun. Blessed be the Bull."

"Blessed be the Bull," the others chanted in unison.

"Let its blood wash over us, like the blood of our enemies. Let it drown the demons at our door. Let it clean the souls of our visitors so that they, too, can see the light of Truth."

The townspeople howled, "*Ia! Ia! Ia!*", while the *pater* raised his sickle over the calf's neck. The animal mowed, trying to break free, but the blade fell in that instant with a mortifying swish.

Nagomi could watch no more. She turned around, passed Heishichi by and ran out of the temple.

CHAPTER XII

The guards bowed deeply, stepping aside and allowing Lord Shimazu Nariakira's entourage into the great tunnel, linking the Kumamoto Castle with the city below.

Katō Kiyomasa knew how to build, he thought, admiring the craftsmanship of the smoothly polished great blocks of granite lining the walls. The tunnel was a unique feature of the castle; not only was it the last ditch of defence in case of a siege, it also allowed complete control over any visitors in time of peace, even those as illustrious as the daimyo of Satsuma. Strong guards were posted at either end, and both gates could be closed instantly, trapping everyone inside.

Lord Hosokawa Narimori waited at the top entrance, twiddling his fingers with a nervous smile on his face.

"Shimazu-*dono*. To what do I owe this unexpected pleasure?"

Less than an hour earlier, Nariakira's ship had entered the Kumamoto harbour. The surprise was complete; there was nobody at the pier to welcome the great Lord, no porters or couriers ready to take the luggage and messages, no soldiers to guard – and control – the passage. This was exactly as Nariakira had wanted it; before anyone in the castle could even think of sending a welcoming party, he crossed the city surrounded only by his own faithful retainers.

Had Nariakira done so in any other domain, it may well have been construed as an act of war; but there were strong ties of friendship between Kumamoto and Satsuma, and Lord Narimori could do nothing but swallow his pride and prepare to welcome the visitors as well as he could.

"There are urgent matters we need to discuss, Hosokawa-*dono*."

"Of course, of course. You must forgive me. I had no time to prepare accommodation for your men."

"There will be no need. I'm not planning to stay the night."

Only the slightest shadow of surprise marred Narimori's face. It was unusual enough for a fellow daimyo to come unannounced; for him to leave on the same day was unheard of.

He's trying desperately to guess what I want, thought Nariakira.

"You have a splendid castle," he said as they climbed out of the tunnel onto the main courtyard. A magnificent view spread from the topmost terrace over the mist-covered mountains towards the distant sea.

"You've seen it many times, Nariakira-*dono*," Narimori replied, his smile twitching even more.

"Yes, and I am always impressed by the work of your ancestors. With a decent garrison, this place would be unassailable."

"Let us hope this needs never be tested."

"Of course, of course. Do you still have that quiet room on the top floor?"

"Always. Do you want to go there right now? I thought a feast might…"

"My men will enjoy the feast while we talk."

The lord of Kumamoto frowned. Nariakira's actions were now verging upon insult to the host.

"And what is this?" he changed the subject, pointing to a large, man-sized piece of luggage which several of Nariakira's porters hauled behind them.

"*Oku,*" the daimyo of Satsuma replied with a broad smile, "a gift."

"I gather you've been busy lately, Narimori-*dono.*"

The two daimyos were sitting alone in the Quiet Room, the most secret place in the castle hidden between the thick walls of the top floor, safe from the prying eyes or ears of any spies.

"I have, but how did you know?"

The eyes of the lord of Kumamoto darted constantly towards the corner of the room where, leaning against the thick supporting beam, stood the mysterious "gift" from Satsuma. There was the faintest of golden glints in these eyes, Nariakira noticed; Hosokawa's skin had an unhealthy, pale hue, and a fresh silken bandage was wrapped around his left forearm.

Did they promise you immortality? More power? My domain?

"It's the only explanation for you not informing me of the recent developments."

Narimori scowled. Lord Nariakira was deliberately pushing the boundaries of proper conduct; the daimyo of Kumamoto had no obligation to inform him of anything. Nevertheless, whenever he didn't, it roused suspicions.

"What… particular developments do you mean?"

"The Immortal Swordsman visited me as well, a few days ago. He told me about the Eight-headed Serpent and the return of the Shard of Fukuchiyama. I trust you are fully aware of the importance of these events."

The lord of Kumamoto was flustered.

"I… I was just going to write you a letter. But you understand, of course, with what happened in Kirishima – many of my retainers died in the fire, such a thing has not happened in two hundred – "

"Some of my men perished there too, Narimori-*dono,*" Nariakira said, nodding sagely. "Terrible tragedy. But let it not divert our attention from what is really important. Have you received any news from the Court lately? You're *closer* to Edo than I am."

Narimori's continuing grimace showed that the play on words did not go unnoticed.

"I know the *Taikun* demands troops from all loyal daimyo. But you were surely aware of that as well, Nariakira-*dono*."

For the first time in the conversation, the lord of Satsuma was caught off guard.

"News travels slowly across the mountains. When did that happen?"

"I only got the summons a week ago."

"And how do you plan to respond?"

"The warriors of Kumamoto serve only the lord of this castle."

Of course. I wonder - how long did you think you could afford to ignore the Taikun's *orders? Perhaps that's what swayed you in the end: fear of Edo is still strong.*

"I wonder what prompted that demand."

"There's a war on in Qin again – and this time in the North. Perhaps the Court is wary of the Barbarians gathering in strength on our doorstep."

"That would be new. They've been ignoring the threat for decades."

"I…" Narimori's voice broke. "I'm sorry, Nariakira-*dono,* but what *is* that thing?"

Nariakira chuckled.

"Of course, no point in keeping you in the dark any longer."

He stood up, came up to the gift, and pulled down the cover. Narimori gasped aloud. The falling fabric revealed an incredibly life-like sculpture – of the lord of Kumamoto himself.

"I had one made of myself," said Nariakira. "It's almost a perfect replica."

"I still don't understand…"

"Oh, allow me to demonstrate."

He turned the key clock-wise and the automaton stirred to life. It looked around, blinked eerily and then opened its mouth.

"Honoured to meet you, Hosokawa-*dono*." Even its voice was a good copy of Narimori's slightly high-pitched timbre.

Nariakira switched it off.

"The *kagemusha* doubles are unreliable and hard to come by. This machine will fool any assassin long enough for your bodyguards to arrive."

"Oh… Oh, I see! It is a great gift indeed, Nariakira-*dono*."

"You don't want to take a closer look?"

Lord Narimori stood a step away from the automaton, cautious of the strange technology. The automatons known to most aristocrats in Yamato were mere toys; there were only a few people skilled enough to create something as immense as this doppelganger.

"Did Tanaka-*sensei* help you with its creation?" asked Narimori.

"I leave details to my wizards," replied Nariakira with a shrug, "but I wouldn't be surprised. Notice the craftsmanship. There are almost as many joints in the hand as in a real one."

While Lord Narimori leaned over to admire the artificial muscles, Nariakira reached again towards the key and turned it – this time counter-clockwise. The automaton came to life again; its hands shot forward, grabbing Narimori's shoulders in a tight grip. A hypodermic needle, hidden in one of the fingers, injected the concentrated venom of a *habu* snake into Narimori's arm. The daimyo struggled briefly but vainly with the onset of paralysis. When the toxin finished its work, the living lord of Kumamoto looked almost indistinguishable from his artificial doppelganger. Only his eyes were different, filled with pain and terror.

"I know you can hear me," said Nariakira. "The poison will not kill you – and the paralysis should pass in a few days. Of course, by then you will be safe in my castle."

He turned a hidden knob at the back of the automaton; the metal grip slackened, releasing the hapless lord into Nariakira's arms.

"I'm sure you'll agree this was a much more elegant solution than, say, sending an assassin. In a way, I'm glad your little bit of thievery prompted me to action. I let you do as you pleased for far too long."

With some effort, he leaned Narimori against the wall beside the machine.

"The automaton will announce your retirement and removal into a mountain monastery, where none shall disturb you but the men I trust. You know which ones I mean – I'm sure my brother supplied you with the list a long time ago... They will also make sure your son is a more... *reliable* ally. The warriors of Kumamoto are famous for their skill and bravery. I need to be sure they are on my side."

He covered the paralyzed daimyo with the cloth and turned the automaton back again.

"I'm sorry you didn't like my gift, Narimori-*dono*. I will order it taken back right away," he said, looking straight in the machine's eyes.

Shigemasa climbed up a narrow stone path in frenzy. The waning moon did little to illuminate the thick, almost jungle-like forest of cryptomeria and camphor trees covering the steep hill. With the two minds struggling for domination, a strange madness was overtaking the boy's body as he ventured upwards through the woods, across the vines and muddied boulders, using his sheathed sword as support.

A small spring seeped out of the rocks halfway up the slope. The stream trickled across the path, wetting the pebbles and boring a watery groove in the sand. Shigemasa tripped on the slippery stones and fell, cutting a deep gash in his head on a boulder. The pain and blood only added to his confusion, as the General trudged on, ever higher and further away from the accursed village.

He stumbled out onto a small, perfectly round glade in front of a dark, gloomy cave. A circle of white round stones stained brown surrounded the glade's edge. There was a dark, foreboding presence here, the air was dense, stuffy and smelled of old blood. Shigemasa took a weak step forward and then fell down, overpowered by the glade's energies.

When he came to, he discovered his hands had been tied up with string. He tried the knots – they were coarse, but strong. He was lying just outside the circle of stones by a small campfire. The Kumaso man was sitting opposite on a large, flat mossy boulder.

"What is the meaning of this?" Shigemasa flailed about. "Let me go this instant! I order thee, savage!"

The Kumaso man patted his beard and smiled softly.

"I always wanted to talk to you, old Spirit."

"Thou shalt die for this insolence." Shigemasa seethed and gnashed his – Bran's – teeth.

"I'm looking forward to seeing my family," the bear-man said, "but it's not yet my time. Neither is it yours."

Shigemasa grunted indignantly and sat up.

"The heretics must die," he said finally, as the silence prolonged.

"Why?"

"They are the greatest foe!" Shigemasa shouted, spittle flowing from Bran's lips.

"Now I know why my spirit could not ascend to the Heavens – and why Fate brought me to meet the boy. It is my duty to rid the Yamato of the last of the heretics!"

"All these people want is to be left in peace!"

"Thou art a fool, savage. They may seem meagre now, but they are cunning and wily. Like a weed, thou let one offshoot live and then one day they will grow over an entire garden."

"So you've met them before."

"I *died* fighting them. But the *Taikun* had prevailed in the end, and we wiped them out!"

The bear-man stopped smiling and stood up. His face twisted in pain and anger, and he swatted his head with his hand in some strange expression of emotion. He grabbed Shigemasa by the hair and snarled in his face, baring his teeth like an angry animal.

"Wipe out. It's all you valley people can do. Wipe out the Heretics. Wipe out the Kumaso. Wipe out the Yōkai. Wipe out anyone that is different… Until only you are left, with your metal swords, and your paper houses, and your *shrines* where the Spirits are imprisoned!"

"There would be no Spirits at all had the Heretics got their way!" the General said, spitting. "They will overthrow the order of things. They will bring the civil war back. I must stop them before it's too late. I have seen the coming Darkness."

Torishi stepped back and laughed.

"You think *they* are the Darkness? *They* are the reason you remain stuck in the mortal world?"

"What else? No demon brought so much foulness to this land as their Warrior God."

The bear-man's look changed from anger to pity.

"I know your kind. You're the hunter that boasts of killing the grey-haired, toothless and clawless old bear. But the *real* beast remains, still threatening the forest."

The General was silent for a while.

"What art thou saying?" he said at last.

"What is your duty, Spirit?"

"To serve and protect the Empire," the General answered without hesitation.

The bear-man ran his fingers through his beard.

"I was the greatest hunter in my village. I thought I was protecting my family, my people. But I failed to see the real danger before it was too late."

The Kumaso returned to his boulder, leaving the General alone. Shigemasa's eyes fell on the stone circle. Only now did he notice that one of the small white stones was roughly carved in the shape of *Jizō*, the bald guide into the Otherworld.

"What is this place?" he asked. "I sense... there was some great evil here."

"I sense it too," said the Kumaso, "but now it's gone."

Shigemasa's thoughts raced. It must have been a place where the heretics performed their darkest rituals; where they summoned their demon servants. But why did Fate bring him here to this circle of black magic so powerful even a remnant of it was making him, a ghost, shiver?

Twenty thousand souls had defended the Hara Castle, he remembered. *Men, women, children.*

The *Taikun* had ordered them all dead. At the end of the siege over a hundred thousand soldiers charged the walls of the heretic fortress. And now all that was left of them was this one little town with one little temple.

He noticed the bright red cloth around the *Jizō* statue, fresh flowers and a cup of saké. He smiled to himself. The Kumaso was right – the old bear was toothless and senile.

The General closed his eyes and prayed to the bald god for guidance. *Jizō* was the protector of lost souls, and who was he but a soul lost between this and another world?

The red dot pulsated in the distance.

He was in a dark place. By now, Bran was able to recognize the red dust plain by the smell of damp earth and the sound of distant, incessant winds.

But there was another light: a translucent flame shimmering with unnatural colours, ghostly blues and otherworldly purples. He started walking in its direction and soon began to make out silhouettes of people in hooded robes standing around the bonfire. They were also wraith-like, made of white and blue light and mists. The wind tore them like clouds.

The scene was surrounded by a circle of white stones and faint phantoms of trees, vanishing into darkness. The ghostly men did not seem to notice Bran as he stepped even closer, intrigued. One of them was wearing the Phrygian cap of a *pater*.

Mithraists. What is this? A vision, but of what... the future? The past?

The bonfire gave out no heat; on the contrary, the closer Bran got, the colder the air grew. Bran's breath became visible; an unpleasant, metallic scent lingered on his tongue.

Something was happening. A body was brought into the circle and thrown on the ground. It hovered eerily a few inches above the red dirt. Then, one by one, the gathered stood above it and cut their forearms deeply with phantom blades. Blood poured on the body like a stream of pale blue light. At last, the *pater* did the same, closing the circle. He raised a brightly glowing talisman showing the horned cross-in-circle, the symbol of the Mithraists. His lips moved in a silent incantation.

Somewhere in the distance, drums began to roll.

Two of the hooded men held the body by its arms and legs; it stirred, twitched and started thrashing about. The *pater* touched its head with the talisman and it quietened. He ordered the men to let go.

Slowly, staggering, the dead man rose from the ground. His body was black with a red tinge, only the eyes shone like golden nuggets. His teeth were long and sharp. He lunged at the priest, but covered his eyes before the talisman's light and bent his knees in a show of subservience.

The drums grew louder, more frantic.

A Fanged, Bran recognized the creature. *This is how a Fanged is created.*

The newly born Abomination looked around the circle, and raised its head, sniffing, hunting. Its glowing golden eyes met Bran's and its muscles tensed.

It sees me!

The creature leapt outside the vision, out of the circle of ghosts with terrifying speed, and suddenly appeared on the red dust plain in the flesh. It was no longer a wispy wraith; its naked skin was pale and bloodless, but its sinews and muscles were all too real, as were the claws and long fangs. Its face was twisted in agony and rage. Before Bran could react, it jumped at him, pinning him to the ground.

They wrestled; the Fanged's teeth tried to reach Bran's neck. He fought back with all his might, but the creature was strong, stronger than Bran, and the claws tearing at his wrists seemed to sap the boy's energy; he couldn't summon a shield or a lance. *Llambed Seal,* he thought in desperation. *Will it work here?*

The drums stopped abruptly and a shadow appeared over Bran and the Abomination: another man, wearing a mask lined with white heron feathers and a colourful kaftan, with both hands raised in the air, holding sharpened bits of steel. He struck at the Fanged between the shoulder blades and disappeared.

240

The creature howled, screeched, and jumped up, trying to reach the blades embedded in its back, but within seconds, a black rot spread from the twin wounds and engulfed its entire body. With an agonizing cry, the Fanged flailed its arms and then exploded in a cloud of grey ash. The blades fell on the red dust with a clunk, their ends twisted and melted.

What in Annwn just happened?

With an effort, Bran remembered the *Egungun* dancer's ritual in far away Ekó, and his father's anger at what he perceived as an assassination attempt.

Not the first time he was wrong, he thought.

He heard steps and turned around, Soul Lance in his hand, this time ready to fight. It was Shigemasa; he seemed weakened and dishevelled.

"Come, boy," the General said with a tired voice. "Time to go back to the others."

They touched hands and Bran woke upon an overgrown forest glade surrounded by polished white stones. The same metallic scent lingered in the air.

His hands were tied up with string; the light of a campfire flickered on the glistening leaves of the camphor trees. Torishi, sitting on one of the boulders, noticed him awake. He observed Bran for a moment, then nodded, stood up, drew his long dagger and slashed through the knots.

THE RISING TIDE

There was no trace of Bran, the path had ended long ago, and everywhere she looked, the wood looked exactly the same.

She was alone in the dark forest; she was tired and lost, her head ached and her stomach rumbled.

What was I thinking? I will have to wait until dawn to get back.

She felt a numb pain in the corners of her eyes and behind her ears. She felt hot.

It's that damn drug. Nagomi was right not to drink it.

She loosened her clothes and staggered on from tree to tree.

I need to walk down the slope... keep straight...

There were lights among the camphor trees, colourful wisps and flashes like the ones showing under closed eyelids. Satō shook her head and the lights disappeared, but not for long.

I'm being poisoned, she realised and giggled. *Why am I giggling? This is terrible.*

She laughed out loud.

Another, greater light appeared behind the trunk of a huge tree. When it moved towards her, she saw that it was the shape of a man.

Is that their God, the Sun? Is that what they see?

The shining man came closer with his hand stretched towards her; he was completely naked. She recognized him at last.

242

"Bran!" she cried. "I'm so glad I found you! Why are you – "

The boy put his finger on her mouth.

"What are you…"

He pulled her towards him and slid a hand underneath her kimono. When he kissed her, his lips were as hot as the Sun.

"I'm fine," Captain Kawamura replied to Nagomi's offer of help. He scratched the roughly bandaged bump on his head.

"I assume it was the boy who hit me, but I didn't see it"

"He wasn't being himself," Nagomi explained for the second time that day. "He has a Spirit within him."

"I wish you'd told me before he got mad," the Captain said, wincing, "we should have locked him in for the night."

He invited her to the cockpit for *cha* and they waited. Not an hour had passed before a quickly moving figure appeared on the pier. In the ship's storm light, Nagomi recognized the *Daisen*.

"Start the engine," ordered Heishichi as soon as he jumped on board.

"What about the others?" asked Kawamura.

"They're not here?" the wizard looked around in surprise. "Doesn't matter. We have to set sail."

"What happened?"

"See for yourself." The *Daisen* pointed at the town. A long, dense line of torches, like a festival procession, snaked along the sea shore silently, slowly moving towards the harbour.

"They're coming to conquer the demons," he said.

"We're not going anywhere!" protested Nagomi. "We have to go look for the others."

The Captain looked doubtfully at the pitch-black forest covering the steep slopes.

"We won't find anyone in the night."

"The ship is more important," the *Daisen* said. "You know your duty, Captain."

Kawamura nodded heavily and disappeared into the engine room. Soon the deck rumbled with the rhythmical beating of the pistons.

The crowd was getting nearer; the first torches were almost at the pier. Nagomi stared into the darkness, hoping – praying – to see anyone returning from the forest. She noticed the Captain untying the mooring ropes.

"No!" she said. "We have to wait!"

"I'm sorry, priestess-*sama*. I have my orders."

Before the last of the ropes unravelled, Nagomi grabbed Torishi's bow and arrows from the bench and leapt overboard onto the wooden pier. She ran towards the head of the procession, which was almost at the harbour.

"Stop! Please, we mean you no harm," she said, catching her breath. "Just let us wait for our friends."

The *pater* raised his hand. The congregation behind him slowed down and began to spread out in a half-circle around her.

"Behold, the servant of the *Deva*!" the priest bellowed, pointing his finger accusingly at Nagomi. "The Adversary takes many guises."

She stepped back, alarmed, and drew her bow with shaking arms, aiming at the *pater*.

"Let us sail away in peace, we won't – "

She screamed as the priest leapt towards her and pushed the bow away; the string twanged sadly and the arrow flew into darkness. He grabbed her by the arm with one hand and drew a long sacrificial knife from the folds of his robe with the other. His eyes gleamed madly. The crowd closed in on her.

"I am a star which goes with thee and shines out of the depths," he intoned. "I spy out my enemies, swoop down upon them, scatter and slaughter them. I – "

She tried to wriggle herself out of the iron grasp. She heard a wild roar and a heavy, earth-shaking thumping, followed by cries of panic. The priest let loose her arm and when she turned, she saw a great black bear charging towards her, sweeping the people aside with swipes of its huge paws.

The bear stood between her and the priest, and growled, baring its teeth, its sides heaving. The priest dropped the knife and backed away, joining his retreating attendants.

"Nagomi, quick!"

She turned and saw Bran standing on the pier beside the *Iroha Maru*, waving at her to follow. He was carrying a barely-conscious Satō on his back.

The bear roared once more and they both ran towards Bran and the ship.

"I was aware of everything," said Bran, drinking *cha* prepared by Kawamura, "but I couldn't reason with the *Taishō*. He would not listen; he went mad with rage. We struggled for control of the body on the mountain path and he was stronger in his rage."

"I wonder what finally made him give up," said Torishi.

The boy shook his head.

"He prayed to the *Jizō* for advice, but whatever happened then was between himself and the Gods. He is silent now. I can barely feel his presence."

"What about Sacchan?" worried Nagomi, wiping the wizardess's feverish forehead with cold, damp cloth. "What happened to her?"

"It's the potion," Heishichi spoke. Everyone turned towards him.

"You let her drink the *haoma*?" asked Bran.

"You know it?"

"I know *of* it. It's the sacred potion of the Sun Priests. They claim it allows them to unite with their Gods."

"Is it harmful?" asked Nagomi.

"It shouldn't be. But it may be a shock to the unprepared."

"I know the smell," said Heishichi. "It's the *maō* plant. They must be getting it from the same source as my supplier."

"What does it do?" asked Nagomi.

"In clear, concentrated form, we use it to keep alert and awake. But this concoction…" He shrugged. "It turned the townspeople to frenzy. They danced naked in the night."

Satō stirred and moaned. "*Bran…don't…*" she whispered.

Bran felt everyone's stare.

"I didn't…" he started, his face burning.

The wizardess woke up with a gasp. She looked around, bewildered.

"Where am I?"

"You're back on the ship," Nagomi said, holding the wizardess's hand.

Satō's wandering eyes found Bran, and the girl let out a stifled cry, covering herself with her hands.

"Whatever you think happened, it wasn't me," he said, trying to sound calming.

"It's true," added Torishi. "I was with him all the time."

The wizardess sighed and lay down again.

"It…it doesn't matter. When can we set off?"

"We are well on our way, Takashima-*sama*," said Kawamura. "Safe in the open sea."

It was their last evening out at sea, a dark, cold, unpleasant twilight. Sailing north, they had left the early Satsuma summer far behind. The wind howled down the funnels and vents, whistling ominously, shackles clanged on the rigging in alarm. The little ship rocked up and down on rolling waves as the paddles struggled to gain a grip on the water and keep the vessel on course.

Bran came out onto the deck to sharpen his Prydain sword. Sparks fluttered in the darkness with every grinding stroke of the blade on the damp whetting stone. Mindless work which allowed his thoughts to wander. He recognized the waters even in the night; the *Iroha Maru* was passing through the bay between Shimabara and Kumamoto.

This is where everything started.

Tokojiro's betrayal and the fight at Mogi, the first quarrel with Shigemasa, the wobbly ferry to Kuchinotsu…

It seems so long ago now.

He recalled the many times he could have died on the journey or become trapped within his mind. It was an odd thought. Before coming to Yamato, he never thought about dying or even coming to harm…

Even after the Ladon *I wasn't really worried,* he thought. *I have the Llambed Seal after all.*

Llambed… his thoughts now drifted back to Gwynedd.

248

They taught us how to kill and not get killed, he realized, recalling how much time and effort he had spent learning combat spells, summoning shields and falling safely off the back of the dragon. While wyverns and gryphons were good for transport and cargo, first and foremost the dragons were, after all, beasts of war. It seemed so obvious in hindsight.

They pretended we were all going to be wyrm lore scholars, he scoffed. *"Sanctity of life" – what a joke! Most of us would end up as soldiers in some dragoon regiment or other. Ready to die for The Dragon Throne. I wonder how many of my class are dead already?*

And that was why his father was so concerned about Emrys. Swamp dragons were perceived as useless in combat. Dylan wished his son to follow in his footsteps after all…

He stopped his work and checked the sword. The runes along the fuller glowed with dull blue. The Prydain blade would not get any sharper; it wasn't as well made as Satō's katana. The sword had drunk so much blood since his arrival in Kiyō…

Every highborn here carries a sword from youth, he thought. *They are all taught how to kill with it. I wonder if they realize what it does to them.*

He sheathed the weapon and looked around. He noticed a figure sitting on the bow in complete silence. It was the *Daisen*, Heishichi, clad in a thick brown coat that protected him from the cold wind.

"You don't carry a sword," said Bran.

"I'm a merchant's son."

"Not even a commoner's *kodachi?*"

"I have no need for crude weapons. I'm the *Daisen*."

Bran leaned against the gunwale and faced the wind.

"What did your master need my dragon for?"

Heishichi smirked.

"Politics. What do you care?"

"His Excellency's assistance was very valuable. I wonder what he wants in exchange?"

"I am not privy to the daimyo's plans."

"Then can you at least tell me why *you* are here?"

"To observe and study," the *Daisen* said. "And to help Captain Kawamura with the ship."

Not to fight, then.

"You still hope you can bring the dragon back to your Master. I told you, it's attuned to *me* only. I won't let you have it."

"Then the beast is of no use to His Excellency."

Should I tell him?

"There may be others."

Heishichi looked up, for the first time genuinely interested.

"How do you know?"

"A skilled dragon rider can sense other dragons if they're close enough," Bran explained.

The wizard stood up.

"What do you sense?"

Bran smiled.

"If I tell you now, I have nothing left to bargain with."

Heishichi's fist lit on fire; his face remained calm, but his scarred cheek twitched.

"Don't play with me, boy. I can squeeze that information out of you."

Bran took a step back and summoned a *tarian*.

"You're welcome to try. You're not an *onmyōji*. Your magic is the same as mine and I grew up learning how to use it."

The Soul Lance shimmered in his open palm. Bran noticed it was at least a foot longer than it had been the last time he'd used it.

"What do you two think you're doing?" the voice belonging to Captain Kawamura boomed behind Bran. "Fighting on my ship? I'll throw you both overboard!"

Heishichi cast the Captain an irritated look and extinguished his flame. He went past Bran towards his cabin.

"It's not wise to make an enemy out of the *Daisen*," said Kawamura.

"I get the feeling we weren't going to be friends anyway," replied Bran.

Satō stepped out onto the jetty and looked around with dismay. The sky was monochromic grey. A flat field of dull-yellow reeds, combed by the breeze spread as far as she could see; the monotony was interrupted by a few decrepit willow trees and tall fishing net poles. The canal into which they had sailed in the morning was boringly straight, its waters murky and dim; the only thing of interest for miles was a lonely, seemingly abandoned, small white-washed teahouse standing beside the jetty. She had never seen a more desolate, empty place.

A long, flat-bottomed boat powered by a single man, standing straight and pushing on a long pole approached down the canal. There was something familiar in the oarsman's towering bulk; as he got closer, Satō noticed the unmistakable purple cloak on his shoulders.

"Dōraku-*sama*!"

The Swordsman pulled back the bamboo hat and grinned at her.

The white-washed teahouse was not abandoned after all. The inside was surprisingly clean and cosy; sitting beside the fireplace sunk in the middle of the floor, Satō almost forgot about the emptiness and bleakness outside.

The six people who came on the ship and Master Dōraku barely fitted into the small room. Satō had to sit close to Bran, conscious of not having taken a proper bath or washing her clothes in days. Every time their eyes met, she was reminded of the strange encounter in the forest. She knew it was just a vision sent by the *maō* plant, but it didn't make her any more comfortable.

Master Dōraku poured everyone saké from a rice straw-wrapped bottle he had brought from the boat and, after raising a toast to their successful arrival, said:

"We have little time to linger. I'll be taking you today to Yanagawa, and we'll pick up the chase from there."

"The chase?" asked Satō.

"I hunted the Crimson Robe for the last few days. They did capture your *dorako* after all," he said to Bran. The boy exchanged glances with Nagomi. "And while it means they're moving slowly, they are far ahead of us already."

"Did you see how the *dorako* was captured?" asked Heishichi.

The Swordsman shook his head.

"They had already left Aso-san when I got there."

"They are moving north," said Bran. "I sensed it last night. What's to the north?"

"The Crimson Robe's island fortress, Ganryūjima" the samurai replied. "If he manages to get there, we'll be in a much more difficult position."

Satō drank her saké in one gulp and put the cup on the floor.

"Then what are we waiting for? Let's go after them!"

THE RISING TIDE

CHAPTER XIII

In Satō's mind this was supposed to be a hot pursuit; but in reality, the flat-bottomed boat advanced lazily up the canal, pushed onwards by rhythmical prods of Dōraku's pole. Her only consolation was that they were still moving faster than they would have on foot through this bleak, inhospitable landscape of marsh, reclaimed land and submerged rice paddies.

Brown-shelled turtles lived in droves in the canal, huddling every boulder or floating log; snakes writhed their way along the boat's edge, and fish popped up curiously, hoping for a crumb. Once in a while the boat passed a village – a few straw-roofed huts, a storehouse raised on pillars and a tiny red-gate of a shrine. Several locals would come out to the bank to watch the boat pass, but they neither smiled nor waved, just stared with tired eyes.

"How long until we get to some civilization?" asked Satō.

"This is civilization!" replied Dōraku, chuckling. "These people are its pioneers. It's a hard life on reclaimed land. But I can see what you mean. Yanagawa is just beyond those hills."

He pointed to a grey, jagged shadow on the horizon. It seemed just as distant as it had when they started. She closed her eyes and sighed.

"Tell us how you defeated those wolves," she asked, hoping a diverting tale of swashbuckling and derring-do would take her mind off the overwhelming dullness.

"I didn't."

"*Eeh?*" She opened her eyes wide.

"There were far too many of them. They destroyed me; tore my body into pieces."

She looked into his eyes to see if he was joking.

"But you still survived?"

"Such is the power of the Curse."

"Then what chance do *we* stand against the Crimson Robe?" asked Bran.

"We can still be stopped," the Swordsman replied with a grin, "and defeated."

A large eel jumped away from under the pole. Satō thought long about what she just heard.

"You call it a Curse," she said at last, "but it seems a blessing to me."

For a moment, the oar in Master Dōraku's hands stopped.

"I would rather die ten times than have this Curse upon me," he said slowly.

"But why? What's so bad about it? You're immortal, powerful, fast —"

"All this and more, Takashima Satō." He stared at her with cold eyes. "But I am no longer *human*. The Curse replaced everything I ever was, turned me into a slave of my addiction and a slave of the man who had brought me to this sad imitation of life. I know you wizards play with blood magic and hope you can control it if used in moderation, but it's a fool's hope. Stay away from it, girl."

As the Swordsman spoke, his eyes turned black like coal, and a cold wind rose about the boat, carrying with it the stench of blood and death. Satō reeled back.

"That... that's not you," said Nagomi quietly, breaking the silence. The priestess was sitting at the bow, with her fingers in the cool water, keeping silent throughout most of the journey.

"That was me for the first ten years, young priestess-*sama*," said Master Dōraku, his voice kind once again. "I *was* a monster. I did things I can never repent of, never forget. My soul is corrupted forever."

"What happened after the ten years?" Nagomi asked.

"I met a *Butsu* priest... but it's a long story. He showed me the path, and taught me how to keep to it. It took me another ten years of meditation and wandering to release myself from the shackles the Curse had put upon me. But even then, the freedom was never complete."

"The wolf," said Bran. "That's why you said the spirits were after you."

257

The Swordsman smiled and nodded.

"What wolf?" asked Satō, disorientated. "What are you talking about?"

"Karasu-*sama* found me feeding on a wolf the night I met you in the forest. I thought I managed to lie my way out back then, but – "

"I always suspected something was wrong," said Bran. "Is that why Shimazu-*dono* called you a renegade? Because you broke your Curse?"

"There's more than that. There is… politics among our kind. I always stayed out of it."

"But you're familiar with the Crimson Robe."

"That's different. I knew him when we were both still alive."

"Can you tell us his name?" asked Satō. "We keep calling him Crimson Robe, but…"

"One of his names was Ganryū Kojirō." He paused; Satō guessed he was checking if anyone recognized the name. But there was no such man mentioned in any of the books and stories she knew.

"And now I must ask you all to bow your heads," the Swordsman said.

"What?"

"There's a low bridge coming," he added, crouching.

Wulfhere blinked repeatedly, trying to get the soot and smoke from his eyes. The wind was blowing the flames of the pyre in his direction.

The funeral was a symbolic one, of course. No search party ever found the Reeve's body – or discovered what happened to Commodore Dylan after he was forced to use the Seal. Banneret Edern was – officially – the last to see the two riders before they disappeared out of sight, pursued by the Qin dragons deep beyond the enemy lines.

Not the Banneret, Wulfhere corrected himself. *Commodore Edern.*

The ceremony over, the small crowd of soldiers began to disperse. Wulfhere limped towards his tent; after the victory at Chansu the camp grew, and petty officers like him now had separate quarters all to themselves. A guard of Qin volunteers stood before the entrance to protect their "hero".

Wulf spotted the familiar dark blue cap and jacket of Li, and slowed down, letting the interpreter catch up to him.

"A touching ceremony," the Qin man said, "and a great loss for all of us."

"Yes," said Wulf, not sure how to respond.

"If a loss it was," Li added.

The interpreter glanced left and right and asked the boy to step aside. They walked up to the sloping bank of a canal marking the southern edge of the Marines camp.

"I will tell you a secret, boy," Li started. "You see, we have some spies among the Rebels. Quite a lot, actually."

He knows.

259

Wulf decided not to tell Ardian Seton everything he had seen, sensing the information he had would prove more valuable as a well-kept secret.

"Listen," Li looked around once again and leaned over to whisper in Wulfhere's ear. "One of our spies saw a Silver dragon heading out to sea, south of Shanglin; it carried two people on its back."

"What are you saying…?"

"The Commodore and the Reeve, we can only guess. But why would they do that, I wonder?"

"A clandestine mission, no doubt," Wulf said, tearing blades of weak grass from the soft, damp ground.

"Oh, that's right!" Li clapped his hands. "But why fly out into the sea? There's nothing out there."

Should I tell him? What can I get in exchange, I wonder…

It was now Wulhere's time to turn conspiratorial. He lowered his voice.

"Banneret… Commodore Edern was not the last to see Commodore Dylan. I was."

A servant climbed down to the water beside Wulf with a mule in tow. The animal lowered its head and started drinking from the canal.

"This is not a good place," said Li. He stood up and wiped mud off his trousers. "Come to the landing glade in an hour."

Li stared at Wulfhere with eyes opened as wide as his arched eyebrows allowed.

"*Aiya!* You spied on your own commander? Why?"

He paced up and down the short landing glade, with his hands behind his back. His golden dragon, coiled on the grass, observed him through half-closed eyes.

"I'm just naturally curious," replied Wulf with a shrug.

He doesn't need to know everything. He had already made his decision; whatever Commodore Dylan was doing, it seemed the Qin would learn about it sooner or later. Wulf's information was valuable only for so long. If he wanted to get something out of what he knew, now was the time.

"My father taught me there is great power in knowing what others don't – and great profit."

Li stopped.

"Your father is a wise man," he said with a nod, "and you're a dangerous boy. But... *Yamato?* Are you sure?"

"You know what it is?" asked Wulfhere.

"Of course! A large island kingdom, east of Qin. Rich and powerful. We have an outpost in one of their cities, where we send one ship per year for some trade. Your Bataavians have a similar arrangement. Nobody else is allowed – few know of its existence."

Wulfhere's curiosity was immediately piqued.

A hidden land? One I've never heard anything about?

261

"And why is it so important that the Commodore went there?"

"If the Dracaland found a way to reach Yamato, this completely changes the balance of power!"

"How is it even possible we didn't find it earlier?"

"They hide behind an impenetrable sea barrier. They call it the 'Divine wind'."

Everyone here hides behind shields and barriers, noted Wulfhere. *People and nations alike.*

"If you already know the way to Yamato, why do you want to follow the Commodore?"

"The Qin ship is not scheduled for another six months. By that time it may be too late: the Dracaland will gain a foothold and will be impossible to remove."

Li tugged on his short, sharp beard.

"No, no. I can't just stand idly by. This war is yesterday's news," he said, more to himself, nodding at the army camp. He then turned east and looked towards the sky.

"I see it. What happens in Yamato now will decide the future. Not only of that kingdom, but also of Qin. Maybe the whole world. I must be there. I must prepare."

"Prepare for what? Are you thinking of another war? This one's not finished yet."

"That's how Empires are forged. Qin has grown complacent for too long. War rejuvenates states. Already the Rebellion is causing changes: we have Western weapons,

262

Western training... But the Court at Ta Du is still reluctant to embrace the modern world. A new war may... I must go after them."

Wulfhere recognized in the Qin man the same cunning and ambition as his own, the same struggle against the odds and mishaps of Fate to prove his greatness.

A kindred spirit.

"You're not just an interpreter, are you?"

The Qin man smiled. Wulfhere ran his hand against the golden scales of Li's dragon, deep in thought. They were small, smooth and shimmering, like flakes of polished stone; the skin was colder to touch than that of a Western mount. The beast lowered its antlered head and purred. One of its long whiskers wriggled in the air as if it was a separate creature.

"I think she likes you."

"*She?*"

The Western mounts were almost exclusively stallions. Females were used only by civilians, or cooped up in hatcheries.

"Naturally. The mares make the best mounts – patient, gentle and hardy. Just what I need for a long journey. Now, about the Commodore... what else have you heard?"

"I will tell you all, if you take me with you," Wulf said, surprising himself as much as Li.

"*You?* You're a Dracalish soldier. Your place is in the army. Why would you want to go with me?"

263

"A Warwick doesn't study history," he replied, at last, with a family saying, "a Warwick *makes* history."

"Well said." Li replied. "I will send for you in the morning. We are not sneaking out like Commodore *Dí Lán*; it will be an official trip. I will present you to the court at Ta Du. The hero of Qiang River."

Wulf smiled.

I can't let Bran take all the glory.

"Are you alright?" asked Li. "I didn't know your race could turn that colour."

"I'm… fine," replied Wulf with great effort. He found it hard to get used to the way the Qin dragon moved in the air. When the weather was good, it swayed from side to side, like a snake on sand; when it had to pick up speed, or face strong currents, it undulated up and down, like a boat in a storm. Either way, the long, serpentine neck he was straddling behind Li, kept bobbing about, causing Wulf to suffer bouts of sea sickness for the first few hours of the flight.

Not seeing the wings flap on either side was disconcerting. Wulf knew all dragons relied on the magic of the Ninth Wind for flying, rather than their wings, but there was something reassuring in the thought that a Western dragon would have always enough lift to glide to safety if the magic failed. The Qin beast looked like it would topple to the ground like a stone – as Wulf had seen happen so many times during this war.

Like all Qin dragons, *long*, this one – "Yuyan" – was much longer than any Western beast; there was enough space on her neck for two comfortable saddles. The rider had little protection from the elements; Li used no *tarian*, and the dragon's breath was not as hot or dense as that of its Western cousins, so they couldn't cruise as high and fast as Wulf was used to.

The sea below them was a featureless expanse of grey, green and dark blue; Wulf had no idea where they were, and could only hope Li knew better. The position of the sun told him they were moving roughly east, but that was where his knowledge ended. In the morning they had passed a few small islets and reefs, but nothing since.

"There is a strong current running from the Tagalogs north-by-north-east," Li spoke, snapping Wulf from a lazy daydream. "No maps show where it ends, but it's the best way to reach Yamato, if one is in a hurry."

"Are we far from it?"

"I'm not sure. I was rather hoping we'd reach some islands by now."

"What?" Wulf sat up, awakened. "Are you telling me we're lost?"

"I'm just an interpreter, after all," Li replied. "Reading maps is not my forte. But judging by the sun's position…"

"*The sun*? Don't you have a compass?"

"We're too close to the Sea Maze," said Li, pointing north, where a thin line of dark, ominous clouds shrouded the horizon. "My compass is no good here."

"Oh, great." Wulf slumped in the saddle. "So much for making history: I'll be the first Western soldier to die on the back of a Qin dragon…"

"Hush, boy. Look sharp. We *must* be close. The sun is bright, the sea is calm; we are bound to spot something."

Wulfhere stared at the navy blue surface until his eyes watered. There was nothing but white ripples on the waves as far as he could see.

"We need to get higher," he said.

"We'll freeze."

"I can put a *tarian* up to shield both of us, though not for long."

Li nodded and pulled on the reins. The golden dragon gracefully coiled upwards and climbed smoothly on the current of the Ninth Wind. Three thousand feet later, Li levelled the flight.

"The dragon likes it here," said Wulf. "It's where she belongs."

"How do you know?"

"Can't you feel it? Through the Farlink?"

"What is *Fá-ling*?"

"Farlink! How do you steer your beast?"

"With these," Li replied, tightening the reins, "and these," he added, waving his legs. "How else?"

Wulf opened his mouth and then closed it. The idea of riding a dragon without a Farlink was preposterous – and terrifying.

She will throw us down any moment… why did I want us to fly so high?

Instinctively, he looked down towards the sea.

"Look," he said, grabbing Li's shoulder. "Over there. Straight ahead."

A column of thick black smoke rose in the middle of the ocean.

A ship on fire.

Chief Councillor Abe felt his knees weaken as he approached the camp of the Barbarians.

We were fools, he realized, *to think we could have done anything to stop them. No wonder Qin gave in so quickly.*

One of the grey-hooded invaders came up in quick, military steps, followed by a small Yamato man: the interpreter. Abe looked to his right, where his own interpreter stood, stiff and formal. Einosuke's nostrils flared and his eyes were unblinking, set forward.

He's fighting the dragon fear. Brave lad.

The man before him cast down the grey hood. He was shorter and older than the other Westerners, but had an unmistakable air of authority about him. He said a few words in his odd language. To Abe's ears it sounded like a mangled, barking version of Bataavian, but he could discern no understandable words. He looked at Einosuke. The interpreter cleared his throat.

"This... this is Komtur Mathiun Perai of the Western Navy of Tyr Gorllewin."

Gorllewin? I've never heard of them.

"I am Abe Masahiro, Chief *Rōju* Councillor to his Illustrious Excellency, *Taikun* Tokugawa Ieyoshi. Do you know what that means?"

"I was made aware of the ruling system of your country by that man," the Komtur replied, nodding at Hotta, who was standing further at the back. There wasn't anyone else in the Yamato delegation; it was crucial for the secret to be kept between as few men as possible.

"I bring a response from the Council," said Abe, handing the Komtur a scroll. Einosuke had spent two nights translating the edict into the language of the Westerners.

The Komtur reached into the inside pocket of his cloak and put on wire-framed spectacles to read the missive. The glasses made him look like a common clerk. It seemed almost impossible that this portly man commanded a squadron of dragons.

He finished reading and nodded.

"Not quite what we came for, but it's good enough," he said. "What is the place you wanted us to relocate to?"

"A small port of Shimoda, thirty *ri* south-west of here."

The Komtur thought about it for a while, then nodded again.

"Very well. But I will need something from you: proof of the *Taikun's* good intentions."

"What do you want?"

"There is a ship coming from our country. It brings supplies."

"We can supply you with everything you need. Food, medicine, meat for the *dorako*..."

The Komtur smiled.

"That's very generous, but there are things you have no way of providing. This ship must be allowed through the Sea Maze."

"Impossible!"

"This is the opening condition. No ship, no negotiations."

One of the beasts growled and raised its head. It licked the air with a long, greyish tongue.

"The dragons are growing hungry, Councillor," the Westerner added.

Let in even more Barbarians? Without the Council's consent... This would be the last decision I ever made.

"Give me a minute," he said and nodded at Hotta Naosuke. The two moved aside to discuss the new development.

"We have no choice," Naosuke said. "Our position is clear: the Council gave us the remit to open the negotiations. That means we have the right to accept or decline any propositions."

"But… that means I have to speak to the *Taikun* about it! Only he can open a passage through the Divine Winds."

"The Westerners can use the Dejima route and sail up the coast."

"And how do you propose to do that? We don't know the route."

"The Kiyō *bugyō* knows it. And he owes us a few favours after the bungling of the Takashima affair."

"That's too risky. The ship would have to go past Satsuma and Tosa!"

"We'll let them know how crucial it is not to be spotted. They seem willing to cooperate."

Abe pinched his lower lip in thought. He returned to the Westerner.

"Where is this ship of yours now?"

"It's stationed near the island you call Tamna. We can contact it swiftly, if need be."

How? That's beyond the Divine Winds!

"Then let them know. We have to make some preparations, but the route will be opened in two weeks. They need to be at least twenty *ri* south of Kiyō by then."

The Komtur mulled it over.

"All right. I accept that."

He turned to the rest of his men and shouted some orders. They started packing up the camp. The Westerner then turned to Abe and spoke briefly.

"He… he wants you to come with him, *tono*" explained Einosuke.

"Wha… what?"

"He wants you to show him the way to Shimoda."

"Give us a few days, and we will have the map ready."

"There's no time for that. My man will translate," the Komtur said, pointing to the small Yamato, who was standing quietly all this time, looking uncomfortable in the big grey cloak of the Westerners.

Abe looked helplessly around. The other Councillor shrugged, his eyes lowered again. *What did I get myself into…?*

"Send horses to Shimoda," Abe told Naosuke, with a sigh. "I will be at the Gyokusen Temple in the town – if I survive this at all…"

Once, in his youth, the Chief Councillor had climbed half-way up Mount Fuji; from there, he could see far across the land, over the forests, fields, towns and little villages, all the way down to the Ashi Lake, glittering like a shard of sapphire among the pine woods. He expected the view from the back of the dragon – when he finally dared to open his eyes – would be something similar.

It was nothing like that.

The earth beneath him moved at a great speed; the forests all blurred into one big green haze, interrupted by brighter spots of what he guessed were villages or open fields. To his left shimmered a brocade strip of the sea, and to his right – the unmistakable cone of the Fuji-san, the only recognizable feature in this fast changing landscape.

He remembered the freezing cold he had endured on the high mountain slope and was surprised at how comfortable and warm the flight was. He could breathe easily. He guessed some invisible barrier protected the dragon riders from the buffeting winds.

"Too fast…" he said.

The interpreter repeated his words to the Komtur. Their dragon was the only one carrying more than two people, but it didn't seem in the least burdened by the additional weight.

"What?"

"I can't tell where we are at this speed."

The Westerner pulled on the reins and the beast slowed. Abe looked down, fighting with the fear creeping into every pore in his skin. They were flying over a flat plain, with the mountains rising to the right, towards Fuji-san. From the height he couldn't even see the individual homes in the villages they passed, just spots of straw-yellow, or grey and blue where the tiled roofs outnumbered the thatches. He tried to remember the maps he had studied when he was still the young Councillor for Maintenance of the Imperial Highways.

We must be over Kanagawa, he thought. *Is this how the Gods see us?*

"Look for a large river and follow it to the sea," he said. "Then we just need to fly west along the shoreline and then due south."

We could govern this land so much better if we had these flying beasts...

Soon his administrator's mind took over the fear.

There's a canal that needs cleaning. And here, a good road — disappearing into nowhere. Who's the daimyo here? I need to send him a stern letter...

"Is that the river?" asked Komtur, pointing to a wide blue string running across the plain.

"I think so. That's the Sagami Bay, anyway," replied Abe. If his calculations were right, they had covered the distance of ten *ri* in less than half an hour. A fast courier needed half a day to reach that far.

Naosuke is right. We need these people on our side. No matter the cost.

THE RISING TIDE

CHAPTER XIV

Satō lowered her head as the boat passed under a water gate in a white-washed wall; beyond it lay a city of red brick storehouses and rich merchant mansions. The hydrangeas were in full bloom, cascading down the walls and bursting in bright blues and purples from under the weeping willows. The water was full of other boats. The oarsmen smiled at them as they passed, waving welcomingly at Master Dōraku, before disappearing into another branch of the criss-crossing network of waterways.

The canals seemed to replace the streets in this strange city. There were inns and teahouses serving the people on the boats; mansions and temples opening onto the water side. Each house had its own little boat. The closer Master Dōraku got them to the town centre, the denser the traffic grew on the main canal, until they had to wait in line before being able to pass under a narrow bridge.

The boat neared another bridge-gate, this time guarded by spearmen and archers. The Swordsman looked up at the Captain of the guards and nodded. The gate screeched open, letting the boat into the Yanagawa Castle.

"You will find lodgings over there," Master Dōraku said, pointing to a long building of grey stone. "Please follow me, Takashima-*sama*"

"Just me?"

"I have something to show you."

The samurai left her waiting in the main donjon's vast vestibule, and disappeared up the great wooden staircase. A minute or so later a grey-haired, white-bearded man climbed down the stairs, assisted by a young boy. It had taken Satō a while to remember where she had seen this face and that clan crest before.

"Tanaka-*sama*!"

The old mechanician patted her on the shoulders.

"My child, I'm so glad to see you well. We were so worried about you."

"We?"

"Many people tracked the progress of your quest. When we heard the dire news from Kirishima... but come, there's somebody waiting to see you."

She followed him up the grand staircase. The castle donjon was decorated sparingly, with a few scrolls and flower vases, except for the third floor, where the walls had been daubed with gold and silver paint.

"Did you ever get to use my glove?" the mechanician asked, as they turned into another corridor. There were very few people in the castle; a few hurrying courtsmen and

276

ladies, and a couple of guards on every level. The daimyo of this province, she guessed, must have been spending the year in his Edo residence.

"Yes, Tanaka-*sama*. It worked perfectly."

"Bring it to me later; I may be able to do some more adjustments. Here we are."

He slid open the door to a small room, with cranes and turtles painted on the walls. In its middle, on a western-style chair sat a bent, shrivelled man, wrapped in blankets. He raised his head slowly.

"Father!"

She ran up to him and kneeled by his side, kissing his hand. He looked at her, but said nothing and there was no recognition in his eyes.

"This is your heir, Shūhan-*sama*," said Master Tanaka. "Satō is here."

"Sa-tō…" Shūhan's lips twitched in a feeble, forced smile.

Satō stood up, kissed her father on the forehead and wiped tears from her eyes. She turned to Master Tanaka.

"Did they torture him?"

"Not physically. The priests found nothing to cure."

"Then what happened?"

"I'm afraid he spent too long under the effect of blood magic; whoever held him captive, was an adept of the Forbidden Art. To make matters worse, Shūhan-*sama* used the Art to send us a signal. That's how we were able to find him, but it cost him dearly. His mind is…how to say it? Blood-addled."

Satō studied her father with terror.

Blood-addled? Is that how it ends?

She noticed his other hand was clutching a jagged piece of bronze metal. The edges were stained dark red.

"What's that he's holding?"

"It's a shard of a mirror. We found him with it, but he refuses to let go. I think it feeds his addiction."

"When will he get better?"

Master Tanaka did not reply; his silence told her enough. She held Shūhan's hand tightly, but dared not look into his crazed eyes again.

"I will avenge you, Father."

She took a slow wander through the castle grounds, under the weeping willows and wisteria waterfalls; the gardens were empty, save for an old gardener cutting the hedgerow into shape.

This is my world now, she thought. *Empty and lonely.*

She stumbled upon an old canal, overgrown with reeds and duck-weed. A single dead fish was floating on the surface. She sat down and wept.

She wept for her father and for herself, for the life she had lost and for the future she did not know. She was an orphan, an exile, and an outlaw, with no possessions other

278

than what she carried with her. Her family name was tainted. If she was a man, she would become a *rōnin,* a masterless sellsword. But as a woman...

She looked at her reflection in the pond. Nagomi was right; even the bandages would not help long. She had been fooling herself, thinking she could play at being a boy forever. Even in Kiyō, her eccentricity was barely tolerated.

Now she was at the whim of other men. If she was lucky, she would be adopted by one of her father's remaining friends and sold off into an arranged marriage.

Marriage? She scoffed, bitterly.

And who would even want me, without a name and dowry?

She had always loathed the concept, but now even that seemed like an unattainable dream. Being a third or fourth concubine of some bored nobleman amused by her feistiness long enough to fill her belly with a bastard child was the best she could count on – if she was *lucky*...

The only other alternatives coming to her mind were a monastery or a house of entertainment. She imagined herself at the beck and call of drunken, red-faced lechers and revulsion rose in her throat.

There were no more tears left in her eyes; she stood up, her mind now clear.

None of this, she decided. *None of these things will happen to me. I am the heir of the Takashima School. As long as I have my sword and my magic, I will carve my own future. A new future.*

She went in search of the grey-stone building where the others were accommodated.

Bran welcomed her with a big grin on his face.

"Look what I got! A messenger arrived with orders from Satsuma... And he brought my ring!"

He showed her the jewel with pride; the blue stone was dim and dark.

"That's... great, Bran."

"What happened? You look like you've seen a ghost."

"A ghost?"

She raised up her anguished face to him. He put the ring away and became serious.

"It's just an expression. You didn't *really* see a ghost, did you?"

"Might as well," she said. "I've seen my Father."

"He's here? In the castle?"

She nodded. She was finding it hard to speak, with tears welling in her throat she was desperate not to show.

Be strong.

"Sit down." Bran took her by the arm and led into the common room. "I'll call for something to drink."

When she finished recounting her meeting with Shūhan, she noticed she had let him hold her hand all through the tale. The waitress brought *cha* and Satō withdrew her hand to grasp the teacup.

"But that's... good, isn't it?" Bran asked. "He's alive."

Is he serious?

"It would be *better* if he was dead. At least he would die like a samurai. What he's now reduced to, it's... ten times worse."

She hid her face in the cup.

"We will get the Crimson Robe... that Ganryū," said Bran. "And make him pay."

"Of course we will," she said.

She woke up with a start. Faint moonlight illuminated the silhouette of a man sitting in the corner of the room.

"Don't fear, child," a familiar voice spoke softly, "it's me."

Is this another vision?

Satō looked at Nagomi; the priestess slept soundly.

"Are you... are you real?"

"I am real. I snuck out of the castle"

"But... you were out of your mind. Blood-addled."

"Because I saw you...I was able to fight the Curse."

The Curse? He can't mean...

"What is happening to you? Wait, I'll light the lamp..."

"No! You can't see me like this. I came to tell you... you have to kill me, child."

"Father..."

"No, listen! You didn't think He allowed me to escape? It was a *ruse*. He's using me. He already knows you're here,

281

and the boy… you should kill me before He… forces me to harm you."

"He… forces you to…?"

His shadow crept a little towards her.

"It now takes all my strength to oppose Him, but I don't know how much longer I can go on."

"I… we can't –" she said, but her hand reached for the dagger she kept under the *futon*.

"I'm already dead…" his voice turned hoarse. "Please… I can sense Him coming…"

His words were pleading, but his tone was unpleasant, slithering. Suddenly he jumped at her and pinned her to the floor; she dropped the dagger. His breath smelled of stale blood, his fingers clutched her arms like claws, fingernails tearing through the cotton of her night shirt. He brought his face near to hers. In the faint moonlight she saw the face she knew so well now contorted in a grimace of pain and fury, his teeth bared, sharp.

"*Where is he,*" he said in a hissing voice she didn't recognize. "*Where's the boy!*"

He was too strong; she couldn't resist his grasp. Her left shoulder – where the Crimson Robe's bronze dagger had hit her – pulsated with agonizing pain spreading all over her upper body. She wanted to scream for help, but the sound stifled in her throat. She felt herself forced to answer.

"In… the room… upstairs…"

"*You will take me to him.*"

"Yes…"

He raised her from the floor and pushed her forward, holding her tight. She felt something trickle down her arm where Shūhan's fingers dug into skin and flesh. Her eyes were full of tears.

The door slid open; a lanky man stood on the corridor, holding a lantern in one hand. His other fist was set on fire.

"Down," ordered Heishichi. She dropped to her knees, feeling the joints strain in her father's grip.

"*Brand!*" The *Daisen* cried and opened his fist; a tongue of flame burst above Satō's head, then another. The grip on her arm slackened and she scrambled into the corridor before looking back. When she finally did, the entire upper half of Shūhan's body was on fire; eerily, he neither flailed nor cried, just stood there, burning down. He reached out a flaming hand towards her; through the flame she could see his mouth move, trying to say something – *I'm sorry? I love you?* – but no voice came from the disintegrating lips.

Satō heard a scream from inside the room.

"Nagomi's still there!"

The *Daisen* threw another ball of flame at the half-burned body, but Shūhan – what was left of him – didn't fall down. He took a staggering step forward.

She heard heavy steps - Torishi came down the corridor towards them. He burst into the room, pushing Shūhan to the floor, leapt over the flames and, seconds later, emerged with Nagomi in his arms. On the way out, he grabbed Satō by the sleeve.

"We must go," he said.

"Wait," she said. "I need to finish this."

She approached cautiously, watching the remains of her father burn. She stretched out a trembling hand.

"*Bevries,*" she said. "*Bevries. Bevries.*"

She kept repeating the spell until Shūhan's body was covered in a thick icy tomb and all her power was spent.

The world around her turned black and she dropped to the floor, exhausted.

Satō played with the *teppō* gun she had received along with the adjusted glove from Master Tanaka after her father's funeral.

"You will need it more than I do," the teary-eyed old mechanician had said.

She unscrewed and screwed the hidden handle repeatedly, finding solace in the clicking sound. She looked around. Everyone in the boat was silent, grim-faced. The only glimpse of colour was the dull light shining off the blue stone on Bran's finger.

"Are you going to be wearing it now, then?" she asked.

"It's the only way to be sure it's not stolen again."

Torishi leaned over to study the ring with interest.

"What is it?" she asked.

"The Little People wore shards of such blue stone around their necks," the bear-man answered.

284

"The Little People?" asked Bran.

"The Ancients," said Nagomi. "His people knew them a long time ago. But why did they do that?"

"Not sure," the bear-man replied with an apologizing shrug, "it may have had something to do with the dragons."

Bran scratched his nose.

"The drawings in the tomb," he said. "So they *did* worship the dragons."

"Yes. The beasts were their Spirit animals, much like the bears were for us."

"What happened to those shards?"

"Gone, like the Little People... stolen, sold for food... there were many who dug up their tombs and looted them."

The bear-man leaned back. Nobody said anything more, only Bran raised his ring finger to the dim sun, letting the cold light play on the jagged facets.

The flat, muddy, reed-covered banks of the Chikugo River passed lazily on both sides. Satō was getting sick of the sight of those reeds, and the weeping willows.

"This is the worst part of our journey," she murmured. "And I thought being lost in the Takachiho forest was bad."

"Not long now, wizardess-*sama*," said Master Dōraku. He had given the oar to Torishi, who alone seemed to be enjoying himself on this mode of journey.

"We should soon reach Kurume, where we swap to horses."

Horses?

"I can't ride a horse," she said.

"Then you are welcome to join me in the saddle. The Kurume horses are exceptional creatures. Descended from the legendary Ikezuki. We're lucky the daimyo is a friend."

Bran moved closer; he and Nagomi were sitting at a bench closer to the bow; Heishichi sat alone in the last one.

"A friend, you say? A friend to whom?"

"Good question, Karasu-*sama*," the Swordsman said with a weak smile. "He is a long-time ally to Nariakira-*dono*'s cause. And since we're wearing Satsuma colours now…"

"Nariakira-*dono* seems to have friends everywhere."

"That's just because we choose our path wisely. To the East, West and North of here, all daimyos are loyal to the *Taikun*. Some even belong to his family. The Kurume is the last safe place until Nagato."

The name reminded Satō of something.

"I had a student from Nagato," she said. "I wonder what happened to him. Hadn't seen him since… since…"

Her voice broke as she remembered the last time she had seen her father alive and well, the morning before she went to Master Tanaka's lecture. Bran reached his hand to her, but she turned him down.

"I'm all right. What is the *cause* that you spoke of?" she asked the Swordsman. "My…" she choked and coughed, "my Honourable Father belonged to some conspiracy he never discussed with me. Was it part of the same cause?"

"It's not up to me to explain His Excellency's plans," Master Dōraku replied.

"We will bring the *Taikun* down. One way or another," said Heishichi from his lonely post, "and wake this land from its sleep."

Satō turned around in shock. This was the first time she had heard somebody speak so clearly and without hesitation on the matter.

"Bring the *Taikun*... that's insane!"

"The Prophecy..." whispered Nagomi. "*The mightiest will fall.* It's all coming true."

"Why is it insane?" asked Bran. "He is just a man, isn't he? How did his family come to such power, anyway?"

Satō looked up at Master Dōraku. As the witness of the beginnings of the *Taikun's* rule, he seemed the most suitable person to tell the story. But the Swordsman nodded at her with a smile.

"Three hundred years ago, a great Civil War ravaged Yamato," she started. "Daimyo against daimyo, local warlords, rebel monks, peasant armies and so on... until a mighty warlord defeated everyone else and united the nation under his rule."

"The first Tokugawa *Taikun*," guessed Bran. "Ieyasu, wasn't it?"

"No, the unifier's name was Oda. Ieyasu was just one of his lieutenants at the time."

"Then how…"

"Ieyasu wielded the greatest weapon of all: patience,"
said Master Dōraku. "He waited until the great Oda and all
his heirs and successors died out or were killed, leaving only
a child of five. He then announced himself a regent in the
child's name."

"There was resistance, of course," continued Satō.
"And an alliance of clans faced him at Sekigahara in the most
terrible battle of all. But Ieyasu won against all the odds.
After that, there was no one left to oppose him."

Bran turned to Heishichi. "I'm guessing the Shimazu
were on the losing side."

"He bribed and cheated his way to victory," the wizard
replied, his face contorted in anger. "He lured the clans with
false promises and divided the allies. And the Tokugawas
have been doing it ever since."

"What happened to the child? The five-year old?"

"Forced to suicide some years after the battle," replied
Master Dōraku. "Along with the rest of the family."

"That's not strictly true," said Heishichi, looking
strangely at the Swordsman.

"Oh, there are other threads of the story, of course,"
Master Dōraku agreed, "but I don't think there is any need
to get into those details now."

Bran stared at the flowing river, mulling over all the
new information, then looked at Satō.

"I thought you said civil wars and revolts like that don't
happen in Yamato."

She shook her head.

"Not anymore. Not under the Tokugawas. The *Taikuns* have all the armies, all the money, all the key castles. They hold children of all the major clans as hostages in Edo. And nobody wants to repeat the bloodshed of the Civil War just to replace one tyrant with another."

"Satsuma seems to think otherwise," Bran replied, nodding at Heishichi.

"Foolish dreams," she barked. "They did nothing for two hundred years."

Heishichi snorted with indignation. "The time was not right," he said. "One day... soon."

"The clans will never support you. To them, a Shimazu is no better than a Tokugawa."

"I don't know much about these things, of course," Bran said with a patient nod. "And this is not my war to wage. But I remember what you've told me about your Father's beliefs. Some might say those were foolish dreams as well."

Satō wanted to scoff with another angry remark, but she held her tongue.

He's right. My Father believed a change for the better was possible in Yamato.

A sudden thought struck her. She turned to Heishichi and bowed before him. The *Daisen* raised an eyebrow.

"I'm sorry, my words were rash. If my Honourable Father thought it wise to ally himself with Satsuma, I am bound to honour his commitment. As soon as this is over, I will return with you to Kagoshima."

A shadow of a smile flickered across the *Daisen*'s face and he bowed back.

Dōraku's eyes narrowed as he steered the boat towards the harbour. Bran followed his gaze towards the castle towering on a low hilltop over the fork in the river.

"That's the *Taikun*'s hollyhock crest on the ramparts. What's going on?"

"It seems a friend is a friend no more," remarked Heishichi. "We should land somewhere else. Look, there are soldiers on the pier."

Dōraku turned the boat about and headed for another, smaller quay beside a tall garden wall. A vermillion *torii* gate on the far end of the pier marked the entrance to a shrine.

"I will wait here, with Torishi-*sama,*" the Swordsman said. "You find out what's happening in the city."

"You really can't step onto a sacred ground, can you?" Bran asked. "Even after all you've gone through?"

"There is no redemption for me," the Swordsman said. "The Spirits are waiting behind that *torii* to tear my soul to shreds."

"Would *that* kill you?"

"I don't know. It might be the closest thing to death. Now go."

There's something he's not telling me, thought Bran. Dōraku's face was surprisingly easy to read, as if so near to a shrine his mask had shattered.

Or maybe I'm just getting better at it.

After all, he now knew the Fanged's deepest secret: his creation. He hadn't asked Dōraku about his vision from Amakusa yet; he had a feeling the samurai would not be eager to discuss his "birth" so openly. But he often thought about what it meant. While the men he saw in the vision were of Yamato birth, they were all Sun Worshippers; probably rebels from Shimabara, like Shigemasa had said. Did it mean the ritual had come here from the West? From... Rome?

"They were using it to raise fallen soldiers at first, but soon discovered that by using blood magic curses they could imbue the walking dead with great power, and keep them under control."

Doctor Campion's words rang in his ears.

Of course – when the Vasconians first came here, the Wizardry Wars were still being fought.

Necromancy. Vanquished and long forgotten in the West – but here, in Yamato…

"Are you coming, Bran?" Satō called him from beyond the *torii* gate.

"Yes, there is a great deal of disturbance in Kurume," said the stocky, square-jawed, balding man. He wore an old, stained set of lamellar armour over his high priest robe. "For one, I'm being held under house arrest here."

It had quickly occurred to Bran that Dōraku had not chosen his mooring place by accident. The high priest of the shrine, introducing himself as Maki Izumi, welcomed them with open arms and led them straight to his study. Heishichi handed him a folded piece of paper marked with the Shimazu crest. Obviously, the man was one of the "friends" the Swordsman had mentioned.

"Edo is in turmoil," said Izumi. "They sent requests for additional troops to all the daimyos. It's almost as if they're preparing for war – or a revolt."

"Preposterous idea," said Heishichi.

"Of course."

"I thought Yorishige-*dono* could be trusted," Heishichi continued. As the official representative of Satsuma, he was the only one talking. Bran was soon lost in the exchange, anyway; the names of the lords and domains mentioned in the conversation meant little or nothing to him.

"He is. But he can't openly defy the *Taikun's* orders! Not with Saga and Kokura on our doorstep. We are but a small, poor domain, not like the mighty Satsuma."

"It's a test of loyalty," guessed Heishichi. Izumi nodded.

"That's why His Excellency keeps me away from the court. He knows my name is not popular in Edo. I'm telling you, *Daisen-sama*, something's stirred the pot. Satsuma must make its move soon, or it will be too late."

"Perhaps it has. Have you read the letter?"

"Ah, the letter, yes. Excuse me for a moment."

The High Priest unravelled the paper and put on a pair of horn-rimmed spectacles, similar to the ones Heishichi wore. His face brightened as he neared the bottom of the page. He finished and smacked a fist on the table.

"Good news?" asked Satō.

"The best news! Finally, matters are moving in the right direction. But, Nariakira-*dono* asks me to provide the bearer of this letter with any help they may require. What is it that you need of me?"

"We need horses," said Heishichi.

"You mean the Ikezuki breed, or you would have just bought some on the market."

"That's right."

The High Priest frowned.

"That may be difficult. All the horses have been requisitioned into the castle, for the army."

"If it was easy, we wouldn't need your help."

Izumi went over to the window overlooking the shrine garden. In this gesture, and in many small others, he reminded Bran of Lord Nariakira.

"I can help you – but under a condition. You must take me with you."

"I'm afraid our mission –"

"No, not on the mission. Just into the castle and out of the city. I need to get away from this backwater place, go to where something important is happening."

"I don't see how that will be a problem," said Satō, before Heishichi managed to open his mouth. Bran caught the *Daisen* give the wizardess an irritated glance.

The High Priest turned around and clapped his hands.

"Splendid. There's an old tunnel leading from here to the castle grounds. It's guarded on the other side, but nothing we shouldn't be able to deal with."

"*We?*" Heishichi said doubtfully. The High Priest smiled and opened a small, narrow cupboard. Inside, on a lacquered stand, rested a splendid sword in a glistening black-and-gold scabbard.

"History was not the only thing we were taught at Mito," he said with a mischievous grin.

Bran bowed before the main altar in the shrine's Offertory Hall, rang the bell and clapped twice, as he saw other visitors do.

The Suiten-gu Shrine was dedicated to the spirits of water and some long-forgotten *Mikado* unfortunate enough to drown in a battle centuries ago. But Bran wasn't here to pray; he wanted to talk to Shigemasa, and being in the presence of other Spirits while doing this made him feel somehow safer. He dared not yet return to the red dirt plain to meet the General face-to-face.

"Tell me, *Taishō*," he said, "You have sworn loyalty to the *Taikun*, have you not?

There was silence at first, and then the familiar bubbling of Shigemasa's ever angry thoughts coming to the surface.

"*And what do* you *know about the* Taikun, *Barbarian? None of this concerns you.*"

"I know his officials would arrest me on sight, and then cut my head off."

Shigemasa snarled.

"*They wouldn't waste a sword on a Barbarian's head. You'd be hanged, crucified or boiled alive, depending on the judge's mood.*"

Bran could feel the General's anger burning. There was some deep, personal grievance buried within Shigemasa's thoughts.

"*I swore fealty to the first of the Tokugawas, yes. But he is long dead, like me,*" he said at last. "*The oaths do not carry into the afterlife.*"

"I need to know you are not going to denounce us. You are now in the company of rebels and traitors, after all."

"*It would achieve nothing. It wouldn't stop the Darkness.*"

Ah. The Darkness.

A pilgrim standing patiently behind Bran coughed. The boy stepped aside, letting the man get closer to the altar.

"I heard you talk about it with Torishi."

"*It's no secret. Even your little priestess knows about it.*"

"Nagomi?"

"All soothsayers see it. The Darkness that gathers around Yamato. Not even the Spirits can peer through it."

"What do you think it means?"

"Nothing good, I reckon. Maybe it's the limit of our prophecies. The Gift is not like your Barbarian science, with measures and numbers."

"Yes. Vague and mysterious — unless you *need* it to be precise."

A drop of rain fell on the pavement beside Bran. He looked up; the silver clouds lined with navy blue gathered above him.

"You never told me that place of red dust was the Otherworld," he said, heading for the grey-stone house.

"You never asked."

"Does it all look like that? Featureless and dark…?"

"That's only the place the living can access. A forecourt of the Otherworld, as it were. And your place is… a bit different to others."

"My place — you mean the tower."

"I've seen castles… mansions… The red-headed priestess' mind is like a fortified temple. But never just a tall stone tower."

"You can see into other people's minds?"

"I could never get past all the walls and wards. Only with you I am bonded enough to break through."

There must be a way to use it, thought Bran.

"Could I reach the place where the Spirits gather?"

"Not without dying first."

"The Kumaso could."

"Those... half-animals," Shigemasa scoffed with resentment. *"I don't know how it works for them. Turn into a bear, for all I know. Why would you want to go there?"*

"It's something Dōraku said... about the Spirits waiting to tear his soul apart."

"You think you'd find a way to destroy the Crimson Robe."

"The Crimson Robe... yes, that's right."

Shigemasa chuckled.

"Oh, I see! Hedging your bets. You're growing clever for your age, boy."

"My father is a diplomat," said Bran, "it must be in my blood too." He couldn't help smiling to himself.

"I like the game you're playing, boy."

The narrow, damp tunnel stretched for a good mile. The road was straight and well lit – two of Izumi's students illuminated the way with paper lanterns – and it didn't take long for Bran and the others to reach its end.

"So what's so special about these horses?" he asked Satō.

"Ikezuki was the horse of Yoritomo," she replied, "a warlord from the Genpei Wars, seven hundred years ago. A foal of a wild mountain mare and a *qilin*. It was said to be able to swim across the sea and run as fast as a flying *ryū*. His brother Yoshitsune used another horse of that breed to hunt dragons."

"And what are they doing *here?*"

"This shrine is dedicated to those fallen in the Genpei Wars," said Izumi, overhearing their conversation. "After the war, Yoritomo gave his horse to us as an offering, and we've been breeding its kin ever since."

A rotting ladder reached a trap door. Izumi approached it cautiously and tried out the first rung. It held.

"Ishi, Bashi, turn those lights down," he ordered his students. The inside of the tunnel turned pitch black.

"The door opens to a small courtyard in the southern corner of the castle grounds," the priest's voice rang in the darkness. "There're usually two or three soldiers immediately by the door, and more in the guardroom further on. But we'd do best not to be noticed by them. Remember, none of your fireworks; we're trying to be stealthy."

"Where are the horses?" asked Bran. His hand rested on the guard of his sword. He didn't like the plan; it was one thing to slay monsters and demons, or even men who were out to get them. But now they were considering killing some innocent soldiers, whose only fault was standing between them and some mounts. Why couldn't they just buy some horses from the market, like Izumi had suggested?

"The stables are on the right hand side, not far from the Eastern Gate. If your friends outside will do as planned," he added, meaning Dōraku and Torishi, "we should be out of the castle in no time."

"Go on, then," said Heishichi. "Open that door."

The door screeched and a narrow strip of dim light appeared in the blackness.

THE RISING TIDE

CHAPTER XV

Shakushain stood on the shore with his arms crossed, watching the dozen grey-clad men struggle to transport a great iron box from an oxcart platform onto the flat-bottomed ferry.

In the cold breeze, they sweated more than the effort required; the beast inside, though now sound asleep and separated by a sheet of rune-scratched steel, still exerted its terrifying influence on anyone who got close. Even from a distance, he felt the chill reaching into his mind, a palpable, primeval fear telling him to run and hide in some dark cave. He could almost see its dark feelers flowing from inside the box. No bear, wolf or wild boar had ever made him feel this way. He was impressed with the way Ganryū's men were managing to hold on to their sanity so close to the monster.

The fear was so strong that only Ganryū himself could board the boat. The others boarded another, smaller vessel, to follow the Fanged towards the small island in the middle of the straits.

Before boarding, Shakushain came up to Koro and crouched down, so that their faces were level.

"Do you remember how we used to race across the Ishikari River?" he asked.

Koro smiled at the memory.

"When we get close to the island, I want you to pretend you've fallen off the boat, dive and swim to the northern shore. It shouldn't be more than five *chō*. Can you make it?"

The little man nodded.

"Why?" he asked.

"I don't like the way Ganryū looks at your necklace. He wants it, I can feel it."

"He does," Koro agreed. "He wants to have a pair."

"A pair?" Shakushain frowned. "What do you mean?"

"The red one puts to sleep; the blue one wakes."

Shakushain looked sharply towards Ganryū; the Fanged was already on the ferry, pushing the vessel away with the long pole. "Do you think he knows?"

"He's not certain. The stone's power is hidden from strangers."

"Good." Shakushain nodded. "One day you'll have to tell me what it is," he added with a smile. He stood up.

"Hide somewhere for a couple of days. I don't think I'll be staying here for too long. And don't worry – I'll make sure nobody follows you."

Satō stepped over the body of the guard, wiping his blood off the blade. She tried not to look at his face; he wasn't much older than her.

He didn't even attack her, just threatened her with a brandished spear. The other guards had charged at the High Priest and his students; they died valiantly, in battle, before Satō even managed to climb out of the trap door. But this boy... he was too afraid to strike, and too dutiful to run away.

"Get him!" Master Heishichi had urged her. "Before he alarms the others!"

A sickening thought fluttered through her mind as her sword fell on the guard's chest.

Is this what civil war is like? Yamato killing Yamato in battle?

She felt herself pushed onwards. The *Daisen* dragged her out of the small courtyard into the open space. She heard shouting and saw dots of dancing light heading towards them from the direction of the donjon.

Soldiers with lanterns, she guessed.

It was too late for stealth – they had been detected.

"In here," cried Izumi. The gate to the long, low building of red brick was locked shut, but only for a moment: in one great burst of flame Master Heishichi released his irritation at being unable to use magic earlier. The smouldering remains of the gate swung open.

The horses inside started kicking and wheezing in panic. Satō stopped on the threshold, overcome by the all too familiar fear.

"Which are the ones we're looking for?" asked Bran. She noticed his sword was still sheathed and it made her feel even more guilty.

303

"The calm ones," said Izumi with a grin. "The big white ones. They should be already bridled. Each of you take one and lead it out. Hurry!"

"We need time to saddle," said Bran.

"Nobody saddles an Ikezuki!" Izumi said with a chuckle. "Don't worry, it'll be all right; you won't feel a thing. You too, boy –" To Satō's terror, he seemed to be talking to her. "Go help!"

She closed her eyes and stepped inside; her entire body wanting to run away. The smell and the noise overwhelmed her. She bumped into something big, soft and warm. She opened her eyes and found herself staring straight into another pair, dark brown and calm, belonging to a giant white horse. Fear took her over.

"Ah, good, take this one, I'll get another," one of Izumi's students said and pushed the bridle strap into her clammy hands.

The animal nudged her with its nose. Satō almost fell down.

What do I do now? Do I just… pull it?

She tugged on the leather strap gently and the animal took a step forward.

"Move, you're blocking the way!" Somebody shouted from behind. The girl shook her head.

Pull yourself together, Takashima Satō.

Every step towards the stable door felt like a mile, but at last she was outside. She saw a full-scale battle in the castle courtyard, with soldiers now running towards them from

304

every direction. Torishi and Master Dōraku were already there, alongside Master Heishichi and the High Priest – the bear-man behind, shooting his bow, the Swordsman in front, whirling the twin blades; she cast a quick glance towards the Eastern Gate and saw it open wide, with several guards lying dead from arrow-shots. She felt sick.

"Right, that's the last one," said Bran, leading another of the white horses out of the stables. He gasped.

"By the Red Dragon's Beard, what's going on here?"

"Release the others," the High Priest commanded, "it will add to the confusion."

Ishi and Bashi ran inside. Moments later, a dozen terrified horses galloped past her, straight towards the soldiers.

"Now! Mount up! *Daisen-sama*, do as we planned."

Master Heishichi spread his hands apart and weaved a complex pattern, shouting a couple of Bataavian spell words in quick succession. A wall of flame rose between him and the castle guards.

Satō felt herself picked up and put onto the back of the horse nearest to her. Master Dōraku leapt in front of her.

"Hold tight!"

"To what?"

"To me!" the Swordsman replied, laughing. She clung to his back and shut her eyes tight as the horse underneath her bolted forward.

She had no idea how much time had passed. Everything was hazy and blurry; her backside and thighs ached with a thousand burns and tears. At last, the horse stopped and she slid to the ground.

They were on the outskirts of the city, just beyond the last line of houses, near the river. Satō saw Bran help Nagomi dismount carefully from the horse she shared with the boy; the wizardess felt a pang of irritation and looked away. She noted that Master Heishichi sat on his mount almost as precariously as she had. She guessed the merchant's son didn't have much practice in bareback riding, either.

Master Izumi and one of his students remained mounted, watching the road behind anxiously. The other boy was missing. There was one more member of the party she couldn't account for… Only then did she notice that Master Dōraku was carrying a bow and a quiver on his back.

"Where is Torishi?"

"He will meet us in two days near Kokura."

"I didn't see him take a horse."

Master Dōraku chuckled. "The Chief of the Kumaso doesn't need a horse."

"Will he know the way? He's never been in these parts."

"He will manage," the Swordsman replied. "And now we'd better go too," he added. "The chase will be upon us any minute. Izumi-*sama*?"

"We part here. I'm grateful for your help," said Master Izumi. "I hope we'll meet again, in Satsuma."

"Is that where you're going?"

"Where else! Oh, and have this; who knows, it may come in useful." He cast the Swordsman a small pouch of red embroidered cloth. "A *Dan-no-Ura* talisman. This one works," he added with a wink, then spurred his horse and galloped south, followed by the one remaining student; Satō couldn't tell whether it was Ishi or Bashi.

"Right. Allow me, please. " Master Dōraku grabbed Satō by the waist and lifted her back onto the horse.

"I hope you don't mind getting a bit wet."

"Why? Where are we going?"

"To the other side," he replied, pointing to the Chikugo River, flowing wide and wild this far from the sea. "Let's see if these horses are really as good swimmers as the legends say."

Bran stroked the horse's snow white neck. Its mane shimmered silver in the moonlight, and its eyes glinted like amber. The horse was silent and serious, just as it had been all night. It never so much as snorted.

He soon learned to appreciate the mount's value. After crossing the river as easily as if it was a garden pond, the horse had now been galloping for hours, without showing the least signs of tiredness. Moreover, the ride was smooth and mercifully gentle on his body, something Bran had been most worried about. He never liked horse-riding much, always preferring the dragon; but this ride, with the road beneath them zooming at incredible speed and the cold wind battering against his head, was as close to flying as he could have hoped. There was even, in the way the horse responded instantly and intuitively to his commands, something resembling a primitive Farlink, a faint buzz of connection. Bran could easily imagine riding a horse like this into battle against a dragon.

He still wasn't sure if getting the horses was worth risking their lives for, rousing the defences of an entire castle and sacrificing one of Izumi's students. As he rode away from the Eastern Gate, Bran had seen the boy fall off his mount with an arrow in the back. Something didn't feel right about it all...

"We've been had," he said to himself.

"I'm sorry?" asked Nagomi; the girl had been clinging desperately to his back at the beginning of their escape, but by now had managed to relax her grip a little, growing steadily used to the new mode of transport.

"We've been used," he said aloud. "This was never about the horses or us catching up with the Crimson Robe."

"Then why...?"

"Politics, I guess. We helped that High Priest escape – obviously he's important to somebody at Satsuma – and disrupted the war preparations by burning the stables and stealing the horses. Maybe even provoked some clash between the lords."

This sounds exactly like something my father would have done, he thought.

308

"*War?* There is a war coming?"

"Haven't you heard what Izumi-*sama* was saying? The *Taikun* mobilizes the troops throughout the country. Even I can tell this is bad."

"You're a soldier. You know how these things work."

I'm not a soldier. I was just raised by one.

"You're the one who foresaw all this," he replied. "You've seen the Darkness."

Nagomi fell silent. Without turning around, Bran imagined her frowning and mulling over what he just said.

"I didn't tell anyone…"

So Shigemasa was right.

"What is it? What did you see?"

"Dark clouds over Yamato. A storm of carrion crows. A bloody dawn."

"I don't know much about prophecies, but that can't be good."

"No, I don't think it is," said Nagomi. She sighed and leaned her head against his shoulders. "There is something else I keep seeing…"

She told him about the three men invading an old man's castle in her dream. Now he frowned.

Grey Hoods! The Rome or…the Gorllewin? They are in Qin… And the green-eyed man – is that…my father? Who's the bearded fellow, then?

"Have you told anyone about this dream?"

"No," she answered. "Not even Sacchan. I dream many dreams."

"And yet you remembered this one."

"This one was different… this one scared me."

Some half an hour later Dōraku's horse slowed down to a trot, allowing Bran to match its speed.

"That's enough for today," the Swordsman said. "These may be half-mythical horses, but they are not immortal – and I bet you are tired too."

Bran nodded, although he felt he could still ride for a few hours more. It was only after he dismounted to help with breaking camp that he felt the pain and numbness in his legs. The girls collected firewood, while he and Dōraku rubbed the horses dry with straw and led them to a small stream and a glade of fresh, moist grass.

"We've covered more ground than I hoped for," said Dōraku patting one horse on the neck. The animals neighed uneasily. "Can you tell where your *dorako* is now?"

Bran leaned against the pine tree and closed his eyes.

"It's closer, but still ahead of us," he said.

And so is the other dragon, he thought. *Far to the north… towards Edo! Did the* Taikun *get a beast of his own?*

The Swordsman frowned. "Ganryū might reach Kokura before us at this rate."

"Then shouldn't we be riding further?"

310

"No, no," Dōraku shook his head. "I can't risk you all being exhausted by the time we confront him."

Confront him?

"We don't even know how – or if – we can kill him," he said, but Dōraku said nothing.

Bran sat under the pine tree, focusing on the black spot inside the campfire flames.

"*Taishō-sama.*"

He waited a while for the General to bubble up.

"*I'm listening, boy.*"

"Have you learnt anything?"

"*I saw your beast again, boy. It's looking rather forlorn.*"

"Forlorn?"

Bran closed his eyes and instantly transported his mind to the plain of red dust. Following Shigemasa's lead, he found the phantom jade dragon shuffling about, dragging its tail across the red sand with its head held low. His heart sank.

It looks sick.

He approached the beast slowly. The dragon raised its head and looked up at Bran, but there was no recognition in its eyes. Lowering its neck again, it trundled on.

We've been through this! What's wrong now? And I even have my ring now –

311

He looked at his hand: the ring was missing. He frowned.

Why is it gone?

Since his conversation with Torishi, Bran had been growing certain that the blue shard was the whole reason behind what, he had thought, was his natural affinity to the dragons.

There was nothing special about me, after all, he had reasoned. *My Farlink quotient, Emrys's obedience… it was all down to this little shard of crystal.*

Dylan had never shown an affinity for having a good contact with his mounts; *he had scars to prove it,* after all. So where would Bran's sudden talent had come from?

Did Ifor know about the stone's power? Did he learn it from that Yamato woman, Ōmon?

He opened his eyes, returning to the real world, and reached into his satchel. He took the medallion out; the sad, almond-eyed face appeared under his touch. Who was she anyway? She didn't seem exotic to him now; he could appreciate her mysterious beauty. She was older than and not as regal as Atsuko, but she was a beauty nonetheless. No wonder Ifor fell for her…

She faced the Crimson Robe too, he remembered.

He chased her all the way to Dejima – all for that little piece of blue stone?

Would Dōraku know…?

He put it back into the bag and noticed Satō approach him.

"Hullo."

"May I –?" she asked. He nodded. She sat down beside him, wrapping her arms around her knees.

"You didn't fight in Kurume," she said.

"I'm not going to kill anyone over some horses," he replied.

She looked at him with a curious expression. "You're always so reluctant to take life. Is this because of what the Western wizards teach about the *mogelijkheif?*"

"You know the theory of potentials?"

"Of course. What Rangaku scholar doesn't? But it's just a theory, and few believe it in Yamato."

"I thought that was it at first," Bran admitted, "but now I think it's something within me. Certainly, the wizards in the Dracalish army have no such qualms." He remembered the bloody history of the Empire, the destruction he had seen in Qin, and his father's personal accounts of war. Dylan must have lost the count of lives he had taken long ago. It did not seem to diminish his powers in the least, but what did he really know about his father?

Maybe that's it, he thought, looking at his hands and imagining the full power of dragon flame surging through his fingers. *Maybe I just don't want to become like him: a man who can kill with a thought.*

"You'll become a *Butsu* monk at this rate," the wizardess said and chuckled softly.

He looked back at her and noticed she was playing absent-mindedly with a small piece of polished bronze.

313

"What's that?" he asked.

She showed it to him. There was a strange rune scratched on the surface; the edges of the bronze were stained dark red.

"My Father had it on him when he… died. I don't know why."

Another man dead because of me, thought Bran.

"Tanaka-*sama* said the rune must have been copied from the Crimson Robe; the whole place where they found him was covered in runes of this design."

"Why did you keep it?"

"Wouldn't you? I thought he maybe… wanted me to have it."

The light of the campfire glinted red off the bronze; the colour of Nagomi's hair.

"So I hear you're not going back to Kiyō," Bran said.

"There's nothing for me to go back to," she replied.

"What about all the things you left behind? What about the Dragon Book?"

She smiled.

"I have *seen* a *dorako*, Bran. What more do I need? Besides, you've already taught me more than any scholar in Yamato will ever learn."

"I wish I paid more attention in school," he said. "I always thought being able to fly well was all that mattered."

"It would be all that matters to me."

314

"My grades were terrible, but they still offered me a baccalaureate," he said with a chuckle.

"What does it mean?"

"More years in school. Had I agreed to that, I would never have come here."

"You wouldn't have lost Emris."

"I wouldn't have met you," he said and looked at her; with her chin on her knees, the back of her neck showed pale in the campfire light. His previous fascination with her nude body now seemed vulgar and barbaric. In Kagoshima, he had learned to appreciate the true beauty of a woman. How much more sensuous was this pale triangle of skin, cut off neatly by the collar of the *kosode* and the black pony-tail. Bran felt the warmth spread from his loins to his stomach and the desire to hold her close. He reached out to touch her. She brushed her cheek against his fingers.

"Tomorrow, can I ride with you?" she asked. There was innocence in the question, belying anything that had ever happened – or could happen – between them.

"I would like that very much."

Bran took the bronze spyglass from his satchel. It screwed open with a screech.

I haven't used it in a while. I almost forgot I had it.

The lens fogged up and, as he waited for it to clear, he studied the view below.

"It's bigger than I remembered," said Dōraku.

The fir-covered hill on which Bran, Dōraku and Heishichi were standing overlooked a narrow, stormy strait, in the middle of which, lay a flat island stretching from north to south. It was shaped like a great ship, narrow at the ends, wide in the centre, a quarter of a mile long and about a hundred yards in breadth. On the southern side it was sheltered from the tides by a reef of jagged black rocks.

Looking further west, Bran spotted tall, white castles rising on hilltops on either side of the narrows, like twin watchtowers guarding the sea passage – Nagato domain's Chōfu in the North and Ogasawara's Kokura to the south, as Dōraku had explained earlier.

At last the spyglass was good for use and he could investigate the ship-shaped island more closely. The entire perimeter was surrounded by a tall earthen wall; most of the land was given to a green meadow, or pasture, with several clumps of wind-bent trees. A rectangular, two-storey mansion stood on a raised mound on the northern tip, with several long, low buildings of white stone scattered around it. The only obvious way onto the island was by a single pier jutting out in the direction of Kokura, surrounded by watchtowers and battlements.

Bran counted at least ten guards in grey uniforms he remembered from Kirishima, wandering around the precinct; he reported this to Dōraku.

"There are more in the watchtowers," the Swordsman said. "These are Ganryū's private troops. His students."

"Students?"

"Officially, this island is the headquarters of a fencing school, Ganryū *Dōjō*. Most of his followers recruit from its students."

"There is a flag up on the mansion," said Bran. "It looks like… an octopus?"

Dōraku chuckled. "An Eight-headed Serpent," he corrected Bran, before turning serious. "That means Ganryū's inside."

I guessed as much. I can sense Emrys down there.

"He flaunts the banner of the Serpent so openly?" asked Heishichi.

"You know what it is?"

"A secret order of assassins and troublemakers. Some say they were behind every failed rebellion against the *Taikun*."

"Not *every*," said Dōraku. "But they were more than just assassins. Each head of the Serpent is an ancient Fanged."

"That banner has not been seen in a century," murmured Heishichi. "Shimazu-*dono* must be informed."

"You've never mentioned it before." Bran turned to Dōraku with an accusing stare.

"Their power is all but spent," the Swordsman said with a shrug. "Ganryū is an arrogant fool to use this symbol for himself."

Once again it struck Bran how much Dōraku knew about the Crimson Robe's affairs.

They've known each other for hundreds of years.

"Were you one of the Serpent?" he asked, putting away the spyglass.

"Never," the Swordsman replied firmly. "I grew apart from the other Fanged long before the Eight gathered for the first time. I was one of the first, really. Me and Ganryū, died and Cursed at the same time. Of course, Chiyome was the eldest of us all, but…" his voice trailed off.

"How did you die?"

Dōraku's eyes narrowed.

"It's a strange moment to ask a question like that."

"I've long been curious – and we might not get another chance to talk about it."

The Swordsman scratched his beard.

"Betrayal. It was supposed to be just another duel; I've won many like it before. But my enemy's blade was poisoned. I smashed his ribs and killed him on the spot, but he managed to scratch me. I suffered in agony for days before finally succumbing to the toxin."

"Was it Ganryū who killed you?"

Dōraku didn't answer, confirming Bran's suspicions.

"We should go back to the others. It's getting late."

"A storm is coming," Bran pointed to the steel-coloured clouds gathering on the eastern sky.

Satō groaned.

"A contingent of skilled swordsmen inside a fortress? Shouldn't we just have asked Nariakira-*dono* for a hundred of his samurai?"

"This is still Ogasawara land," replied Dōraku. To her surprise he seemed to have taken her seriously. "Nariakira-*dono* would never agree to use his banners in what would be an open declaration of war."

"We need an *army* just to get inside. We've already faced the Crimson Robe once, and we've failed! With all the wizards of Satsuma and warriors of Kumamoto on our side."

"You didn't have me," the Fanged replied with a grin. "But what I'm most worried about is you, Karasu-*sama.*"

"Me?" asked Bran.

"Can you guarantee your *dorako* can be controlled this time?"

Bran gazed in the direction of the island fortress, then shook his head.

"I can't. I don't know what kind of power the Crimson Robe has over my beast. What I *can* guarantee is that, if it does turn against us, I will stop it."

Dōraku tapped his fingers on the hilt of his sword.

"No matter now. Let's get down to the beach."

Satō followed him down the path, but noticed Nagomi didn't move from where she was standing.

"What is it?"

"I'd only be in the way…"

"Don't be ridiculous."

"She's right," said Bran. Satō grimaced at him. *Don't!*

"We can't risk her life again," the boy continued. "She'll be safe here until we come back."

Torishi sniffed. "There's death in the air tonight."

He had arrived in the morning, having run all the previous day.

Nagomi stood up straight.

"I'm not a coward. I want to help, but I don't know *how*."

"Against Ganryū you are as useful as anyone, if not more, princess-*sama*" Dōraku boomed over Satō's head. "You wield the power of the *kami*. That's the best weapon against the likes of us."

"Tell me then, Dōraku-*sama*, what should I do?"

Dōraku shook his head.

"This is not my domain. It must flow from within you – when the right time comes."

Nagomi nodded and passed Bran, who shook his head. The priestess turned.

"Well, what are you waiting for?"

By the time they reached the shingle beach, the wind had picked up, surging high waves billowing against the shoreline. The storm clouds covered the sky with a black shroud, and any minute it was going to start raining. The white horses pricked their ears nervously.

"We're too late," decided Master Dōraku. "Not even the Ikezuki can swim in that weather. Let's get back to the camp and wait it out."

"No." Satō stood up, defiant. Since Shūhan's death she had been pushing away the thoughts about her future and focused on destroying the Crimson Robe, that cursed *creature* that destroyed her father and her life along with him. The very thought made the blood run hot in her veins.

And there was something else, too… some force pulling her towards the island fortress, a deep yearning. She needed to heed its call.

She put on the glove and studied the blue-glowing dial. Just as she had guessed, the oncoming storm was filled with magical energies.

"We've delayed too long. We go tonight."

"Don't be foolish, girl. Look at the waves. The tide is rising."

"We go tonight." Her voice was sharp and strong, leaving no room for objection.

"I am heir to the Takashima *Dōjō*. I will not be held back by wind!"

Master Dōraku opened his mouth to oppose her, but seemed to change his mind. He looked at the horses, then at Torishi.

"Are you up to it, Last of the Kumaso?" asked Dōraku. "No man swam the Kannon Strait in the storm before."

Torishi smiled.

"What about a bear?"

The Swordsman laughed.

"Very well then! At least the guards will be less watchful in this foul weather."

CHAPTER XVI

The ship rolled gently on the waves of the Inner Sea. The weather outside was as fine as anyone could expect at this time of year – which wasn't good news for the boat's Captain trying to reach Chōfu, the capital city of Nagato, before the end of the month.

Shōin didn't mind. He had plenty of time. He was sitting cross-legged, alone, staring at the four cups of water before him. His cabin was a luxury he badly needed, but could barely afford, even after selling all but one of his books to the antiquarian in Kiyō. Each cup was marked with an elemental rune at the bottom. The cups were borrowed from the ship's cook. The runes he had scribbled himself.

He couldn't focus on the magic; as so often lately, he was wondering what had happened at the Takashima *Dōjō*. An accident with a magic artefact, was the official explanation for Master Takashima's death – but then, what happened to Takashima-*sensei*? Why didn't she return to the school after the incident? And what of the other boy in the class, that annoying Keinosuke? Shōin never learned the answer to any of the questions. With the closing of the *dōjō*, he had no reason to say in Kiyō any longer. The school's sudden bad reputation reflected on its students, and no other teacher of *Rangaku* wanted to take him in. It was time to return home and start preparing for the take-over of his father's business.

This did not mean, however, that Shōin was going to give up his studies. He knew he had talent; *sensei* had said so herself. It would have been improper to squander it. That's why he was now playing with the water cups, desperately trying to clear his mind enough to execute a spell – any spell.

He was trying to discover his affiliated element, just as *sensei* had taught him:

You will choose your element, eventually, or rather, it will choose you. You will find some of the transformations are easier to perform, some invocations don't require as much effort.

He stretched his palms over the four cups, imagining the flow of magical energies through his body and down to his fingers; he was summoning a raw power, without focus. If his calculations were right, one of the cups should react to the magic faster and stronger.

But it seemed his calculations were wrong. This wasn't the first time he had tried the experiment; time and again, the results were the same: the frost rune made the water freeze, the fire rune made it boil; the water in the air cup bubbled up and the earth cup's thin clay walls cracked. All at the same time and, as far as he could tell, with identical intensity.

There was only one logical explanation to what was happening, but Shōin refused to acknowledge it. *Perhaps I'm too young and inexperienced,* he thought. *Perhaps my affiliation did not yet fully manifest. Maybe the difference is there, but too small for me to see.*

He bit his lips and felt the familiar jolt of power run through his hands; with each try, it came quicker and more powerfully. The four cups under his fingers burst into pieces.

A gentle bump announced the ship's arrival at Chōfu, and jolted Shōin out of his meditation. He looked around; the shards of a dozen cups were strewn all over the cabin's floor, among the densely scribbled sheets of paper. The cook had refused to give him any more, so he had to try to mend the pieces together for his continuing experiments. The pieces broke into even more shards, until he had to forget trying to work with water altogether and start on just the broken bits of clay. He didn't need the water as a conduit anymore, anyway; the clay itself melted, froze, whirled in the air or dissipated into dust under his fingers.

He gathered his notes, picked up his only remaining book – the small handbook of basic spellwork from Takashima *Dōjō* – and the bundle of clothes, and stepped outside into the sun for the first time in over a week.

As he waited his turn to step down onto the pier, Shōin noticed the crew and other passengers giving him frightened glances. He leaned overboard and looked at his reflection in the water. He saw a famished boy, with sunken cheeks, unkempt hair and deep blue bags under his eyes.

That's strange, he thought, calmly. *No. That's not me. I just need to rest and eat a proper, dry-land dinner. It's the sea.*

And then he remembered the words of Satō-*sensei* and shook his head.

"Their life energy is spent too fast. They die young."

The familiar yellow clay walls of the Chōfu castle town spread welcomingly before him, like mother's arms. It had been two years since he had last seen them; he was eager to reach home.

"You, boy!"

Shōin walked on, recognizing neither the voice, nor a reason why anyone should call him.

"Hey, you, with the book!"

He stopped, turned and saw a man in the drab overcoat, marked with a red pentacle – the uniform of a Kiyō policeman. He was accompanied by another, younger man, supporting himself on a bamboo stick; a nasty scar ran across the left side of his face underneath a black eye-patch.

They pursued me all the way here? Impossible…

"That's a Takashima book, isn't it? I recognize the crest."

Shōin dropped his bundle of clothes, clutched the handbook to his chest – and ran. The policeman behind him swore and launched in pursuit; but this was Shōin's home town. He knew every nook and alleyway. He zigzagged in the narrow streets, past the merchant's houses, over the canal bridge, up the temple hill. He hid behind the pine tree and looked down the street. The policeman was nowhere to be seen.

Who was this? What did he want?

"Kuso!"

Doshin Koyata returned to the harbour, swearing and panting. He found Tokojiro kneeling, rummaging through the boy's belongings.

"Leave it, we're not thieves."

"If we don't pick it up, somebody else will," replied the interpreter. "He will be looking for these things."

"It's just some spare clothes. He'll get new ones."

"These may not be easy to replace," said Tokojiro. He stood up with effort and handed Koyata several sheets of densely-written paper.

"Some notes."

The *doshin* browsed through them quickly.

"Magic." He shrugged. "I have no idea what any of this means."

"Neither do I, but I recognize this hand-writing," Tokojiro said, pointing to a comment scribbled on the margin in red ink next to a set of complex runes: *Good thinking, but the last line is all wrong. Check your equations.*

"That's the Takashima girl," said Tokojiro. "The same as in the dragon book."

"So I was right. It *was* a Takashima crest."

"Of course. The boy must have been one of the school's students."

Koyata scratched his nose, trying to remember his Kiyō investigation.

"There were two boys in the youngest class... one was a son of an aristocrat; that couldn't have been him. These are merchant clothes."

"Why does it matter who it is? Why do you care?"

Koyata looked at the bunch of papers in his hand.

"You're right, it probably doesn't matter. It's just... it feels somehow ominous to meet that boy here, of all places. So far from Kiyō and everything we've gone through."

"All the more reason to leave this wretched place," Tokojiro said with a grimace. "When does the Naniwa ship set off?"

"Tomorrow morning. You should go to the guesthouse, get some rest. I'll stick around, ask the locals. I may find somebody willing to deliver these things to the boy."

"You're not in Kiyō anymore, *doshin*. This isn't one of your *cases*."

Koyata smiled.

"I can't help it. A policeman is never off-duty."

Shōin followed the Mōri clan retainer nervously across the moat, up the sloping ramp, through the heavy wooden gate and up the stone stairs.

He had never been to the Chōfu Castle before. In fact, he had never been inside any castle. The only reason a member of the merchant class like him could be summoned to a daimyo's residence was to be punished or interrogated.

Which one was the case here, he wondered? *And why the secrecy?*

The retainer said nothing about the purpose of his visit when he had come to take Shōin away from his father's workshop.

He was led to a grand chamber at the third floor of the castle where he was told to wait for the lord of the castle to talk to him. Shōin lay prostrate on the straw mat floor, desperately trying to remember what he could have done that was of such importance to the daimyo.

He heard soft steps and the rustle of silk.

"Get up," he heard a calm, but firm, voice. He sat up. A young man, no more than thirty years old, was staring at Shōin from the podium at the other end of the room. His mouth drooped a little and his cheeks were sunken; there was a sadness and world-weariness in the man's eyes, surprising in one so young.

"But you are just a child!" the man said. He shouted to somebody hiding behind the paper wall: "Are you sure that's him?"

"Yes, *kakka*," another voice replied.

This is the daimyo of Chōshu? This is Mōri Takachika?

"How old are you, boy?"

"I'm… fourteen, *kakka*."

The daimyo shook his head. He stood up and came closer to Shōin. He was holding some pieces of paper in his hand.

329

"Are these yours?"

Shōin looked up. *My notes!*

"Yes, *kakka*."

"I found myself in possession of these a few days ago. Somebody was asking around in Chōfu for the owner of these papers."

"I… lost them at the harbour."

"Did you *really* write all these yourself?"

"Yes, *kakka*. Some of it is just notes from school…"

"Where did you learn magic?"

"At the Takashima *Dōjō* in Kiyō."

"Why did you leave?"

"The school was disbanded. The headmaster died in an accident, and my teacher has gone… missing."

"Hmm."

The daimyo returned to his podium and browsed through the papers.

"It says here you think anyone can be taught *Rangaku*. What does it mean?"

"The scholars in Kiyō think you need to first show affinity to some of Yamato's old arts – fencing, *onmyōji*, archery, the way of *cha* – before attempting to learn the Western magic," explained Shōin. "Even the Takashima method, advanced as it is, involves weeks of unnecessary training with the sword, *kakka*."

"So you don't believe that's the way."

"I think anyone with the tiniest bit of talent can start learning *Rangaku* straightaway. It is, in fact, much simpler than our ways. Even a commoner like me could grasp the basics in a matter of weeks. Of course, that's just a theory…"

Lord Mori nodded slowly.

"I have a school here in the castle. You may have heard of it – Meirinkan."

"Of course, *kakka*. One of the three finest in the country."

The daimyo smiled.

"That may be, but without a *Rangaku* faculty it's quickly becoming obsolete. All my wizards are old and useless – or spies for Edo and Satsuma. I had my court mage read these notes. He could barely follow the more complex theories. I need someone whom I can trust. Can I trust you, Yoshida-*kun*?"

"I am your servant, *kakka!*" Shōin cried out and beat his head against the straw mat in awe. To be spoken to in this manner by the daimyo of Chōshu himself was a privilege almost too great to bear.

"You will establish a faculty of Western learning at Meirinkan. All my resources are at your disposal. You cannot fail. The tide of war is rising – and I'm going to need an *army* of wizards soon."

THE RISING TIDE

The evening sky darkened quickly under the thickening cover of the storm clouds. The horses treaded carefully into the foamy surf of the rising tide, their manes flowing in the wind. Bran sensed his mount's hesitation. He caressed it on the neck, trying to calm it down. He lit up a faint flamespark and looked around to see how everyone else was doing; he noted that Heishichi did not yet move from the beach.

"What's he doing?" he shouted to Dōraku over the wind.

"Leave him. His orders are just to observe."

Bran wanted to add some nasty remark, but a sudden tall wave washed over him, almost throwing him and Satō off the horse. They were now out into the open waters of the strait, and the sea heaved and tumbled all around them.

This is insane. I should've known it's suicidal.

Another spray pummelled him. He felt Satō's hands slipping off his waist and caught her just before she fell into the water.

"We must go back!" he shouted to her, "before it's too late!"

"No!" She clung closer. "Hold my hand tight. Don't let go."

"I don't think that will…"

"Just do it."

He grasped her wrist with all his strength. He felt her wiggle about for a moment, and then heard her cry a spellword in Bataavian.

"Hoor mij, zee! Hoor mij, elementen! Kalm jezelf!"

He looked back – she was holding her sword aloft, pointing it into the waves. Her hand was clad in a leather glove, with several bits of metal sewn to it, gears and dials. She shouted the spell two more times; with her third cry, the waters around the horse calmed as if somebody had poured oil on them.

Bran saw Dōraku lead his horse behind them into the corridor formed in the wake of Satō's spell, followed by the bobbing black shape of Torishi's bear form.

It was an impressive feat, but Bran wondered how long Satō could sustain the spell, and in what fighting shape she'd be once they reach the island. Her jaws were clenched in determination; sweat mixed with rain on her face. The corridor was beginning to taper as the force of the sea battered against the magic barrier.

Half-way through, the horses began to struggle; they were now in the middle of the mighty current linking the inner sea in the south-west with the Great Ocean to the north-east.

A boat would have trouble crossing this strait, not just these poor animals.

But something else drew his attention among the waves. In the blue darkness he saw a white mist, whiffs of smoke and whirls of haze coming out of the billows.

"Can you see that?" he shouted back to Dōraku and Nagomi. The Swordsman looked up and nodded with a frown.

"There are faces in the water!" cried the priestess. The mists formed into human forms, masks twisted in anger, dying, agonized expressions.

"It's just like the Cave in Suwa," said Bran, "They must be spirits of the dead!"

"It's the wights of *Dan-no-ura*!" Dōraku shouted back. "Those who drowned in the battle!"

The commotion was beginning to break Satō's concentration. Her sword arm dropped and the corridor between the raging waters was now barely the width of a horse. Sea spray blew again in Bran's face, salt getting in his eyes.

"Why are they so angry?" he heard Nagomi ask. The spirit faces were twisted in fury. "Are they serving the Crimson Robe?"

"No," replied Dōraku, "these are forces more ancient and more powerful than any Fanged. They hate all the living. They must have been awoken by the storm."

"They're not attacking," said Bran, "maybe they're just trying to scare us away."

"It's the talisman from Suitengu," Dōraku said, reaching into his sleeve for the embroidered pouch. At the sight of the amulet, the wights pulled away. "But it won't hold them forever."

As if in response, the wights returned a moment later, and in greater numbers. A few flew past Bran, flashing bared teeth and staring with bulging eyes. A rogue wave broke through Satō's barrier and washed over the horse.

Bran put up a *tarian*, hoping to at least protect himself and the wizardess from the cold and waves; he couldn't do much for the others.

"What do we do? We can't go back, we're more than halfway through. Satō can't fight both the waves *and* the ghosts."

"*Let me out, boy*" a voice spoke in Bran's head.

"It's no time for your tricks."

"*Don't be a fool. If you drown, I'll be stuck here forever.*"

Bran thought fast. The wights were growing bolder and more aggressive with every minute, and Satō's safe passage corridor was beginning to waver, along with her strength and determination. Nobody else seemed to offer any solutions.

"What do you need?"

"*The priestess's help. And the talisman.*"

Bran leaned back.

"Give that pouch to Nagomi, quickly," he shouted.

"*Tell the girl to meditate as if she was at the Waters.*"

The priestess thought Bran's hasty explanation over and then nodded.

"I understand."

She closed her eyes and started chanting. Her body then seemed to glow with a soft, fuzzy light, her copper hair rose in an unseen wind. Dōraku, sitting in front of her, stirred uneasily and his face tensed as if in great pain.

335

The light around Nagomi grew in all directions. When it reached Bran, he felt a jolt and a buzz, and then Shigemasa was no longer in his head.

We must be as visible as a lighthouse.

The boy's neck was beginning to hurt from looking over his shoulder. The light solidified, forming the semi-translucent shape of a samurai, imposing in full armour, holding a broad *naginata* halberd, blade down, ready to strike.

Shigemasa shouted an ancient challenge. The wights understood; they poured at the General in droves, drawn to the light like moths to a flame. The halberd slashed through their wispy bodies with ease. The *Taishō* laughed, elated, launching himself into battle.

Bran spurred his horse; the animal picked up the pace. By the time they reached the reefs and shallow waters nearer the island, it was foaming at the mouth and heaving. Bran let the horse climb the rising sea bottom until the water reached only up to its chest. Then he dismounted into the cold water with a splash.

Satō slumped and slid off the horse, half-conscious. He grabbed and held her until she could stand on her own again, then sat her on a flat, black rock.

"You were brilliant," he whispered in her ear and kissed her on the cheek. She waved him away, exhausted. The sea resumed its rage around them, and they were drenched to the bone, but they were now sheltered from the worst of the storm by the reefs and a spur of the island's shore.

Dōraku led his horse by the reins into the shallows, half-wading, half-swimming. Nagomi lay on the animal's back breathless, legs and arms hanging down its sides. The light around her dimmed into a faint aura. Shigemasa waved his *naginata* a few more times before fading away and Bran heard his thoughts again.

"Glorious battle! We must do it again some time, boy."

Glad somebody enjoyed it…

"You seem exhausted," Bran said to Dōraku. The Swordsman looked at him with heavy eyes and attempted a weak, shrug-off smile.

"The girl's power is… quite astonishing," he replied.

So Nagomi can hurt you so much even without trying to… Bran thought with surprising satisfaction.

A great black bear was the last to wade into the shallows away from the horses. Together, they strode up to the ochre-daubed wall surrounding the island. The water here reached only up to their knees and, at last, they could rest.

We're about to go into battle, and there's not one of us that doesn't look exhausted, Bran thought, taking stock of the company. He knocked on the wall; it was a solid, thick earthenware construction. Even at his best he couldn't hope to burn it through with magic.

"What now? I think I forgot to bring my battering ram."

"There's a secret entrance not far from here."

"How do you know?"

"I helped build it," Dōraku answered. "I told you, me and Ganryū go back a long time."

So you keep saying…

"Perhaps you could share some hints as to how to defeat him."

The Swordsman scratched his beard.

"He's got a penchant for theatrics. I've always told him it would be his doom, and I'd love to see this prediction come true."

"*Theatrics?* That's it? No weak spots, no secret spells or talismans?"

"Salt helps, if you've got some," Dōraku replied with a grin, "but you don't get to live for three centuries without taking care of all your weak spots."

With the flamespark's light reduced to that of a candle, Bran moved carefully along the ochre wall, touching his way.

"There's a depression here," he said, "a finger's breadth."

"That will be it," said Dōraku. "Torishi-*sama,* give me a hand with this one. It's bound to be a bit rusty." Torishi, now back in his human form, was grumpy and silent. Water trickled down his naked, scarred body in thick rivulets. The two strongmen pushed against the wall with all their strength. A narrow crack appeared at first, then the outline of a door. Sea water rushed in, helping the gate to swing open.

Bran's horse had to lower its head to cross the threshold. Beyond the wall lay a beach of white pebbles, now licked by the tide flowing in through the secret door, and a slipway with a single flat-bottomed boat tied to a mooring post. A thick line of trees and bramble separated the cove from the rest of the island.

"This isn't very secure for a fortress," remarked Bran, eyeing the wall with suspicion.

"It would only open for one of the Fanged," explained Dōraku. "Looks like Ganryū still uses it from time to time."

"Why would he need to sneak away? He's the lord and master on this island."

"He doesn't trust even his own students."

Bran helped Torishi close the gate and then followed the rest of the company onto the beach. The island was filled with magic – nasty, dark power which made his sensitive body sick. Satō lay down on the pebbles and closed her eyes, catching her breath. Dōraku helped Nagomi off the mount and laid her beside the resting wizardess.

Torishi unravelled a bundle of his belongings tied to one of the horses. He put on the loincloth, bark-spun tunic and the head-scarf and tied the long dagger to his waist. He strung the bow and checked if the arrows were loose enough in the quiver. He then knelt by Nagomi and caressed her copper hair.

"Little priestess." These were his first words on this side of the strait. He reached into a small wooden box he carried with him and took out several sprigs of some herb.

Somehow, they had managed to remain dry throughout the ordeal. He crushed the herb under her nose.

Nagomi gasped and woke up. Torishi smiled and moved to Satō to repeat the procedure, but the wizardess pushed his hand away and sat up on her own.

"I'm fine. I just need a few minutes to catch my breath."

She twiddled a brass knob on her glove.

"Quite a performance, wizardess-*sama*," said Dōraku. "Your Honourable Father would have been proud."

She nodded.

"Are we safe here?" asked Nagomi.

"Ganryū wouldn't want his men to come here. But there will be guards just beyond those trees."

"I assume you have a plan," said Bran.

"Your *dorako* will be kept somewhere in Ganryū's residence; perhaps in the garden. All we need to do is charge the mansion's gates and break through."

"You make it sound easy. But there's a small *army* between us and the mansion, and two watch-towers overlooking the place."

"We'll try to sneak as far as possible. If stealth fails, I will lead the charge with Torishi-*sama*. That should keep most of Ganryū's men occupied."

"Are they just swordsmen? No mages, no *yamabushi*?"

"No. Ganryū is jealous of power. He's the only one allowed to use it on the island. I think he's afraid others would use it up," Dōraku added with a quiet chuckle.

Bran noticed Satō trying to stand up, and leapt to her aid. The wizardess held a hand to her forehead.

"Are you alright?"

"I… yes. This place… can you feel it? I smell blood," said Satō and shivered.

"At least we know it's definitely the right place," he said with a forced smile.

"Have you rested?" Dōraku asked. He had just finished tying up the horses to the mooring post. "We'd best be going."

Satō nodded. Like Torishi before her, she too readied her weapon. The sword slid in and out of the sheath with ease. Bran did the same; there was some resistance at first.

Eh…I forgot to oil it, he thought. *It will rust badly.*

He saw Nagomi pull out the remains of her paper-tasselled wand, ruined by sea water. She eyed it sadly and threw it away. Satō came up to the priestess and gave her a dagger.

"I don't really – "

"Just in case," said the wizardess. "I have my gun."

"I wouldn't even know how to use it."

"Press here," said Satō quietly, touching Nagomi's chest, "if it comes to the worst. It's a swift death."

Dōraku turned to the group and gave them a long, solemn look. His hands rested on the hilts of his twin blades. He hid his face in the shadow of the purple hood.

"We're ready," said Bran.

CHAPTER XVII

The trees provided them with shelter for about twenty yards, but the grove ended abruptly, opening onto a long and narrow courtyard running across the length of the island. At the far end, the white-washed walls of the two-storey mansion loomed in the faint light of the stone lanterns beyond a loose bamboo hedge.

The fortress was asleep but for the lone watchtower, its light directed outside the island at the sea; the other tower, Bran remembered, stood watch over the pier on the southern end of the island. The entire central courtyard was bathed in pitch black darkness. In the occasional distant flash of lightning Bran could make out some long, low buildings on the right-hand side.

"It looks so quiet…" he whispered.

"Make no mistake – they *will* be expecting us," said Dōraku. "Be prepared. I'll try to get us as close as possible without them noticing."

Bran tried to use True Sight and immediately regretted it; it was like looking into the heart of an explosion. The island was covered with dense energy flows, some ancient, some new; a rainbow of bright lights and colours too painful to bear. He shut his eyes and shook his head, waiting for the after-image to dissipate.

The Swordsman bid them all crouch and sneak along the western edge of the courtyard, past the hedgerow, along what looked like the training grounds. Bran walked carefully among the straw poles for practicing sword cuts, archery target boards, dummies of soft wood for spear and halberd training, empty weapon racks. The closer they got to the centre of the island, the darker it got, until they walked almost blind, touching their way.

The noise of the wind and storm drowned their footsteps. It started raining in earnest again, a fierce shower battered against Bran's face. The gravel beneath his feet turned to slushy mire.

They were almost half way across the courtyard when a lightning strike bathed the island in a bright white light. Five shadows were cast against the white gravel, five silhouettes cut out sharply by the flash, for just an instant, a blink of an eye.

Bran heard the rustle of the bush on his left, and the sound of many sandal-clad feet on the mud; Dōraku's blade swished in the darkness, and somebody fell down with a cry. Another lightning blasted even closer, and in its light he saw a dozen or so swordsmen in grey clothes, charging at him from all sides. He flashed a flamespark, reached for his sword, and felt a thud on the back of his head.

Satō drew her thunder gun and aimed it at the nearest group. The blinding-white lightning leapt from one man to another;

three warriors fell at once. The wizardess herself almost fell, stunned by the recoil. She looked behind; she was being surrounded. Twenty, thirty swordsmen were heading towards her, pouring from the direction of the low stone buildings. She pulled the trigger again, but the charge was not yet full and the weapon's electrodes sizzled in vain. She thrust it back into her sash and drew the sword.

With mighty swipes of his fists, Torishi made his way through the enemy and reached Satō just as her frost-covered blade cut side-ways through the first of the spears, splitting it in two. Another warrior fell with an ice-lance embedded in his chest. The bear-man grabbed her at the waist and, despite her protests, dragged her behind, punching his way back towards Master Dōraku, who was fighting what seemed now like fifty men at once. Satō noticed Nagomi, cowering behind the Swordsman, clutching the Spirit Light in her hands.

Against all reason, he seemed to have the upper hand in this battle. There was a half-circle as wide as his two ruthless swords could reach where none of the attackers dared approach. At least a dozen bodies lay sprawled on the ground beneath his feet.

"This is like Ichijōji all over again!" Master Dōraku cried, and laughed.

Ichijōji! The story in Master Kawakami's book – the nameless swordsman...

Was that... him?

Seeing Master Dōraku now she could easily believe what she had once thought was an exaggeration. The attackers numbered less than a hundred this time, but it wouldn't have made any difference if there were twice as many. The Swordsman enjoyed himself immensely, taunting the warriors, threatening them with pretend attacks and licking the bloodied blades of his swords. When he stepped forward, the crowd rippled back in fear. He was like a bear cornered, not by a pack of hounds, but by a swarm of rats. In desperation the archers tried to pierce him with arrows but he simply sliced the missiles in half.

"Come on!" he goaded, laughing, "Is this the best the Ganryū *Dōjō* has to offer? Do I fight children or men?"

His blades whirled around the spears and halberds, and broke through steel chains. He jumped and rolled, slashed high and low, turned and twisted, dodged and parried. None of the enemies' blades even touched his clothes. The smell of blood mixed with rain and mud.

"If only I could fight like that..." said Satō, filled with profound awe, forgetting about the danger for a moment.

Torishi grunted. "He lost his humanity to gain this power."

"If that's what it takes," she whispered, shaking.

"Where's Bran?" asked Nagomi.

"They took him – towards the mansion!" said Satō.

"Go get him then!" Master Dōraku yelled. He moved forward, cleaving a corridor through the enemy as if he was cutting a path through the bamboo grove.

"Kumaso, lead the way." His eyes glinted gold for a moment, then turned black. His face contorted in a fierce, blood-thirsty grimace.

"They will stay here, with me," he seethed through bared teeth, glinting black and sharp in the light that shone from the watchtower.

Satō darted towards the residence, still a hundred yards away. Arrows twanged about her from the balcony of the watchtower. She saw Torishi draw his bow and, not even slowing his run, let two arrows lose one after another. Two archers fell to the ground.

They reached a small wicket gate in the bamboo fence. Torishi kicked it in with ease. A pair of guards appeared on the path beyond the bamboo fence, their spears lowered against the intruders. Torishi roared, grabbed the shaft of the nearest spear and pulled it. The helpless soldier stumbled forwards, his face meeting the bear-man's head with a bloody result. The other guard struck at Satō, but the wizardess deflected the spear's blade and cut him across the chest with ease. The guard fell back with his arms thrown apart.

The path climbed up the raised mound through an azalea thicket beyond which lay the door of the mansion; a thick slab of ancient, riveted bronze. Its frame was scribbled in odd runes. The markings glowed bright blue. The dial on her glove twitched when she ran her finger along them.

Torishi barged against the door with his shoulder, but it didn't budge.

"The runes," said Satō, pointing to the door frame. "Like on my father's shard."

She took the piece of bronze from her sleeve and put it up to the door.

"Hand me the dagger," she asked Nagomi.

With the tip of the blade she copied the rune onto the door's surface. Nothing happened. Satō cut her finger and pressed it to the scratch. A jolt ran from her hand, along the shoulder, to the place where the bronze dagger had hit her. The copper conduits on the glove buzzed and sparked. The rune drank her blood greedily; the markings on the frame glowed purple. The door swung wide open.

They ran out onto a small square garden surrounded by a shaded veranda. A tall, broad-shouldered figure awaited them, casting a huge black shadow in the light of a burning brazier.

Silently, the enemy approached. He had a beard almost as thick and bushy as that of Torishi, and long, black, braided hair; his clothes bore similar ornaments to those of the bear-man, but were more elaborate and colourful. Several bronze bracelets jangled on his wrists. He was unarmed, but poised to strike. She noticed beads of glass and polished stone tied into the man's beard and hair.

Satō raised her sword, but Torishi put his hand on the blade and pushed it down. He stepped forward, his face grave, his fists clenched. The two giants seemed like long lost brothers.

"*Irankarapte, nipa,*" said the bear-man.

"*Irangarapte na,*" the other one replied, raising his fist to his chest.

"You know him?" Nagomi whispered. Torishi shook his head.

"He's my kin. Of those who departed north and lost their unity with the Bear."

The two hairy giants stared at each other for a long while.

"I cannot let you pass," the Northerner said.

Torishi grunted. "Then I will fight you."

He then turned to Satō and Nagomi.

"Go. I shall join you later."

Torishi had never told the young cubs of how he had wandered about the forest for days and months, slowly losing his human mind along with the will to live.

He wanted to forget about his wife dying a slow and painful death, her skin covered in bloody blisters; about his daughter, the last child buried in the burial pit. When the hunters finally found him, he had been resolved to die with no regrets. He let them trap him.

Since he first met the three youths, he had sensed a greatness inside them; courage and strength they themselves had not even begun to realize. The Spirits had confirmed his suspicions; *go with them,* they said. *Help them fulfil their destiny.* Once, he had resolved to die because he had no reason to

349

live. Now he wanted to live, because they had given him a reason to die.

He met his opponent's gaze.

"Why are you with the *Shamo*?" the Northerner asked, not unkindly. "I know what they did to your people."

"I am not here with the *Shamo*," replied Torishi. "I am here with three young cubs that need help. Why are *you* here? Do you not know who lords over this island?"

"I know he is a demon that feeds on blood," the Northerner said, laughing. "How is that different from any other *Shamo*?"

"What will you gain in exchange for your service?"

"He promised me he would help unite the tribes of the North and drive away the *Shamo* from our mountains and forests."

"And you believed him?"

"Of course not. But he also promised me a great hunt, and a good fight. And on those he delivered."

He looked the bear-man over and nodded in appreciation.

"You seem strong. I hope you Southerners have not forgotten how to brawl."

"There are no more Southerners. I'm the last of the Kumaso."

"Pity. But don't think I'll go easy on you because of that."

"I might think that. The bear won't."

Torishi laid his weapons on the ground and raised his arms high with a roar. In a flash of lightning, the great black bear appeared, the glistening fur quickly soaking in the rain. He felt his reason slowly give way to bloody instinct.

The Northerner let out a joyous cackle.

"A worthy opponent, at last!"

He leapt forward and grappled with Torishi in a deadly embrace.

Satō crossed the courtyard and broke through the door in the northern wall. There was another corridor here, dark, narrow and winding.

The corridor seemed empty, but she stopped. They were in enemy territory, and there had to be traps and ambushes waiting if the Crimson Robe expected their arrival. She was not trained in True Sight, but her senses had grown sharper ever since she had first stepped on the island, as if she was somehow growing attuned to the energies of the place.

"Look out!" she cried and pulled Nagomi down to the ground just as a pair of darts zipped above their heads. The *shinobi* assassin in a tight black uniform leapt down noiselessly from the top-right corner. The chain-and-sickle weapon whizzed through the air inches from Satō's neck. The wizardess rolled aside and jumped to her feet, her sword in her hand.

Between the black facemask and the dark blue hood she could only see the eyes of the assassin, seething with fury, concentrated.

It's the kunoichi *woman from Kirishima.*

Satō accepted the unspoken challenge and stepped forward.

"I will give you a fair duel," she said. "But this one's just you and me."

The assassin narrowed her glinting eyes, looking at Nagomi as if she had only noticed her now.

"I killed you once already, priestess," she said. "Twice would be bad luck."

"I can't leave you alone," said Nagomi.

"You must," replied Satō. "Somebody has to save Bran."

"But I'm —"

"My patience is running out," the assassin seethed through her mask.

"Go!" Satō pushed Nagomi towards the darkness of the corridor. The assassin made no move to stop the priestess as she went past her.

When Satō had entered the hall, the *shinobi* had thrown *three* poisoned darts at her. Two she managed to avoid, the third embedded itself in her left thigh. The numbing poison was slowly spreading through the entire leg.

A sudden, unwanted memory came to her now. The master of one of Kiyō's best fencing schools, humiliating her in the test match, breaking her leg with the wooden sword. He had done it to teach her a lesson; Satō easily surpassed all other applicants, but she had to be shown her place. A girl could never be a swordsman.

It had been this contempt which forced her on the path to years of lonely, arduous training of both magic and swordsmanship; fighting against straw dummies, wooden boards, and her father's illusions, she pursued perfection. Had she been a boy, it would have been enough for her to be of average skill; but as a female, she had to be the best to be considered equal.

But that was all theory and mock fighting. Nobody in Kiyō wanted to spar with her. The men deemed it beneath them, the boys weren't skilful enough.

The month-old wound in her shoulder throbbed with heat, like a second heart.

All this knowledge and training would have been for nothing, she thought, *had I not met Bran and gone off on this quest...*

She had got a chance to try herself against the bandits, the *rōnin* and the hunters... She stood her own against Master Kawakami and that old annoying Spirit in Bran's head. She had gained more experience and confidence in the last month than in her entire life. At Kirishima, just for a second, the wizardess had glimpsed what it would have been like to achieve self-mastery, the unity of purpose and means which had been, until then, only a theory in Shūhan's writings.

And now, at long last, she faced an opponent of equal skill in a proper duel.

Another woman.

The assassin's dark, cold eyes studied Satō in silence, as they both circled each other slowly, looking for an opening. The sickle whooshed on the end of the chain rhythmically like a pendulum. The tight uniform clung to her taut, supple muscles, leaving no doubt as to her physical prowess. The wizardess wondered briefly if the *shinobi*'s life had been as difficult as hers.

Worse, probably, she thought. *She ended up here.*

"Who was the man in Kirishima? Your lover?"

The pendulum stopped.

"He was my everything."

"I'm sorry. It was the heat of the battle."

"Enough."

There was a barely noticeable flinch in the assassin's stance; she was ready to strike. Satō focused on the single point at the end of her sword. She felt the energies of the island go through her like freezing winter wind. The countless, ancient spirits of those who had died in the many battles fought over the Kanmon Strait; and the new, evil force brought on by the Crimson Robe's dark deeds. She knew now why he had banned anyone else from using magic here – and what power had been calling her to the island: his presence alone made it a miniature magical nexus, the *mogelijkheit* of the place almost as strong in its concentration as the Takachiho Mountain.

354

She no longer needed to speak out the spells. She didn't even need to use the needle in her glove: all the power of her blood, that trickling down her knee, the one making her left palm slippery or that running through her veins, was now at her disposal. In the darkness of the narrow corridor, she and the blade became one; a streamlined conduit of magic. Her senses sharpened, her movements magically enhanced.

For a brief moment, in a flash of concentration, the wizardess saw the world the way the Scryers saw it. She saw all the points in time, all the possible outcomes of the duel. At last, before what might have been her final battle, she became what Takashima Shūhan had wanted her to be; the samurai wizard.

And when the *shinobi*'s sickle blade struck for the first time – her sword was already there.

The winding corridor was eerily quiet. On one side there were rooms Nagomi dared not enter, on the other it ran along the back garden. Lightning flashes painted the shadows of the trees on the semi-translucent paper windows. The monotonous noise of the rain shrouded the faint sound of blades clashing back in the mansion where Satō fought her deadly duel. The smell of freshly blooming peonies lingered in the heavy air, seeping through the cracks in the wall.

Nagomi touched her way forward; the corridor turned left, then right, then split in two opposite directions. The wall in front of her was made of solid oaken planks, and there was nothing on either side that could help her choose.

She pulled the Spirit Light and studied the way the orange flame danced in the beaker. A sudden chilling gust of wind blew from the right-hand wing, bending the flame. She turned there and, after twenty paces, she reached a dead end; the same plain oaken wall. She was ready to turn back, but the cold wind made the orange light flicker again – and it seemed to be seeping *from the wall*.

She could hear steps running towards her from the other end of the corridor: guards, she guessed. She moved the dancing beaker up and down the wall, looking for the source of the draught. There was a narrow slit in one of the planks. She drew Satō's dagger and pushed it in. Something clicked, and the wall slid open, revealing a cold, narrow, stone staircase leading straight down, into even blacker darkness.

Hearing the guards approaching the place where the corridor split, Nagomi took a deep breath and stepped onto the first stair. The wall slid noiselessly behind her.

There were no more doors to pass. The staircase led her to a long hallway lined with flat slabs of white stone. A hundred or so paces later, she reached a large square room with walls and floor of the same material, made bright by a single flaming brazier.

A broad ramp led out of the room on the opposite side; between this puzzling gateway and Nagomi stood a huge, ornate, steel-walled box, with only a narrow opening at the top.

The priestess felt a paralyzing fear creeping over her, as if oozing from the box. Her knees buckled under her and her teeth chattered. She hugged the Spirit Light close and withdrew until her back touched the cold stone wall.

What monster is this…?

And then she remembered. She had seen this place before – in a dream, in Kagoshima.

Emris! I found Bran's dragon!

Gathering all her courage she stepped forward.

Maybe if I could open it… I could release it? Would that help?

She touched the steel wall. It was cold and vibrating slowly as the beast within breathed. It belonged to a Fanged – how would a demon like that make sure only he could open the container? She looked the box over, pressed and pushed the coiling, snake-shaped carvings, tugged and pulled on the runed walls, all to no avail.

What trickery or magic would he use?

Then she had an idea. She took a hairpin and pricked her finger. A large drop of blood appeared at the tip. She pressed it against the wall of the box. The metal glowed purple for a moment, absorbing the red liquid, but nothing else happened.

Not enough, she thought desperately. She took the dagger and slashed her left palm deeply. She cried out; it hurt and bled a lot more than she expected; a thick stream of red liquid trickled down her wrist and forearm.

Suddenly, she felt she had become the focus of somebody's attention. The torch light dimmed, the air grew cold and stale; Nagomi's breath quickened. The primeval fear she had felt before was replaced by the terror of the Otherworld. Drawn to the blood like hungry *koi* fish in the shrine pond, malevolent, tortured spirits were swirling all around her. She put her palms together and spoke a quick prayer with trembling lips. Her hands glowed with weak blue light, and the air nearest her cleared enough so she could breathe freely again.

In a hurry she smeared as much of the blood as she could onto the surface of the metal box. The wall glowed again in the shape of a magic rune, much brighter this time, and something inside clicked.

Clutching her bleeding hand, Nagomi opened the door. A wave of hot, stale air rushed from the inside, as if from a furnace. She saw the shadow of a massive, heavily breathing beast. This was the first time she had seen the *dorako* up close. She had never imagined anything so big could live on land, much less fly. The beast lay asleep, bound in thick steel chains.

Strangely, now that she could see the dragon, her fear lessened. The evil spirits perished, as if unable to withstand the monster's presence. The priestess approached the beast closer. Its scales were warm to touch and smelled of brimstone. She studied the chain and discovered it was all one length of metal links, wrapped around the beast's body, with no padlock or knot. She pulled on it with all her might, but it didn't budge. The sleeping dragon growled and shuddered. Its claws contracted, scratching the iron floor of the box. She jumped away.

A distant thunder rolled above, its rumble reaching the underground room magnified by the echo. The dragon stirred and the snake eyes flashed open. Fear was beginning to grip her in its cold grasp again; the dragon's jaws could easily snap her in half, its claws shred her to pieces...

But she didn't step back. She watched the monster stand up shakily. With a shrug of its massive shoulders and flap of muscular wings, it ripped both the chain and the steel box apart as if they were made of paper.

The priestess was resolved to die.

With dorako *at Bran's side, the battle is as good as won.*

She closed her eyes and felt the dragon come closer.

Seconds passed and nothing happened. Surprised, she opened her eyes; the dragon gazed at her patiently. It lowered its neck beside her.

"You... you want me to...?"

The dragon snorted. Nagomi clumsily mounted the beast's neck. Not sure what to hold on to, she grabbed one of the long, sharp horns protruding from the dragon's head. As soon as she did that, Emrys turned and shot through the ramp, into the stormy night outside.

THE RISING TIDE

CHAPTER XVIII

"Wake up, boy!"

A nagging voice prodded Bran slowly into consciousness. His first feeling was a strange, numbing pain, difficult to localize.

"Careful. Don't open your eyes yet."

"Why…?"

"I can sense He's near. Pretend you're still asleep."

"It hurts…"

Bran twitched his hands and felt thin blades piercing deep into the skin on his forearms and shoulders. Something sharp was stuck in his neck as well, pulsating in the rhythm of his heart.

He half-opened one eye. His head was spinning. He was sitting in a high metal chair in a small room, encircled by bright candles. Bronze needles and tubes of oiled canvas were sticking out of his arm. Spiked bracelets kept his wrists and ankles safely in place.

He couldn't see much else without opening his eyes fully; but he could sense a dark, cold presence in the room.

361

"This room feels exactly like that place above the heretics' town," observed Shigemasa.

"He's draining me…"

"He's changing you into one of his own!"

Bran strained to focus; with clenched fists and gritted teeth, he summoned a *buckler* along his left arm. He gasped as the magic shield cut through the tubes and tore the needles out of his body. Blood spurted from the open vein.

"You're awake," a freezing voice spoke. Bran opened his eyes fully. The Crimson Robe was sitting cross-legged on the floor before him, outside the circle of candles, underneath a fresco of an eight-headed serpent outlined with black paint on the clay-daubed wall. He held the glowing orb of red crystal in his hand. The great two-handed sword lay by his right side – and Bran's Prydain blade at his left, along with the satchel and all the items from inside were laid out neatly, the blue ring among them. The Fanged was studying the medallion with great interest when he noticed Bran stir and gasp.

"Fascinating," he said. "I wonder just how much she told your grandfather."

How does he know?

The Crimson Robe gestured at somebody beyond Bran's field of view. Something moved, slithering and shuffling in the periphery of his vision, a bright orange robe on a dark, withered body; an odd smell of lacquers and essential oils licked his nostrils. A skeletal hand, covered with dried up skin, browned with age, picked up the needles and tubes from the floor and hovered over Bran's arm, still protected by the *bwcler*.

"You can't keep that shield forever," the Crimson Robe said. "How do you like my chair? It's an old Western design. Vasconian, I believe."

A Roman device! A remnant of the Wizardry Wars.

The Fanged was right – Bran could feel power flow from his veins along with the blood, and through the wounds inflicted by the bronze spikes on his hands and legs. Even a powerful wizard would not last long in this trap.

But I'm not a wizard, thought Bran. The Crimson Robe did not know everything. Bran was a dragon rider; the source of his power was his mount. And Emrys was somewhere near. He could feel it again, just as close as in Kirishima. And just like then, despite the same veil, the envelope of dark energy separating them, the dragon's life energy flowed towards him – a narrow trickle but enough to sustain whatever the chair drained from him.

There was something else, very faint under all the layers of spent energy, hunger, and fear; an undercurrent of longing, like a sad, wistful song hummed in the distance; the dragon was lonely and miserable. These weren't the feelings of a *feral* beast at all!

"Why are you smiling?" the Crimson Robe asked, irritation slipping into his voice. Bran became serious. The Fanged stood up, picking up Bran's sword and weighing it in his hand. The runes on the blade glowed a sickly pale blue.

Theatrics.

"Tell me, have you come here to *duel* me, boy? Sword against sword?" The Fanged raised his eyebrow in mocking surprise. "You would die in one second from my swallow-tail cut," he said with a sneer.

Bran recognized this sneer. It was the sneer of one who believes himself superior to all around him. Wulfhere and his bullies always sported this grimace on their pure-blood Seaxe faces; always stronger, faster and more self-confident than Bran. But this time, there would be no teachers coming to help, no roofs to leap from...

"What's the matter, boy? Fear got your tongue?" Crimson Robe said in the prolonged silence.

He dismissed the creature holding the tubes and needles and stepped forward. Bran said nothing. He was breathing heavily, his mind focused.

Just a little bit closer...

Ganryū leaned over to examine the contraption. Bran rejoiced quietly in his confusion – and what he was sensing from Emrys. The dragon finally noticed his rider's presence; the sad song turned into one of joy and welcome. The link wasn't yet strong enough to summon the Dragonform, but maybe...

The Crimson Robe straightened, his golden eyes studying the boy with annoyed curiosity.

"Why are you – "

"*Rhew!*"

A narrow, blade-like tongue of dragon flame burst from Bran's open palm. The Fanged covered his face with the wide sleeve of his robe. Fire enveloped him, as Bran continued to feed it with the dragon's energy. The bluish flame poured ceaselessly from the outstretched hand. At last, when he was certain that no thing, living or dead, could survive so much heat, the boy let go, exhausted.

The scorched remains of the robe fell to the floor. Ganryū's skin peeled off in burned patches, the ends of his black hair were singed white. The sickly-sweet stench of charred flesh and boiled blood filled the room. But the Fanged was still alive. He spat out bits of flesh and loose teeth.

"You ruined my robe, Barbarian. It will take a lot of blood to dye a new one."

At the flick of his fingers, the straps and bracelets snapped open. He dropped the sword with a clang and raised Bran from the chair by the neck.

His eyes turned black, his fangs glistened.

"I will drink you dry, and then move on to your friends. I will leave the priestess for last, so she can watch you *all* die."

The boy lifted his head and looked straight into the demon's jet-black eyes.

"Fooled you."

For a moment, Ganryū's eyes reverted to gold as he looked at the boy with confusion. Bran pressed his right palm against the Fanged's chest. The blade of the Soul Lance pierced the demon through.

"*Gwrthyrru!*"

The spell ran down the lance; the push threw Ganryū ten feet back against the wall. The red jewel dropped from his hand and rolled off into the corner of the room. Bran fell to the floor, his consciousness slipping away.

The Fanged shook his head, half-stunned, and jumped at the boy with a furious snarl.

"You'll pay for this!" he yowled and Bran felt a terrible, paralysing pain he didn't know existed as fangs tore his skin and hot blood gushed from a vein. Ganryū lapped it up and spat it out in Bran's face.

"Just as I thought, disgusting. Now I'll have to drink a Yamato girl to get rid of the taste."

He stood up.

My shirt's all wet, the boy thought, dying.

And then the roof exploded.

The dragon carried Nagomi high into the storm; she held on for dear life to his scaly neck, swathed in the beast's hot, brimstone-smelling breath, too scared to open her eyes. After a few seconds, however, the fear passed, replaced by a rush of excitement. She looked down at the mansion and the garden below her and laughed. She had never experienced anything more exhilarating than this.

"*Bran!*" she remembered. The dragon roared and banked sideways, almost dropping her; she grabbed the horns at the beast's neck.

"I'm sorry if it hurts," she said, but the dragon paid no attention. It swooped down towards a small square building in the middle of the garden, the size of a tea pavilion.

The dragon landed, crushing a wall and part of the roof with its weight, its wings spanning almost an entire length of the hut. It lowered its neck so that Nagomi could slide off it to the floor, trembling. She stepped over what looked like a pile of bones wrapped in skin, covered in a monk's robe, half-crushed by the rubble, and looked around.

It took her a few seconds to guess that the tall, half-burned, naked man standing over Bran's mangled body was the Crimson Robe himself. The demon cursed and looked around the room, barely noticing the dragon. A large round jewel, glowing weak red, lay in the corner. Nagomi recognized it in an instant.

What through blood stone can you see?

Emrys roared and spat a lash of flame, but failed to stop the Fanged from reaching the stone. The stench was sickening. The demon's hand was now little more than strips of fried meat hanging off the bones, but there were enough muscles and tendons still left for him to grab the jewel strongly. The jewel shone blood red.

The dragon flapped its wings and breathed fire again, but something was wrong. It swayed from side to side; for a moment the beast rose, towering over the Fanged, but then it dropped to the ground with a fleshy thud.

The Fanged stared at Nagomi with eyes black as night.

"*You.*" He drew and pointed his great sword at her. He seemed to have no difficulty wielding it with only one hand.

The discarded scabbard clanged on the stone floor. "I know you. You saw me take the orb from Mekari."

She stepped back.

The Prophecy. It was him!

She thought about the glowing white light she had summoned during the sea crossing; the pain it had caused Master Dōraku...

But before she could even start the chant, the Crimson Robe leapt across the room with inhuman speed and landed several feet from her, raising his two-handed sword. She cowered before the falling blade.

Time slowed down to a crawl. A humming noise filled Bran's ears, and milky white mist shrouded the world around him.

He felt dirt under his feet. He stooped down and picked up a handful. It was the colour of iron ore; he was somewhere on the red-dirt plain again.

He wandered blindly through the mist until the ground beneath his feet started to rise. He found himself on a hill top. There were other peaks rising from the white mist, and an entire mountain range on the horizon.

A wind blew, parting a tunnel in the mist. Somebody was coming through.

"*Taishō!*" Bran shouted. The General picked up the pace, climbing up the hill the boy was standing on.

"You've made it here, boy," he said.

"Where is *here?*"

"This is the place you wanted to see. Where the Spirits dwell."

"You mean I'm... dead?"

"Not yet. Then you'd be beyond those mountains," the General said, pointing to the jagged peaks. "But you've not long to go."

"But I can't die... I need to save Emrys! And Nagomi... and Satō... everyone's relying on me!"

"Calm down, boy. I'm not looking forward to spending eternity on this island. The wights of *Dan-no-Ura* make for poor companions. I'm here to help you."

"Can you really do that? Can you bring me back from the dead?"

"I told you, you're not dead yet! First, we need to find your beast. Can you sense where it is?"

Bran closed his eyes and focused as he had done so many times before. Instantly, he picked up a faint buzz.

"Over there," he said, pointing towards a nearby hill, split in two by a dark gorge.

The phantom Emrys waited for Bran at the saddle of the gorge, sitting on hind legs bent like a sphinx, wings spread wide on the ground.

Its sage eyes followed the boy as he neared the beast cautiously. Bran reached out his hand, but the dragon flapped its wings and leapt aside.

"What's wrong, Emrys?"

He ran up to it again, and again the dragon raised its wings. Bran jumped and grabbed the horns on its neck; the beast whinnied and shook its head up, glaring at the rider with mad, bulging eyes, like a frightened horse.

"Ease!" cried Bran, sending soothing thoughts through Farlink. "Ease, Emrys!"

But the beast was in panic. It launched into the air with Bran clutching at the horns. Bran managed to hook a leg around its neck and gain a firmer grip. He could feel his signals reaching the dragon, but there was no response.

"Perhaps it doesn't want you to fly it," cried Shigemasa, observing the scene from a safe distance.

"What do you mean?"

The General shrugged. "It's your mount."

Bran clung to the dragon's green scales with his entire body and dug deep into the beast's mind, past all the barriers and past the dumb, beastly bewilderment.

Like a jewel hidden in the darkness, Bran found the dragon's true feelings. The connection was still there, faint and erratic; the beast had fought hunger, exhaustion and its feral nature, still loyal, still, amazingly, steadfast and obedient. Just as it had always been – ever since Bran had got the ring …

The ring.

Bran looked at his hand. The blue stone was missing again.

What does that mean?

And then it dawned on him. The ring he got from Lord Shimazu was a fake; a forgery. That's why he wasn't able to use it anymore.

Of course. He's keeping the stone for himself. But that means…

He remembered the first time he had flown Emrys; it was just a brief flight over the Caer Wyddno; he'd flown above the town earlier, with Dylan, so he hadn't thought anything would surprise him. But the way the wind felt around him that day, the exhilaration of altitude and speed, the freedom, it was like nothing he had ever dreamt of before. It had taken Bran just a few flights like that to establish a strong, special bond with the jade green dragon.

Dylan had always dismissed his story as fanciful.

"You were just an impressionable child," he'd say. *"No rider your age had ever achieved a Farlink. You were imagining things."*

Did I have my ring then, on that first flight? He tried to remember. No, he wouldn't have got it for at least a year.

The beast flew on its own over hundreds of miles of featureless sea in search of Bran. It struggled to find his rider and remain in contact through weeks of entrapment and bondage. This connection was not the result of some magic stone. There was no other dragon like Emrys. And Bran wanted to repay this loyalty. He had crossed an unknown land, fought powerful enemies, all to find and free Emrys from its shackles.

"I will not give up yet," he whispered and closed his eyes.

He sensed an impulse coming now from the phantom dragon, almost a message; Emrys was *telling him what to do*.

"Dragon Form? Here? Now? But... Oh, I see. *Y Ddraig Ffurf!*"

He felt his body disappear, melt and fuse with that of the phantom jade dragon.

Bran saw Ganryū's blade fall on the priestess and shot his head forward; he wanted to bite the Fanged through, but miscalculated and instead punched him through the wall into the garden outside.

Bran leapt after him. Unused to having wings, and struggling to stay aloft, he swayed from side to side. His claws caught in the rubble and tumbled down. He shook his head, stunned, but picked himself up. He saw Ganryū stare at the gem in his hand in surprise and disgust, trying to comprehend why it didn't have any effect on the dragon.

"No matter," the Fanged decided. "I don't need *this* to kill you all."

He let go of the gem and grasped the sword in two hands, raising it flat above his head.

The boy spewed fire. The pure dragon flame was nothing like the poor imitation Bran had tried before. Hot like the Sun itself, it burned the rest of the skin and flesh off of Ganryū. What stood now in the garden was a blackened skeleton covered with patches of scorched muscles and tendons, staring at the dragon from empty eye sockets. But the Curse still powered the Fanged, and he still held the sword firmly with blazing hands.

"Is that all you've got?" the lipless mouth said and laughed. Bran heard in the voice the buzz of the Otherworld he had heard a long time ago in the roar of the skeleton dragon. Ganryū leapt high and struck. Bran dodged, but the sword grazed his neck, cutting through the celadon scales. The wound burned as if doused with acid.

A magic blade! I must be more careful.

He leapt into the air and flapped his wings a few times to stay aloft. The chaotic Ninth Wind of the island buffeted him about, like a paper toy. He swooped down and snapped his jaws, but Ganryū rolled safely aside and Bran's teeth only caught dirt. He flew back up but not before the magic blade struck again, leaving a deep, bleeding gash.

Ganryū could not reach him in the air, but Bran did not dare to get close to the great sword. His flame could not cause the Fanged any more harm. It was stalemate.

Nagomi lifted Bran's head; he was covered in his own blood and there was no heartbeat in his chest. A torn, gaping wound on his neck left no doubts to his fate. The dragon rider was dead.

She did not cry. All the despair and panic floated away, leaving just an empty shell behind. Her mind withdrew, fleeing from all the pain and suffering. The world around her turned hazy, distant.

A streak of white fur leapt out from the mist. A white fox coiled around her legs and nudged her sleeve with its long, slender nose. Nagomi stood up and pulled the Spirit Light from within the folds of her priestly robe. The orange flame burst brightly, clearing the darkness.

Bran heard a beautiful chant coming from the pavilion. He looked down and squinted, the dragon's eyes blinded by the bright white light. Nagomi's voice, clear, pure and strong, filled the garden. Her skin glowed with the sacred light, reflecting the one dancing in the clay beaker she was holding. Her body was ablaze; she was a naked pillar of light. The white flame surrounded her and spread in a spherical wave, her copper hair raised by the hot wind. The sphere grew, encompassing the entire pavilion and the garden around it, until it reached Ganryū. The Fanged cried out in pain, dropped his sword and covered his ears.

"The screech! Make it stop!"

He stepped back.

"It burns!"

But it was too late. His body froze as the divine whirlwind of light and fire tore into the bones, causing him to howl in agony. He reached out the skeletal hand at Bran.

"Make. It. Stop."

The smouldering knuckles clenched into a fist as the Fanged gathered all his remaining power and struck back. The holy flame withered, pushed away by the darkness of his cursed soul.

374

The chanting stopped; Bran heard her abrupt cry, the sound of shattering clay, and felt himself torn away from the dragon back into his own body.

The world was bathed in dazzling, warm light. The white haze receded only enough for him to see outlines of what was going on around him. His body was strangely weightless, wispy and... fragrant? There was no mistake, his skin – strangely pale, glowing white – smelled of cherry blossom and incense. The walls of the pavilion – what was still left of them – were shattered and half-melted, as if after some enormous explosion.

"Focus, boy. You have not won the fight yet," a familiar voice spoke beside Bran. The General's spirit hovered in the air the same way it did back at the straits.

"Pick up the sword," the old ghost ordered. "Kill Ganryū."

"But..."

"Trust me. Pierce him with your blade."

The boy picked up his weapon and stepped over a smouldering crossbeam into the garden. The Fanged turned his attention from fighting off Emrys and stared at Bran, nuggets of gold gleaming within the terrifying, scorched skull.

"You're only prolonging the inevitable, boy. You can't kill me. Nobody can kill me!"

He let another cone of dragon flame wash over his charred bones and raised his *nodachi* sword at the boy.

"Can't you see? You will all die here. You, your beast and your little priestess."

Bran grabbed the sword's hilt with two hands and, with a desperate cry, charged and thrust it straight into Ganryū's chest.

The blade wedged between the ribs where the creature's heart would have been if it hadn't already turned to ash, and Bran had to let it go to dodge the edge of the *nodachi* falling beside his head. Ganryū gloated, but the laughter died in his throat.

The General, a pale white waft of smoke, a phantom of mist and vapour clad in ghostly armour, appeared beside Ganryū, reached for the sword and wrapped his hands on the hilt.

"Your Curse, demon. I will take it upon myself. It's the only way."

"No! You can't..." cried the Fanged, but it was too late. The sword in his chest turned black. Ganryū fell to his knees.

"No!" he repeated defiantly.

He looked past Bran, towards the mansion gate where Dōraku stood, observing the scene in silence, his two swords dripping with blood.

"Shinmen..." Ganryū whispered, "...you are... late... again."

His skull cracked and shattered, and he crumbled to the floor in pile of ash and loose, old bones.

The General's spirit beamed with heavenly radiance, and his ghostly face was, at long last, content and fulfilled.

"Farewell Bran ap Dylan gan Cantre'r Gwaelod. You are a real samurai now. Take care of Yamato for me."

"Farewell, Itakura Shigemasa-*dono*."

The spirit vanished in a haze of wisps and a twirl of raindrops.

"Emrys," Bran commanded. "I know you can hear me now. Come to me."

The dragon landed before Bran. It was wounded in several places. Thick, dark red blood oozed where Ganryū's blade cut the deepest. Bran touched the dragon's warm scales. Emrys purred with joy. At long last, they were united.

Bran's world swirled and turned cold, empty and dark.

Drops of icy rain fell on his face. Bran was lying on the wet, muddy ground. When he opened his eyes, he saw Emrys leaning above him. The beast nudged him with its warm nose like a worried dog.

"It's all right. I'm all right," he croaked, reaching out to pat the beast's snout.

Somehow, Ganryū's crystal orb was in Bran's hand. Its surface, smooth like glass, was cooling rapidly, but still warm to touch. He hid it inside the sleeve.

He stood up slowly, achingly, and looked around. In front of him was the wicket gate where Dōraku had held back the entire army of Ganryū's students. There was blood and gore everywhere, slowly washed away into the gutters by the rain. Corpses, whole and hacked, entire body parts and bits and pieces, slashed away by the Fanged's blades.

Bile rose inside his throat as the morbid smell of death and flesh penetrated his nostrils, mixed with the heavy, damp scent of rain and salty sea air. He bent forward and retched. He felt sorry for the warriors. They were followers of his enemy, and as such, his enemies; but, in a way, they got involved in this battle where they stood no chance. So many of them had perished without even learning the name of a man who killed them.

Those who remained alive were now standing in a half-circle around Bran and his dragon, grim and defeated, rain trickling down their lowered heads, their weapons thrown down in hopeless surrender. The dragon rider could not look into their sullen eyes for long.

Turning around, he saw Dōraku standing beside Emrys, silent, his face a featureless mask, the rain washing away any signs of battle. The Fanged held unconscious Nagomi in his arms. She seemed as faint as after Kirishima, but her skin had a healthy glow and there were no visible injuries.

Torishi and Satō walked slowly from the direction of the mansion. The bear-man glanced at the boy, but if he was surprised to see his Prydain face, he didn't show it. The wizardess limped, supporting herself on Torishi's shoulder. Her *hakama* was soaked in blood, her face covered in bruises and cuts.

"You're alive!" shouted Bran. His heart felt suddenly lighter. "I thought –"

He stopped, seeing another man appearing from behind, a hairy giant similar in gait and posture to Torishi. His skin was slashed and torn, but he stood straight and looked the boy proudly in the eyes.

Bran rushed to help the wizardess down the path. She smiled at him weakly, absent-mindedly.

"Who's that?" He nodded at the giant.

"One of Ganryū's men," she replied.

"I have no reason to fight you anymore," the hairy giant said. "I will depart for the North tomorrow."

"Are we letting him go?" Bran asked Torishi.

"He fought honourably," replied the bear-man, "in defence of his Master. Why should I begrudge him?"

"How's Nagomi?" asked Satō.

"She seems fine. We won. And we're all alive."

"We're all alive," repeated Satō in disbelief.

THE RISING TIDE

CHAPTER XIX

Azumi parted the azalea bush and looked carefully around. A blue magpie screeched in the hydrangeas. It was dawning.

She had the right to feel angry, robbed of her right to avenge Ozun. But she knew she had been almost unbelievably lucky. Not only did she manage to survive meeting that terrible man with twin blades again and flee, the intruders succeeded in *destroying* the Crimson Robe!

She always sensed the plan was too complicated to succeed; she had been telling him that all the time.

"Why not just kill them all when they arrive?" she boggled.

"The boy is the prize," the Crimson Robe had explained. "I need him alive, and separated from Dōraku and the priestess. Without them, he'll be helpless."

She shook her head; *everything went wrong.* The dragon broke free. The priestess reached the boy in time. And then the unthinkable happened: the Curse had been reversed... it seemed these children were indeed favoured by the Gods.

And now she was free, released from the Fanged's dark grip. She could start her life anew...

Without Ozun.

The Master's death meant the *yamabushi* could no longer be brought to life. But –

There is another Fanged. The one with two blades, Dōraku. And where there were two, there could've been more.

What did Shō say before he died? "I serve one of the Eight Heads."

Ganryū's banner. Eight-headed Serpent. A faint hope quickened her breath.

They will send somebody here to investigate, she thought. *They will be looking for survivors…*

She picked up the basket containing Ozun's head, tied it onto her back and stepped onto the garden path. After a few steps she stumbled over something. A pile of blackened bones and the charred and twisted remains of a sword still smouldering with dark vapours and glowing a faint, ghostly light. Some remnant of the battle. She picked it up carefully through her sleeve; it pulsated with heat.

This is bound to attract their attention.

Azumi moved stealthily through the garden, around the mansion and onto the courtyard, hiding among the target dummies. She passed a group of grey-clad *rōnin* sitting on the wet ground in the rain. They weren't even tied up; the Swordsman's watchful eye was enough to keep them from running away.

The Fanged turned around and faced Azumi.

He can see me, she realized; her hair stood on end. There was no way she could hide from those golden eyes. Had he interrupted her duel with the wizard girl the night before only to feed on her now?

But the Swordsman made no move.

He's... letting me go!

She ran the rest of the way, across the courtyard and through the thicket separating the secret cove from the rest of the island. Through an opening in the ochre wall she saw five of Ganryū's students rowing the small boat out into the sea; there was no other way off the island. She picked up the pace. They spotted her, but did not stop. One of them turned towards the shore – she recognized Hajime by his broken nose, the leader of the Crimson Robe's assault squad, and his finest student. He stood up on the stern and watched her wade in the shallows after the boat. Salt water attacked her wounds with a thousand needles and clawed its way into her eyes. Blinded and in pain, she tripped; the weight of the basket on her back pushed her down and the sea closed over her head.

A strong hand grabbed her and pulled her, bubbling and struggling onto the boat.

"Stop making so much noise," the leader barked. "For an assassin, you're terribly clumsy."

Bran finished bandaging Satō's left forearm. It was one of the many wounds she had suffered in the duel. He wrapped the girl's hand in an herbal poultice, prepared by Torishi to draw out any poison, and tightened the linen wrappings. The girl hissed.

"Careful!"

"I'm sorry. I've always been clumsy with this sort of thing. How's the leg?"

"A little better, but it hurts when I walk. What about you? You're not looking so great yourself. Your neck…"

"I'll be fine," he said. "Just a little sore."

He rubbed the great, ugly torn scar running across his neck and collar-bone. Nagomi's light had brought him to life and healed the shattered muscles and tendons, but was not enough to restore the mutilated skin torn by the cursed claws and fangs.

"Dōraku says it may never heal," he added. "But I don't care. I'm just glad to be alive. Nagomi's not going to be sleeping for three days again, is she?"

"She woke up. What exactly happened up there?"

"I… I'm not sure. It was all like a dream. She channelled tremendous amounts of power. Brought me back to life, held Ganryū enthralled…"

"I can't believe she got to ride the *dorako*. Remember, you promised to take me too!"

"I know." Bran nodded. His head remained in the nod a little too long; a lump grew in his throat.

"Let's go see Nagomi," he said, standing up quickly.

They walked across the gravel courtyard arm in arm; Bran thought she was squeezing him a little bit tighter than was needed just to support herself – but couldn't tell for sure. Ganryū's students were digging graves for their slain comrades under Torishi's command. Bran remembered the dozens of hacked corpses lying on the dirt in a pool of blood.

I don't think I'll be able to forget it.

Satō stopped before the nearest set of graves and bowed.

"They fought bravely. They deserve respect," she said.

Bran bowed too, but out of pity he was feeling for every life lost during their quest.

Respect? They served a blood-thirsty demon and were willing to die for his sake. They were stupid or greedy. I have no respect for any of them.

"What happened to the *kunoichi* woman?" he asked.

Satō shrugged.

"She fled when Dōraku-*sama* arrived. She must have got off the island in one of the morning boats."

"You don't know? What if she's still hiding somewhere?"

Satō shook her head. "It's over, Bran. Don't worry."

They entered one of the low stone houses Dōraku had commandeered into an infirmary.

"How do you feel?" Bran asked, sitting down by the priestess's bed. She was wrapped in Satō's travel cloak and a thin blanket.

385

"I feel... strange. Weak. It's not a bad feeling though, more like... when you sit in a nice hot bath for too long and it wears you out. I'm all warm inside."

"What do you remember?"

"Not much... I was in a world of bright white fog..."

The Otherworld.

"You saved us all. You saved me," said Bran. "I... don't know how to thank you."

"It wasn't me... it was the power of the *kami* —" Nagomi gasped and reached her hand to touch Bran's face. Her hand was warm.

"You look —!"

Bran nodded.

"Itakura Shigemasa-*dono* is no more. Without him, I have no power to change the way I look."

"What are you going to do now?" asked Nagomi. "You will be arrested the moment we get off this island."

"Arrested?" Satō laughed. "He's got a *dragon* now — I don't think he has to worry about *Taikun's* men."

"I haven't thought of all that yet," Bran answered. "Everything's still... for now we all need to rest, bathe, eat," he added with a forced smile.

"A bath!" Satō clapped her hands. "Where do you think it is?"

"I'll go ask Dōraku. I needed to talk to him about something anyway."

386

He found the Fanged alone in a shack by the training grounds, sitting by a low table, smoking his long pipe and browsing through some papers.

Dōraku looked at Bran curiously.

"You can't change anymore," he said.

"No. That's gone with the *Taishō*."

"But you still speak our language."

"It seems I haven't forgotten anything."

The Swordsman nodded. "That's something, at least. How are the others?"

"They're all fine, I guess. They could use a bath, though. And some more food."

"There's a kitchen for the guards," Dōraku pointed to a small building, plastered white, "and a bathhouse attached to it. What about your *dorako*?"

"It's fine too. The wounds heal fast. It killed one of our horses, I'm afraid. I'm really sorry about that..."

The Fanged nodded.

"Sad, but understandable. The beast must not have eaten for days."

Bran scratched his cheek.

"I thought one of your kind cannot be killed."

Dōraku put the pipe away.

"Yes, who would've thought that would work? Another soul taking the Curse upon itself voluntarily…"

It must have given even you a fright.

"What will happen to Ganryū's men?" asked Bran.

"Left or preparing to leave. As soon as we finish the burials. I let them go, save for a few who will carry the wounded. There's a supply ship coming in today from Kokura, it should take the rest of them to the mainland."

"And the Ogasawara Clan? You said it's their land…"

"We'll be out of here before they get curious. Don't worry, boy, I'm sure the Ogasawaras will soon have more important things to lose sleep over. As will everyone else in Yamato. I read through some of these papers," Dōraku said, gesturing to a pile of documents before him. "I fear there may be no stopping the war after all."

"What are these?"

"Letters and documents from Ganryū's private chest. I hope they will give me some clues as to what the others are planning."

"The others – you mean the Eight-headed Serpent?"

"You remembered," said Dōraku with a smile and tapped his pipe on the table.

"So they are not a spent force after all."

"No, I suppose not. They must be hoping to gain something from the approaching chaos."

You knew all the time.

"Will this help?" Bran took the red gem from his sleeve. "I wish I knew what it really was."

Dōraku turned the jewel in his fingers, puffing the pipe.

"They call these the Tide Jewels. They are as old as Yamato, if not more. Each holds a different power; I don't know what this one did exactly, apart from apparently being able to influence your *dorako*. Heishichi-*sama* will know more."

The Swordsman handed the orb back to Bran, but the boy refused it.

"It's yours," said Dōraku. "Think of it as the spoils of war."

"I have no need for it. If you don't want it, give it to… Satō."

The Fanged put down the papers and stared at Bran in silence.

"I had hoped you would at least take some time to rest," he said at last.

"I've made my decision. The longer I stay, the more painful it will be for me to leave – and the more chance you have to convince me otherwise."

"Have you told the girls?"

Bran shook his head. "No. But I can't stay here. Do you understand?"

The Fanged nodded.

"This is not my home. This is not my world! And now I can't even disguise myself as one of you anymore. I have to go back."

"You don't have to explain. Are you leaving right now?"

"Yes. I have everything prepared."

"Do you know the way?"

"I know where West is."

The Fanged shook his head. "You'd soon get lost in the open sea. Here, take this," he said, giving Bran a rolled piece of paper.

"I found it in the chest along with the letters. It's a map drawn in Western style. I wish I knew how Ganryū came into its possession."

Bran unrolled the scroll.

"We are here." Dōraku pointed to a spot on the map between two of the largest islands. "You should go south-west along the coast – that way you'll have navigation points all along your route. Then when you get to Hirado turn due west, crossing the Divine Winds – hopefully – until you get to Tamna Island – that's Chosun land, but remote and sparsely populated. It's only a hundred *ri* from there to Qin."

"What's this?" Bran lifted a piece of paper which had fallen from the map as it was unrolled. The Fanged glanced at it.

"It's the copy of a missive from the *Taikun*'s High Council."

"And how did Ganryū get *that?*"

"Good question. The Serpent must have spies high in Edo. The letter is not a day old."

"Won't you need it?"

"I know what it says. But it might be of interest to your people."

Bran rolled the letter and the map and opened his satchel to put them in. This reminded him of something.

He took the medallion out and showed it to Dōraku.

"Did you know her?"

The Fanged studied the thaumaturgic image.

"Who's Ifor?"

"My grandfather."

"Your grandfather, eh? And he was…?"

"A sailor on MS Phaeton. They met in Kiyō."

"What strange fate."

It looked like Dōraku wanted to add something else, but he must have changed his mind for he just smiled wistfully.

"Then I guessed right – you knew her."

"I helped her flee Ganryū. Last I saw her she was safe at Dejima."

"So you didn't know the Crimson Robe found her eventually? That he attacked Dejima?"

Dōraku shook his head. "I was… otherwise occupied. What happened to her?"

Bran felt strange describing the events of the past to this being, so much older and wiser than himself.

You always seem to know everything.

"MS Phaeton arrived in Kiyō at the same time; she fled on board. I think she sailed to Prydain with my grandfather."

The Swordsman let out a short laugh.

"I wish I could have seen Ganryū's face."

"Why was he after her?" asked Bran.

"She was the last guardian of the Shard of Fukuchiyama."

"The Shard of – you mean my ring?"

Dōraku nodded.

"It was a part of some powerful artefact Ganryū was trying to collect. Another Tide Jewel, perhaps. He always chased after trinkets like these – and that was reason enough for me to try and stop him."

It's obviously more than just some trinket, Bran thought. *The daimyo of Kumamoto wanted it as well, and now…*

"Now Nariakira-*sama* has it."

"So the copy didn't fool you for long. We couldn't risk it falling into wrong hands, you understand…"

"I don't really care." Bran waved his hand.

This is not my war.

"The stone belongs here, in Yamato," he said. "To me it was just a memory of my grandfather. This will suffice," he added, shaking the medallion. "I must be going now."

Dōraku stood up and the boy bowed. The samurai bowed back and reached his hand out to Bran.

"I know this is how you Westerners bid farewell. Farewell, Bran-Karasu-*sama*."

The boy shook the Swordsman's hand.

"Farewell Dōraku-*sama*. Tell Nagomi and Satō, I..." Bran fought back tears welling up in his eyes. He shook his head. "No, don't tell them anything. I hope they will understand."

Shakushain stood among a dozen or so students of the Ganryū *Dōjō* on the pier, waiting for the supply ship to carry them back to the mainland.

They all seemed dejected and broken. They had been caught in the fight between demons, so there was neither shame in defeat, nor obligation to die or avenge the Crimson Robe. They were his students – but not his retainers after all; and now it was time for them to search other schools and other masters.

The ferry's Captain was surprised to see them, and even more surprised and disappointed about the news that there would be no more need for his services. Shakushain guessed he was already calculating how to recover his losses and where to move on with his business.

THE RISING TIDE

I wonder how Koro is faring. He remembered the last time he saw his small, dark face – under the waves of the Kanmon Strait as they waved at each other: Koro swimming away with strong beats of his short legs, Shakushain strangling one of the grey swordsmen who jumped into the sea with him.

"The currents of *Dan-no-ura* are deadly," he had explained then.

They were half-way to the shore when the wind and waves around the boat stopped. The sail fluttered and hung impotently. The Captain grunted and gave the few crewmembers an order to row across the flat surface of the Kanmon Straits. Shakushain volunteered for oar duty; at least it was something to keep his mind and body occupied. He hated being idle.

Several of the students noticed the odd silence and came up to the edge of the boat.

"Hey, look at this, what's going on?"

"The water is calm only around the boat. There's waves further out."

"That's not natural. Do you think it's the ghosts of *Dan-no-ura*?"

"They only ever come out on stormy nights..."

"Maybe the Master's death brought them out."

"What's this?"

One of them pointed to the sky. Shakushain looked up. A bright, blazing light appeared in the clouds and was falling towards the ship at great speed.

"It's going to hit!" somebody cried. "Jump out!"

But it was too late. The fiery missile struck the boat, shattering through the decks and hull. A ball of flame engulfed the ship and everyone on it, before dissipating in the cold water in a cloud of hot steam.

The waves and wind returned.

Torii Heishichi brushed the wooden boards of the pier with a sandal-clad foot, erasing the Falling Star character he had drawn in white chalk. He was breathing heavily, cursing his bad health. He adjusted his spectacles, wiped a trickle of blood from his nose and looked at the sea with satisfaction.

It was the first time he used it in the field: the first native Yamato spell; not copied and learned from *Rangaku* books, but created from scratch through the combined efforts of the wizards of Kagoshima. Written in Qin characters instead of Western runes, spoken in Yamato Spell Tongue instead of Bataavian. And it worked perfectly. Where mere moments ago a large supply ship was rowing towards the shore, there was now nothing but silence and emptiness. Only a few smouldering wooden boards bobbed up onto the surface.

Excellent.

"No witnesses," he repeated the daimyo's order to himself.

Bran buckled the saddle-bag packed with a little food for the journey, checked the reins, bridle and harness, tightened straps and buckles. He improvised the tack from bits and pieces he had found in Ganryū's stables. He patted Emrys tenderly on the snout. The dragon answered with a low, welcoming grunt.

"I bet *you* can't wait to leave this place."

The dragon snarled.

"I'm really sorry for everything you had to go through," said Bran, stroking the thick, scaly neck. He felt guilty for abandoning the dragon – and enraged at those who forced them to stay apart.

"I'll make it up to you somehow, I promise. And..." He put his arms around the neck and pressed his forehead against the scales. "I'm so proud of you, Emrys. I really am." The beast purred and puffed a little wisp of grey smoke.

Bran jumped on the dragon's back – no horse saddle was big enough to fit Emrys – put on the goggles, and lightly squeezed the beast's sides with his knees. It felt great to be able to fly again.

From the moment they departed the island, Bran noticed something was different. Emrys reacted to commands faster and more smoothly than ever; the sensory feedback was far stronger: Bran felt the wind on his arms as if they were wings; his eyesight grew sharper, and he could swear he started feeling the magical energies on his skin without the need for True Sight.

Could it be...?

He leaned down, touching the green scales just like he had in the Otherworld the night before, and closed his eyes.

He whispered the spell words and felt his mind meld with that of Emrys in a soft flash of light.

He became aware of all the minute details of the land below: individual people on the roads and in the fishing boats, sharks and tuna in the ocean, black kites in the sky. He saw the currents of magic running through the air and sensed the flows of the Ninth Wind. He heard the buzz of a distant Farlink, the one he had been sensing for days, now far clearer and precise, coming from the North; *four riders,* he could tell with remarkable precision. Finally, he felt himself on his back, a light enough burden, clinging precariously to his neck.

The strain of trying to reconcile being in two places at once made him dizzy and Bran let go of the dragon's mind, returning to his own body.

Nobody's ever done anything like this before, he thought. At least, he'd never heard or read of a Farlink gone so far, or of such strange use of the Dragonform – and if there was any subject he knew about, it was the dragon lore. Something had happened to him and Emrys in Yamato's Otherworld, something unique; was this Shigemasa's parting gift?

He patted the dragon on the neck and breathed deeply.

THE RISING TIDE

CHAPTER XX

The lights of the city twinkled in the distance like a second Milky Way low over the horizon. In the darkness, these flickers and the dark shadows of tall hills above them outlined a wedge-shaped, narrow bay.

Samuel lowered the peculiar twin-lens spyglass he had borrowed from the Admiral and handed it back to him.

"How do you like the Porro glasses, *Doktor*?" asked Otterson.

"Curious invention," replied Samuel. "Not as good as a magical spyglass, of course, but impressive for a Roman device."

"This is the finest harbour I've seen in these waters," the Admiral said. "Such a waste."

"What happens now?"

"In the *morgoen* they will spot us."

Diana was not able to submerge since the accident, and with the damaged rudder was no longer as nimble as it once was.

"I hope they will send a pilot to guide us into the harbour."

"What if they attack?"

"The *spion* said the Yamato have no *kanoner* that would break through this hull," the Admiral said, patting the steel plate.

"He also said they have no mistfire ships."

Otterson frowned.

"With our two *kanoner* and a *torpeder* launcher we should be fine. But I'd rather avoid starting another war. Let's hope they'll be... how you say... *resonlig*?"

"Reasonable," offered Samuel.

"Yes. Let's hope the Yamato officials will be reasonable."

The Admiral knocked at the hatch with his staff. It screeched open.

"*Amiral...*" Samuel said quietly, "what is behind the door of bronze?"

Since his discovery, he had been dreaming of the hidden room – dark, heavy dreams of something, or someone, trying to break free.

Otterson looked sharply at Samuel, then back at the twinkling city in the distance.

"It's a weapon, *Doktor*. One that I hope never to have to use."

Satō left Nagomi in the infirmary and went outside; Bran and Dōraku were nowhere to be seen. The courtyard was eerily empty and quiet.

She passed the wicket gate and climbed the path through the azalea thicket before entering through the rune-covered door into Ganryū's abandoned mansion. She walked through the narrow, dark, silent corridors. Some of the rooms along the way were opened wide, or even broken into – by the staff of the mansion, trying to loot as much as they could before fleeing, she guessed. There was a fortune scattered on the tatami floors: gold, jewels, overthrown vases, ancient scrolls torn off the walls. An iron-bound chest, still locked. A collection of antique weapons. A cabinet of exotic wood, one of its doors hanging loose from the hinges, another stolen. Satō passed it all by, barely taking notice. She could sense Ganryū's Curse still lingering on all this treasure and she didn't want to have anything to do with it.

On the wooden boards where she had fought the assassin she noticed the stains of spattered blood; she crouched to touch it. There was more of it than she remembered. *It was a long fight. If Master Dōraku had not come, I wonder...*

She touched her left shoulder. The pain was still there, faint but distracting. The blade with which Ganryū had wounded her was not of his making, so there was no reason to believe the injury would disappear after his death. Still, she was a little disappointed.

The patterns of magic she could sense in the mansion had been dissipating since the Crimson Robe's demise, and were now barely noticeable. Though the wooden walls looked solid, she had a feeling the building will soon fall apart without the blood energy supporting it. Unless some other demon or wizard took the island for his abode, in time there would be nothing left to tell the tale of the Ganryū *Dōjō*.

In the garden, among the scorched trees and cratered ground, the remnants of the battle, a few hydrangeas valiantly sprouted blue and purple buds. Satō followed the path to the ruined pavilion. Rubble and ash were strewn everywhere, some still smouldering and crackling with the energy of the powerful magic.

She picked up one of the still sizzling pieces of rubble. She didn't need Nagomi's power of sightseeing to know that what happened last night had been just the first battle of a coming war. She tried to reconstruct what the fight may have looked like, based on what Bran had told her in the morning.

The Crimson Robe stood there, she imagined, *and Bran faced him here. Alone. And stood his ground.*

Bran may not have been a Yamato, and he may have been reluctant to kill, but he had fought as bravely as any samurai. He had proven his worth ten times over.

Why was I so hard on him?

Repeatedly spurning his advances must have hurt him.

Was it all just because he was a foreigner?

"A proper Yamato boy", she scoffed. "Is that really what I wanted?"

She wasn't sure herself why it was that way.

Was I afraid he'd disappear, like Nagomi's father?

The more Satō thought about it, the angrier she was at her former self. *I promised myself a new future,* she remembered. And what better chance for a new future could she have than with Bran? For a moment, she clung to the idea of getting help from daimyo of Satsuma. But how much assistance would Lord Nariakira *really* offer, and how much would she have to bargain for it? She wasn't so naïve to think he would do anything for her out of good will. Once again she had to face the humiliating reality of being a woman in Yamato. What other man would appreciate her resolve and independence better than a foreigner, who came from a country ruled by a woman?

How could I have been so stupid?

She stood up from the rubble, resolved to seek the boy out and tell him what she had just decided. A cross-shaped shadow passed over the garden; she looked up, just in time to see the jade-green shape disappear into the clouds.

Bran flew along the coast, just as Dōraku had advised him, but far enough from the land not to be seen by anyone below. The rain clouds parted and the sun was shining at his back. He did not try the mind meld again – he resolved to try it when he was somewhere safe.

He tried not to think of his decision to leave Yamato. There would be plenty of time for regrets later.

It was the right thing, he kept telling himself. *What else was I supposed to do?*

He was going home, or at least in the direction of home. In a few days he would reach Huating, and then he'd try to find out what had happened to his father and the rest of the Marines. Some of them were bound to have survived... He hadn't thought about Qin in a long time. What state was the Empire in now? What happened to the rebellion?

Whatever was going on, he was certain Dylan – if he was still alive – was right in the middle of it.

By evening, Bran reached an archipelago of small islands around a narrow bay. He unrolled Dōraku's map to make sure he was in the right place. As he did so, a monogram in the corner of the cartouche caught his eye. Four Roman letters: P.F.V.S.

Nagomi's father.

He studied the map more carefully. It was drawn with a strong, yet precise hand. The shoreline was rendered in great detail but, inland, only certain geographical features were marked: roads, mountain passes, river crossings and local fortresses. Garrison sizes were noted in thin black ink.

This is a military map. He was *a spy after all!*

He couldn't read any more in the quickly falling twilight. It was time to look for a place to stay the night to rest up before next day's long flight across the Divine Winds. Bran chose to land on one of the uninhabited islets, far from the ship lanes and human settlements, and lay among the roots of a great cedar tree, covering himself with a cloak.

He quickly fell asleep, still tired after the night's events.

He wasn't sure how, or even *if*, he could fly across the Divine Winds. Emrys had done it, but the beast was riderless and confused. The storm certainly *looked* imposing: an impenetrable wall of black clouds, torn through with howling, hurricane-speed winds. Thunder struck so densely that at times it formed webs of blue light encompassing the entire horizon. Through the holes in the clouds, Bran saw torrential rain and streams of hail. Flying closer, he noticed something else, a sight now almost familiar: the white light wisps of trapped Spirits, thrown every which way by the wind.

There must be thousands of them here, he thought. *Tens of thousands. Have they all drowned at sea?*

He took a deep breath and looked over his shoulder, towards Yamato. *This is it,* he thought. *Once past this, there will be no going back.*

What if I am never able to return? He swallowed hard. Never again see those cedar forests? Never walk on the cobbled streets? Taste the food? Smell the air?

He would be like Nagomi's real father, forever torn between two worlds, unable to see his loved ones again. He shook his head.

It's different now, he realized. *Sooner or later, Dracaland will move into Yamato. And when it does… I could become a diplomat. Not a spy, not a soldier like father, just a mediator and interpreter. I know the language; I understand how they think…*

Bran wondered what Dylan would say about his travels across the foreign and hostile land in pursuit of a dragon.

He would tell me to forget all about it and find an easier way to return home. Look, I will buy you a Highland Azure, he would say, now let's bribe the captain of this ship and have him sail us to Huating!

Bran chuckled. He thought he did rather well, all things considered. At least he managed to stay alive.

Emrys snorted and shook its head.

"All right, all right, we're going…"

He spurred Emrys higher, hoping to fly over the worst of the rumbling storm. At around five thousand feet, the clouds began to thin enough for the dragon to risk flying through. Enveloped by the cocoon of warm air – a by-product of the dragon's metabolism – and protected by a light *tarian,* Bran braced himself as he and his dragon braved the hurricane.

The Spirits from the storm below climbed towards him; their faces were white masks twisted with anguish and fury.

I could use Shigemasa and his halberd now, he thought. As they got closer, he started to recognize some of them. There was the bird-like *tengu* goblin; here, a reptilian *kappa* sprite. White foxes and raccoons, and other beings he had not yet heard about.

All the magical creatures, he realized with a shudder. *Yōkai! Is that what's happened to them?* Trapped in the Divine Wind, sentenced forever to harass those who would dare to sail to Yamato without the *Taikun's* permission?

He increased the power of the *tarian* and climbed another couple of hundred feet, out of the range of the damned Spirits swirling below like a shoal of frenzied sharks.

It took Bran half a day to cross the hundred or so miles of the Divine Winds and catch the first glimpse of the Tamna Island. Both he and Emrys were exhausted and eager to land somewhere, anywhere. The island on the horizon was welcomingly large, forty miles across at least, with a great volcano rising into the clouds right in the middle. As he got closer, Bran spotted a few more small islets to the north, looming through the haze – and a squadron of ships anchored in the open sea.

They were undoubtedly Western ships; one large, black mistfire ironclad, and a few auxiliary vessels around it. A couple of large dragons flew overhead. Bran's heart started beating fast. It could only be a Dracaland fleet! Home!

He wanted to fly straight towards the ships; but then the sun glimpsed through the clouds and reflected off the wings of the beasts.

They were onyx black.

Bran slowed Emrys down and had it hover in place high above the surface of the sea, at a distance – the dragon's light green scales made for a good camouflage against the clear sky. Black wings... there were no black dragons. Not in Dracaland, not in Midgard, not even in Varyaga...

A hooded man flying over the wall. Nagomi's prophetic dream. Were these the dragons he had felt before? No, the distant buzz had definitely been coming from within the Divine Winds barrier, somewhere in Yamato. But it was of a similar nature to what he sensed now; these riders must have been a scouting party – or reinforcements...

He studied the squadron through his spyglass. Only when he saw dots of people moving on deck did he realize how immense the flagship of the flotilla was. Half as big as *Ladon*, its deck was wide and flat, a typical dragon carrier. Bran was wondering how many dragons such a giant ship could accommodate, when one of the beasts landed on the wide deck. This gave him a size reference, as dots of the crew surrounded the dragon to take it to the stable.

Impossible. It must be a trick of perspective...

He pointed his spyglass to the other dragon still circling the fleet, looking for a rider on its back. At first he thought there was none, before noticing the tiny silhouette clinging between the massive shoulder blades. That dispelled any doubt.

Compared to these black winged monsters even Afreolus was small. A tiny dragon like Emrys was like a kittiwake next to a gannet. Only a secluded and secretive nation could have managed to breed such terrifying monsters in secret, a nation such as... He tried to spot the design on the ship's banner flapping in the wind; he couldn't see it clearly, but was almost certain it was the horned circle-and-cross sigil of the Gorllewin.

He remembered seeing the crest in Bharata, and later in Qin. *Scouts and spies, all over the Eastern Oceans. I wonder if father ever guessed what they were really after. But their dragons... How did they manage to hide* these *monsters?*

He turned the spyglass back to the ship; the lens blurred momentarily, as if a wisp of mist had obscured his vision. A second later the mist was gone, and Bran found himself looking at a snow-white, fat, squat beast sprawling

408

on the deck: a *Snaellander,* just like the ones he had seen in Fan Yu.

Glamour, he realized. *Like the Shadowclouds. The four from Qin must be the ones I sensed in Yamato.*

Suddenly the white dragon launched again, turning back into the jet-black and sleek beast mid-flight. The other mount stopped circling around the squadron and turned towards Bran and Emrys.

They saw me.

The Tamna Island was not far, but the dragons approached at great speed. Bran dived down, towards the rocky shoreline; the surface of the island was pock-marked with ancient craters and lava streams, overgrown by thick jungle. There were plenty of places to hide.

Why would I hide? The Gorllewin are not the enemies of Dracaland.

Something inside him wanted to get as far away as possible from the enormous black beasts. Emrys lunged among the tall trees of the island with the two pursuers on his tail. Now Bran could really test the newly gained ability to control the dragon's body as well as his own. Zigzagging between the mighty tree trunks, avoiding the rocky outcrops, skirting past stone pillars and arches, he was getting steadily away from the black dragons, which were too big to follow him into the narrow crags and crevices.

But Emrys was getting tired; it had been an exhausting day already, and the small dragon could not keep flying for long. Bran swooped to the bottom of one such crevice, deep and tight, ending in a large cave with walls of smooth, glittering crystal. He landed Emrys in front of the cave and led it inside. His heart thumping, he pulled out the letter Dōraku had given him and read quickly through the brief note.

It was addressed to the commander of a ship stationed near the Tamna Island; a description of the opening of negotiations between the Great Council of Edo and the invading Western force. The proposals were surprisingly lenient: opening of ports, trade monopoly, full diplomatic liaisons. Bran tried to wrap his head around it; everything he had heard in Yamato pointed to the Edo government being ready to fight any foreigners to the death if need be, to keep them off the "Sacred Land". Was it all a façade? It seemed the *Taikun* was ready to sell his nation to the highest bidder. Bran knew now what the price of this purchase was.

He imagined the *Taikun's* samurai riding the mighty flying beasts into battle, supported by modern navy and army built with the help of the Grey Hoods. No rebellion against them would have a chance to succeed. Satsuma and its allies would not last a day, crushed and trampled under the claws of the black dragons.

And what are the Grey Hoods getting in the bargain? Trade opportunities? No, that can't be enough…

A vision from Amakusa, the dark, forgotten ritual of necromancy, flashed through his mind. Bran swore loudly and crushed the piece of paper in his hand. He felt manipulated. Dōraku knew what was in the letter when he had given it to him. He had planned the route for his return home as well, so that the boy would "chance" upon the Western fleet near Tamna. But what did he expect from

410

Bran? Turn around, hand over his dragon to Satsuma? Die in a war he didn't care about?

Emrys snarled and growled. Bran heard the rush of wind from the enormous wings. One of the black dragons hovered over the crevice.

"This must be the place," the rider shouted. Bran was surprised at first to hear him speak in a mixture of Seaxe and Prydain, until he remembered the Gorllewin had started as the colony of Gwynedd several centuries ago. He heard the other dragon fly near, and they both landed almost on top of the cave.

"Come down and see if he's really here. Be careful."

One of the riders appeared in the cave's entrance brandishing a broad sword with an eagle-shaped hilt. He threw back the hood of his grey greatcloak; his hair was fair and cropped short, shorter even than the Dracaland military style. He saw Bran and Emrys and jumped back.

"By the Bull's Horns, who the hell are *you*?"

"What is it, Thorfinn?" the other rider cried.

"You'd better come down and see for yourself! *You* – " the rider waved his sword at Bran, "out!"

Easy, Bran ordered Emrys silently and stepped into the light. The other rider came down to take a good look at him.

"What are these funny clothes he's wearing?"

"I've no idea," replied the first one, Thorfinn. "But he's definitely not from around here."

"I thought we were supposed to be the only ones."

"Maybe the narrow-eyes are playing on several fronts."

"I don't like this whole endeavour. We should have just stayed in Huating."

"Have you not read the first squadron's reports yet? Huating is a goner! I'm sure the rebels have overcome it by now, and we never got anywhere with those Black Lotus guys. Yamato is more eager to cooperate."

Huating a goner? What about Dylan and the Second Regiment?

"I wouldn't trust any of the narrow-eyes. Qin, Yamato, Nam, they're all the same, lying heathen bastards. I'm sure they're plotting something against us even as they sign the treaties."

"That's not for us to discuss, ensign. What do we do with him?"

"Take him back to the ship. The Vice Komtur will want to have a word. You – " the rider turned back to Bran and pointed to one of the black dragons. "Dragon. Now. Understand?"

"I can fly on my own," the boy replied. This took them aback.

"You speak our language?"

"I speak *Prydain.*"

They exchanged looks.

"What are you doing here, boy?"

"I am a Dracalish soldier and I will speak to your Commander only," Bran said defiantly. He wasn't afraid of the two riders; he had already assessed them. Like all Old

412

Faithers, they bore no magic weapons or shields. Thorfinn wielded a gunpowder pistol of complex design, but obviously did not deem the unarmed boy enough of a threat to draw it. Even if they knew how to draw upon their dragons' power – and something in their gait told Bran they weren't ready to do so – the boy was confident he could fight his way out, if need be. Would he be able to flee the black beasts? He looked at one of the dragons peering curiously over the crevice; its head alone was as big as half of Emrys's entire body. The beasts had already proved themselves resilient in pursuit.

I would need to kill the riders to be sure of escaping...

But now he was intrigued. He wanted to learn what possible reason had brought the Gorllewin to these seas.

And there was something else the riders had mentioned... *Black Lotus.* The tattoo on the saboteur's arm... Bran never forgot that image. Did the Grey Hoods know who caused the *Ladon*'s disaster?

The riders looked at each other again and shrugged.

"All right. Mount up," said Thorfinn. "But no tricks; you stand no chance against the Black Wings."

"And wherever you were heading to, you can forget about it now," added the other. "You're coming with us. All the way to Yamato."

THE RISING TIDE

CHAPTER XXI

Hotta Naosuke entered a vast underground chamber lit only by a few torches; the flickering light outlined six silhouettes in the shadows – four men and two women, all clad in long, flowing robes and wearing masks of demons; twisted faces painted in garish colours.

They stood in a circle in the middle of the cavern floor, waiting. One of them, wearing the white robe, stepped into the centre.

The Speaker guides the ceremony, but is not the leader, remembered Naosuke. *All Heads of the Serpent are equal, but one.*

There should have been seven of the celebrants; today one of them could not come. And there was only one reason why a Head would miss the Gathering.

"Today, our circle is broken," the Speaker boomed. "Today, the unthinkable has happened. One of us will never again grace us with his presence; never again grant us his wisdom and strength. Mars's Curse has been lifted!"

A murmur spread about the circle. They had already guessed what had happened.

"A war is upon us," the Speaker continued, "we are being attacked once again, and in our very heart. Ganryū was one of our finest and bravest. He will be remembered.'

"He will be remembered," the others repeated in unison.

"What about Mars's plans?" asked one of the Heads, wearing a golden robe and a black and yellow horned face of an *oni*. "Have they failed? It would be a major setback to our cause."

"Some have," the Speaker replied, "but not all. Some are still going strong."

"Who will replace him?" asked one of the women, her robe silver, and her mask a pale fox's head.

The Speaker clapped his hands.

"Initiate, come forth!"

Naosuke put on his mask – it was a blank, white, featureless surface with only holes for eyes and mouth – and stepped slowly out of the shadows.

"Show yourself."

He lifted his mask and bowed with pride. He had dreamed of joining the Eight-headed Serpent ever since his recruitment into the ranks of the Fanged twenty years before. He never actually imagined it would be possible, not before decades or centuries passed – a Head would have to be destroyed or retire before another took his place. And yet, here he was, the youngest, the least experienced of them all.

"Your name and position, Initiate."

416

"Councillor to His Illustrious Excellency, *Taikun* of Yamato. Hotta Naosuke."

The others murmured again.

"Who will vouch for the Initiate?" the Speaker asked.

"I will," said a tall, broad-shouldered man in the robe woven of metallic thread shimmering in the light of the torches like fire, and the mask of a leopard. When Hotta had first met him, in the library of the Mito school, the man had been using a common samurai name; here, in the Circle, he was known as Jupiter of the Bronze Robe, the master strategist of the Serpent.

"I confirm that Hotta Naosuke has passed his tests and is ready to join our ranks," said Jupiter.

The Speaker nodded and asked:

"Are there any here who would object?"

Hotta cast a quick glance around. None uttered a word.

"Then, as is our custom, Initiate, step into the circle in place of the one who has created you. You will take his name and position as yourself: Mars, of *the Crimson Robe*."

Naosuke took his place in the half-circle, his hands nervously squeezing the ends of his fresh robe. It still smelled of the sacrificial blood with which it had been infused. At the Speaker's gesture, the remaining Heads began the ritual of Recognition. One by one, in a line, they approached Naosuke and showed him their faces without masks. That way the new Initiate was able to learn the identities of all of them.

"Yui Shōsetsu, Saturn of the White Robe," said the Speaker, the last in line. Naosuke recognized every name; they were all ancient, hidden in the shadows behind fallen plots and failed rebellions.

And me among them. Me, Hotta Naosuke, aged thirty-nine.

He knew he was lucky; had Ganryū succeeded in turning Takashima Shūhan before his demise, it would have been the old wizard standing in Naosuke's place.

Luck is also a talent.

After the entire procession passed, the six Fangeds stepped aside, letting Naosuke approach the wall of black, semi-opaque crystal. He stepped forward with a deep bow. Behind the crystal, in the flickering light, he saw the Armour: a cuirass of polished steel plate of old *Nanbando* Western style, topped with the pointy helmet and the long silver feather.

There was another man standing next to the Armour, behind the crystal; he was not a Fanged, but looked more like a demon in samurai clothes: seven feet tall, muscular, and... dark as night. His skin glistened like polished mahogany. He observed Naosuke with great white eyes in silence.

So it's true. Oda does have a black samurai for a servant.

Two flames lit up in the eye sockets of the Armour's metal mask.

"*Hotta.*" A dark, chilling voice spoke. "*A clan of traitors.*"

"It... it's an old story, Master..."

"*Quiet. Your ancestor's betrayal brought me my first victory.*"

Naosuke felt the eyes study him all over.

"Blood red is the colour of your clan."

"Yes. The Red Devils of Sekigahara."

"How fitting. You may yet be of more use to me than Ganryū. His arrogance and recklessness were always troublesome, and his plans needlessly elaborate. And now it seems we may not require his trinkets after all. When you're done with the ritual, I want you to tell me all about your dealings with these... new Westerners."

The flaring eyes grew dim and then vanished. Naosuke turned around and stepped into his place in the complete circle. The Speaker then presented Naosuke with his new mask: a green and black *tengu*, a mountain goblin.

"The wheel rotates," the Speaker intoned, "the spoke is replaced. The ox cart rolls forward. Our journey continues."

"Our journey continues," the others repeated. Naosuke was a little late with the unison murmur. He noticed a scorning glance from one of the masked Eight.

No matter, he thought. *I am part of the Serpent now. Nothing can change it. Now all my plans can be set in motion.*

He remembered the last words of the Prophecy his Master, Jupiter of the Bronze Robe, had revealed to him, all those years ago:

> *The Eight-Headed Serpent rises,*
> *But the Storm God's sword is sheathed.*
> *At the breaking of the world*
> *The Mightiest will fall*
> *And his dying cry will break open*
> *The Gates to the Other World.*

JAMES CALBRAITH

APPENDICES

GLOSSARY OF TERMS

(Bat.) — Bataavian

(Yam.) — Yamato

(Pryd.) — Prydain

(Seax.) — Seaxe

aardse nor *(Bat.)* spell word, "Earth Tomb"

amazake *(Yam.)* a traditional sweet drink from fermented rice

ardian *(Seax.)* the Commander of a Regiment in the Royal Marines

banneret *(Seax.)* the Commander of a Banner in the Royal Marines

bento *(Yam.)* a boxed lunch, usually made of rice, fish and pickled vegetables

bevries *(Bat.)* spell word, "Freeze"

biwa *(Yam.)* fruit of loquat tree

blodeuyn *(Pryd.)* spell word, "Flowers"

bugyo *(Yam.)* chief magistrate of an autonomous city

bwcler *(Pryd.)* magical shield covering a fighter's arm, a buckler

cha *(Yam.)* green tea

chwalu *(Pryd.)* spell word, "Unravel"

Corianiaid *(Pryd.)* a race of red-haired dwarves from Rheged

cwrw *(Pryd.)* beer

dab *(Pryd.)* creature, thing or a person

daimyo *(Yam.)* feudal lord of a province

daisen *(Yam.)* chief wizard

dap *(Pryd.)* the same size and shape as something

dengaku *(Yam.)* a meal of grilled tofu or vegetables topped with sauce

denka, —denka *(Yam.)* honorific, referring to the member of the royal family

derwydd *(Pryd.)* druid

dōjō *(Yam.)* school of martial arts or fencing

dono, —dono *(Yam.)* honorific, referring to a noble man of a higher level

doraco *(Yam.)* Western dragon

doshin *(Yam.)* chief of Police

dōtanuki *(Yam.)* a type of katana, longer and heavier than usual

draca hiw *(Seax.)* spell word, "Dragon Form"

draigg *(Pryd.)* a dragon

duw *(Pryd.)* a swearword

dwt *(Pryd.)* a young child

egungun (Yoruba) a holy spirit, also a shaman dancer representing Egungun

enenra *(Yam.)* a spirit born of smoke

faeder *(Seax.)* father

fudai *(Yam.)* an "inner circle" clan; one of the vassals of the Tokugawa Taikun before the battle of Sekigahara

futon *(Yam.)* a roll-out mattress filled with rice husks

gaikokujin *(Yam.)* a foreigner, non-Yamato person

genoeg *(Bat.)* spell word, "Enough" (to mark the end of a continuous spell)

gornestau *(Pryd.)* magical duel

graddio *(Pryd.)* school graduation ceremony

gwrthyrru *(Pryd.)* spell word, "Repel"

hakama *(Yam.)* split trousers

hamon *(Yam.)* visual effect created on the blade through hardening process

haori *(Yam.)* a type of outer jacket

THE RISING TIDE

hatamoto *(Yam.)* the Taikun's retainer, samurai in direct service to the Taikun

hime, —hime *(Yam.)* honorific, referring to women of high position

igo *(Yam.)* a board game for two players, using identical black and white tokens

ijslaag *(Bat.)* spell word, "Ice Layer"

inro *(Yam.)* a wooden container for holding small objects, hanging from a sash

inugami *(Yam.)* a dog spirit

jawch *(Pryd.)* a swearword

jutte *(Yam.)* police truncheon

kabuki *(Yam.)* a form of classical dance theater

kagura *(Yam.)* a type of theatrical dance with religious themes

kakka *(Yam.)* honorific, referring to lords of the province or heads of the clans

kambe *(Yam.)* a shrine servant taken from an adjacent village

kami *(Yam.)* God or Spirit in Yamato mythology

kanpai *(Yam.)* Cheers!

kappa *(Yam.)* a water sprite, reptilian humanoid

katana *(Yam.)* the main Yamato sword, over 60cm in length

kaya *(Yam.)* a bright yellow wood used for making igo boards

kekkai *(Yam.)* a magical shield, similar to tarian

424

kimono *(Yam.)* official layered robe of the noble class

kirin *(Yam.)* a chimerical creature of Qin, body of a deer and the head of a dragon with a large single horn

kodachi *(Yam.)* a short Yamato sword, less than 60cm in length

koenig *(Seax.)* the monarch of the Varyaga Khaganate

kosode *(Yam.)* basic, loose fitting robe for both men and women

kun, —kun *(Yam.)* honorific, referring to young persons of the same social status

kunoichi *(Yam.)* a female shinobi assassin

kuso *(Yam.)* a swearword

lloegr *(Pryd.)* Dracaland east of the Dyke

llwch *(Pryd.)* spell word, "Dust"

long (Qin) Qin dragon

mam *(Pryd.)* mother

mamgu *(Pryd.)* grandmother

Matsubara *(Yam.)* the family of katana swordsmiths

metsuke *(Yam.)* inspector representative of the Taikun

mikado *(Yam.)* the divine Emperor of Yamato

mikan *(Yam.)* fruit of tangerine tree

mithraeum (Latin) temple of Mithras

mitorashita *(Yam.)* worshippers of Mithras

mochi *(Yam.)* a sweet made of rice gluten

mogelijkheid *(Bat.)* magical potential

monpe *(Yam.)* workman's trousers

naginata *(Yam.)* a polearm formed of a katana blade set in a bamboo shaft

nodachi *(Yam.)* a large, two-handed sword, over 120cm in length

noren *(Yam.)* a curtain hanging over the shop entrance, with the logo of the establishment

oba (Yoruba) chieftain

obi *(Yam.)* a silk sash wrapped around the waist

obidame *(Yam.)* a buckle for tying the obi sash

oden *(Yam.)* a type of stew

omikuji *(Yam.)* fortunes written on a strip of paper

onmyōji *(Yam.)* a practitioner of traditional Yamato magic

onmyōdō *(Yam.)* traditional Yamato magic

oppertovenaar *(Bat.)* overwizard of Dejima

pilipala *(Pryd.)* spell word, "butterfly"

proost *(Bat.)* Cheers!

rangaku *(Yam.)* "Western Sciences", study of Western magic and technology

rangakusha *(Yam.)* a practitioner of Western magic

reeve *(Seax.)* the Staff Sergeant in the Royal Marines

rhew *(Pryd.)* spell word, "frost"

ri *(Yam.)* measure of distance, approx. 4 km

rōnin *(Yam.)* a masterless samurai

ryū *(Yam.)* a Yamato dragon

Saesneg *(Pryd.)* (slur) Seaxe

sakaki *(Yam.)* a flowering evergreen tree, used to produce **sacred** paraphernalia

sama, —sama *(Yam.)* honorific, referring to peers of the same social status

sencha *(Yam.)* popular kind of tea

sensei, —sensei *(Yam.)* honorific, referring to teachers and doctors

shamisen *(Yam.)* a three-stringed musical instrument

shinobi *(Yam.)* assassin

shōchū *(Yam.)* strong liquor (25-35% proof)

shōgi *(Yam.)* strategic board game similar to chess

shukubo *(Yam.)* accommodation for temple pilgrims

sokukamibutsu *(Yam.)* a self-mummified monk

stadtholder *(Bat.)* the ruler of Bataavia

swyfen *(Seax.)* a swearword

tabako *(Yam.)* tobacco

tadcu *(Pryd.)* grandfather

tafarn *(Pryd.)* tavern, inn

tafl *(Pryd.)* strategic board game, played on a checkered board

taid *(Pryd.)* grandfather

taikun *(Yam.)* military ruler of Yamato

taipan (Qin) leader of a trading company

Taishō *(Yam.)* field marshal, commander-in-chief of all the forces in the field

tarian *(Pryd.)* magical shield surrounding entire body

tengu *(Yam.)* a forest goblin

tenpura *(Yam.)* small fish and vegetables fried in batter

teppo *(Yam.)* a "thunder gun" — hand-held lightning thrower

terauke *(Yam.)* a passport produced by an affiliate temple

tono, —dono *(Yam.)* honorific, referring to a noble man of a higher level

torii *(Yam.)* wooden or stone gate to the shrine

tozama *(Yam.)* an "outer circle" clan that was forced to become the vassal of the Tokugawa Taikun after the battle of Sekigahara

tsuba *(Yam.)* a handguard of the katana

twinkelbal *(Bat.)* sparkleball; a stone used for thaumaturgy practice

twp *(Pryd.)* insult, "stupid, simple"

tylwyth teg *(Pryd.)* Faer Folk, a race of tall, silver- or golden-haired humanoids

waelisc *(Seax.)* (slur) Prydain

wakashu *(Yam.)* an "unbroken" youth, a virgin

wakizashi *(Yam.)* a short sword used as a side arm, 30-60cm in length

xiexie *(Qin)* "thank you"

y ddraig goch *(Pryd.)* Red Dragon

yamabushi *(Yam.)* an ascetic mountain hermit

yōkai *(Yam.)* evil spirit, demon

yukata *(Yam.)* casual summer clothing, simple light robe

GLOSSARY OF CHARACTERS

GWYNEDD

CANTRE'R GWAELOD

DYLAN AB IFOR o Cantre'r Gwaelod

b. 2566 a.u.c. Ardian of the Second Dragoons Regiment of the Royal Marines. Married to Rhian ferch Rhys.

Mount: Highland Silver, Afreolus (*Unruly*)

BRAN AP DYLAN o Cantre'r Gwaelod

b. 2590 a.u.c. A graduate of Dracology at the Llambed Academy of Mystic Arts.

Mount: Rhos Jade, Emrys (*Ambrosius*)

ROYAL MARINES

EDERN mab Gwyn

b. 2526 a.u.c. Banneret of the Second Dragoons Regiment of the Royal Marines. A Tylwyth Teg.

Mount: Highland Silver, Nodwydd (*Needle*)

GWENLLIAN ferch Harri

b. 2577 a.u.c. Reeve of the Second Dragoons Regiment of the Royal Marines.

Mount: Highland Silver, Tywyll (*Dark*)

WULFHERE of WARWICK

b. 2589 a.u.c. Ensign of the Twelfth Light Dragoons, descendant of Richard Warwick the Kingmaker.

Mount: Highland Azure, Eolhsand (*Amber*)

HYWEL AP CADELL o Llyn

b. 2590 a.u.c. Flight-Leader of the Twelfth Light Dragoons

Mount: Eryni Ruby, Taran Goch (*Red Thunder*)

BROUGHTON REYNOLDS

b. 2542 a.u.c. Rear Admiral of East Bharata and Qin Station

QIN

TSENG KUO-FAN "BOHAN"

b.2564 a.u.c. An eminent Qin official, general and scholar, commander of the Eastern Army.

LI HUNG-CHANG

b. 2576 a.u.c. A scholar, officer and translator. Personal aide to Tseng Kuo-Fan.

YAMATO

KIYŌ

MIZUNO TADANORI

b. 2563 a.u.c. *Bugyō* – Magistrate of Kiyō. *Hatamoto* retainer of the Taikun.

KOYATA JŪMONJI

b. 2570 a.u.c. *Doshin* – chief of police – of the Merchant's District in Kiyō

ISHIDA TAKUYA

b. 2566 a.u.c. Lieutenant of *Doshin* Koyata

HIRATA MITSUYU

b. 2574 a.u.c. Lieutenant of *Doshin* Koyata

TSUKINARI SHIGEZAEMON

b. 2578 a.u.c. Captain of the guards of Kiyō Magistrate

BLACK RAVEN SOMERLED

b. 2577 a.u.c. Cast-away, teacher of Dracalish

TAKASHIMA

TAKASHIMA SHŪHAN

b. 2544 a.u.c. A *Rangaku* scholar, head of the Takashima School of Wizardry.

TAKASHIMA SATŌ

b. 2589 a.u.c. Heir of Takashima School of Wizardry.

SUWA SHRINE

HOSOKI KAZUKO

b. 2567 a.u.c. High Priestess of Suwa Shrine.

NAMIKOSHI TOKOJIRO

b. 2581 a.u.c. An interpreter of Dracalish language.

ITŌ NAGOMI

b. 2591 a.u.c. An apprentice at the Suwa Shrine.

IKŌ

A servant girl at the Suwa Shrine

434

DEJIMA

HENDRIK CURZIUS

b. 2566 a.u.c. Oppertovenaar (Overwizard) of the Bataavian outpost of Dejima.

GERHARDUS FABIUS

b. 2559 a.u.c. Captain of the Soembing

SAKUMA

SAKUMA ZŌZAN

b. 2564 a.u.c. A scholar of *Rangaku*.

SAKUMA KEINOSUKE

b. 2594 a.u.c. A student at the Takashima School of Wizardry.

HOSOKAWA

HOSOKAWA NARIMORI

b. 2557 a.u.c. Daimyo of Kumamoto domain, tenth lord of Kumamoto Castle.

KUMASO

TORISHI KAYA

b. 2569 a.u.c. Chieftain of the last village of the Kumaso People.

TOSA

TAKECHI HANPEITA

b. 2582 a.u.c. Samurai of Tosa Domain

JAMES CALBRAITH

SATSUMA

SHIMAZU NARIAKIRA

b.2562 a.u.c. Daimyō of the province of Satsuma, lord of Kagoshima Castle.

SHIMAZU ATSU

b. 2589 a.u.c. Adopted daughter of Shimazu Nariakira, princess of Satsuma.

TORII HEISHICHI

b. 2557 a.u.c. *Daisen,* Arch-wizard of Satsuma.

KOMATSU KIYOKADO

b. 2588 a.u.c. A samurai of Satsuma.

ŌKUBO MINEKO

b. 2591 a.u.c. A court servant girl in the court of Satsuma.

SUGIMOTO YOSHIO

b. 2566 a.u.c. An earth-wizard from Satsuma, student of Torii Heishichi.

KUMAMOTO

MAGONOJO ITSUNEN

b. 2579 a.u.c. A monk at Honmyōji temple, host of *shukubo*.

MOTOMENOSUKE INGEN

b. 2570 a.u.c. A monk at Honmyōji temple, cook of *shukubo*.

IPPONIN

b. 2538 a.u.c., d. 2606 a.u.c. Previous abbot of Honmyōji temple

CHIZONIN

b. 2565 a.u.c. Current abbot of Honmyōji temple

SOZAEMON FURUHASHI

b. 2567 a.u.c. Fifteenth abbot of the Unganzenji Temple

KATŌ KIYOMASA (I)

b. 2315, d. 2364 Founder of Kumamoto Castle, general, one of the *Seven Spears of Shizugatake*

KATŌ KIYOMASA (II)

b. 2570 Captain of the Guards Regiment at Kumamoto Castle.

GENSAI KAWAKAMI

b. 2577 A retainer of the Kumamoto Domain. Master swordsman.

HŌJŌ

YOKOI SHŌNAN (TOKIARI)

b. 2562 a.u.c. A scholar and reformer at the Hosokawa's court in Kumamoto.

MOTODA NAGAZANE

b. 2571 a.u.c. A student of Yokoi Shonan.

ITAKURA

ITAKURA SHIGEMASA

b. 2341, d. 2391 a.u.c. Daimyo of Fukōzu Han in Mikawa Province, commander of Taikun`s forces during Shimabara Rebellion.

TOKUGAWA

KAYAMA YEZAIMON

b. 2547 a.u.c. Daimyo of Uraga, commander of coastal defences of Edo Bay

MORIYAMA EINOSUKE

b. 2573 a.u.c. Interpreter of Dracalish at Edo court, school friend of Tokojiro Namikoshi

MASAHIRO ABE

b. 2572 a.u.c. Chief Senior Councillor in the Taikun's government

HOTTA NAOSUKE

b. 2568 a.u.c. Senior Councillor in the Taikun's government

MAKINO TADAMASA

b. 2552 a.u.c. Senior Councillor in the Taikun's government, chief of Edo defences.

KUZE HIROCHIKA

b. 2572 a.u.c. Senior Councillor in the Taikun's government.

MATSUDAIRA

MATSUDAIRA NOBUTSUNA

b. 2349 a.u.c. – d. 2415 Commander of the Taikun's forces in the final victory over the Shimabara Rebellion.

MATSUDAIRA TADAKATA

b. 2565 a.u.c. Senior Councillor in the Taikun's government.

MATSUDAIRA NORIYASU

b. 2548 a.u.c. Senior Councillor in the Taikun's government.

MITO

AIZAWA SEISHISAI

b. 2534 a.u.c. A scholar and a thinker of the Mito School.

NOBUMITSU AOYAMA

b. 2560 a.u.c. A student, later scholar at Mito School

TENKŌ TOYODA

b. 2558 a.u.c. A student, later scholar at Mito School

SAGA

NABESHIMA NAOMASA

b. 2568 a.u.c. *Daimyo* of the Saga Domain.

SHINPEI ETŌ

b. 2587 a.u.c. Retainer of the Saga Domain.

TANAKA

TANAKA HISASHIGE

b. 2552 a.u.c. A scholar of *Rangaku* magic, mechanician and thaumaturgist.

TANAKA DAIKICHI

b. 2598 a.u.c. Heir and apprentice of Hisashige Tanaka.

ARIMA

ARIMA YORISHIGE

b. 2581 a.u.c. Eleventh daimyo of Kurume Domain

MAKI IZUMI

b. 2566 a.u.c. High Priest of the Suiten-gu Shrine, retainer of Arima clan, scholar and revolutionary

HEIAN

MUTSUHITO

b. 2595 a.u.c. Crown Prince of Yamato

KŌMEI

b. 2576 a.u.c. 121st Divine Mikado (Emperor) of Yamato

EIGHT-HEADED SERPENT

OZUN

b. 2581 a.u.c. A renegade Yamabushi priest

AZUMI

b. 2585 a.u.c. The last of the line of shinobi assassins of Koga

SHŌ IKU

b. 2566 a.u.c. Last heir of the royal family of Nansei Islands

SAITŌ HAJIME

b. 2587 a.u.c. Student of the Ganryu Dojo, commander of its 1st Squad.

SHAKUSHAIN

b. 2569 a.u.c. A native warrior from the northernmost island of Ezo

KORO

b. 2558 a.u.c. A man of the ancient native race of Ezo, friend of Shakushain

UNRYŪ KYŪKICHI

b. 2575 a.u.c. Sumo wrestler from Yonogawa. 10th Yokozuna

TYR GORLLEWIN

MATHIUN PERAI

b. 2547 a.u.c. Komtur of the Western Navy of Tyr Gorllewin.

VARYAGA KHAGANATE

FRIDRIK OTTERSON

b. 2568 a.u.c. Varyagan admiral, Captain of the *Diana*.

MAGNUS INGVARSSON

b. 2549 a.u.c. The ship's doctor on *Diana*.

HJALMAR NOBELIUS

b. 2554 a.u.c. Varyagan inventor and thaumaturgist, creator of the *Diana*.

THE RISING TIDE

Thank you for reading *The Rising Tide*
If you enjoyed it, why not leave a comment on Amazon or
Goodreads?

The Year of the Dragon cycle contains the following volumes:

The Shadow of Black Wings

The Warrior's Soul

The Islands in the Mist

The Rising Tide

The Year of the Dragon: Books 1-4 Delux Edition

www.ingramcontent.com/pod-product-compliance
Lightning Source LLC
Chambersburg PA
CBHW070859260626
47162CB00007B/2506